I0818301

STRANGER 456

A THRILLER

ALSO BY PETER LANCE

First Degree Burn

The Stingray

1000 Years For Revenge

Cover Up

Triple Cross

Deal with the Devil

STRANGER 456

A THRILLER

PETER LANCE

TENACITY MEDIA BOOKS

STRANGER 456

Tenacity Media Books
244 Fifth Avenue Suite 2454
New York, N.Y. 10001
212-203-6123
212-591-6029 (fax)
www.peterlance.com

book design realized by Walton Mendelson
www.12on14.com

cover design by Wells Moore
www.welzmo.wordpress.com

ISBN-13: 978-0-9962855-2-0

To Mallory Lance who constantly surprises me
with her intelligence, tenacity and heart

Sors immanis et inanis, status malus, vana salus semper dissolubilis, obumbrata et velata michi quoque niteris; nunc per ludum dorsum nudum fero tui sceleris.

Fate, monstrous and empty, you are malevolent. Well-being is vain and fades to nothing. Shadowed and veiled, you plague me too. Now, through the game, I bring my bare back to your villainy.

—Vulgate text: the *Burana Codex,* circa 1230 AD

PART ONE

1

THE PSYCHOPATH WHOM THE FBI SUSPECTED of killing thirty-seven women leaned in over the autopsy table. The body of a female lay face up. Blonde, in her early twenties, her green eyes were opaque in death. The young woman's arms lay open at either side of the stainless steel table. Her inner wrists had been stitched with sutures which the killer had used once he'd removed the trochar and the last drops of embalming fluid.

When he was finished making her up, he would transfer her body from the table to a gurney on a sheet of opaque plastic so as not to bruise her skin. He needed to pose her before lividity turned her perfect white belly to purple. But first he had to mark her—to designate her position in his master work.

He looked across at his table of instruments. When he found what he wanted, he switched it on. There was a sharp whirrrr that resonated against the 40 foot walls of the cavernous space. It was empty now and dimly lit except for a wall of scaffolding on each side that ran up the 4 stories to the roof. The space had been designed as a charnel house, but the killer thought of it now as his church. His basilica.

He dipped the tip of the tattoo needle in indigo ink. Then, ever so gently, so as not to bruise the nape of her neck, he turned the subject's body over and swept her mane of blonde hair forward. Finally, with the precision of a neurosurgeon cauterizing a tumor, he leaned in and etched a series of tiny letters at the base of her neck: J:20:14–18.

When he was finished, the killer ducked under the scaffolding and walked into his office where he scanned a wall. It was covered with pictures. There were snap shots, drivers licenses and missing person photos from seventeen states. Dozens of faces of men, women and children of every age, size and weight.

Each one of them had been marked with a Sharpie in the same sequence as the tattoo: I 6:8–12, D 32:6–22.

The killer never thought of these people as victims—merely subjects—and now, on the bottom row, he found the DMV registration of the woman he'd just embalmed: Marlee Jane Hofstadter. She'd been a sophomore at the University of Indiana. On October 28th she'd vanished from a laundry room in the basement of the Alpha Chi Omega sorority house.

The killer removed the push pin that fixed her license to the wall and used a Sharpie to inscribe the same combination of letters and numbers on its face: J:20:14–18.

When he was done, the killer unlocked a metal file cabinet and pulled out a journal; a brown banker's ledger that he'd covered in duct tape. He flipped through pages illustrated with drawings of celestial creatures locked in unnatural acts with devils and other beasts. The illustrations of demons and angels fornicating were interspersed with rows of numbers.

Finally, on a page next to the name of Marlee Jane, he recorded the tattooed sequence.

There were two places on the killer's own body where he, himself, had been inked. An inch under his left wrist, below his cuff line, was the same set of numbers and letters he'd inscribed on his subjects: M 10:31.

On the bottom of his right foot there were three tattooed letters: W.A.R. the initials of his hero's adopted name: W. Axl Rose. The killer had never known his own parents. He'd been raised in a series of foster homes throughout the Midwest. But in his early teens, he came to identify with the lead singer in Guns N' Roses who had survived an abusive childhood.

Since he'd found his true calling, the only people the killer ever talked to, had *died* before they even knew his name. He was a loner, an enigma, with no social ties. He had no friends or associates, not even a pet. But as he spoke to his inner demons and filled out the elaborate pages of his journal, he began to use a corruption of Rose's first name: Axel.

Now, as he finished writing, he felt a jolt to his frontal lobe. It was as if a nail gun had shot a four-inch projectile into his brain. He almost blacked out for a moment, then gritted his teeth and recovered, rushing across to an old wooden desk and pulling open a drawer full of medicine.

There were prescription pill bottles from pharmacies across the far west—part of the booty recovered from his subjects.

Axel searched frantically for a vial of Oxycontin, but had to settle for prescription strength Midol. As the next spike drove into his choroid plexus, he popped the cap and dry swallowed a handful of capsules.

Hyperventilating, he dropped to the floor and pressed his fingers into his skull. He bit his tongue to distract himself and slowly willed his pulse to go down. Sitting in the corner of the half-darkened office, he tried to focus and then remembered that the makeup job had to be done before the subject's white skin began to mottle. He pulled himself up and held out his left hand.

Still trembling, he willed it to stop. Then he placed his index and middle fingers against his neck, forcing his pulse to subside.

When he was calmer, Axel walked into the embalming room and found the makeup he'd recovered from the young "Indian woman" whose wallet contained a Nevada license that read "cosmetologist."

On two consecutive nights he'd watched her park her blue Olds Alero in the employees' lot of the MGM Grand in Las Vegas where she worked preparing the showgirls. In the neon light off The Strip he couldn't be sure of her precise skin color, but he coveted the makeup bag that she carried in and out of the casino each night. It was just after two a.m. on the third night, when he followed her home and waited until she made her regular stop for beer and cigarettes at a 7-Eleven.

Hiding now in the shadows of the empty lot, he popped open her trunk and climbed inside with the hood ajar. He cut the wire from the lock that would have ignited a *Trunk Open* light on her dash and broke the bulb on the inside of the hood so that when she opened it to retrieve her dry cleaning, she would barely have time to react before he was on her.

Minutes later, the woman emerged from the store carrying a plastic bag. She got into the Olds and drove off. Axel held the trunk closed and waited until she pulled into the garage below her condo a few blocks away. She got out and he heard the snap of her stiletto heels on the concrete of the garage floor.

She began to walk toward the rear of the car, but then stopped. He heard her unzip a purse and pop the cap off a vial. It was probably lip gloss. He felt himself getting hard as he thought of her checking her reflection in the driver's side window while she made herself beautiful for her boyfriend inside.

It was moments like this that excited Axel the most; knowing before his subjects did, that they had only minutes to live.

2

AS HE WATCHED HER ENTER THE 7/11, Axel noticed that the "Indian" makeup artist was wearing a leather miniskirt with thigh-high black boots. When she came out, he could see the mesh top that covered her black push-up bra. There was a turquoise choker around her neck. Navajo jewelry that might be worth something. He rubbed himself, thinking how she really exploited that Native American thing. Her vanity plate even said LTL BEAR.

Now, as she moved to the back of the car and put her key into the trunk, he sprung open the hood and pressed the Taser against her belly. Zap. 50,000 volts ran through her body. Then, with the quick, rehearsed moves of a predator expert in abduction, he grabbed her by the hair before she dropped. At this point he didn't want her to crack her skull on the concrete.

Easing her down, Axel climbed out and flex-tied the woman's wrists behind her, duct-taping her mouth closed. Once she was within his control, he flipped open her purse and saw that the name on her license was Rosario Dominguez.

Axel was disappointed. She was a mixed breed. An eighth or a 16th "Native" at most. Her eyes bulged with horror as he flipped her face-up on the Olds trunk hood and brandished the pistol-like Taser.

He flicked on a penlight flash that would give him a truer sense of her skin color. He had only another 15 seconds before she'd recover enough strength to start struggling, so he opened her makeup bag and moved the flashlight left, then right to look for a cotton swab and some alcohol.

Just then, in the distance, he heard the sound of a gate opening. Another tenant was driving into the condo complex. So he hit her with another 50,000 volts. A third hit and she'd go into cardiac arrest, so he flicked off the light in the dark and waited until the car passed.

Ten seconds went by and it was quiet now. Axel found the cotton and sprayed a tiny pool of alcohol on it to wipe away the makeup from her cheek. She was just coming out of the second jolt and apoplectic with fear. But she failed his test.

He needed white Europeans to complete his work and this was an olive-skinned Latina who liked to lie by the pool. The bodies he coveted had flawless skin; as close to alabaster white as this tan obsessed culture would allow. Rosario Dominguez would just have to die in obscurity, left out of his grand design.

For a few seconds, the blood drained from Axel's cock and he felt weak—even boy like. But as the woman began to struggle, he began to get hard again. It was never about lust for him. It was always about control.

Just then, the cell phone rang in her purse. It must have been the boyfriend wanting to know where she was. That carton of Camels and six of Miller Lite had been for him. She was coming out of the second jolt now, kicking with her spike-heeled boots; fighting for her life. But she was worth nothing to Axel now. Her genetic fate had been to be born too dark. So he flipped her onto the trunk, face down, and snapped her neck.

He waited to see if he felt it. But he didn't. More often than not, when he snuffed the life out of someone, Axel experienced a palpable shudder, as if the soul had been lifted out of the corpse. The phenomenon was different with each kill. Sometimes it would happen, sometimes it wouldn't.

Soon he began to theorize that the good—those directed toward the "white light"—would escape, but the damned would remain. Earth would become their purgatory.

Now, since he felt no sensation with this woman who put makeup on showgirls, Axel reasoned that she would be here to stay. He lifted her body up and laid her gently inside the trunk so as to avoid any telltale contusions that might be inconsistent with a mugging. He scanned the exterior of the Olds to insure that the garage was clean; pausing for a few seconds at the sound of a police siren a few blocks away.

When the threat passed, Axel drove to a self service parking garage near the 7/11. He'd left his van on the bottom floor, so he pulled the Olds into a dark corner space next to it and retrieved his murder kit. It was a black rolling duffle from Eagle Creek. A trophy he'd taken after the abduction of a male teenage runaway he'd seen stepping off of a bus in St. Louis. Inside the bag was a series of tools. He used some for abduction and others for wiping his crime scenes.

His tool of choice for fiber removal was a portable battery powered Arrowhead Trace Evidence Vacuum. It collected fibers down to 0.3 microns and most importantly, it was quiet.

Preparation was everything with Axel. The key to his longevity as a serial killer. He'd found the garage location on the first night he'd followed the "Indian" makeup artist and he was careful to insure that this ground floor was free of surveillance cameras.

Now, after pulling her lifeless body from the trunk, he laid her face-up on the floor of his van. He'd already covered the floor, ceiling and the walls of the old Econoline with non-static plastic sheets. Axel went back to the Olds and took out her dry cleaning, vacuuming the plastic bag and hanging it on a hook inside the Alero's back seat.

He then used the vacuum's white flexible hose to clean every square inch of the trunk's interior. Since he always wore surgical gloves, his own prints were never an issue. But he took particular care to make sure that he'd collected the tiny shards of glass from the bulb he'd broken inside the trunk's hood.

When he was finished, Axel put the vacuum back into its carrying case and went into his murder kit for a brand new loofah. He opened it and leaned in over the body, pulling up the woman's black mesh top to reveal the marks that the stun gun had left on her belly.

Gently now, Axel rubbed the exfoliator across her stomach, creating an abrasion that would obscure the Taser scars. As he'd dropped her to the floor, she'd smudged her lip gloss, so he went into that zippered purse she was carrying and redid her lips.

This touch was unnecessary, considering the way that Axel was going to leave her, but it always excited him when he got close enough to a woman's body to paint it, living or dead. Just then, her cell phone rang again and he knew that he wouldn't have much time before the boyfriend began to look for her. It wouldn't be for love, he was sure. The bastard would be angry that she was late with his alcohol and smokes. He couldn't have had much concern for her safety, because he'd made her stop at the 7/11 in the dead of night. But

Axel couldn't risk a 911 call under any circumstances. So he closed the back door of the van.

He was about to jump into the driver's seat when he remembered her makeup kit. He grabbed it from the back seat of the Olds, then got into the van and exited the garage. At the time he'd driven in, the barrier had been up, so he didn't have to take a ticket or risk dealing with a parking attendant. There was a camera that photographed the license plates of exiting vehicles, but that caused him no worry.

Without being reckless, Axel exuded the confidence of a professsional who understood the risks inherent in his work. He was always three moves ahead of the police, so when it came to disposing of this body, he knew that he had little fear.

3

ONCE LISTENING TO THE TAPE of a confession by Henry Lee Lucas, Axel had learned how to obscure the numbers of the license plates on the vehicles that he stole. His technique—a refinement of Lucas' trick—was to cover two of the plate letters with mud and spray them with a transparent adhesive so that the dirt wouldn't wash away. Even if the cops associated the exiting van with the Olds on the lower level, it would take them too much time to I.D. the Dodge Caravan which he'd stolen from a used car lot in Utah the day before.

He had made his first kill as a child, setting a fire that burned his brutal foster parents to a crisp. As he got older and killed again, Axel came to realize that like any discipline, repetition and practice led to greater skill.

He'd once read a monograph by Dr. George Crile, former head of the Cleveland Clinic, who associated this phenomenon with what he called "function lust." Professionals were drawn to do what their skill sets permitted, and as their learning curves improved, they were driven to do *more*. Thus, surgeons tended to *cut* versus following a less invasive form of therapy. Trial lawyers were prone to litigate rather than settle. While most people who killed were one-offs, committing only a single homicide in their lives, the serial killer knew no bounds. With each abduction and body drop he became more proficient.

For this reason Axel studied technique. He researched the most notorious SK's who were, by definition, the most prolific. He read every news account, downloaded clippings from the web and pasted them inside his journal, hungry for the kind of forensic edge that would allow him to take his killing spree to exponential new levels.

Just as athletes became trivia junkies when it came to sports statistics or actors memorized the most obscure details from Broadway or Hollywood, Axel immersed himself in the methodology of murder. He paid homage to the serial "masters," but except for a few of them, he thought of himself as far superior. He'd studied Latin since the sixth grade in Catholic School and the term that described him best was "sui generis." Literally translated, it meant a species that defines its own genus or kind.

Most of the others hunted in a specific victim class, killing in succession, one victim after another, until they died or were caught. But Axel defied the cliché, killing *dozens* in a single month; taking a cherubic little boy on a Monday morning and an obese septuagenarian female the following afternoon. With each kill he seemed to vary his M.O., defying any profile. And so the repeated use of vans bothered him because they were the stereotypical mode of transit for serial killers.

From time to time, he would steal a Lincoln Navigator, an Infiniti QX56 or a Mercedes M-Class. But they were tricky because expensive vehicles were prone to have Lojack, the auto theft recovery system. He loved the Chevy Suburban, but most late GM models now carried Onstar. The last thing he needed was to be moving a corpse across state lines and spot the flashing lights of a State Trooper in his rear view mirror.

So while he hated to be lumped into a class with lesser predators, Axel tended to steal older Dodge Caravans and Ford Econolines—many with body damage that wouldn't be missed. When it came to the abduction and transit of human beings, there was just no better vehicle than the side loading van.

But even if the Las Vegas P.D. had dusted off the Utah plates and linked the missing Caravan to the auto theft in Provo, Axel was confident that no one in uniform would connect it to the "robbery- murder" of the faux Pocahontas who worked at the MGM Grand.

Rosario Dominguez was a nobody. When they found her body in the alley outside, she'd be just another statistic. In fact, the cops would be anxious to clear the murder so that it didn't negatively impact their homicide stats.

Axel was certain that no detective would go the extra distance of trying to run a smudged license number through the NCIC crime database. As he'd honed his skills at hunting humans, he'd studied forensics and come to know the law enforcement mindset. Like any enterprise, it was odds-driven and in this city of Las Vegas, which thrived on the odds, he knew that no investigator would spend more than a few hours working an apparent mugging.

The Caravan rolled out of the garage and Axel turned into the alley that opened onto the next block by the 7/11. There was a dumpster outside the back of a Chinese restaurant and on the way to pick her up, he'd noticed that the halogen security light above the restaurant door was out.

He pulled beside the dumpster and slid open the side door of the Dodge. He yanked out her body, boots first, and dropped her hard onto the pavement. Crack! He could hear the sound of the fracture at the base of her skull. This time he didn't care what kind of debris trail he left.

Street robberies were messy and once her body was found he was sure that the cops would view theft as the apparent motive. As he cleaned out the cash and credit cards from her wallet, Axel saw a small pool of blood begin to thicken in her long black hair.

Then, without even looking back at her, he got into the van and drove off. He'd drop her wallet into a mailbox nearby—a common ploy for street robbers—then pawn her jewelry when he got back to the Midwest.

Rosario Dominguez was Axel's 232nd kill in five years.

Now, months later in the cavernous space, using her makeup kit, he covered the circles under the eyes of Marlee Jane Hofstadter. They were dark gray contusions; in a woman this young, usually the sign of excessive alcohol consumption.

As he used a concealer on the beautiful coed, Axel imagined her sipping Apple Martinis in a little black dress at some Alpha Chi mixer. He rouged her lips the color of a perfect young vagina. Then he put her in the beautician's chair and set her hair, before moving her body out into his church.

Posing her now with her arms up, wrists turned so as not to show the sutures, he rouged the nipples of her breasts and shaped her stitched-up smile into an almost erotic taunt before he took out his Nikon and began taking shots.

Flash! A close up on the nape of her neck. Flash! Her labia open like the petals of a lily. Flash, Her blond hair still full and shiny. Flash! The nails of her toes painted the deep red of blood. Flash! Flash! And then, as he did with each of his subjects, he widened her eyes and tried to imagine them lit up and conscious. But he couldn't.

She was an empty vessel. No matter how he tried to breathe life into them—no matter how gorgeous he made them—richer, healthier and sexier than they'd ever been in life—Axel could never find the fire in their eyes—that essential spark of humanity.

And he knew that in the end, as he laid in the final jewel of his masterpiece, the last one—this redhead—no matter how the clock ticked against his completion date—she would have to be taken alive.

4

FOUR DAYS after he'd photographed Marlee Jane Hofstadter, Axel was roaring across State Route 906 in the ski town of Snoqualmie Pass, twenty-eight miles east of Seattle, Washington. It had rained around 4:30 p.m. as darkness settled in and a sudden drop in temperature had turned the two-lane mountain road into a ribbon of asphalt and glass.

This time he was driving a 1999 Ford Econoline that he'd lifted from a lot in Missoula, Montana the night before. It had body putty on the left side.

By eight p.m. the first snow of the season had started to fall. Except for his stop to change rides, Axel had driven straight through from his lair 2,100 miles to the east. He had only three weeks left to finish his magnum opus before a wrecking ball threatened to destroy his life's work, so he was amped up and edgy.

The migraines had become more and more frequent and the prescription strength Demerol he'd been taking had rendered him dizzy and nauseous. He tried Relpax, Topamax or Imitrex, the dedicated anti-migraine inhibitors, but they left him exhausted, so he'd begun downing meth: crystal, ice, even capsules of Desoxyn; any strength he could get to stay up and in it.

As a consequence, the slightest provocation would set him off—a dangerous condition for a serial killer who needed to harvest his victims in the shadows. But the conflicting cocktail of downers and uppers that raged through his system caused eruptions that he couldn't control.

The van passed the entrance to the Summit at Snoqualmie, a ski resort still closed for the season. The narrow two-lane ridgeline road had no lights, and when Axel pulled around a darkened bend, he started to nod off.

Just then, the van crossed the median, but the horn from an oncoming car blared and Axel quickly snapped back.

The snow was getting thicker now and he switched on the wipers, but the driver's side blade in the stolen Ford was broken, so he could barely see through the windshield.

Trying to stay alert, Axel searched for a good metal station on the radio, but reception was bad up on the ridgeline road, so he flipped open the center console and found the iPod Touch he'd taken off a young music student in Kansas earlier in the year.

The playlist had been largely classical and he'd dumped it in favor of Metallica, GNR and Iron Maiden. But there was one piece that he couldn't stop listening to: *Carmina Burana*, Carl Orff's orchestration of the *Burana Codex*, a manuscript found in a Bavarian monastery in the early 1800's.

It was a collection of 228 poems compiled by a series of writers who'd corrupted the lyrics of the Latin-Germanic vernacular to celebrate the dark side of the Catholic Church. The music was composed in the Ecclesiastical Latin meter, but the content was bawdy and profane—the work of 13th century Goliards, a cadre of young monks who denigrated the faith.

Axel was so taken with the pulsating chant that he'd memorized the lyrics to the most popular of the verses: *Oh Fortuna.*

Fate, monstrous and empty, you are malevolent.
Well-being is vain and fades to nothing. Shadowed and
veiled, you plague me too. Now, through the game,
I bring my bare back to your villainy.

That's how he saw much of his life—monstrous, empty and driven by fate. Though he never knew his natural parents, Axel had been blessed. He was tall, muscular and gifted.

After the death of his foster parents in that fire, a child welfare agency had tested his I.Q. and he'd spiked at 160—a genius level of intelligence. He'd shot or swallowed virtually every drug in the Physician's Desk Reference, but he never smoked or drank and he'd run at least ten miles a day since he'd made the cross country team in junior high school.

He had the piercing blue eyes and angular jaw of a rock star and he was ripped—there wasn't an ounce of fat on his speed riddled body. All the better for when he met the redhead, the young woman he planned to take with him through history.

Axel turned up the music as the Orff piece blasted out across State Route 906. A sign blew by that said SNOQUALIMIE 6 MI. He checked himself in the rearview mirror and flipped down the visor which held the Polaroid he'd found in that tattoo parlor near Long Beach. The girl in the picture was eighteen, sitting astride a Harley in a black leather halter and chaps, holding onto her "old man" with one hand as she flipped her middle finger to the camera with the other. A sexy, defiant young bitch with a tat of the Angel of Death on her shoulder.

He'd been trolling ink parlors for months, searching the web for a woman like this. He'd data mined all the social media sites starting with Facebook. After killing a State Trooper in Missouri, he'd stolen the cop's NCIC Password and started searching DMV databases nationwide.

The female he needed would be a rare find. Most redheads were covered in freckles, a genetic trait caused by a concentration of melanin in their skin. Under the sun, the blemishes got darker.

But the model he needed, had to be a natural redhead with flawless skin the color of milk. Until he'd found that Polaroid in the ink parlor, all of the redheads he'd seen had left him cold.

"Hell on wheels," he said to himself, as he ran his thumb across her pouty little mouth in the picture, knowing that before the night ended he'd meet her in person.

Axel was doing seventy now on the narrow road and he looked away for a second as he pulled the Polaroid off the visor and shoved it into his pocket. But when he looked back, he found himself driving head-on for a logging truck coming the other way.

SCREEEEECH. The big semi hit its breaks and the driver blasted his air horn, screaming out at the van.

"Fuck you, you fucking fuck."

Axel heard the taunt as the big truck blew by him and something in him snapped. Hyperventilating with rage, he pulled to a stop at a turnaround. From the cup holder on the dash, he found a couple of rocks of crystal and dry swallowed them. He buckled his shoulder belt, then slammed the van into gear, spinning it into a sharp one-eighty, pedal to the floor, as he roared back after the truck.

In a matter of seconds he was ten feet behind the driver who spotted this maniac in the van in his side mirror. The driver gave two more blasts on his air horn, but that only made Axel angrier, and he pulled alongside the truck doing eighty in the oncoming lane. Roaring up next to the cab, he turned up the iPod full blast and practically spit out the lyrics at the driver:

"O fortuna velut luna, status variabilis. Semper crescis aut decrescis, vita de-stabilis..."

Now the driver was worried. Clearly this guy in the van was whacked.

He speeded up and pulled ahead, checking his side mirror. He was about to jump on his CB radio to call the local Sheriff when...

VAROOOOM... Axel pulled ahead, cutting in front of the logging truck's headlights and hitting the brakes, whereupon...

BOOOOM!!! The big semi demolished the van's bumper, forcing it to skid across the median and flip, rolling side over side as it broke through a guard rail, at which point...

SMASH! a huge Douglas Fir branch pierced the van's windshield, holding it precariously 100 feet above the gorge below as the right tail light blinked and the profane Latin lyrics blasted out from the iPod.

"Nunc obdurat. Et tunc curat. Ludo mentis aciem egestatem!"

Inside, Axel was pinned against the wheel, bleeding all over the airbag which had deployed just in time to keep the wheel from crushing his chest.

He was semi conscious, but the crank was keeping him awake and amazingly, as the van's horn blared, he kept muttering the lyrics like some crazed mental patient on animal tranks.

"Felix et beatus, nunc a summo corrui, gloria pri-va-tus."

When the truck driver realized what had happened, he skidded to a stop and jumped out. He raced across the road with a hand-held searchlight and saw the mangled guard rail.

"My God."

The snow was really beginning to come down now, and as he panned the light above the rail, he spotted the blinking red light of Axel's turn signal.

With the snow falling and the wind beginning to pick up, the van dangled on the branch. To the truck driver it looked like an enormous Christmas tree ornament about to slip off and drop into the gorge.

He rushed back and jumped into his cab, keying the mike on his C.B. "Breaker Breaker, this is Weyerhaeuser Driver two-two-four. Repeat. Whiskey Delta two-two-four. Located at mile marker one-five-two on State Route nine-zero-six. There's been a crash. Repeat. A vehicle is hanging from a tree outside the guard rail about a mile west of the ski basin. Request immediate air evac... Do you copy?"

He waited for a response, but there was none.

"I can't get cell phone service up here. Is anybody *copying* this?"

The driver stared through the snow at the van.

"If somebody doesn't get up here soon, that thing's going down... Do you read me? Please. Come back at me... Please..."

5

When the phone rang, down at the Snoqualmie Station, Sheriff's Deputy Maddy Bergstrom was about to knock off for the night. Buddy Beecham, a wheel-chair-bound Iraq war amputee who spent his days monitoring CB broadcasts, called to say that there was an emergency up by the ski summit.

When he played a tape of the logging truck driver's alarm, Maddy felt a dull cold sensation at the base of her spine. She'd been on the job for less than a year now and though she'd trained for airlift mountain rescues, she had never done one under blizzard conditions.

She immediately called the Sheriff, her father, Mike Bergstrom. He was on street patrol in the small resort town of 6,300. Maddy was his second Deputy. Just that morning, Eddie Gomes, who ranked above her, had taken off for a fishing vacation in Cabo San Lucas. So they were short staffed.

Sheriff Bergstrom was an ex-Marine pilot who'd flown the MH 60 Seahawk during the Gulf War. After he'd put in his twenty, he'd retired and moved with his wife Shauna, his son Billy and his daughter Maddy, then ten, to Washington State where he'd been raised.

In this ski town, the work they did was mostly search and rescue with some occasional fire evac. The County had an old Bell Jet Ranger that they'd requisitioned from the National Guard after the Mt. Saint Helen's eruption in 1980. The Sheriff prided himself on his mechanical skills, and he'd restored the chopper to what he liked to call "combat readiness."

But the only real "combat" they encountered, came from the ungrateful skiers who they pulled off the mountain each season. Maddy had come back to Snoqualmie after a few years of "finding herself," and only took the job after her brother Billy was killed with his Marine unit in Fallujah.

Their mother had died from ovarian cancer in 2005 and after that, Billy had become his father's right arm. An Eagle scout and multi-letter athlete, he'd earned a hockey scholarship to Wash State, which he lost when he blew his knee out the night before graduation.

Deciding to take a few years off, Billy joined his dad in uniform and went through a kind of basic training more rigorous than anything his father had endured on Paris Island.

Always a severe man, the death of his wife seemed to harden Sheriff Bergstrom. He was a particularly tough task master, especially with his daughter, and the independent Maddy decided to rebel. By her junior year, the clash between them turned her from a cheerleader hopeful to a black-haired Goth and by the middle of the 12th grade, with a nose ring and a Mohawk, she just left.

Billy's death three years later was the precipitating event that sent her into rehab. When she finally got clean, Maddy came home, the prodigal daughter, bound to put on a uniform and take her brother's place.

But now, after eleven months under her father, she'd begun to rethink that plan. No matter how she excelled at the job, it never seemed to be enough for him. She'd even taken a rigorous six week course at the North Cascades Mountaineering School – graduating at the top of her class.

The final involved scaling a sheer, six-story wall with a pick ax, harness and rope. Maddy was only the second woman in the program's history with the upper body strength to pull her way to the top.

But even that accomplishment seemed to pale, when she hung the framed certificate on the wall in the hallway at home next to Billy's medals, trophies and sports page headlines. Besides, nothing could match his ultimate commendation: the Bronze Star that had come from the Department of the Army in a frame with the black slash of a posthumous decoration.

So now, as the Bell Jet Ranger roared through the oncoming blizzard, Deputy Maddy Bergstrom, twenty-two, sat in the co-pilot's seat checking the harness over her Nomex jump suit and nodding quietly as her old man ran the numbers:

"We're gonna have about a three minute window," he said, over the radio that she picked up in her SPH-5 helmet receiver. "That gives you one shot down and if it's hung up at all, you're not gonna have the Hurst tool to help you."

"I *know* Dad." Maddy was a climber and he didn't have to tell her that the "jaws of life" were too heavy to deploy on the Goodrich hoist and winch. But he wouldn't let up.

"So if the door's jammed and you can't break the window to get the harness around him, it's an abort. No questions. Are we clear?"

"Yeah. We're clear."

"I want you up and away from that thing, because right now, from what that trucker reported, even if it's still hung up, you are talking about eighty-five hundred pounds of dead weight that will take me, you, and this bird to the bottom of that gorge. Do you copy?"

"Dad I get it. Just *chill*. O.K.? I can do this."

Maddy angled the search light below and just then…

"I see it. Outside the guard rail at four o'clock."

"Then get down there. I can't hold her long."

Maddy winced at the snap of his tone. Then she rolled open the side door and clipped the winch line to the harness.

"Two, maybe three minutes," he yelled. "This is starting to blow."

The wind buffeted the chopper as he eased off on the winch controls and she dropped… down, down, about thirty feet to the edge of the guardrail. Maddy had no way of knowing that the young man she was risking her life to save, had killed another 42 people since he'd broken the neck of Rosario Dominguez in Las Vegas.

The branch of the Douglas Fir that was holding the van was starting to move, as piles of snow from the tree above, plopped down onto the Econoline's roof. By now the battery was dead and the rear blinking light had gone dark.

Maddy pushed out from the guardrail and swung herself toward the rear bumper of the van. Catching onto it, she pulled herself along the driver's side and came to the front door. Fortunately, the victim had rolled down the window, so she didn't have to smash it, but as she switched on a spotlight clipped to her helmet, Maddy was suddenly startled when she saw Axel's face, covered in blood.

"Sir? Can you hear me?" She had to shout over the deafening roar of the rotor blades up above. "Sir, we're here to get you out. Can you *hear* me?" But there was nothing from Axel, so Maddy reached through the open window and felt his neck for a pulse. Good. He was still breathing.

"He's unconscious," she said over the radio. "But his pulse is racing."

"Then jump on it. Get him clipped," said the Sheriff, barking orders down at her, as he struggled to steady the chopper and keep an eye on the winch.

Maddy lowered her voice and shot back, "Easy for you to say Dadeee.... The goddamn thing's hangin' by a threa—"

"What? Didn't copy—"

"For*get* it, Dad."

Maddy tried the door handle. Good, it opened easily. The windshield was demolished, but the frame hadn't been bent. Gently, she opened the door with one hand and pulled out a pair of surgical scissors with the other. She cut the bloody seat belt away quickly, then pushed back the airbag and began the precarious process of getting a harness around the victim, when suddenly, another pile of snow dropped onto the roof and the van dropped another foot.

"Oh shit."

Maddy backed off. If she'd been tethered to Axel when the van dropped, she might have pulled down the chopper.

"What's wrong?"

"It's O.K. Can you give me another foot?"

The wind was really beginning to whip through the trees and the snow was blinding. The Sheriff was ready to abort the mission, but his daughter was in a better position to assess the risk, so he hit the winch control. She dropped another twelve inches and got back inside the open door, close enough to get a harness around Axel's shoulders. She felt each of his arms to see if they'd been broken and then slipped the harness under them, gently moving him forward and dropping the harness behind him, so that she could clip the two ends together across his chest

As she leaned in to clip a carabiner onto the harness, she could smell the blood on his face. And then... CLICK... Just as she got him tethered, another pile of snow hit the roof and the van fell from the tree... careening down, as the chopper pulled Maddy and Axel out.

Dangling with him now on the line, she looked down as the Econoline fell end over end until it hit the bottom of the gorge and exploded in a fireball.

"Up and out," she said, signaling for her father to hit the winch, and the two of them rose up through the trees, the chopper banking slightly east over the mountain road.

Now, as they were getting closer to the helicopter, Maddy pulled out a penlight flash and opened one of Axel's eyelids. She was checking for pupil dilation, when suddenly, he woke up and eyed her. For a split second there was a look of recognition on his face and Maddy was startled.

"Hey. Are you O.K.? Can you hear me?"

But then, he closed his eyes and seemed to drop back under as the two of them spun on the winch line moving up towards the Bell Jet Ranger. Finally, when she was parallel to the door line, Maddy climbed onto the struts and swung inside with her victim. She unclipped him quickly and strapped him down on a body board, rotating her index finger and signaling that she was...

"Good to go." Without a word, Sheriff Bergstrom pulled back on the stick and they took off. Maddy didn't see it, but for an instant through the blood, Axel flashed the hint of a smile. He was holding something in his hand, but then, just before Maddy rolled the door close, he let it go and it flew off into the storm.

It was the Polaroid of that defiant redheaded biker check that he coveted. Somehow, as he drifted back under, Axel knew that he'd already met her.

6

By land or by air, the distance between the crash site on State Route 906 and the Snoqualmie Valley Hospital was just over 26 miles—a virtual straight shot as the crow files along Interstate 90.

Under ideal conditions, the modified Bell Jet Ranger that Sheriff Mike Bergstrom was flying could have made the run in just over ten minutes. But the snow storm's ceiling was 2,000 feet and he had to get up and over it. Otherwise, the old model 206L, known to chopper jocks as "The LongRanger," would ice up and they might all go down.

It was almost twenty-five minutes before he was able to land in the parking lot outside the E.R. He'd radioed ahead and two volunteer paramedics from the town Fire Department were standing next to a gurney awaiting the crash victim.

The lone attendings working the E.R. that night were Dr. Harminder Singh, six months out of residency at Chandigarh Medical College in the Punjab region of India and L.P.N. Amber Jensen, a blonde, Scarlett Johansson look-alike who had recently submitted her pictures to Maxim and was awaiting a call back. She'd known Maddy since junior high.

The hospital's lone radiologist was at a convention in Tacoma, and Rory, the X-ray tech wasn't answering his cell, so once Axel was rolled into an examination area, Dr. Singh did a gross examination to look for fractures. The victim was still unconscious, but his respiration, blood pressure and heart rate all were stable.

After the initial check of his vitals nurse Jensen drew blood for a workup. When she was finished, she sponged off the blood from Axel's face and cut off his clothes with a small pair of scissors. When she eyed his body, Amber rolled her eyes and called out across the E.R. floor. "Hey Maddy. You've gotta see this guy."

The Deputy Sheriff was still in her Nomex jumpsuit. She was over at the E.R. desk, filling out paperwork when Dr. Singh came up behind her and nodded to a Physician's Assistant who was busy filing charts. "Do me a favor and find Rory. I've got to get some films of this patient."

"Try the Kegger," said Amber coming up to the desk. She retrieved the number of the local bar from her cell phone and showed it to the Assistant. Then she elbowed Maddy and nodded toward the gurney at Axel. "You gotta take a look at your man, girl. He's ripped."

"Didn't notice."

"You mean when the two of you were just dangling up there from that chopper and you were holding onto him for dear life, you didn't *feel* anything?" She held her hands up, four inches apart and then widened them to six inches, grinning.

Finally, Maddy stopped writing and turned to her.

"You're right Amb. As soon as I swung open the door of that van and saw him slumped over that bloody airbag, he *had* me." For the first time, she cracked a smile. "No, I'm serious, the dating possibilities in law enforcement are endless."

Amber laughed and started to bump fists with her, when Maddy's cell phone began to ring. She checked it and winced. It was her father, pacing outside by the chopper.

"How much longer?"

"A few more seconds Dad."

"You know the drill." He nodded to the Bell. "We've got to get her back and into the hanger before we're socked in."

"Be right out."

"Is the suspect still under?"

"You mean the *crash* victim?"

"I didn't like that tat on his wrist. Looked like prison ink."

Maddy grimaced at his paranoia.

"Dad, it was done with a *professional* needle."

"And you're an expert on tattoos—Oh right. Belay that. I forgot that you *were*." His reference to her drop-out past, stung Maddy and she didn't have a comeback. "Is he still unconscious?"

"*Totally*," she said, eyeing the gurney.

"Did you search him?"

Maddy nodded and looked down at a tray full of Axel's pocket litter: a couple of tabs of prescription meds, some chewing gum and a Bic pen. "Affirmative. No I.D. His wallet must have gone down with the van." This time she got no response.

"Dad?"

By now, the impatient Sheriff was heading inside. As he pushed through the E.R. room doors he said, "What's the first rule of police work?" Amber raised her hand as if to volunteer. "Make sure the donuts are always fresh?" This time Maddy didn't laugh.

"No. The road to hell is paved with—"

"Assumptions," said Maddy.

Her father was looming over her now. "Alright, listen up. I can get the bird in on my own. I want you to stay with this guy and watch him. I'll be back with the Unit when I've buttoned her up."

"O.K. Dad." Maddy was anxious for him to leave.

"Remember what I used to tell Billy?"

"Yeah. Retreat is not an option."

"You're damn right.

Amber gave him the "thumbs up" sign and Maddy nodded. The Sheriff started to leave, then stopped.

"By the way."

Maddy gritted her teeth. "Yeah, Dad?"

"That was one righteous pull you made tonight." He gestured toward Axel. "You saved that man's life over there." Maddy started to light up. A compliment for once.

"Thanks Da—"

Then he cut her off.

"Only next time, if we ever encounter a vehicle that close to a drop, you inform me *first*, and *I'll* make the call. You damn near took us all down." And with that, he turned on his heels and walked out.

Nurse Amber walked up and put her arm on Maddy's shoulder. "No wonder you ran away." She hugged her. "Cheer up girl. Tomorrow night at the Kegger, the Jager shots are on me."

7

HALF AN HOUR LATER, Axel was still unconscious. They'd moved him to a bed in a corner of the first floor E.R. Once Rory had been pulled out of the bar, X-rays were taken of the chest, spinal column and extremities. Dr. Singh was in an anteroom off the E.R. checking the films on a light box.

In a break room off the E.R., Maddy was feeding quarters into a coffee machine, while Amber used a file on her nails.

"So how long have you been up now?"

Maddy checked her watch. "Twenty three hours and change. Pulled a double last night. I was on my way home when we got the call."

She pushed the button on the machine for a macchiato with an extra shot of espresso.

"That's just what you need to get you to sleep, girl. You think he'll let you go home?"

"Doubt it," said Maddy. "Not until he's *sure* that our van driver doesn't have any outstanding wants or warrants."

Amber flashed a mischievous look. "Hey, come here." She walked over to Axel's bed and lifted the sheet. "You've got to see what this guy's carrying." Maddy was about to take a peek, when Dr. Singh came out of the ante-room carrying a file.

"The blood work came back. Call your father."

Minutes later, Sheriff Bergstrom was at the foot of Axel's bed, awaiting word on his condition.

"What can you tell me about him?

"If I knew his date of birth, I'd buy Lotto tickets and play the number.

"Meaning?"

Dr. Singh eyed the X-Rays.

"Minor contusions, no fractures and zero brain trauma, thanks to the airbag and your daughter." He nodded to Maddy as Amber, offered another fist bump, but, trying to keep it professional, Maddy didn't respond.

"Anything else?" demanded the Sheriff.

"Yeah," said Dr. Singh. "He's also got enough HGH and meth in his system to send a hockey team to the Stanley Cup."

He handed him the lab report. Without even checking it, the Sheriff cocked his head toward Maddy.

"What did I tell you?"

"Did I say you were *wrong* Dad? I just said he was—"

"Hung, right?" Amber, elbowed Maddy who looked away.

"He's also an UNSUB," said the Sheriff, using cop speak for *Unknown Subject*. He eyed the doctor again. "Other than the tattoo on his wrist—that M 10:31—did you find any scars or other identifiable marks? Something that might help with the I.D.?"

"Just this," said the doctor, approaching the bed and pulling the sheet away, revealing the W.A.R. tattoo on the bottom of Axel's foot. "What's it mean?" asked the naive nurse Amber.

"What's it *usually* mean?" asked the Sheriff. "War…"

"No Dad. They're initials" said Maddy, looking away. She was almost ashamed that she knew the significance.

"For what?" demanded her father.

"W. Axl Rose..."

"As in Guns N' Roses?" asked Amber. Maddy nodded.

"Wait a second?" recalled the Sheriff. "Isn't that the band who dedicated some song to Charles Manson?"

"Actually it was *written* by him," said Maddy. "They put it on the *SI* album."

"You mean they *profited* from that maniac?"

"No Dad. They gave the royalties to the son of one of his victims."

Maddy was suddenly defensive.

"And you think that mattered?" The Sheriff eyed her, for a response, but she stood silent. So, he started pacing, delivering orders like he was commanding his old flight squadron.

"O.K., here's what's going to happen. First, Dr. Singh is going to get him into a room on the highest floor of this building where we can lock him down. Second, Deputy Bergstrom, is going to post herself outside his door after cuffing him to the bed."

But Amber came to her defense.

"Sheriff, she's been up for more than a day."

"It's O.K.," said Maddy. "That's the job."

"Damn right," said the Sheriff. "You'll man your post until we can get him printed and get a response from the NCIC. Until then, we hold him as a DUI."

"Why?" asked Amber, "'cause you don't like his taste in music?"

"No," said the Sheriff, eyeballing her defiantly. "Because he almost *killed* a truck driver up on that road, because he was legally *intoxicated* and because—I *said* so."

He turned to Maddy. "Now make it happen." And with that, he stormed out.

As soon as he went through the E.R. doors, Maddy looked at Amber. "You don't even have to say it."

"Oh yeah, I do," said Amber. "Your dad is an asshole."

8

It was just after 7:00 a.m. when the morning shift arrived on Three-East, the upstairs ward where Dr. Singh had locked Axel into a private room.

Maddy had been in a chair outside the door all night. Her father had brought her a uniform to change into earlier and there was a line of empty espresso cups on the table next to her. But as much as she'd tried, she could not stay awake.

Just then, she felt a gentle pinch on her cheek as Doris Gibbs, the head floor nurse, woke her up.

"Up and at 'em Hon. Your Dad's on his way." Nurse Gibbs had been an old friend of Maddy's mother and she felt the need to protect her. The young Deputy had barely gotten to her feet to wipe the sleep from her eyes when her father came around a corner.

Looking sharp in a freshly pressed uniform, he was walking with the confident gait of cop whose hunch had paid off.

"I hate being right."

"What'd you find out?"

He nodded toward Axel's room. "Our boy in there is looking at Grand Theft Auto and interstate flight at a minimum"

"Based on what?

"The van that went down matches the precise color make and model of a ninety-nine Ford Econoline stolen from a lot in Montana Monday night. Surveillance camera caught this…"

He showed her a grainy black and white fax from the car lot of a man the same height and build as Axel. The picture was too dark to be definitive for an I.D.

"What's that prove?"

"That I was right to have you cuff him." Just then, he spotted the cuffs in a holster on Maddy's uniform belt.

"Christ, tell me you followed orders."

He peered through a small glass window into the room, but the bed was half-covered with a curtain.

"Dad it was late. He was so far under that I—"

"Open it up," He bellowed the order to Nurse Gibbs.

"Fine, Mike, just lower your voice."

She pulled her keys out and put them into the lock, starting to open the door, when Sheriff Bergstrom pushed past her. Rushing in, he pulled back the curtain around the bed.

"Oh Lord…" said the nurse as she came in behind him.

The bed was empty and the bed clothes had been stripped. The Sheriff drew his weapon, a 9 mm Sig-Sauer, and double-handed it, pushing into the bathroom and pointing it left then right. He tore back the shower curtain.

The room was empty.

Suddenly, Maddy rushed to the third-story window. The bed sheets had been torn and tied into a makeshift escape line. It ran down the outside of the hospital.

Axel, the homicidal crash victim, was gone.

Maddy just stared out the window, as her father paced back and forth behind her. "God*damn*it Maddy, what have I told you since the day you got back here?"

Maddy's voice was low and she was trembling.

"You are not cut out—"

"*What*? Speak up!"

He rushed up behind her and spun her around. There were tears in her eyes now.

"You told me—you said, 'Maddy, you are *not* cut out for this work.' Dad I'm sorr—"

"Sorry doesn't cut it. If we weren't so short staffed I'd suspend you right now.

"Dad please..."

"No! I want you to get home and clean up. Be back at the Station in twenty minutes to get out the BOLO." He looked over at the empty bed and Axel's escape line. "We'll deal with the rest of this later."

Maddy tried to reach out for him, but he backed away. Then he turned and walked out. She stood at the window and watched as he exited the hospital and got into his Unit. Before he opened the door he just leaned against it and shook his head.

She could almost hear him asking God why it was Billy who had to die first.

9

THE BERGSTROM HOUSE was a modest three bedroom ranch on the outskirts of Snoqualmie. The Sheriff had grown up in the same neighborhood and he'd played sandlot ball in the area where the house had been built as part of a six home subdivision. During summer cookouts he used to joke with his wife Shauna that he'd built their outdoor grill right over his old home plate.

Captain Michael Bergstrom, U.S. Marine Corps Retired, was a happier man then. After years of overseas duty away from his family, he was home every night. He'd met Shauna at a Camp Le Jeune dance just after he got his officer's bars and in 20 years of marriage, he'd never even glanced at another woman.

For Maddy, her early years in Snoqualmie had been happy. Her dad didn't seem to favor Billy back then. He'd taught her to cast a spinning rod, throw a fast ball and how to pin any boy her size in a wrestling match. He always seemed to have a smile on his face. Nothing bothered him back then.

That afternoon when her mother had missed the car pool and wasn't at school to pick her up, he told Maddy everything would be fine. The local G.P. couldn't figure out what was causing such distress in Shauna's abdomen. He ran a battery of tests and reasoned that it had to be gastrointestinal. After all, she was only forty-five and so healthy otherwise. Even then, Maddy's father assured her, "God would never do harm to a woman as good as your mom. He doesn't work that way."

But then, on the day he came home with her mother from the diagnostic clinic in Seattle, her father looked white. The color had drained from his face and there was a look of angry pain that had stayed with him ever since.

That was the day he'd learned that his beloved wife had cancer of the ovaries. The oncologists had given her three months to live.

Up to that point, Maddy's father had literally flown through life. Even under fire he never lost his cool. Old Marine buddies used to come to the house to try and cheer him up after the funeral and they'd tell tales of Mike Bergstrom and how "he never lost the stick." Hand-held RPG's would be coming up at him out of the desert and he'd keep that Seahawk steady.

Now, with the death of his wife, he felt vulnerable. He feared not so much for himself but for his two children. If fate could reach out and bring such a healthy young woman's life to an end, what else might happen? Where was God now?

But instead of hugging his kids and letting them know how much they meant to him, Sheriff Mike took on the role of protector. He became a kind of angry Drill Instructor, trying to prepare his children for the worst, the way the DI's had forced him to crawl under barbed wire during Basic on Paris Island.

Growing up, Maddy barely remembered him drinking anything but an occasional beer. Now he turned to whiskey; Jack Daniels at first, and when that didn't cut it, Wild Turkey 101. Billy responded to the new regimen by trying to outdo his father. He made his bed every morning with tight military corners, begging his dad to bounce quarters off the mattress.

He blew through Scouting in three years, amassing every merit badge in the *BSA Handbook*. He pushed himself physically, scoring more letters than any single graduate of Snoqualmie high—nine in five sports in three years of J.V. and Varsity.

The one time that Billy allowed himself to break loose—the night of his senior prom—he'd gotten wasted at the Kegger and crashed his jeep. The next day he had to call the hockey coach at U. Wash and tell him that he'd have to forego the scholarship. It would take another year for his knee to heal.

The frown lines on Mike Bergstrom's face got a little deeper that morning. Somehow, the luck he'd enjoyed all his life had gone away. He was no longer invincible. There were dark forces out there and the Sheriff felt that he'd have to protect his children from them at all costs. Maybe that's why he was so gung ho for Billy to join him at the Sheriff's Station and so worried when his son ran off to Seattle and enlisted in the Corps.

Maddy thought about all of this as she stood in the corner of the shower, trying to wash away Axel's blood and the guilt she felt at letting him escape. Her father had only given her twenty minutes to get back and she'd spent the first ten of them weeping, the second child, who had tried to fill her brother's shoes and failed.

When she turned off the water, Maddy squeezed her long red hair and put it up to dry in a towel above her head.

She grabbed a short silk kimono from a chair just outside the shower door. Since she spent her days dressed as a man, the robe was the one luxury she'd allowed herself. She'd seen it in a vintage clothing store in Seattle and she wore it at times when she felt particularly vulnerable. After she'd gone through rehab,

Maddy hadn't touched alcohol or any drug stronger than Advil, but right now her head was throbbing, so she went to the medicine cabinet in her father's room where he kept a bottle of Vicodin. This was one day she would need it.

Then, on the way back into her room, when she opened the door to her closet, her heart stopped. There, on the full-length mirror, someone had written these words with her lipstick:

FATE, MONSTROUS AND EMPTY…

10

SUDDENLY, AXEL LUNGED OUT from the hallway and grabbed her from behind by the hair. He was dressed in one of her father's uniforms. "I knew it," he said. "A natural redhead."

"What? What are you doi—"

Before she could finish, he flung her face-down on the bed, grabbing the belt from the robe and tying her wrists behind her. He ran the back of his hand across her face.

"Your skin—it's pure alabaster."

Maddy was struggling to pull away, but he had his knee on her back. She looked across the room and spotted her holster, but it was empty. That's when Axel reached behind his back and pulled out her Smith & Wesson. "Take off the robe. Let me see it."

See What? What are you talking about?

"You know what I mean…"

He spun her around and pulled the robe down, exposing her shoulder. There, where the Angel of Death tattoo had been, she had a scar. "You had it *removed*…" He grabbed her by the hair. "Does your old man know who you ran with? Did you *tell* him?"

Axel leaned down and whispered in her ear. "If there's one thing I hate, it's people who defy their own nature."

"What do you know about *anything*," said Maddy, practically spitting out the words.

"I know about *you*."

"*How*?" She was playing for time. Weighing her options. "How did you know I ran with the Nomads? How do you even know I *exist*?" He jerked her up from the bed and pushed her against a wall, holding the gun with one hand and her throat with the other.

"You can't be somebody you're not. Just accept it. There's outlaw in your blood."

Axel licked her ear as she struggled. Maddy spit in his face, but he only smiled and pushed against her. He was rock hard now. Wide-eyed, Maddy was fighting to get free, but Axel squeezed her throat, putting more and more pressure on her windpipe, so she stopped struggling, before she blacked out. With less resistance now, Axel shoved her gun in the belt behind his back. He ran his free hand down across her breasts, toward her panties.

Maddy was sure he would try and rape her, when just then, the phone rang on the bed table.

Back at the Station, Sheriff Bergstrom was worried. He let it ring, once, twice and then heard Maddy's answering machine switch on.

"This is Maddy. Leave it at the beep."

Now she and Axel could hear her father's voice: "Maddy, I need you back here ASAP. We got a hit from NCIC. The Staties in Indiana pulled a partial print at the scene of a home invasion in Bloomington. Sorority house. There's a freshman coed still missing."

Back at the station, Mike Bergstrom eyed a snapshot of the missing coed on his PC. It was Marlee Jane Hofstadter, the dead blonde Axel had photographed at his lair.

"Maddy. Maddy, it's Dad do you copy? Pick up." The phone line went dead and she knew, he'd be on his way over. If she didn't do something soon, Axel would kill them both.

Mike Bergstrom, rushed out of the Sheriff's Station carrying a Mossberg 500 pump. He jumped into his unit, a Tahoe SUV and pulled out, engaging lights & siren. The Bergstrom house was only ten blocks away and now in the bedroom, Axel heard the sound of the oncoming unit. He let go of Maddy's neck and grabbed her hair from the back. "To be continued," he said. "You're coming with me."

He spun her around and untied the belt on her wrists. Then he grabbed the handcuffs from the belt on Maddy's uniform, sitting on a nearby chair. "You should have listened to your old man last night."

"What? You heard that? You were awake?"

"Baby, do the math—or should I say, do the *meth*. You heard that Paki doc tell you how much crank I was on."

He slapped one of the cuffs on Maddy's right wrist. He was about to cuff her left when, she looked across the bed and spotted her Search & Rescue kit with the surgical scissors she'd used to cut him out of the van. Before he could get the second cuff on, Maddy jerked away and in one, swift move, rolled across the bed, grabbed the scissors and jammed them into his thigh.

"Argggh!" Axel winced from the pain. "This is *not* a good time for me to have scars…" He pulled out the scissors and dropped them, lunging at her with his bloody hand and catching the edge of her robe, flipping her onto the floor. Maddy pushed back with her feet to get away, but Axel grabbed her ankle, pulling her toward him. He slid his hand up between her legs, catching hold of her panties.

Four blocks away, the Sheriff's unit was closing in.

Back in the bedroom, Axel ripped off the panties and lunged for Maddy's neck with his other hand, but she groin kicked him, sending him doubled over, into a corner, whereupon, she escaped and went into the hallway, rushing down to a gun cabinet. It was locked, so she smashed the glass with her elbow and pulled out a double barreled Remington and a handful of 12 gauge shells.

Back in the bedroom, Axel took a moment to recover, then jumped up. He was about to rush out into the hallway when he heard the unmistakable sound of Maddy clicking the shotgun shut after she'd loaded it. He slammed the door closed and locked it, then hit the floor as… BOOOOM! Maddy blew a hole through it.

Axel looked around and spotted the keys to Maddy's unit, another Tahoe parked outside. So he pulled her Smith and shot out her bedroom window, jumping through it and rolling on the ground to the door of the cruiser, just as she emerged from the house and fired the second barrel… BOOM! Maddy blew out the left side window of the unit. She heard the sound of her father's siren approaching from the north.

But Axel slipped inside the front seat of the Tahoe and jammed the keys in the ignition. Ducking down, he slammed it into reverse, while Maddy stood on her porch and reloaded. Now as he roared back out of her driveway, he spun it south away from the arriving Sheriff's unit; when Maddy raced down from the porch into the street and fired another round… BOOM!… blowing out the Tahoe's rear window. By now, Axel was halfway up the block and away.

For a moment, she just stood there, half in shock. She was naked beneath the robe now and there was blood on the hem where he'd grabbed her. She rubbed her shoulder where the tattoo had been. Starting to shiver from the shame of letting him escape a second time, she dropped down onto the curb.

As her father's unit roared up in front of her, Maddy put her head in her hands. Next to the day when her mother died, this had been the worst 24 hours of her life.

11

Exiting the scene in a speeding police unit, Axel had two advantages: first, with the sirens blazing and the roof rack flashing he encountered zero traffic resistance as he followed South East Snoqualmie Parkway toward I-90.

Second, the only other Sheriff's unit available to chase him was now parked in front of Maddy's house and Mike Bergstrom had all he could do to keep his daughter from commandeering his *own* vehicle and taking off after the fugitive psychopath.

Realizing that the stolen Tahoe with the huge super-graphic SNO-3 on the roof would be easy prey for the State Troopers or Bergstrom's own chopper, Axel decided to forego the interstate and drive south, south-west on Highway 18.

He would dump the Tahoe at a truck stop under cover of darkness. So he searched for a place where he could get it off the road and out of sight.

He found what he was looking for about two miles north of the town of Hobart. There was a Kings County Public Works facility that stored sand for snow removal near the junction of 18 and Hobart Road. Since he'd gone through the guard rail up on State Route 906 the sun had been out all day and the temperature had been in the high 40's. Most of the highway snow had melted and the DPW yard was deserted. There was a large shed area where mounds of sand were piled under a corrugated metal roof.

He backed the Tahoe underneath facing the road, and turned up the police radio, alternately monitoring the Snoqualmie Sheriff's channel and the State Police band. In the trunk of the unit, he found a series of state maps and a Rand McNally Road Atlas which he used to plot his escape.

There were truck stops in either direction that would allow Axel to hitch a ride east, but as he studied the Washington State map, he spotted Issaquah, a bedroom community of 24,000 which held a special significance for him.

On July 14th, 1974, two women—Janice Ott and Denise Naslund—went missing from a heavily crowded beach area in Issaquah's Lake Sammamish State Park. Seven weeks later, their skeletal remains were found in a forest off nearby I-90.

To Axel, Washington State was hallowed ground. It had produced two of the most prolific sexual predators in history: Gary L. Ridgeway, otherwise known as The Green River Killer and Theodore Robert Bundy, aka Ted.

Starting in 1982 Ridgeway had strangled more than 48 woman—mostly prostitutes—near SEA-TAC strip, the 17 mile highway of motels, B joints and massage parlors near Seattle-Tacoma Airport. He later admitted to 71 homicides.

But while he outdid Bundy in volume, his crude style and isolated lifestyle couldn't match Ted, the smooth, handsome psych major who worked as a GOP campaign aide and a rape counselor while simultaneously abducting coeds, decapitating them and enjoying post mortem sex with their bodies. Bundy was so audacious that he actually kept the heads of some of his victims at home while he entertained his otherwise "normal" girlfriend. Using crutches and a phony cast, he'd lure his victims to his brown VW Beetle, then drop his car keys. When the unsuspecting women bent down to retrieve them, Bundy would knock them unconscious with a crowbar.

He'd push them into the Volkswagen, from which he'd extracted the front seat, and keep them sedated with a garrote until he got to his dumpsite.

From 1974 to 78 he bludgeoned and strangled 28 females in Utah, Colorado and Florida, but his last two Washington killings took place in Issaquah, just miles from where Axel was now waiting. This was the town that put serial murder on the map. And it was out of homage to his handsome role model that Axel chose to dump Maddy's unit up there.

The clock on the Tahoe's dash said 5:45 p.m. as he pulled out of the DPW shed and drove north under cover of darkness to a truck stop near N.W. Gilman Boulevard and the entrance to I-90.

Along a reinforced concrete wall on the north end of the lot he spotted a row of tractor trailers parked for the night. There was just enough room to squeeze a vehicle in behind them. So Axel parked Maddy's unit at the far end of the row. It would be morning before anybody found it.

Working in the dark behind the trucks, he took off the Sheriff's jersey and used a razor blade he'd found in the glove box to cut off any law enforcement markings.

He excised the Sheriff's Department patch from the sleeve of the outer jacket, then cut off the yellow stripes running up each leg of his pants.

Finally, he grabbed Maddy's Smith and Wesson and shoved it into the belt at the small of his back. Just before he walked out into the light of the truck stop, he pulled her panties from his pocket and rubbed them across his face.

Moments later, Axel spotted a long tractor-trailer hauling brand new Nissan Xterras. He jumped onto the back of the truck and hid among the vehicles as the driver turned East on I-90 toward Montana.

Later that night, minutes after they passed through Spokane 280 miles to the east, Axel felt the spikes shooting into his brain. Fighting off the migraine, he buried his face in the trophy he'd taken from Maddy.

He needed her now, the way a diabetic needed insulin; this redhead with the perfect white skin. How defiant she'd been. Even when he'd had her by the throat, she wouldn't yield. Now, as he fought to lower his pulse rate and control his respiration, he began to plot a scheme for getting her back.

12

By 8:30 P.M. THAT SAME NIGHT, Maddy sat in a room at the Sheriff's Station used for questioning suspects. Just hours after she'd returned to work, a black Chevy Suburban had pulled up outside and three men had jumped out flashing FBI ID's.

Two of them were from the Seattle Field Office, but they were merely playing chauffeur to the lead agent: SSA Ron Killebrew, a late 50's Bureau pit bull with a brush cut, a raspy Southern drawl and a smoker's cough. He was the Supervisory Special Agent who ran the BAU, the Behavioral Analysis Unit at the FBI Academy in Quantico, Virginia.

That morning, Sheriff Bergstrom had issued an all points or "be on the lookout" for the tattooed UNSUB linked to the Indiana sorority abduction. An hour later, Killebrew had boarded a Gulfstream Five at the Quantico Marine Base. He'd arrived at SEA-TAC by early evening.

Another ex-Leatherneck, Killebrew immediately bonded with Maddy's father. After debriefing him, he asked to speak to the young female Deputy alone. The Sheriff put them in the interrogation room because it had a one-way glass mirror and he wanted to observe his daughter's questioning.

It was a small ten by twelve foot room and the overhead fluorescents were harsh. Maddy was seated at a grey metal table on a hard metal chair.

Killebrew put an Olympus digital recorder in front of her. He had a briefcase open nearby and Maddy strained to see a folder marked with the FBI logo. Across the top in blue printed letters it said STRANGER 456.

Before he began, Killebrew sat in a chair across the table from her and studied Maddy. He took out a package of Marlboros and a Zippo lighter with the Ball and Anchor insignia of The Corps. He waited to see if Maddy would object to him smoking and when she didn't, he took out a cigarette and put it behind his right ear.

He flicked the lighter on and off a couple of times, then put it back in his pocket. The whole time, he stared at Maddy with a smirk on his face. Finally, he leaned forward and pressed the RECORD button on the Olympus. A small red light came on and he got up from his chair. He walked to the back of the room, studying himself in the two-way mirror. With his back to Maddy, he started out slowly.

"Let's get the I.D. on tape first, O.K.?"

His accent said North Carolina. Maybe Georgia.

"Sure," said Maddy. She leaned in over the recorder:

"Deputy Bergstrom, Madeline C., Snoqualmie Sheriff's Department."

Inside, she was nervous, but she kept her voice steady.

"Years on the job?" Killebrew was still facing the window.

"Less than one... About eleven months."

"Formal forensic training?"

"None. This is mostly S&R work up here agent..."

"Supervisory Special Agent."

"Oh yeah. I forgot. All you guys from The Bureau are special."

Killebrew smirked, then turned to face her.

"You know Ms. Bergstrom—I'm gonna address you as MIZ because, in my book, after your performance, you don't qualify for any title associated with law enforcement. So Ms. Bergstrom, answer me this: when your father told you to cuff this offender, why did you disobey a direct order?"

Maddy looked down at the digital recorder and switched it off.

"Is this an interview or an interrogation?"

"That's entirely up to you darlin'. Now answer the question, and please, don't touch my recorder."

He switched it on again. Maddy eyed him for a few seconds and exhaled hard. Finally, she said, "I was tired. I'd just come off a double shift. I'd almost died up on the mountain trying to save that man's life. He was apparently unconscious and didn't appear to be a threat."

"Damn that was one, two, three, four, excuses," he said, counting them on his fingers. "The next time I get hauled up on Capitol Hill and have some Committee Chairman up my ass, I do believe I'm gonna take you along."

Maddy decided to leave that one alone.

"So, after he'd escaped from the hospital and showed up at your house, you just let him go..."

"Hardly. I put a hole through my bedroom door to stop him."

"Nonetheless, the suspect escaped."

Killebrew was moving closer now, starting to circle the desk.

"Did he say anything about a journal?"

"No. If he had it, it would have gone down in the van."

Killebrew nodded. "O.K."

He went to his briefcase and opened another file. It had a small head shot of Maddy clipped to it. "According to your jacket, you put on a uniform after your brother died."

The reference to Billy made her uneasy.

"What about it?"

Maddy seemed more vulnerable now. She looked up at the one-way mirror, knowing her father was behind it burning a look into her. Killebrew opened another file on Billy.

"William Bergstrom. Takes a leave from his post as your father's Deputy in 2008. Marine corporal. Caught by a sniper in Fallujah leading his unit to safety."

He stabbed at Billy's picture in his Marine dress blues.

"Goddamn hero. What made you think you could live up to him?"

Finally she recovered some spunk.

"Is this The Bureau's approach to interrogation? Humiliate the subject and she'll open up? The only reason I agreed to this was so you'd show us his file." She strained to see it. "Is that him? Stranger 456? Who the hell is he?"

Just then, the door opened and Sheriff Bergstrom walked into the room. "Show some civility, Maddy."

Killebrew smiled. "No. I get it. It's understandable she'd be a little prickly. After all, the man stripped her, took her weapon and escaped in her unit." With that, Maddy got up and started to exit.

"I don't need this shit, O.K.?"

But her father stopped her.

"Sit down, Deputy." He stood in front of her, blocking the door.

Maddy was about to walk past him, when Killebrew opened a file and started tossing down pictures of women. All kinds: hookers, teachers, runaways, nurses, coeds. Finally, he threw down a surveillance shot of Axel.

"We don't know his birth name. He's listed in BAU's suspect files as Stranger Killer Four Fifty Six, but he likes to call himself Axel."

The Sheriff nodded at Maddy. She'd been right about that one. He turned back to Killebrew. "Please, continue."

"We've traced him back to age seven when his parents died in a fire." He pulled out a shot of a fire charred Illinois bungalow.

"I thought you said you didn't know his birth nam—?"

"He was adopted. The fire turned out to be arson. The little fucker stabbed them with his Cub Scout knife before he drowned them in gasoline and lit the match."

He pulled out a series of shots of Axel from surveillance cams and ATM's.

"He grew up in five different foster homes," said Killebrew. "He'd kill their pets first, then he'd threaten their children."

Maddy swallowed hard now.

"I've been tracking this fiend for more than a year. So far, we've tied him to the abduction of 37 females."

"Abduction?" asked Maddy. "You haven't found—"

"Any bodies. Not a hair. Not a fiber. The only crime scenes we have are the points of abduction."

"Which means," said the Sheriff, "if they're dead…"

"That would make him the most audacious serial since Green River…" Killebrew nodded to Maddy. "And you were a hair's-breadth away from becoming his latest pin-up."

Humiliated, she tried to turn away, but he kept pressing.

"That's right Deputy. You should've cuffed him to the bed. You should've nailed his fucking door shut and called the State Police to get another unit on the street outside his window."

Maddy looked to her father for support, but he shook his head. She was on her own. Finally, Killebrew leaned over the desk and put his face inches away from hers.

"'Cause of you we just lost Teddy Bundy from the Class of 2012."

13

THE SEMI CARRYING THE NISSAN XTERRAS drove nonstop for more than ten hours before pulling into Billings, Montana around five a.m. The temperature had dropped to near freezing, but Axel had been able to pry open the rear door on the SUV closest to the end of the truck and he'd had a relatively comfortable ride under the circumstances.

The truck driver parked at an all night gas station off I-90 and slept in his cab for a few hours before taking off around eight a.m. His final destination was Grand Forks North Dakota.

By the time he arrived at Paulson Nissan Subaru, a dealer on Gateway Drive near the junction of I-29, it was 6:00 p.m., almost a full 24 hours since Axel had escaped from Washington State. This time, fate, not so monstrous and empty, had been with him.

The SUV dealership was just 2.9 miles from the Amtrak station on Demers Avenue in Grand Forks, a half hour walk at best. Axel had used the onboard laptop in Maddy's unit to check the timetable for The Empire Builder, Amtrak's sleeper train that traveled west to east between Seattle and Chicago. It was due to pull out that night at 8:15 p.m.

He got to the station an hour early and scanned the crowd of travelers waiting to board the eastbound incoming train. There were two college kids with U.N.D.

sweatshirts and backpacks, a young mother with her baby in a snuggly and a businessman he'd overheard talking to a ticket agent about his fear of flying.

The clock was ticking for Axel. He was broke and on the run. By now, a fugitive warrant would have been issued for him, making him subject to immediate arrest. Though he'd escaped from Snoqualmie before they'd gotten to the point of a mug shot, he'd been printed and run through the National Crime Information Center. The Bureau would be looking for him throughout the northwest. He needed to get home right away, so he scanned the station for a target of opportunity.

He spotted her luggage first.

The woman was sitting on a bench next to a Redcap who had a rolling cart filled with three separate Louis Vuitton suitcases. She was a brunette in her late 50's. Dressed in a Burberry trench coat under a red fox hat; her boots were alligator. Probably Prada. Underneath her trench coat, she was wearing an Hermés blouse. Her suede skirt was from Chanel, he was almost certain.

Axel brushed past her and noticed that she wore a pearl choker and diamond stud earrings. He could swear that her jewel encrusted watch was a Patek-Phillipe. For years now, he had financed his murder spree by robbing his "subjects;" taking whatever he could from them in the way of cash and jewelry. He read Vogue and Harper's Bazaar every month so that he could keep up on the latest styles from the runways of Milan, Paris and New York.

He'd even taken an online gemology course so that he could separate the paste from the genuine "bling" and he got an erection just thinking about how this woman was going to finance his trip back home.

Now, as the train approached the station, an announcement came over the P.A. "Your attention please.

Announcing the arrival of Amtrak's Empire Builder, with service to Chicago, stopping at Fargo, North Dakota, Minneapolis, Minnesota and Milwaukee, Wisconsin. It will be ready for boarding momentarily on Track Eleven."

Axel made his way down to the track and slipped onboard ahead of the woman and her luggage. Inside the station he'd heard the Red Cap tell her that she'd be in compartment twenty-eight.

Moments before the train pulled out, a Porter led the woman down a corridor in the Number Two Sleeping Car. As the Red Cap loaded her luggage into the compartment, the Porter asked her if she wanted her bed turned down.

"Yes, please," she said, tipping the Red Cap as he exited. "You can call me in the morning before we reach Milwaukee."

The Porter smiled and unlocked a pull-down bed across the compartment. He lowered the shade on the door to the corridor.

"The dining car's open 'til ten, miss. Would you like me to make you a reservation?"

"No, I've eaten, thank you. But can you ask them to bring me a cocktail?"

"Surely Miss. What would you like?"

"A double Grey Goose martini. Rocks, extra olives. Very dry."

She handed him a fifty. "Keep the change."

The porter eyed it and he tipped his hat. "Thank you Miss. Very Generous. Be here shortly."

When he left, the woman locked the door behind him. She opened her smallest piece of luggage, a beauty case with her initials, M.P. near the latch. From the bottom of the case she took out a document on legal sized paper. It had been filed that day in the Superior

Court of Grand Forks. The caption said: "In the Matter of Nathan W. Purloff Petitioner vs. Miriam A. Purloff. Respondent. Dissolution of Marriage."

She'd been served by her husband's attorney on her way to what she thought was a reconciliation meeting.

Nathan had been a history professor at the University of Wisconsin in Madison when they'd met. He was 15 years her junior. Her father had left her a fortune after the sale of his dry goods business in Milwaukee.

Young Nathan had a mind like Thomas Friedman's and a swagger like Richard Gere's. He had simply dazzled her. They'd had five good years until he took the visiting lecturer job at the University in Grand Forks.

That's when he'd lost his mind to a blonde teaching assistant named Heidi. She was twenty three and he actually confessed that he wanted her to "bear his children."

Nathan wasn't even apologetic about being such a cliché. But what was worse than the betrayal was his threat to take half. Wisconsin was a community property state and this sonovabitch and his whore were going to take fifty per cent of what her father had spent a lifetime building.

Miriam Purloff didn't want to think about it. She just wanted to get to sleep after having a Xanax and couple of vodkas.

There was a knock on the door. A waiter with the drinks. He set down a tray with a small shaker, a plastic cup full of ice and a cup full of olives. Then he presented her with two more small bottles of Grey Goose.

"Compliments of the Porter," he said. Miriam pulled out a twenty and handed it to him. The waiter beamed.

"Thank you, Miss. He said you were a generous tipper."

"Better you than my husband," she said. The waiter smiled, a bit confused and exited as she locked the door behind him.

She sat down and looked at herself in the beauty case mirror; unbuttoning her blouse. Underneath she was wearing a black bra and panties. A little silk set from La Perla that she'd hoped her husband would enjoy. But now this.

She eyed the legal papers, then checked her Blackberry for any e-mails; hoping that maybe he'd decided to reconsider. But there was nothing. Only junk mail and a message from her lawyer to call her when she got home to Milwaukee.

She picked up the tiny shaker and shook it. Then she poured a drink into the cup full of rocks and took a sip.

As the train moved west through the North Dakota night, Miriam Purloff turned to stare out the window. She wasn't sure what she would do with her life now that the younger man had left her. She downed the first martini, then opened up one of the Grey Goose bottles and poured it directly into the cup.

She stared at her reflection in the window for a moment and frowned. No amount of surgery or Botox could reverse the aging process. The numbers were simply against her.

Miriam opened the second bottle of Grey Goose and started to mix it with the contents of the shaker, when suddenly, she heard a child weeping. The sound was coming from the next compartment adjacent to her bathroom.

The crying stopped. Then started again. So she got up and placed her ear against the wall by the bathroom door. The crying grew more intense. She was about to knock on the wall, when she heard the sound of a man clearing his throat. My Lord, she thought, could some child be in distress? She wasn't sure what to do, so she decided to open the bathroom door. Maybe that way she could hear it more clearly. But then, as she put her hand on the door latch, she stopped.

"Oh God," she said, feeling a chill. The weeping was coming from inside her own bathroom.

14

MIRIAM SHOOK WITH FEAR. She turned toward the outside door. But before she could reach it, the bathroom door sprung open and Axel lunged out at her. He was holding a bath towel rolled up lengthwise, with his hands on either end. Quickly, he swung the towel over her head like a garrote and began to choke her.

The towel was so tight that Miriam was unable to scream. As she started to struggle, Axel jumped up on the seat so that he was above her, pulling her upward with the towel acting now as a kind of terry cloth noose. Her body began to tremble. Her legs kicked, her arms flailed and she gasped for breath. But within seconds, as he closed her wind pipe, she blacked out.

Axel held the towel tightly for another few moments until he saw the eight ball hemorrhages in her eyes.

He listened for any sound in the corridor, but all he could hear was the staccato clack of the train as it moved across the tracks. So he dropped her body gently to the floor.

When he looked at the divorce papers and read the affidavit of her husband, he decided that he'd done the older woman a favor. As a gesture, he would redo her makeup before he left her.

Axel had all night now to rifle through her luggage, but first he stripped her of the jewelry. He found a small velvet bag in which she kept a silver Cartier travel clock and he filled it with the pearls, the diamond earrings and the watch. He'd been right. It was a white gold Patek-Phillipe Calatrava encircled with diamonds.

In her Fendi purse he found a wallet with a driver's license. She had a Milwaukee address. He found the key to a Mercedes, which she'd probably parked in the station garage and a small makeup kit with bottles of Xanax and Darvocet. He allowed himself a swig of vodka as he swallowed a couple of mood stabilizers. Then he wiped the tears from his eyes.

As Axel lay in wait for the woman, the sadness that he felt in that bathroom had been genuine. He had no feelings for his impending victim. But after the long night locked in that SUV, he was overcome with a deep depression.

He was worried that he would not have enough time to complete his work before his lair was destroyed in the demolition for the highway to come.

The next morning, as the Empire Builder pulled into Milwaukee, the Porter knocked on the door to compartment 28.

When he got no response he used his pass key to get inside. Everything seemed in order. All of her luggage was stowed neatly beneath her bed, which she'd apparently slept in. But when the Porter opened the bathroom door, he rocked back.

Miriam Purloff was naked except for the black La Perla bra and panties. She'd been propped up on the toilet, her head resting against the window. Her eyes were open and she had been made up as if she was about to go out for a night on the town. But as the astonished Porter gazed down at her, he noticed that something had been written across her belly in eyeliner. It said:

MAKE ME AN INSTRUMENT OF THY PEACE

Five minutes later, Axel was moving through the parking garage attached to the Amtrak station, pressing the unlock button on the Mercedes remote. He got no response on the first floor, so he walked up a flight of stairs. On the second floor, near the exit ramp, lights flashed on a lavender CLK63 Cabriolet. He thought to himself, "Maybe the nuns were right and there actually is a God."

By 7:00 a.m. Axel was roaring down I-94 south. He had the top down and he was pushing buttons on Miriam Purloff's CD changer. Retching at her taste in music, he ejected discs by Julio Iglesias, Andrea Bocelli and Neil Diamond, tossing them over his head, out of the car onto the interstate.

He stabbed at the radio tuner until he found 1240 AM, a metal station that was blasting *Rock You Like a Hurricane* by the Scorpions. Just then, he raced past a sign that said CHICAGO 91 MILES.

From there he'd continue south on I-57, through Manteno and on to Kankakee, the town where he was born. He'd passed his new home years before, but rediscovered it after surfing the web for techniques on euthanizing animals.

One of the links had brought him to a news story on the demolition of the old Armour meatpacking slaughterhouse down on Rural Route 17. A new highway spur was going in right through the plant which had been vacant since 2010

It was the precise space that he needed. There was a furnace where the carcasses had been burned. It vented out into a nineteen-story brick stack that was so high, any smoke from the bodies he'd dispose of would dissipate in the wind that blew across Kankakee County.

The slaughterhouse itself was an extraordinary four story space. It was T-shaped like an old cathedral with an enormous central room he called his nave. The free standing concrete walls were four stories high and the ceiling was unobstructed by beams—a two-inch thick expanse of white concrete reinforced with rebar.

He was able to steal electricity from an old 220 line that ran along route 17 to power the street lights. They'd long since been turned off as that section of 17 was condemned, but there was still juice in the cables. Best of all, the plant was 100 yards away from an old Illinois Central railroad canal—a twenty foot wide concrete channel with three feet of draft that was part of an old irrigation system. It connected into a network of canals and waterways that flowed south from the Chicago River, fed by Lake Michigan.

In a small Boston Whaler, Axel could move in and out of the Windy City virtually unnoticed as he claimed the subjects for his masterpiece. He had a series of vehicles that he kept hidden in containers parked along the riverbanks on Chicago's south side. To avoid identification, he would routinely spray paint them and switch the license plates.

With the slaughterhouse as his base, he moved with impunity across the Midwest, mostly at night, locating his victims, abducting them, killing them, embalming them on site and then moving their bodies up into his basilica before they were corrupted, post mortem.

It was a fiendish plan that took extraordinary stamina, tenacity and great organizational skill and he was close to completion.

But as he got home and hid the Mercedes in an old garage on the property, he went into his office and checked the calendar. He had only two and a half weeks left to paint Eve and he'd come back from Washington alone.

He had to lure her back here at all costs. There was no other woman who could take her place with him up on that ceiling.

15

Back in Snoqualmie, Maddy Bergstrom took her anger out on a heavy bag. She was trying to purge the guilt; throwing punches and side kicks as if the six foot 100 pound Everlast bag hanging from the gym ceiling was Axel himself.

She felt his knee on her back. She could smell the blood on his face. The fact that he'd touched her private parts and taken an intimate article of her clothing made her sick. She'd been blindsided and outgunned.

For the last year she'd been telling herself that her father was wrong, that she could do this job at least as well as her brother had, but this predator had proven her wrong. And if the humiliation of losing him twice wasn't enough, she had to sit still for that self-righteous prick from the FBI—Killebrew.

Then, in return for subjecting herself to his abuse, what did she get? Nothing. Not a single lead she could work. Typical of The Bureau, he'd refused to share the files.

Maddy had offered to resign, but her father had been surprisingly forgiving. She shouldn't keep punishing herself, he told her. The failure to cuff him was one thing, but who could have foreseen what happened at their house? The Sheriff blamed himself for not anticipating the threat to his daughter who'd gone home on his orders to face possible rape and abduction.

There was no amount of police work or training that could prepare an officer for an evil like Axel, he said, assuring Maddy that she would get through it after she took some time off.

But even her father's forgiveness had troubled her. Would he have prescribed the same course of R&R for Billy? She doubted it.

If a man had been violated and robbed of his pride, the first order of business would be retribution. Men didn't turn tail and run—they got back on their horses and tracked down the bad men who'd attacked them. That was the code. The lawman's way. So it was her father's "girls don't belong in this line of work" attitude that hurt her the most.

Now as she punished the heavy bag, Maddy kept running the incident through her mind, trying to remember some detail that would help her pick up the scent and get back on the hunt for this psychopath. Finally, it hit her: one of Killebrew's questions, "Did he say anything about a journal?" and her response, "It must have gone down in the van."

It had been seventy-two hours since Axel's escape and today was the day that her father was going up to the gorge with a tow truck to bring down the burned-out wreck. Killebrew and an FBI forensics team were due to link with him at the town impound garage. The meeting was set for 2:00 p.m.

Maddy stopped punching and checked the clock on the gym wall. It was 1:55. She thought about the consequences of interfering in the investigation. She'd lose her badge for sure and she might even get charged with obstruction of justice. But none of that mattered as she thought about Axel; how he'd forced her face down on the bed and ripped open her robe.

So she took off running—out the back door of the gym—down an alley and up over a fence as a pair of FBI Suburbans rolled down Route 202 toward the garage.

When she got to the rear of the garage at Southeast Newton Street, she scaled a chain link fence and slipped inside. The fire-ravaged van was in an isolated corner on the ground floor. Deputy Eddie Gomes, who'd been called back from vacation, was just finishing cordoning it off with yellow crime scene tape.

From where she was standing, Maddy could look through the first floor of the garage to the entrance.

The two Suburbans had just arrived out front. Eddie was walking out to greet them and she could see the roof lights of her father's unit pulling up. She knew that she would have almost no time to do this, so she raced across the garage floor and under the crime scene tape.

One of the Econoline's back doors had broken off in the crash, so she jumped inside, checking under the seats, in the glove box and under the dash which had been scorched by the flames. She could hear Killebrew's raspy drawl now as he got out of the Suburban and handed her father a federal search warrant.

Maddy moved to the back of the van, and found a burned-up Eagle Creek rolling duffle. Inside, she found the fire-scarred remains of an evidence vacuum, a container of flex-ties and a crowbar: Axel's "murder kit." But nothing else.

"Seal it off. I want a full quadrant search," said Killebrew as the forensics team prepped to come inside.

Maddy had seconds left, so she crawled out of the van and slid underneath it, checking the undercarriage. Nothing in the wheel wells. Nothing around the brake housings. And then she spotted it: the spare tire well. She pulled herself over to it, getting soot on her face as her heart pounded. The cover on the wheel well was ajar. Instead of fitting tight to the chassis to protect the spare tire, it was cocked, on an angle. It must have been damaged when the van dropped into the gorge.

Maddy looked down and saw the forensic team approaching. Their shoes were covered in non-static boot covers to preserve the integrity of the scene which she was now violating. But she had one last shot.

She reached up inside the wheel well and felt it. Some kind of book wrapped in duct tape. She pulled it out and rolled out from under the van, hiding between the burned-out Econoline and the back wall of the garage.

Now, just as Killebrew and his team came up to the crime scene tape, she slipped out the back entrance. Keeping her head low, she did a broken field run down the alley. When she got to the end, she went back over the chain link fence and dropped down behind a dumpster, hyperventilating.

Biting into the duct tape, she peeled it back, frantically unraveling the package like some methed-out archaeologist who'd just cracked a mummy's tomb.

Then, when the tape was gone, she came to a series of black Hefty garbage bags—each one wrapped around the other. For finishing first in her Cascade class, Maddy had received a belt buckle knife with the school logo.

She popped it off now, carefully cutting the bags away. The plastic had melted in the heat from the fire, but had otherwise protected the book hidden inside the metal wheel well. Finally, when she got to the last layer of plastic, she ripped it away to reveal: a brown banker's ledger full of numbers and filthy drawings.

Axel's journal.

16

THAT NIGHT, working alone in the Sheriff's Station, Maddy pawed through page after page of Axel's scribbling: an elaborate system of letters and numbers interspersed with pictures of angels in sexual acts; seraphim and cherubim coupling with demons and mythological beasts. He had whole chapters full of news clips and analyses on the most notorious serial killers: DeSalvo, Heidnik, Gein, Lucas, Corona, Berkowitz, Williams, Bianchi and Buono.

In the middle of the book there was a table grid of the major unsolved serial killer cases in the country from the late 1990's on. The table contained each killer's nickname, the location of the murders, the suspected number of deaths along with the name of the chief investigator in each case.

Case	Area	From	Victims	Investigator
Pig Sty Killer	Des Moines	1999-01	39	T. Hastings
Blunt Force Killer	Wichita	2001-03	28	P. Abrams
Bus Stop Strangler	Nashville	2005-07	26	R. Killebrew
Ohio River Killer	Dayton	2007	22	T.C. Forbes
Gay Bar Killer	Kansas City	2008-09	10	M. Grimes
Dismemberer	O.K. City	2008	15	R. Killebrew
Field Killer	Galveston	2009	21	T.C. Forbes
Child Snatcher	Pittsburgh	2008-09	26	R. Killebrew
Railroad Killer	Midwest	2006-08	34	T.C. Forbe
I-80 Killer	Ill.-Ind.	2008-10	44	T.C. Forbes R. Killebrew

Maddy noticed that next to FBI Agent Ron Killebrew, the investigator who came up most often on the list was Thomas C. Forbes, a senior FBI Agent who was listed with Killebrew on the recent series of Midwest truck stop-prostitute homicides dubbed "The I-80 Killer" case.

She turned to her Macbook Pro and did a Google search for "T.C. Forbes." A dozen URL'S appeared along with a series of headlines. Reading Forbes' c.v. to herself, she took notes in a yellow legal pad as various pictures and newspaper headlines flashed across the laptop's screen:

"Forbes, Thomas C., FBI Quantico. Behavioral Analysis Unit. Born 2/18/65." There was an FBI I.D. photo of Forbes as a young Special Agent.

"Northeastern undergrad. Criminal Justice College. Master's Thesis at Emory on the Atlanta Child Murders. Consultant on Gacy and Dahmer." Pictures of John Wayne Gacy and Jeffrey Dahmer.

"Ph.D. Kennedy School at Harvard '06." A shot of Forbes up in Cambridge. "Returns to Bureau '07. Point man on the I-80 killings. Wounded during an arrest attempt… Killebrew gets assigned to the case and then…" A Washington Post headline:

BAU AGENT ON I-80 CASE EXITS FBI.

"He's out." Maddy printed out a Seattle Post-Intelligencer profile on Forbes under the headline:

SERIAL HUNTER TO TEACH AT U. WASH.

She went to the University Website and punched his name into the Faculty Directory. His "Introduction to Homicide" class met on Tuesdays and Thursdays.

It was now Wednesday. Maddy couldn't believe her luck, but after reading and re-reading the journal, she knew that Axel would describe it as "fate."

She asked her father for a leave day and, now that Eddie Gomes was back, the Sheriff was happy to oblige. He had no idea that she'd stolen Axel's journal and was continuing to work the case.

Dr. Forbes taught the criminology course in a lecture hall with stadium seating. The next morning, Maddy arrived about ten minutes into his class using the entrance at the top of the hall.

Down below, Forbes was limping slightly. There was a large screen behind him filled with images from a Power Point presentation. Next to that, a large white board where he made notes projected to the entire class.

The light was in his eyes, so he didn't notice Maddy ducking into a seat in the back row.

In person Dr. Forbes hardly resembled his web photos. He was dressed in an old sport coat over a denim shirt and wrinkled corduroys. There was a three-day beard on his face and he was using a nine iron as a kind of cane.

Now in his mid 40's and still ruggedly handsome, he spoke rapidly and aggressively. At that moment, he was looming over a sophomore student named Ward who was seated in the second row.

"So when you registered for Homicide what were your expectations, Mr. Ward? Coast with a easy C? Maybe pick up a copy of last year's Blue Book exam on Facebook? I mean, come on, you had to know the course was murder…"

There were a few titters from the students. Ward looked flustered as Forbes pressed on.

"Didn't anyone give you my rap sheet?"

Ward nodded nervously. "Yeah. Sort of."

"Which version Mr. Ward? Forbes, the burnout who brings his Beretta to class? Forbes the sadist who feeds on undergraduates or Forbes the defrocked agent with a chip on his shoulder the size of Jody Foster?"

More laughs from the crowd. But Ward was slumping down in his seat. Maddy thought of the blistering treatment she'd received from Killebrew. But Forbes wouldn't quit.

"Come on son. You're prepping for a career in law enforcement and this is the Fort Bragg of Criminology. Basic training. Get past me and you'll never die in combat. But don't ever come into my class unprepared!"

He slammed the golf club down on the floor and Ward jumped from the sound. Squirming now, he stared down at the textbook: Fisher's Techniques of Crime Scene Investigation. He hesitated, then suddenly, Dr. Forbes jumped onto the first row of seats.

"The sphincter tightening Mr. Ward?"

In the back row, Maddy winced at his heavy-handedness. She hated the guy already. He was another sadist like Killebrew. She wanted to run down, grab the nine iron and throttle him with it.

Down below, Ward was almost pissing his pants as he eyed the book for the answer. Finally, he gritted his teeth and took a shot...

"Patech... a... Petechial hemorrhages."

Suddenly, Dr. Forbes lit up. "Bang! That's it, Mr. Ward. The first indication of death by asphyxiation."

Ward breathed a sigh of relief as Dr. Forbes jumped back down and wrote a number on the white board: a big "88%."

"Now let's talk about clearance rates. You've read the stats… Eighty-eight. That's the percentage of conventional homicides that are solved. Most people kill once and only once in their lives. And they kill for a…"

He held his hand up to his ear waiting for a response and the class sounded out in unison: "Motive…"

"Exactly… So as soon as you hit the chalk mark and I.D. the victim, ask yourself where he worked, who he owed money to and who he was fucking." He paused as they let it sink in.

"You draw a straight line between the dead guy and his known associates and you'll wrap it up. In 88% of the cases you'll be downing Cuervo shots with your partner within 48 hours post-mortem."

The class was taking furious notes now and he waited another ten seconds before slamming down the head of the nine iron on the floor to get their attention.

"*However*… The serial killer is a different breed. He's a stranger. Typically a white male; late 20's to mid 30's. Above average intelligence. He may be an XYY with an extra male chromosome. Almost always, he's a victim of severe abuse as a child."

Now, Dr. Forbes' rapid fire delivery began to slow. "He starts young; mutilating animals, setting fires, wetting his bed. The full MacDonald triad. In his early teens he's looking in windows. Peeping Tom shit. But as he gets bolder, he graduates to serial rape and then…"

He paused now and turned to face the white board, not just lecturing hypothetically, but channeling his own awful memories.

"His first one is usually close to home. Easy prey. A hooker; a hitch hiker. Some runaway girl that nobody misses. When he makes his first kill he'll often bolt the scene, tossing out pieces of evidence; wracked, not with guilt, but the fear of being caught. He'll lay low. Enter a cooling-off period and then, he'll begin to troll for another. In this hunting phase he goes into an aura. He'll get smashed to kill the pain, then speed up on meth to get hard. Pretty soon he starts crossing jurisdictions; selecting a victim in point A… Capturing her in point B… Snuffing out her life in point C and dropping her body in point D…"

He drew the letters A, B, C, D in a quadrant on the white board, getting more and more somber as he thought back on the terrible images of his own career.

"Ladies and gentlemen, you add *time* and *distance* between point A and point D and you'll find that the clearance rate will drop to less than five per cent." He turned to face them.

"And why? There's no motive. He's a phantom. You have no fucking idea who this man is or where he'll strike next."

The class sat transfixed now as Dr. Forbes stood there, almost frozen in his own past. He gripped the podium and looked out at the faces of a hundred kids who would never know the horror that still haunted him. Even at thirty feet away at the top of the lecture hall Maddy could see his hands trembling as he tried to steady himself.

Turned off by his bitterness at first, she began to understand him now. This man was nothing like Killebrew. He was vulnerable and capable of self reflection. She could barely wait to show him Axel's journal.

17

MADDY WAITED OUTSIDE as Dr. Forbes exited the lecture building and crossed to an old BMW R-75/5 motorcycle. He stowed his briefcase in a saddlebag and climbed on, about to kick-start it, when she stopped him.

"Dr. Forbes. Deputy Bergstrom, Snoqualmie Sheriff's Department." She offered her hand, but he turned away.

"Got your message on my voice mail."

"So I was wondering if maybe you could take a look—"

But he cut her off. "Sorry. I don't consult anymore."

He kick-started the bike, ready to take off, when Maddy stood in front of him.

"Fine. I just thought, you know, since Killebrew's all over it, tha—"

"Ron Killebrew? BAU at Quantico?"

Maddy nodded. Dr. Forbes shut off the bike and burned a look into her. Finally, he gritted his teeth and nodded for her to get on.

He kick-started it again and popped the clutch, screeching off, tearing across the campus, zig-zagging in and out of students, then up onto a sidewalk and down an embankment as Maddy held on.

She leaned forward and yelled over the engine noise: "You don't wear a helmet?"

Dr. Forbes, smiled and looked back at her.

"At my age, a man rides a motorcycle for one of two reasons: to pick up girls or to service a death wish."

"My Dad says that at *your* age they're both the same thing."

Stung by the remark, Dr. Forbes suddenly braked the bike and skidded to a stop.

"That's good. Next time send *Dad*. I don't have time to play."

He nodded for her to get off, but Maddy pressed him.

"Look, I'm sorry. I wouldn't have come all the way up here if I didn't need your help. Please. It was a stupid thing to say."

"You're right. It *was*."

Dr. Forbes eyed her, deciding whether or not she was worth it, and then…

"It was also *true*. Hang on."

He left rubber as they screeched forward, ran a red light and roared off.

Dr. Forbes' house in the U. District was a bit like its owner—well worn and full of memories. As he tinkered in the kitchen trying to open the only bottle of Chardonnay he could find, Maddy examined his bookshelf.

He owned dog-eared copies of Geberth on *Crime Scene Investigation*, DiMaio's *Gunshot Wounds*, *Tire Impression Evidence* by McDonald, William Bodziak on *Footwear Impressions* and Dr. Cyril Wecht's *Cause of Death*.

The man's brag wall was immense: covered with citations and plaques from a half dozen different law enforcement agencies. There were framed pictures of Forbes with every FBI director since Louis Freeh in 1994. The opposite wall of his office was stacked shoulder-high with files from police departments across the country requesting his help. A third wall contained a series of framed newspaper headlines on every major serial murder case since The Son of Sam.

As he sat at his desk paging through Axel's journal, Maddy decided not to tell him that she hadn't touched alcohol since she'd gotten out of rehab. Besides, she didn't think a lecture on sobriety would be appropriate, given the half dozen empty bottles of Percodan on the credenza behind him.

So she sat quietly, nursing the white wine.

While he read down through Axel's elaborate number and letter system, Dr. Forbes kept rubbing his thigh. Almost unconsciously he grabbed a pill bottle, popped the top and swallowed a capsule. Finally, he closed the Journal.

Maddy couldn't wait for his evaluation. "So?"

Dr. Forbes picked up his wine glass and took a sip. He nodded across the office.

"See that stack of files against the wall? Some are cold cases ten years old. Positive DNA matches and I don't even have time for *them*..."

"I just need an opinion. His journal is like a scrap book. There's a profile on every serial murderer since The Boston Strangler."

"And you want to know if he's a star fucker, or if Killebrew was right and you unleashed a psychopath?"

Maddy nodded with guilt. "Something like that."

Dr. Forbes handed the journal back to her and turned away.

"You don't want to know..."

"Oh, yes I do." She started to get up, but he slammed his golf club-cane down on the floor.

"No!"

Maddy sat back down.

Forbes got up and started pacing.

"You have no idea what it's like to be on the trail of a predatory killer who won't stop." He was circling the desk now, lecturing her the way he'd talked to his students: angrily and aggressively, using the framed news stories on the wall to make his point.

"No matter *what*, he's always ahead. The more bodies he drops, the greater the public hysteria, so you end up choking on the intake."

With the golf club, he pointed to a headline from the *New York Daily News*:

SON OF SAM EVIDENCE GLUT

"You're overwhelmed by a thousand false leads. Every morning you come into the office to find the families of victims he's abducted. They're praying for some kind of hope, but you have none."

He nodded toward a story from *The Seattle Times*:

TED KILLER DISAPPEARS.

"Other cops pass you in the hall and turn away. The brass doesn't want to *know* you 'cause the killer's still out there and you're an embarrassment to the department."

He tapped a framed piece from *The San Francisco Herald Examiner*:

ZODIAC KILLER STILL AT LARGE

"The press dogs your every move. You wake up dreading the next body drop. Meanwhile, the killer gets bolder. Every murder that goes unnoticed is a challenge for him to go on. He's out there laughing at you. Why? Because *he* calls the play."

Dr. Forbes sat down in a chair next to Maddy.

"In ninety-five out of a hundred cases you lose, Deputy Bergstrom. The murder stops *only* after the killer exits your jurisdiction or he gets hepatitis or AIDS or he's arrested on a lesser charge and ends up in stir."

He moved closer, inches from her face now.

"In this line of work, rarely, if ever, do you have the satisfaction of making a collar. Even with amateurs..." He nodded to Axel's journal. "And this man has a Ph.D in serial death. He's studied. He's on an accelerated learning curve. From his knowledge of forensics and his classical references, I'd say he's got an IQ in the high one-fifties. And given the meth in his system he's killed since you lost him. Of that, I'm certain."

Maddy winced. He was rubbing his leg now from the pain...

"I happen to think Ron Killebrew is a fraud and an empty suit, but he's right about this one. You were lucky. Give it up. Be glad he fled when he did. He's not your problem anymore."

"Oh yes he is..."

"Well, he's not *mine*." He looked over at the stack of files. "I'm just... tired."

Maddy nodded toward the Percodan bottles.

"You mean *bitter*, don't you?"

She grabbed her files, got up and exited, doing her best to keep her game face on until she reached the street. When she was sure he could no longer see her, Maddy leaned back against a tree by the curb and began to weep.

18

BACK IN HIS LAIR, Axel was up on the left scaffold, pressed into a corner of the huge space, painting a face on the ceiling using a digital picture as a reference. It was the face of Marlee Jane Hofstadter, the blonde coed from Alpha Chi. Axel had set up a series of enormous speakers in the space below. Driven by an iPad, *Welcome to The Jungle* by Guns N' Roses blasted in the background.

Now, as he painted, Axel grew frustrated. Despite the clarity of the picture, the woman, in death, had her eyes closed and he was representing her on the ceiling as if she were alive.

"Eyes, damn it. Open your fucking eyes."

He bellowed at the picture, then threw his brushes down and slid down from the scaffold on a nylon climbing rope.

He went into his office and crossed to his file drawer full of cards marked with the mysterious letters and numbers. He ran through a pile of sketches; line drawings of faces he was about to paint. One was the outline of a 12 year-old girl in repose. But he needed a model.

Growing more agitated, Axel stormed over to his wall of "missing person" pictures. He looked for a face that would match the sketch, but he couldn't find the right subject. Next to the wall was a Kankakee Daily Journal. The headline from a page-one story said:

DEMOLITION SET FOR HIGHWAY

Finally, Axel moved to a calendar and checked the date: December 15th. It was now only two weeks away.

He walked back into the nave and looked up at the centerpiece on the ceiling: the place where his portrait of Eve would soon go. In order to execute it, he would have to get back the surly biker chick-cop that he'd left up in Snoqualmie.

On the long truck ride out of Washington State, he'd conceived a plan with perfect symmetry He would use one of his subjects to lure back the redhead—the 12 year-old girl that he needed.

Back at the Sheriff's station, working alone, Maddy wouldn't give up. She was paging through Axel's journal.

Running down his list of open serial cases, she focused on the latest series, "The I-80 killings."

Using her Mac laptop, Maddy accessed the NCIC database. She ran a search for the available I-80 case files. A series of crime scene photos downloaded as jpg files; shots of the truck stops along the U.S. interstate where the killer had murdered the hookers. There was a map of the highway system and a series of files describing trace evidence retrieved at the scenes.

Maddy stopped when she came to an FBI #302 memo written by then Special Agent T.C. Forbes. It listed a chronology of the murders that took place at the I-80 junctions of I-65, I-57 and I-55, the North-South interstate routes.

Now, running her index finger down the I-80 list in Axel's Journal she zeroed in on a repeating number pattern: 55.57.65 55.57.65. She looked back at the numbers on the screen from Forbes's #302: 65, 57, 55 65, 57, 55. Axel had them in the opposite order of the I-80 killings and Maddy shook her head at his mistake.

"Goddamn copycat and you couldn't even get the sequence right." She printed out Forbes' #302. For the first time, she felt that she had something she could go back to him with.

The next day, she stopped at the local Starbucks and picked up a tall black drip coffee and an Apple Fritter. It was the donut-in-disguise that her father craved. The door to his office was closed, so she knocked. He looked up and waved her in. She walked in, put down the coffee and handed him the bag. The Sheriff peeked inside and smiled.

"You must be after a major favor to offer a bribe like that."

Maddy approached him sheepishly. "I wanted to see what you thought… About my request for a lea—"

"The answer's affirmative."

Maddy was shocked. "What? Yes? Oh Daddy, thank you. You won't regret this, I promis—"

But he cut her off. "*If* you use the time to get out of here for awhile. Go down to Florida and visit your grandparents. Get some sun. Take a course; anything to get your mind off of this, but you are *not* going after that maniac. And that is final."

Maddy leaned over his desk.

"Dad I'm ready. I've read everything on serial death that's in print. Cleckley. Ressler. Keppel. All the FBI monographs."

"Right, and I read all the flight manuals before my first solo. Then I took off in that T-38 from Pensacola, circled the base and damn near augured in."

"You're not even giving me a chance—"

"To do what?"

Maddy turned away and bit down on her lower lip. He could see that she was fighting back tears. Her years of frustration at trying to please him were coming to a head. The Sheriff got up from his desk and moved toward her.

"Just try to understand, honey. We lost your mother, then Billy." He nodded to a family picture on his desk. "I can't go to another funeral."

Back in the Kankakee slaughterhouse Axel was using the Toshiba laptop he'd taken off a salesman in Dallas. It had a Verizon wireless card that he paid for each month with a Paypal account he'd established under another hijacked identity.

He logged onto Facebook and scrolled through dozens of files, searching for a young female subject.

Finally, he came to the page for Ginny Kendrick, a 12 year-old girl with fair skin and long dark hair, braided into pigtails. In one photo she was wearing a sweatshirt that said Chase Prep Chicago.

Three days later in Snoqualmie, Maddy was ready to give up. She'd left repeated voice mail messages for Dr. Forbes with no response. She'd e-mailed him several times. Nothing. So she slipped Axel's Journal into an envelope and addressed it to: Ronald Killebrew Special

Agent In Charge Behavioral Analysis Unit FBI 4000 Potomac Road Quantico, VA 22134.

The package sat on her desk most of the morning. Then, just after noon she looked out the Station window and spotted the mail truck making the daily delivery. So she grabbed the package and ran out to hand it to the driver, Travis Olson.

She'd gone to high school with him and he was always hitting on her. "Hey Maddy. Haven't seen you at the gym lately. You workin' nights?"

Maddy nodded. "Something like that. Listen, I want to send this Priority with a Delivery Confirmation. Can you figure out how much postage I'll need?"

Travis smiled. "Absolutely."

He weighed the package on a small scale, eyeing the address. "FBI huh? Official stuff?" Maddy smiled.

"O.K. It'll be $9.60."

She handed him a ten dollar bill and he gave her the change.

"So it'll get there Priority?"

"Absolutely. Figure two to three days."

He printed out the postage and stuck it to the envelope, then cancelled it, round-dating Maddy's receipt for the Delivery Confirmation. Then he handed her the Sheriff's Department mail and she started to take off.

"Catch you at the gym."

"Thanks Trav. I'll see you."

Maddy headed inside, idly flipping through the bills and the other mail, when she came to a small padded manila envelope. She turned it over casually and then froze. On the front, decorating the handwritten address like an illuminated manuscript, was one of *Axel's drawings*. The package had been addressed to her.

Suddenly, Maddy took off running, yelling after the truck.

"Travis wait.... TRAVIS!"

The mailman skidded to a stop, whereupon Maddy reached in and grabbed the package addressed to SSA Killebrew.

"Sorry. I need it back."

She ran to her Unit, which they'd recovered from that truck stop in Issaquah and radioed Eddie Gomes at the Station inside. She asked if he could cover for her, then put the Tahoe into reverse and took off.

Minutes later, Maddy was parked behind a billboard on Route 202, just West of town. She found a forensic kit that she kept in the console and pulled out a pair of latex gloves. With the knife from her belt buckle, she carefully opened the package.

Maddy felt sick. Inside was a pigtail cut from the hair of a teenage girl. There was a barrette at the end of it that said "Chase." The postmark on the envelope read "Chicago." There was a *Sun Times* piece with a shot of the 12 year-old girl Axel had located on Facebook.

The headline said:

CHASE PREP STUDENT STILL MISSING

19

ALONG WITH HIS COLLECTION of victims photos, Axel maintained an assortment of license plates. Many of them had been taken from cars, vans and SUV's he'd hijacked with the owners still in them. It was a technique he employed most often with women. He used Henry Lee Lucas's dirt-over-the-numbers trick so that he could recycle them on the vehicles he'd take with him to collect other bodies. There was an enormous garage connected to the slaughter-house where Armour's refrigerated trucks had been parked. It was now filled with more than a dozen trucks, vans and sports utility vehicles.

While he waited for a response from Maddy, Axel was still more than twenty subjects short of the number he needed to complete his final work. He had less than two weeks to go before the demolition, so he'd have to amp-up his murder spree. Right now he had an immediate demand for a black-haired model for a panel depicting a scene from Genesis. She had to be full figured, with angelic features and skin that was virtually albino-white—a difficult combination.

But he'd found a candidate during one of his visits to Nic's, a tattoo parlor off Rush Street on the near North Side. This woman had auburn hair, but she was otherwise perfect. She had the bone structure of a runway model but it was somehow hidden inside a size 14 body. Axel wondered if there had ever been a period in her life when she'd attracted men. If he had the time and energy he'd cut the flesh away himself to find out. But he was under the gun.

Her name was Christie Sloane. It only took him a few minutes online to find her. The tat that Nic's had drawn in the center of her back was so unique.

It was a glass, v-shaped perfume bottle with a top in the form of a crystal crown. The logo on the bottle had a lion with a serpentine tale sitting atop another crown. In script across the amber-colored liquid on the bottle's face it said: Clive Christian.

A brief search on his laptop revealed that Christian made the most expensive perfume in the world: Imperial Majesty. His limited edition of five bottles was priced at $215,000 an ounce and three had already sold. Christian also produced a more "affordable" scent called No. 1. An ounce of that retailed for $2,300.00 and there was only one place to buy it in all of Chicago: the perfume counter at Saks Fifth Avenue on North Michigan. The store closed at eight.

Axel decided to use a black 2011 Land Rover LR-4 that he'd picked up when he'd abducted a thirty-five year old real estate agent in the tony Detroit suburb of Bloomfield Hills. He'd found her on the Sotheby's website. Her name was April Potter; a dead ringer for a seraphim that he needed for a corner of his work. When he'd called in to inquire about whether she might show him a listing, the chatty receptionist had volunteered that April was taking off that Sunday night for a two week vacation to Prague.

Alone? asked Axel. Oh yes, said the receptionist. She's single. That meant nobody would miss her when he walked into the vacant Tudor she was showing. He waited until she took down the "Open

House" card atop the Sotheby's sign and followed her inside.

Bloomfield Hills was only a five hour drive for Axel across I-94. So he left the stolen van he'd arrived in two blocks from the house and took April Potter in her own SUV. With the rear seats folded forward, the sporty LR-4 had more than ninety cubic feet of storage space, so Axel was able to fit her in amid her own luggage and return her body to the slaughterhouse without having to embalm her onsite.

That was 13 days ago and he hadn't used the Land Rover since. So, he switched plates and took the Rover to a drive-through car wash off I-57 on his way to Chicago. This was the kind of vehicle one expected to be parked outside Saks on Michigan Avenue.

He got there at 7:45 p.m. From the driver's seat Axel was able to look through the first floor window directly to the perfume counter. The hefty, angel-faced Christie, wore a white smock with the Saks logo. At 7:55 p.m. he saw her packing up for the night.

Axel followed her to a parking garage on North Wabash and waited until she pulled out in a small Mini-Cooper. She drove East and turned left on Rush Street, heading north. A few minutes later she drove into a garage in the bar district and paid the $3.00 flat rate. He entered behind her and parked nearby as she pulled into a space on the lower level. Through the tinted windows of the Land Rover, Axel watched as Christie changed from a turtle neck work sweater into a silk blouse. She got out of the Mini, dropped the calf-length skirt she'd been wearing and pulled on a tight spandex miniskirt. It was two sizes too small for her, but it didn't matter. He felt an erection coming as she used the mirror to paint her lips, transforming herself from shop girl to bar slut.

Christie took out a small bottle of Christian No. 1 that Axel was sure she must have stolen. As if to increase her chances of landing a man, she anointed her breasts and that magic place between her legs. She dabbed a touch of the scent under each of her ears and shook out her full head of auburn hair so that it spilled seductively over her shoulders.

Finally, she replaced the flats that she'd worn all day with a pair of four-inch heels. Axel could hear the spikes click as she exited the basement and took the elevator to the first floor. As soon as she was gone, he walked to the Mini and sprayed Crazy Glue into each of her door locks. He got back in the LR-4 and waited another twenty minutes until a spot opened up next to Christie's car and he pulled in beside it. He noticed a security camera that swept the garage, but he calculated that if he took her on *his* side of the Rover, there would be a blind spot. The bar scene must have been dead for Christie that night because she came back in less than an hour. She had a disappointed look on her face and she was slightly tipsy in the heels. One too many Lemon Drops, thought Axel.

The overweight perfume girl had to struggle to find the car key in her purse and she didn't notice Axel standing in the shadows. Finally, she located the keyless remote and hit it. The lights flashed on the little car, but the doors didn't unlock. She tried it again. Nothing. "Damn it, not tonight," she said to herself as she moved to the driver's side and tried to insert the key into the lock. But it wouldn't go. "Oh God, why me?" she said, stamping her heels. And then, before God could answer, Axel was on her, pressing the stun gun to her neck. Zap! He caught her under the shoulders before she could hit the ground.

He waited to make sure that there was no other activity in the garage, then rolled her into the back seat of the LR-4. Christie was zaftig, but she was also short—about five foot two, so he was able to get her under the cargo cover with the rear seats up without bruising her precious skin.

Just before he took off, Axel opened the top of the rear door and covered her mouth with a white handkerchief soaked in methyl tri chloride. That would keep her quiet until he reached Kankakee. But just to be sure, he flex-tied her wrists together. Next, he went to her purse and found the coveted bottle of fragrance. Axel pulled off the crystal crown cap and waved the bottle under his nose. He got hard almost instantly. Clearly it was worth the $2,300.

Then he gazed down at her ass in that spandex mini. He'd always liked plus-sized girls because they were so hungry. Axel reached down and ran his hand along her ass. The spandex skirt felt silky and taught. He pulled her toward him, using her spike heels as handles, then spread her legs and played with her breasts. Axel wished he had more time. She'd looked so disappointed when she'd come back from the bars. He wanted to give her something to remember. To take her right there. But he was on a mission.

Besides, he had to save himself for the Deputy Sheriff from Snoqualmie who would surely be on her way.

20

As soon as she'd finished reading the story on Ginny Kendrick's abduction, Maddy headed for I-90 West to Seattle. She radioed Eddie Gomes that she had a personal "emergency" and told him that she would work a double shift for him starting in the morning.

She hit rush hour traffic, so it was just after 5:00 p.m. and dark when she screeched up outside Dr. Forbes' house. She grabbed the package and the file she had with Axel's journal and ran up the steps to his porch, stabbing at the doorbell. No answer, so she pounded on the door. Finally, Dr. Forbes came downstairs in pajama bottoms. He was naked on top.

He hadn't shaved since the last time she'd seen him and clearly he hadn't bathed. As soon as he opened the door, Maddy pushed past him and went inside. The place was a mess. There were empty bottles of Tsingtao beer and Chinese food containers everywhere.

"Don't tell me," said Forbes as she stormed into his office. "You I.D.'d the guy who did Jon Benet Ramsey, or was it Natalie Holloway?"

"Axel… I found him." Maddy was earnest and pumped. The cop he was 20 years ago. Forbes eyed her, impressed at her audacity.

"Slow down. What are you telling me?" He's in Chicago." She held up a see-through evidence bag with Ginny Kendrick's pigtail.

"O.K. You've got my attention."

For the first time in days, Maddy smiled.

Minutes later, she had the journal opened on the doctor's desk along with the *Sun Times* clipping and the envelope with Axel's drawing. She stabbed at the news clip. "You see, Chicago. He wants me to go there. A girl's missing..."

"By now she's dead," said Forbes.

"Oh God. Are you sure?"

Maddy eyed a picture of Ginny from the newspaper.

Dr. Forbes nodded.

"But why would he send this to *me*?"

"He's a young male and he wants to impress. Clearly you got to him." He looked at the pigtail with zero emotion, tossing the evidence bag back to her.

"Could you do me a favor and stop acting so *callous* about this?" said Maddy. "We're talking about a 12 year-old girl."

"Would you feel any less guilty if his next victim had terminal cancer? You got struck by lightning, sweetheart. The chances of running into a virus like Axel are one in a billion. Trust me. You don't want to see him again."

"Oh no. Maybe *you* can live with the fact that you let a serial go, but I can't."

"Christ, you really know how to stick the knife in, don't you? Call Killebrew."

He got up and reached for a Percodan bottle on the credenza, but Maddy grabbed it.

"No! Look at Axel's journal. He's all over the I-80 killer. You're the only one who made contact..." She gestured toward his old leg wound and opened a file on the I-80 case, showing him the crime scene pix and the evidence that she'd downloaded from the NCIC.

"Only he got it wrong. See..." She shows him a map.

"Look at the numbers he's written. This sequence: Fifty-five, Fifty-seven and Sixty-five correspond to the North-South routes that cross I-80 West to East. According to your #302, the killings went East to West. Axel is so precise, but he blows a detail like that. That means he's vulnerable."

Suddenly, Dr. Forbes sat back down. He began flipping through the pages of Axel's journal, comparing them to the I-80 files and shaking his head. "I don't believe this."

"What?"

"When I was working this I knew that the press might get hold of my #302, so I transposed the numbers to weed out the copy cats. The women *were* killed West to East."

"But how would he *know* that?" demanded Maddy. Dr. Forbes was already on his feet. He crossed quickly to a drawer and pulled out his Beretta, then slammed in a mag.

"Unless..." said Maddy getting it, "Axel's the I-80 Killer."

Forbes nodded. "He started with prostitutes. Easy victim-class. Farm team ball. Now he's throwing in the Majors."

Maddy jumped up to face him. "Does that mean you're gonna help me now?"

"What do you think?" Forbes started rubbing his thigh near the place where Axel had stabbed him. "This fucker ruined my golf game. It's time for payback."

PART TWO

21

THEY RENTED A FORD CROWN VICTORIA at O'Hare. It was just after 9:30 a.m. the next morning when Maddy and Dr. Forbes pulled up outside Chicago Police Headquarters at 3510 South Michigan. A media gang bang was in progress. All the local stations were there: *WMAQ, WBBM* and *WGN* along with reporters from the *Tribune* and *Sun Times* shoving mikes at Captain Winston Jamal, the severe, early 40's ex-black Muslim who ran the Chicago P.D. Homicide Squad.

The City had been shaken for days over the disappearance of Ginny Kendrick, the young girl from Chase Prep and now the roommate of Christie Sloane had reported her missing. Her car had just been found in a garage near Rush Street with the door locks glued shut. A police forensics team had turned up markings on the garage floor consistent with a struggle.

An aggressive, blonde reporter for BBM, named Deborah Schilling wanted to know from Captain Jamal if the abductions of the two females were related?

"We see no link at this time," he said, lying.

"Then why involve Homicide?" she demanded.

"The Mayor considers these missing persons cases to be a top priority," said Jamal. "We have the most bench strength in Homicide, so he's called us in."

Schilling had the mike with the Channel 2 logo inches from Jamal's face and she wouldn't let up.

"Since these are possible kidnappings, have you notified The Bureau?"

"Naturally, they're in the loop," said the Captain. "Now that's all I've got. Anything breaks, you'll be informed."

Inside the Homicide bullpen all hell was breaking loose. Uniforms and plain clothes detectives were working phones with missing posters of Kendrick and Sloane in front of them.

As Captain Jamal walked in, a female Sergeant named Edmonds nodded toward Dr. Forbes and Maddy who were standing outside his office.

"Yeah, I got their text," said Jamal. "Tell them I don't have time."

Sergeant Edmonds crossed the bullpen to brush them off, when Maddy held up the see-through evidence bag with Ginny's pigtail. Suddenly, the buzz in the room cut to silence. As soon as Capt. Jamal saw it, his jaw dropped.

Moments later, he was seated at the head of a long table in a conference room that had been converted into a temporary control room for the two missing cases.

Pictures of Ginny and Christie lined the walls. The table was covered with files. Three senior detectives sat around it listening. Dr. Forbes stood at the opposite end of the table from Captain Jamal and briefed them. Maddy sat in a chair at his side as he held up an out-of-focus ATM camera photo of the I-80 Killer.

"This is the only known photo we had when we were investigating I-80," said Forbes. "It was taken from a cash machine camera at one of the truck stops. I've asked the Washington State crime lab to compare DNA from fibers found at the I-80 dump sites to blood samples taken after the suspect's crash in Snoqualmie."

He nodded to Capt. Jamal. "If there's a match, I guarantee, you'll be the lead guest on Anderson Cooper 360."

Jamal was an accommodating talking head, but the prospect of catching the notorious I-80 killer intrigued him even more.

"Any leads on his victim selection?"

"From the missings out west," said Maddy, "we think he's using driver's licenses." At this point she hadn't told Dr. Forbes about how Axel seemed to know her.

"That wouldn't explain Ginny Kendrick," said the Captain.

Just then, there was a knock on the glass window of the conference room door. Sergeant Edmonds poked her head in and nodded toward the bullpen.

"The Feds are here."

Maddy looked out through the glass conference room wall.

"Oh Christ."

A pair of special agents in blue field jackets with large yellow FBI letters were mulling around. Next to them was Ron Killebrew, the SSA who'd grilled her.

"It didn't take him long," said Forbes. "Ronnie never met a press case he didn't like."

Minutes later, Killebrew was pacing back and forth in front of Captain Jamal who was seated at the desk in his office. Killebrew closed the door so they could talk privately.

"With all due respect Captain, Forbes is a pill-popping washout and the girl's a rookie."

"Yeah, but she was inches away from the suspect who took Kendrick, and Forbes worked I-80.

"So what?"

"One of those truck stops was in southern Cook County. This may be the break we've been after."

He got up and started to exit, but Killebrew tried to stop him.

"Ask Forbes why he left The Bureau."

Capt. Jamal kept going so Killebrew followed him out into the bull pen and kept it up.

"Ask him why he washed out after I-80."

Just then, Dr. Forbes confronted him.

"Why don't *you* tell him Ronnie? Tell him why I left The Bureau…" He turned to the Captain. "See, I had the audacity to question the god of profiles."

"What are you talking about?" asked Jamal.

"The foundation that the BAU is built on," said Forbes. "The notion that every serial killer has a signature; a particular set of traits that can be isolated and identified to predict his next move. Well it's bullshit."

"Don't listen to him," snapped Killebrew.

But Forbes wouldn't stop.

"Tell him about Atlanta, Ronnie." He turned to Captain Jamal who was sitting on the edge of a bullpen desk. "Wayne Williams was dropping bodies on land. He was killing young African American boys."

"You don't have to tell *me*," said Jamal. "I was ten at the time and even up here in Chicago it had me terrified."

"Yeah, well Williams got wind that The Bureau had found a fiber," said Forbes, "so he started dropping the bodies in the river. It didn't fit the profile, so *Killebrew* here convinced everybody that there were *two* of them. Not just *one* serial killer but two, and Williams kept up his murder spree."

Dr. Forbes was getting more and more agitated now. His leg was beginning to hurt him and he was starting to limp.

"Now take this guy Axel—Stranger 456. Given his previous victim class you wouldn't expect him to abduct a little girl. But he's dynamic; willing to change his M.O."

"For what reason?" demanded Killebrew.

"So we don't fucking catch him, Einstein," said Maddy, getting right in his face.

"Oh really?" said Killebrew. "Then answer me this: If he fled your jurisdiction and he wants to keep doing this, why in hell would he contact *you*, a cop, and entice you here to Chicago?"

Killebrew had led them into a trap. Maddy didn't have an answer for that one. Neither did Forbes.

"You don't *know*," said Killebrew, "because neither of you has a clue what makes this guy tick. Furthermore, there isn't a shred of evidence tying Stranger 456 to I-80.

"Oh, yes there is…" said Maddy.

"What is it? Show me." But Dr. Forbes put his hand on her arm. He wasn't ready to give up Axel's journal. So Maddy stood mute as Killebrew leaned in on Jamal.

"You've got to listen to me Captain. I counted half a dozen T.V. trucks downstairs. Brian Williams is flying in and I'm trading calls with Diane Sawyer. I suggest you pick up the phone and get the Mayor on the line. Ask him who he wants running point on this case: a Percodan addict and some local uniform or the F, B, fuckin' I?"

Capt. Jamal eyed Dr. Forbes and Maddy and shook his head.

Round one to Killebrew.

22

Less than an hour after he'd taken her from the garage near Rush Street, Christie Sloane was flex-tied to a beautician's chair in Axel's lair. He'd sedated her with a highly diluted mixture of water and chloral hydrate administered via an IV drip.

As she started to come to, Christie felt light-headed and spacey. She looked up and saw magnificent images on the walls and ceiling above her. Pictures of angels and saints. She could smell jasmine. All around her scented candles had been lit. It was a kind of dreamy place.

But then, when she tried to get up, she realized that her wrists were tethered to this chair and there was a needle in her arm. Oh God. Now she remembered blacking out in the garage and riding in some dark vehicle. Her heart started to race. Where was she?

And then this handsome man leaned over her. Late 20's. Piercing blue eyes. Rock hard abs. He was naked, except for a pair of silk pajama bottoms. Where could she be?

"Hello Christie," he said. "I know this all seems like a bit of a shock, but you've been selected."

"For… what?" she asked, her voice trembling.

"A kind of makeover," he said.

"Is this a reality show?"

Axel smiled. "In a way, it is. You see, you've been chosen to model for me. You're going to be part of something very important. It won't take long, and when I'm finished, I'm going to send you home. You'll have nothing to worry about."

He gently removed the IV, then tipped her back so that her head was at the edge of a basin. It was red porcelain. Axel had stolen it along with the other beautician's equipment from a Supercuts salon in Racine, Wisconsin.

"After I do your hair, I'm going to let you go."

Christie was about to say something else, but he had her back now, massaging her scalp as the warm water poured over her thick auburn tresses. She was so doped up that she didn't know what to think, when Axel picked up a remote and turned on the iPad. An acoustic piece began to play throughout the huge space. *Every Rose Has Its Thorn* by Poison. The voice of Brett Michaels emerged from the speakers.

We both lie silently still in the dead of the night…

After washing her hair, Axel handed Christie a silk mask to cover her eyes. He put the IV back in, and she drifted off as the seductive music continued to play.

"I'm going to transform you. Just trust me. You'll see."

Now, as he began to dye her hair black, the chorus of the Poison classic kicked in.

Every rose has its thorn. Just like every night has its dawn…

It took Axel another hour to turn the Michigan Avenue clerk into a vision. He dried her hair. He painted her lips a bright crimson. He did her eyes with mascara and eyeliner and applied the subtlest powder to her cheeks.

Finally, when he was finished, he woke her gently and produced a large mirror so that she could see his work for herself. She looked positively angelic.

"Do you see what I mean, now?" he asked her, keeping his voice low as he turned off the drip.

"I can't believe it," she said.

"Here, I want you to put this on." Axel handed her a white silk robe. He cut the flex-ties and helped her stand. She was still shaky, but he put her right arm over his shoulder as he led her out onto the faux marble floor.

For the first time, bizarre as all this was, Christie Sloane was starting to relax. Being heavy all of her life, she wasn't used to this kind of lavish attention, especially from a man who looked like a movie star and with a body to die for. Besides, he'd made her look so beautiful.

Now, as Axel turned the music off, he grabbed a digital camera and began posing her, shooting frames as if she was some kind of runway model.

As the camera flashed, she looked up at the ceiling. She could see clearly now: there were classically painted renderings of men, women and children. Finally, she got the courage to ask…

"Am I going to be part of that?"

"That's why I brought you here, Christie. I have an important place in the work reserved just for you." He pointed up to an empty space in the middle of the nave.

The perfume clerk felt a strange combination of emotions: apprehension at having been abducted, but a kind of excitement over how he'd been able to change her—transform her was more like it. She felt glamorous, worthy for the first time, of Clive Christian No. 1.

But still . . .

"There's something I just don't understand," she asked.

"What is it?"

"How did you even *find* me?

"Do you really want to know?"

Christie nodded, so Axel exited into his office and returned a few moments later with a Polaroid. It showed Christie, bending over at Nic's, flashing the perfume bottle tattoo.

"When I saw that, I had to have you."

Suddenly, Christie got defensive.

"Where . . . did you get that?"

"At Nic's, honey. They do beautiful work."

Axel reached out and pulled the top of her robe down.

"Let me see the original."

Christie was scared now.

"No. I want you to take me home." She pulled the robe around her and tightened the silk belt.

Axel stopped smiling.

"Show me the *goddamn* tattoo."

He smashed the mirror and lunged forward with one of the broken pieces, slitting open the back of the robe.

"Now let me show you *my* work."

He moved the mirror piece toward the back of her neck and pulled her hair away so that she could see the tattooed number he'd branded her with: H 12:22-26 . . .

Christie's heart started racing.

"What did you *do* to me? What *is* that?"

"Something to remember you by. I needed you alive. Even after embalming, the lividity bleaches out the skin. And the eyes... With the others, the eyes were just dead."

She was terrified now. "What others?"

Axel pulled a curtain away, revealing his stainless steel autopsy table and the embalmed body of 12-year-old Ginny Kendrick.

Suddenly, Christie got up and started to run.

There was a scaffolding at the edge of the huge space, and she ducked under it. But Axel reached in and grabbed her by the hair. He ripped off what was left of the robe and wrapped it around her neck, starting to choke her, watching her die the way a cruel boy might snuff the life out of a butterfly.

Finally, just as she was at the edge of death, he forced her eyes open, leaving her to stare up at him, wide-eyed.

Later, when he'd finished with the digital camera, Axel carried Christie's body over to a blood stained metal cart. It had once been used by Armour workers to move sides of beef.

He loaded Ginny Kendrick onto to the cart in the opposite direction, so that the young girl's painted toenails touched Christie's white face. With the life gone from their eyes, Axel saw these two females as nothing more than meat for the furnace.

He rolled the cart out of the nave and up a ramp onto a loading dock outside. The temperature in November was in the low twenties and Axel was still naked on top. But he didn't care. Leaning over both bodies, he breathed on them so that he could see his breath congeal for a moment on the pupils of their eyes. First Ginny and then Christie.

He pushed the cart to the end of the loading dock and came to the furnace. The door was six feet wide and opened sideways. When he undid the latch, he felt the heat from the flames licking out.

The fire singed the hair on his forearms as he rolled each of the bodies inside. Then, when they started to burn, Axel slammed the door shut and looked up at the smokestack towering 190 feet above him.

He could just catch sight of their ashes as the sparks blew south toward Champaign.

23

When Dr. Forbes had agreed to chase Axel with Maddy they didn't have a lot of time for logistics. Maddy used the Samsung 4G wireless router linked to her MacBook Pro to do an online search on their way to Seattle Tacoma Airport. As an ex-special agent who'd spent months at a time in the field, Forbes recommended that they find a motel.

They needed to book three adjoining rooms, one for each of them with a "war room" in between where they could work the evidence. The place should be cheap, he said, with great ingress and egress. The location should be as close to downtown as possible but with access to the Interstate so that they could move quickly if they got an out of town lead.

Security would be an issue, if Axel attempted to make a move on Maddy, so Forbes suggested an L-shaped motel in the 1960's style with the rooms wrapping around a parking lot where they could keep an eye on their vehicle. They should be on the second floor with access to their rooms only from the front along a walkway that they could also watch.

Maddy found it on cheapmotels.com. The Traveler's Inn on North Waukegan Road in the suburb of Niles, Illinois. It was perfect. The rooms went for $49.00 a night. They were 14 miles from The Loop and centrally located between I-94 and 294, the two major north-south interstate routes.

In rush hour traffic they could be downtown in 35 minutes and if the hunt took them out of state they could get to O'Hare in under ten minutes on Touhy Avenue. The Sports Bar & Grill next door even delivered food until the kitchen closed at 11:00 p.m.

Before she'd unpacked, Maddy was in the middle room taping pictures of Axel's two suspected abductees on the wall along with the I-80 crime scene photos. When she finished, she knocked on Dr. Forbes' door which was ajar.

From his bathroom he told her to come in. He was lining Percodan bottles on the ledge of the sink. Maddy eyed him in the mirror as he rubbed his scruffy week-old beard.

"There's a point in every case," he said, "where the cop starts to resemble the killer."

"Don't flatter yourself, Doc. For a psychopath, Axel's pretty hot. He's also clean shaven."

Maddy disappeared for a minute, then returned with a disposable Bic razor and a travel-sized can of shaving cream.

"Are you trying to change me already?"

"Nope," said Maddy. "I just don't want to scare off any potential witnesses." She exited as Forbes rubbed his chin.

Minutes later he emerged clean shaven and sporting a fresh denim shirt above his khakis. He looked ten years younger.

"Damn," said, Maddy, getting up. "You clean up nice."

Forbes nodded, then walked to the window facing onto the parking lot below. He closed the blinds, then examined the door lock. Not satisfied, he went to his carry-on bag and pulled out a small hammer and three wooden shivs."

"Are we starting a fire?" asked Maddy.

Forbes ignored her, then used the back of the hammer to jam a shiv under the war room door.

"That door lock wouldn't stop a six year old.

"O.K. and what happens when we want to leave?"

Forbes bent down and used the claw end of the hammer to flick the shiv free. Then he went into each of the bedrooms and tapped shivs under the other doors.

"It's just about slowing him down, that's all. If he wants to get in here, he will."

"O.K." she said. "So let's get him first."

She started to line up the evidence—pumped and ready to do battle, but Dr. Forbes stopped her.

"Look, neither one of us wants to admit we're irrelevant. But you have to know what we're up against."

"Like?"

"We're off the res. We have no jurisdiction. We'll be lucky if we don't get busted for carrying." He tapped his Beretta in a paddle holster at the small of his back. "The Bureau has 12,000 agents and every forensic toy there is. We've got a motel room, some old files—"

"A Kinko's down the block and a Mr. Coffee. We're set."

Maddy was inches away from him now; an earnest, attractive young woman who had no real idea what they were facing.

Forbes confronted her.

"I need you to *listen* to me."

"Absolutely, Obi-Wan…"

Suddenly, he grabbed her by both arms.

"Stop it *will* you? There's a man out there who pisses ice water and he's gonna make a run on you."

Maddy was trying to show strength.

"Is this where I'm supposed to get scared?"

Dr. Forbes eyed a picture of Christie Sloane and nodded ominously.

"Yeah."

Later that night, Maddy slept in her room with the door to the war room open. Dr. Forbes sat in a corner with his Beretta next to him. The digital clock read 2:10 a.m.

Just then, lights flashed from a car pulling into the lot below. He got up and looked through the curtain. It was nothing. His leg was bothering him, so he sat back down. He pulled out a Percodan bottle, but decided to hold off.

A few hours later, Maddy rolled into a deeper sleep while inside the war room, Forbes checked the digital clock. It was 4:25 a.m. and his leg was really killing him. This time, he dry swallowed a capsule.

Later, it was dead quiet. In the distance, there was the faint sound of a police siren. But Forbes didn't hear it. He was asleep.

Suddenly a shadow passed by the war room window. Whoever was outside, tried the handle on Maddy's door and pushed against it, but the shiv held it closed.

It was 6:30 a.m. when Maddy's alarm went off. She stretched and climbed out of bed, moving into the adjoining war room to find Dr. Forbes still asleep in the chair.

"Wheels up at seven, Doc." She was about to wake him, when she noticed that the shiv in her door was ajar.

She went to her bag and pulled out a 380. Ruger. Then she found Forbes' hammer and pulled the shiv away from the door. Cautiously she opened it and then froze. Push-pinned to her door was the same kind of manila envelope that Axel had sent her with Ginny's pigtail.

"Oh no..."

Maddy quickly scanned the balcony and swept the parking lot down below. Then she went back inside and pulled out a pair of latex gloves from her forensic kit.

"Get up doc," he's been here."

When Maddy showed him the envelope, Forbes sprang to his feet. It was illustrated with a drawing—a rendering of Maddy with angel's wings. Axel had depicted her bending over her bed with her ass up, as if she was waiting to be fucked.

She started to open it, but Forbes gestured for her to wait. He held the envelope up to a light to see if it had been booby trapped, but there was nothing visible inside.

Finally, he nodded and Maddy slit it open with her buckle knife. Inside, were the panties that Axel had taken from her.

24

"SERIAL KILLERS ARE MADE, not born." That was the opening sentence in a long monograph that Dr. Forbes had planned to turn into a book before the I-80 killer had stabbed him. He didn't know it at the time, but the hooded figure who jammed the blade into his femur was the living embodiment of that dictum. Axel had been born, like all children, with a pure soul and an innocent heart. He carried no extra Y chromosome as so many mass murderers did. His mother had been a prostitute who'd used crack cocaine, but she'd been in prison and clean throughout most of her pregnancy, so there were no residual drugs in her system at the time Axel was in utero.

He was born at the Decatur Women's Correctional Center. The name on his birth certificate was Bobby Leroy Cole. But since his mother had another year to go on her sentence, baby Axel was sent into foster care. At the age of four weeks he was placed with a couple named Tingley in the farming town of Mattoon, Illinois. From that point on, fate became truly monstrous for little Axel.

Roger Tingley had been a sugar cane farmer in Thibodaux Louisiana. He'd met his wife Dotty, a Mattoon native, during a booze-sodden Mardi Gras week in the mid 1970's. They'd struck it rich in 1979 during the "Arab oil crisis" when the Government subsidized ethanol production. The cane crop on Tingley's 60 acre spread yielded five times the return he'd gotten from granulated sugar, but when the bottom fell out of the market in the early 80's, he lost the farm that had been in his family for six generations. Humiliated, Roger tried to stave off foreclosure by setting up a bootleg ethanol distillery. But his short career running grain alcohol bought him a sixteen month stretch at the State Penitentiary in Angola.

During his time inside, Dotty was "saved" by the evangelicals and when Roger got paroled, they moved into the five bedroom ram-shackle farm house in Mattoon that her daddy had left her. It was 1982. With no marketable skills and a $30,000 IRS bill for back taxes, the Tingleys began taking in foster children. By the time baby Axel arrived in his state-issued bassinette, they had six other troubled juveniles ranging in age from two to thirteen—all white and all the progeny of criminals. It wasn't illegal back then for a paroled felon to run a foster home, even a raging alcoholic like Roger. He got his revenge for the broken life he'd led, by disciplining even the youngest of the kids with a barber's strop used for sharpening straight razors.

At the age of three, due to a bladder infection that had been neglected for months, Axel began wetting his bed. Dotty responded by locking him in his bedroom closet with a radio outside his door. Every night he'd fall asleep on the closet floor to the preachings of some fire and brimstone minister who blamed all of God's "infamy" on that "harlot in the Garden" from Genesis.

On his first day of kindergarten, Dotty made little Axel wear his urine-soaked underpants to school. What beatings didn't come from his classmates, he got from his older "brother" Raymond who had an I.Q. in the low 70's. "Ray Ray," as they called him, got a book on taxidermy for his eleventh birthday, along with a skinning knife.

He used it to stuff squirrels he'd trap in the yard. When Axel started "acting out," Dotty began calling on Raymond to discipline him. Night after night he'd be locked in the closet with Raymond outside holding the key and brandishing the knife; threatening to come in and cut off his "pee pee."

When Axel tried to fight back, Roger would whip him or sic Raymond on him. By the age of five, Axel had sustained two jaw fractures, a broken right wrist and a broken left arm. The Tingley's covered up the abuse by telling hospital authorities that the little "devil" had hurt himself climbing trees.

The only outlet that Axel had back then—his only refuge—was his imagination and the strange ability to draw that God had given him. He still believed in Jesus in those days. In fact, he covered the inner walls of the closet with drawings of Biblical figures, imagining what they looked like as the evangelical preacher's sermons blared from the radio. Sometimes he'd find little note pads and make flip book animations of angels carrying him off from the dreadful house. Soon, he began to perfect a plan for escaping himself.

A few days after his fifth birthday Axel swallowed a handful of salt at breakfast, inducing vomiting so he'd have an excuse to stay home from kindergarten. While Raymond and the other kids were at school, he gathered up all of "Ray Ray's" mountings and put them in the middle of his parent's bed. Roger was out at an A.A. meeting and Dotty was at a prayer service when Axel found the can of lighter fluid and lit the match. A neighbor saw the smoke and the blaze was quickly knocked down by the local F.D., but Axel was sent back to Kankakee to a juvenile holding facility run by the Illinois Department of Children and Family Services.

He was put into a "ward" with a dozen older juveniles, most of them habitual offenders from the south side of Chicago. With his deep blue eyes and blond hair, Axel was almost "pretty" back then. So the older boys tied him to his bed and raped him repeatedly until he escaped. For the next two years, he moved through four different foster homes. He learned to box at a summer youth camp near Evansville and was tested by a DCFS psychologist who wrote the words "near genius" in his file. But if there had ever been any hope of rescuing this boy, the system had long since abandoned him.

A victim since birth, Axel now began to punish others; starting with insects. He stole a magnifying glass from a teacher and used it to burn ants and other bugs. He found that he loved the smell of their tiny burning bodies, so he experimented with matches and disposable lighters. By the time he reached his last foster family at the age of seven, he'd graduated to killing stray dogs and cats.

Childhood was a terrifying period for Axel. He was in an unending state of war. He could never remember a moment when he'd felt safe or comforted. To the foster families he was nothing but a check every month. To his siblings he was a competitor for the shitty scraps of food they'd dish out. To the string of therapists and "counselors" who'd get his file, he was just another case in the endless parade of unwanted children spawned by poverty, addiction and crime.

By the time he was sent to St. Timothy's, Axel was a hardened sociopath who spent every waking moment thinking about his revenge. The abuse continued at the orphanage as one particularly sadistic nun tried to stop the bed wetting with a wooden yardstick.

But Axel soon learned that the Catholic Church was an institution that inspired the best and the worst in humankind. In his church history classes, the sisters exposed him to the Renaissance along with the Inquisition. As an altar boy during Holy Week he lit the Pascal Candle which bore the Greek letters for Alpha and Omega—the beginning and the end. It was this strange duality that all Catholics lived with: the love that they felt for the Prince of Peace and the contempt they had for the clergy who had spent centuries corrupting His simple message. Dark and light. Birth and Death. Good and Evil. They now existed on one plane for Axel and it was no longer the straight line of beginning and end, but a circle.

In this dark Catholic orphanage where Axel spent so many awful nights, he also perfected his artistic gift. He developed the skill to paint like the masters. It was here that he first conceived of the master work that would convey his message. It would be an icon so epic that the world would have to take notice and for once, they'd begin to understand the unmitigated cruelty that comes from treating little children like animals. Maddy, the defiant Deputy Sheriff, would help him perfect that message. Like him, she understood the concept of redemption. She had fallen and risen and she would come for him now. Their union was inevitable. If death was the price she paid for her place with the others in the painting, then so be it. He was on a trajectory now and he didn't have a minute to lose.

25

BACK IN THE WAR ROOM at the Traveler's Inn motel, Dr. Forbes was pacing with his cell phone.

"Goddamnit, will you tell me how I can be 15 miles from downtown Chicago and not get a signal?"

He crossed to the night table by his bed and picked up the land line, punching in numbers.

"Who are you calling?" asked Maddy.

"Your father. You're going back."

"No way." She grabbed the phone and slammed it down.

"Look, you might as well face it," said Forbes. "Killebrew's right. I'm a washout." He pointed to the empty envelope from Axel. "Look how close he got. That wouldn't have happened if I was on my game."

"All the more reason for me to stay," said Maddy. "You said it yourself—we've got limited resources. We're not gonna find him unless *he* comes to us."

She started to exit the room, when he stopped her.

"What are you not telling me?"

"Let me go."

"No. I want to know why he wants you. The same question Killebrew asked. Why would he bring you here to Chicago?

"I told you. I don't know."

She tried to pull away, but he grabbed her.

"I checked your sheet. Back when you were eighteen, you had a felony bust for possession. It was heroin."

Maddy broke away from him and started to go for the door, but he caught up with her.

"What the hell were you doing with *smack*?"

She hesitated, deciding whether to open up. Finally…

"Alright. Just sit down and I'll tell you."

She nodded for him to take one of the seats in the room. When he did, she walked over and sat down across from him. She closed her eyes and exhaled, letting her breath out really slowly, as if she was deciding how much of the full truth to tell. Then, finally, she opened up.

"After my mom died, I had a really rough time. My brother Billy was Daddy's boy and I couldn't do anything right. Do you know what I mean?"

"I guess."

"Yeah, well, you had to be there… Anyway, I took off."

"Where'd you go?

"I hitched with a girlfriend down to Portland. One night we talked our way into a bar and met some guys."

"What *guys*?"

"The kind that'll buy an eighteen year-old girl whatever she wants."

"Including Horse?"

"No. It was coke at first. Some pills. We did some X. These guys had Harleys. Some really gorgeous rides. They were on their way to a rally in Austin, so we went."

Dr. Forbes leaned over and took her wrist. He started to pull up the sleeve on her sweater, but she pulled away. Finally, Maddy pulled up the sleeve herself, exposing the bend in her elbow. It was scarred with injection marks.

"You don't get tracks like that from Ecstasy, honey."

"No. You don't." She looked away. "Seems like I'm always letting some man get the best of me."

"Are you going to finish?"

"Yeah..."

Maddy pulled her sleeve back down and got up, walking around the room as she told it.

"The guys with the Harleys wanted to stop near L.A. Some place out in Antelope Valley. They said they had to pick up something to bring to Texas."

"Out there it had to be meth, right? That's were the labs are. All the tweakers."

Maddy nodded.

"Go on."

"My girlfriend split with this other guy and the one I was with gave me some kind of Roofie. Next thing I knew, I woke up in a shooting gallery out near Banning. The sonovabitch had sold me to a guy in the Nomads he owed money to."

Maddy was biting down hard on her lower lip now, trying to keep from losing it. Forbes seemed touched.

"Did your father have any idea?"

"I didn't have the guts to call him."

"So at that point you were strung out on heroin?"

"Yeah. The habit was three dimes a day. The fucker in Banning wanted to put me on the street to turn tricks."

Forbes shook his head. "How'd you get out of it?"

"They sold me again. This time to a guy from the club down in Pedro. But he wasn't so bad. He just wanted sex. That was it. Not for money. Just the two of us."

"What was his name?"

"Bradley. An ex-Army Ranger. He got busted for bringing an AR-15 back from Afghanistan. Dishonorable discharge. But he seemed, you know, decent, at first. I rode with him for a month. Got the habit down to a nickel a day." She still didn't feel comfortable enough to tell him about the tattoo or Axel's fixation with it.

"So how did you end up in rehab?

Maddy sat down on the edge of the bed.

"We got pulled over by the Highway Patrol one night down by Long Beach. Brad was carrying felony weight and he had an outstanding warrant. They arrested me for possession and gave me a choice: Phoenix House or the Woman's House of Detention."

Dr. Forbes had interviewed a lot of witnesses in his day and he could sense it when something was missing.

"I still don't get it. One day you're born to raise hell and the next day you're in uniform?"

Maddy got up and turned away from him.

"No. It was after I got out of rehab. I wouldn't have come home if Billy hadn't—Anyway, I made it through the Academy in Kings County. Took the mountain rescue course in the Cascades. I started boxing. Did some defensive training. I was trying to become my brother. Only now—"

"What?"

"I'm *half* the girl trying to be *twice* the man he was." She was close to tears. "Are you satisfied?"

Forbes just sat there without saying anything.

"Doctor, answer me. I saw the way you were with that student. You don't know when to let up. Are we done?"

"Yeah. We're good."

"You're sure?"

Forbes nodded.

"You don't want to see the tracks on my *other* arm?"

Just then, he got up to face her.

"Look, I said I was satisfied."

He cocked his head toward the evidence on the walls. "I'm willing to keep working this with you. I just don't want to see you get—"

"What? Hurt? Sorry Doc, but I've already got *one* old man who thinks I can't cut it. I don't need two."

And with that, she opened the door and rushed out.

Forbes went after her, but by the time he got out to the balcony she was halfway down the stairs.

"Maddy. Come on. You don't want to be out there alone."

He was shouting down to her as she ran into the parking lot.

"Hey. I told you I was sorry. Come back."

He started to run after her, but his leg was really killing him now. By the time he got to the bottom of the stairs, Maddy was gone.

26

AS SOON AS SHE'D EXITED THE MOTEL, Maddy began walking south on North Waukegan Road until she hit West Touhy Avenue in Niles. She was carrying a few hundred in cash and she had the Ruger .380 in a paddle holster under her sweater. She caught a cab on West Touhy to the Park Ridge Metrarail station and headed for the Loop via commuter train.

Maddy had now been outmaneuvered by Axel three times and on the train ride downtown she decided that the only way to redeem herself was to take the fight to him. The Postmark on Axel's original package to her contained the Zip Code 60614. It had been mailed through the P.O. at 2643 Clark Street on the near North Side. Her plan was to get some media attention in a location close to Clark Street that was visible and draw him in.

In the stall of a Starbucks restroom near the Post Office, she examined the Ruger semi-automatic. Under TSA regs, law enforcement officers were permitted to fly with their weapons broken down in checked baggage on the condition that they notified the airline at the time of check in.

The Snoqualmie Sheriff's office used Remington Express Hollow Point ammunition as standard issue and Maddy had brought three mags along with her to Chicago. But on the way in from O'Hare Dr. Forbes introduced her to a more lethal round: The Glaser safety slug. These were Teflon-jacketed loads full of tiny lead BB's designed to explode on impact with meat. They had incredible stopping power.

Forbes insisted that she carry them during their pursuit of Axel, since he'd been so cranked up on meth at the time of his seizure in Snoqualmie. If he came at her again, counseled Forbes, Maddy would get one shot to drop him and if she didn't, he'd keep coming.

Now in the Starbuck's bathroom she ejected the ten-round mag from the Ruger, inspected it and slammed it back in. She racked the slide and put one in the chamber. Then she walked a few blocks to a Kinkos and bought some time online, searching the three local T.V. stations to locate that blonde reporter who had been so aggressive with Captain Jamal.

Her name was Deborah Schilling. She worked for *WBBM*, the CBS station, and her bio on the Channel 2 website was impressive. Schilling was an ex-print reporter from the *Sun Times* who'd won a Pulitzer Prize and half a dozen other awards for her dogged investigative work. Maddy used her cell to leave a message on Schilling's voice mail at Channel 2:

"Ms. Schilling my name is Deputy Sheriff Maddy Bergstrom. I'm in Chicago in pursuit of the suspect who kidnapped Ginny Kendrick. I've actually been in *touch* with him..." Maddy chose her words carefully now, not wanting to say too much, but letting Schilling know that she'd actually *met* the kidnapper.

Then she dropped the bomb that would surely send a Channel 2 news van her way: "We have reason to believe that he's tied to a series of homicides, not just in Chicago, but nationwide." Maddy left her cell number. She could almost hear the alarms going off over at *WBBM* when Schilling picked up the message. She also knew that there would be hell to pay with Capt. Jamal and the Chicago P.D. for the end run; not to mention Killebrew. But if she didn't stop Axel now, more people would die.

Maddy had to let the killer know where she was and she didn't want to involve Dr. Forbes. He'd already been wounded by the psychopath. This was one collar she'd have to make on her own.

She did a Google search of the 60614 Zip Code and saw that the most prominent nearby landmark was the Chicago Zoo. It was located in Lincoln Park along Lake Michigan at the intersection of North Clark and Armitage ten blocks south.

Three minutes later Schilling called back. Maddy said she'd meet her near the Zoo entrance in an hour. She wanted to make sure that the interview was in a public place that would be easy for Axel to recognize. But one where she might get him alone after dark. There was another advantage in talking to the reporter from Channel 2. The interview would also run on 780 AM, *WBBM*'s all news radio station, increasing the odds that Axel would hear it.

Schilling arrived with her crew around 3:00 p.m., early enough for the piece to run on the 5:00 p.m. evening newscast. She exited a blue Channel 2 van with a cameraman and a field producer. Though Maddy was out of uniform, she showed Schilling her Sheriff's badge and I.D. from Snoqualmie. Schilling pulled out a spiral Reporter's Notebook and did a pre-interview; taking notes in shorthand.

Maddy explained how Axel had been in her jurisdiction and escaped. She gave very few details except to say that once he'd fled, he'd sent her some hair with proof that it had come from Ginny Kendrick. She left out any mention of Dr. Forbes or why Axel had sought her out in the first place. Her one condition for doing the interview was that Schilling identify the location where it was shot.

The cameraman set up on a tripod, framing Schilling and Maddy wide so that the Zoo entrance was in the background. Schilling told her that she'd make sure her producer used a "lower third," title with the address: 2001 North Clark.

"This is Deborah Schilling, reporting for Channel 2 News from just outside the Chicago Zoo. I'm with deputy Maddy Bergstrom from the Snoqualmie Sheriff's Department in Washington State. She contacted me today with a startling story."

Schilling turned to Maddy with the microphone. "You say that the suspect the police are hunting now in the abduction of two Chicago females may, in fact, be a serial killer?"

"That's right," said Maddy focusing on Schilling rather than looking into the camera lens. "He uses the alias Axel and he literally sent me a portion of hair from one of the victims."

"Can you be more specific?"

"Not right now. We need to withhold that kind of detail. What's important is that the public understand just how dangerous this man is."

"Can you describe him?"

"Yes. He's a white male, in his mid-twenties; about six foot two; 180 pounds. The suspect has brown hair, blue eyes and an athletic build. There's a tattoo of a series of letters and numbers on the back of his left wrist." She pointed to her own wrist to show the position.

"Can you give us the actual letters and numbers."

"Not at this point."

"Have you shared this with the FBI?"

"Definitely. There's an agent from Quantico in Chicago right now. But if you don't mind, I'd like to make a personal appeal to this suspect." Schilling was a bit thrown by that, but she said, "Sure. Go ahead." Maddy now turned to face the lens.

"Listen Axel, there's some unfinished business we need to discuss. I want you to know that I'm here and that I'm willing to meet you one on one. If you come in now. If you stop whatever it is that you're doing—these abductions—these killings, I'll do what I can to make sure you're treated fairly. If you make contact, you have my word that I'll meet you alone."

Schilling waited a beat to make sure that she was finished and motioned, out of frame, for the cameraman to focus on her.

"Call it an offer, call it a taunt, but this tenacious Deputy has flown two thousand miles to Chicagoland to stop what she says may be a serial killer. We'll keep you up to date on this story as it breaks. This is Deborah Schilling, Channel 2 News outside the Chicago Zoo on North Clark Street."

As soon as she finished and they stopped taping, Maddy asked Schilling how soon the interview would be available to the public. Schilling said that they fed the video back to the station live. It would hit radio within minutes after she did a wrap around for 780 AM.

A few minutes later it would appear on their website which was linked to CBSNews.com. Very shortly, this would be a national story. She could almost guarantee that the interview would lead the five o'clock broadcast with an update at 5:30 and 10:00 p.m. If this guy Axel had any media awareness, he'd get the message.

She asked if Maddy would mind coming back to the station. She'd like to hook her up with a sketch artist to get a drawing of Axel.

But Maddy was anxious to get away. She wanted to call Dr. Forbes with a heads up on the off chance that Axel might try and make another move on the motel. She knew that Schilling would want to stay close to her and she needed to get away from the crew, without alienating them. So Maddy took Schilling's cell number and promised to call her if the killer made contact. She then crossed North Clark and drifted into the foot traffic on West Armitage.

Just after 4:00 p.m. she ducked into a storefront and started to dial Dr. Forbes' cell phone. But she stopped. She knew that he'd read her the riot act for going to the media. After that he'd want her to let him back her up as she drew Axel in.

But she'd promised the killer she'd come alone and she was sure that if Axel found Dr. Forbes waiting in the shadows, he'd finish what he'd started at the I-80 dumpsite and kill him.

If Forbes had been careless enough to let Axel get the best of him *then*, with his addiction to Percodan, he was certainly no match for him now. Besides, Maddy felt that she had an edge on Axel. She didn't believe that he'd kill her right away. He needed her for something and she'd exploit that weakness, dropping *him* before he could take her.

So she sent a text message to Dr. Forbes, telling him to watch Channel 2 News at 5:00 and to go to their website immediately. She would meet him later.

But before that message ever reached Forbes, Axel had already seen the interview and he was finalizing his strategy for abducting Maddy in the Park.

Back in his lair, he kept his laptop on at all times. He'd set up an "as-it-happens" Google alert for any coverage of the subject "Chicago abductions." By now, the web master of Channel 2's site had streamed the video of Schilling's interview. Axel was up on the scaffold finishing the image of Christie Sloane when he heard the loud audible alert.

The deputy had been smart to pick Lincoln Park for a rendezvous, he thought. It was public enough for him to observe her from a distance while checking to see if there was any police presence nearby. Maddy assumed that he'd be coming for her in a van or an SUV. But she'd underestimated him again.

He couldn't wait to see her. He lay down on his bed and rubbed himself, thinking about how excited he'd be when he tattooed those letters and numbers on *her* neck.

27

THAT AFTERNOON, Maddy went into the Nike store on Michigan Avenue and picked up a pair of running shoes, some sweat pants, and a windbreaker.

In the Water Tower Place mall she found a Radio Shack and bought a package of foot-long flex-ties in the hope that she'd tighten them around Axel's wrists later that night.

As soon as the Schilling piece ran on Channel 2, Dr. Forbes had called her and she'd let him know that she was safe. He begged her to let him pick her up in the Crown Vic, but she insisted on facing Axel alone.

She shut off the phone after that, and when she turned it on again around 11:00 p.m., her voice mailbox was full. *WBBM* had run her phone number at the end of the story at 10:00 p.m., so most of the calls were from other reporters who wanted to talk to her, or Axel wannabes. But the killer himself had yet to make contact.

It was just after midnight now as she ran north through the Park past the Zoo. She stopped to catch her breath on a path opposite the Reptile House and checked the Ruger one more time.

Then, as she turned to start running, Maddy thought she saw a figure move in the shadows behind her, but when she looked back at the lighted path, there was nothing. So she headed north toward Diversey Harbor.

The figure in the dark hooded sweatshirt held back until she turned a corner, then he sprinted along a parallel path to get ahead of her.

Now as Maddy got close to the Boat Basin, she stopped at a water fountain to take a drink. For a second, she thought she heard footsteps, but when she stood still to listen, all she could hear was the wind coming off the lake.

She took off running again. This was her third time through the park and she was beginning to feel that her plan had been a failure. Did she actually think that this nutcase would come here to find her?

She was ready to call Forbes to come and get her, when she passed close to the Boathouse at the edge of the Marina and BANG!

The hooded figure who'd been chasing her, lunged out and cold cocked her. "Stupid bitch," the figure said, looming over her. "What kind of asshole goes running in this park after midnight?"

Maddy was on the ground looking up at him, but an overhead light was shining in her eyes so she couldn't see his face clearly under the hood. Just then, she pulled out the Ruger and came up with it.

"Get the fuck down."

The figure backed into the shadows by the Boathouse and mocked her. "I was on you fifty yards back and you didn't make me 'til now."

"Do what I TELL you," said Maddy. She went into a Weaver stance and doubled handed the weapon.

"You better *shoot* me," the figure said. "Otherwise I'm gonna take that gun, shove it up your tight little ass."

"I said get down Axel, NOW!"

But as she moved forward to grab him, the figure kicked the gun from her hands. He turned and delivered another kick to her sternum, knocking her back.

Maddy got up and started jabbing; working the figure over with a series of crosses like she used on the heavy bag back in Snoqualmie.

The figure threw another kick at her, but Maddy grabbed his foot and dropped him. She slammed him down on his face and pulled out a pair of flex-ties to cuff him.

"What did you do with my goddamn Smith?"

The figure didn't answer. Maddy had her knee on his back now, pulling his arms back and cuffing his right wrist with the plastic tie, the way Axel had bound her with the belt of the robe in her bedroom.

"See how it feels, you sonovabitch?"

She was about to close the flex-tie around his left wrist, when she spun him into the light and realized that this wasn't Axel at all.

The guy was black. Just a mugger.

"Who the hell are *you*?"

"For sure not the muthafucker you're lookin' for *bitch*."

"What the fuck are you doing here?"

"What do you think? Jackin' you girl. Least I was… What are you? Some kinda undercover?"

"Stay down," said Maddy. She spotted the Ruger and moved to retrieve it. The mugger was lying in the shadows. He didn't move.

Maddy picked up the gun and walked into the light. Double handing it now, she pointed it down at the guy.

"Alright get up. You can go."

But the guy didn't move. All Maddy could see were his legs extending out from the shadows.

"Hey! Are you listening to me, man? I am cutting you *loose*."

The guy was just laying there. Maddy couldn't get a good look at him, so she pulled out her cell phone and it lit up.

With the Ruger in one hand and the phone in the other, she moved toward the guy cautiously. And then, when she was close enough to see his face, she bent down. His body was trembling. It was like he was in some kind of shock.

"Hey, are you alright?" And that's when she heard it. CLICK. The sound of the hammer opening on the Smith & Wesson that Axel had stolen from her.

Fear shot through Maddy's heart. Then she heard his voice.

"You didn't have to go to all that trouble to talk to me on the news," Axel said. "I would have found you anyway."

Maddy felt the steel of the barrel against her neck. She didn't have a chance against him unless she could turn around and disarm him.

"Look, obviously you want me for something," she said. "Why don't we just discuss it like civilized peo—" But before she could get the word out, she felt an extraordinary pain against her neck. She lost all muscle control and just dropped.

Axel reached around her with both arms so that she didn't fracture her head when she fell. He had the Smith in one hand and the stun gun in the other.

He dragged the mugger by the feet into the light. The guy was just starting to come out of it now, so Axel hit him with a second jolt and then a third, sending a fatal shock to his cerebellum. He kicked the guy's body off the dock and into the Boat Basin, then pulled Maddy into the light and eyed her.

"Every time I get two feet away from you I get hard."

She was starting to emerge from the Tasering, so Axel pulled out another flex-tie from her windbreaker and bound her wrists in front of her. She looked at him now, wide-eyed with fear.

"You know that was *kind* of you to describe me as 'civilized,'" he said. I mean, I know you didn't *mean* it, but I felt, like, you know, maybe under different circumstances, we might be able to—*connect* in some way."

He shoved the Smith into the belt behind his back and bent down to flex-tie her legs. Maddy was fully alert now. She spotted the Ruger, inches from her face in the shadows. As Axel reached down to pick her up, she turned and grabbed the gun with her two flex-tied hands, but he saw it and pulled it away, tossing the .380 into the water.

"You know this is getting embarrassing. That's the *second* weapon I've taken from you and this is what? Like the *fourth* time you've been punked. I just want you to know that I HATE IT when you show me such weakness. I want the bitch back. I want that black leather whore on the Harley saying 'fuck you' to the world."

"Cut me loose and you'll meet her," said Maddy. "Drop the stun gun and the Smith and I'll have you by the throat." Axel was carrying her now. He had both arms under her as Maddy struggled to break free. "Oh yeah. There she is. That's the animal inside Maddy coming out." He was grinning now.

"You know," said Axel, "there's a part of me that would like to give you that chance. Let you punish me. Beat my face to a pulp."

He stood her up fully erect, leaning her against the Boathouse wall so she could keep her balance. For a moment Maddy was hopeful. Maybe she could talk him into giving her a running chance.

"You want me to hurt you?"

"Why not? On one hand I deserve it, but on the other hand I've got this project that I have to finish and I need you to help me. You're just going to have to wait." Axel walked to the edge of the dock where he had a 16 foot Bayliner runabout tied to a cleat. He reached down into a cuddy cabin in the bow and pulled something out.

"Til when?" said Maddy, thinking she might have an opening. "When can I punish you?" Axel loomed over her with what he'd grabbed from the boat. It was a roll of duct tape.

"In the next life."

And with that, he ripped off a piece of tape and covered her mouth. Grabbing her hair with his right hand, he picked her up by her belt with his left. As Maddy struggled to break free, he carried her to the Bayliner and set her down on the floor of the boat.

Then, to Maddy's horror, he unzipped a black plastic body bag and rolled her inside. She was fighting for her life now, bound hand and foot, so he took out the stun gun and zapped her a second time. The last thing she heard was the zipper closing across her face.

28

THE 156 MILE CHICAGO RIVER was a testament to the triumph of 20th century engineering over nature. The river had originally flowed East into the Lake, which was the source of the Second City's drinking supply. But by the mid 1850's sewage and other industrial pollution had turned the waterway into a public health nightmare. Back then "the stinking river," as Chicagoans called it, produced multiple outbreaks of typhus and threatened the city's growth.

So at the turn of the century, the river's flow was remarkably reversed, using a system of locks and canals. The river now flowed due West from the Wrigley Building under a network of 38 movable bridges. It merged with the Skokie River in the town of Morton Grove to the south. The series of canals and irrigational channels then spilled into the Des Plaines River and flowed south toward the Gulf of Mexico.

It was on this highway of water that Axel got into and out of the city from the Loop in downtown to his lair. And now, as the days closed in on his terrible plan, he would require Maddy and three more dead souls to finish it.

Ten minutes after he'd abducted her in the Park, she woke up in the body bag. The second jolt from the Taser had induced a sudden increase in the enzyme Troponin T in her system and she'd barely escaped cardiac arrest. Now as she came to, she could see a sliver of light at the mouth of the bag where Axel had opened the zipper so she wouldn't suffocate.

After putting her into the Bayliner he'd exited Diversey Harbor and gone south along the lake to the mouth of the Chicago River at the Michigan Avenue Bridge. From there he'd steered the runabout West along the riverbank to a dock area below the Franklin Street Bridge across the river from the Merchandise Mart.

Adjacent to the dock was a small container yard used by the city's Parks Department to store recreational equipment. In the off season Axel had quietly requisitioned two of the steel storage units and he put Maddy into one of them as he hauled a five gallon gas can down to the Bayliner to refuel it.

Now, inside the bag, Maddy used the thumbs of her two bound hands to push the zipper back. She had no idea where Axel was or how much time she'd have, but the opening in the top of the bag gave her just enough light to find her belt buckle knife.

She slit the flex-ties, freeing her hands, then bent over and cut the ties binding her feet. Cautiously now, Maddy crawled out of the body bag and brandished the tiny knife as she moved toward the container door.

It was open just a crack and she still couldn't see Axel, so she pushed it open a few more inches. Now, light spilled into the container and when she looked back, her knees buckled.

There were three more body bags on the floor. Maddy sucked in hard. What in Christ's name was he doing? She dropped down to the floor and quietly pulled back the zippers on each of the bags. Lying in the first one was a heavy-set woman in her 50's.

In the second one, a two-year-old boy, with the face of a little cherub. He stared up at her wide-eyed in death.

From the third bag, she detected a rancid smell. Opening it, she found an old derelict. His clothes were stained from a combination of vomit and cheap wine.

Now outside, Maddy heard the sound of an old rusty gurney. Axel was pushing it toward the container. She figured that he was going to use it to haul her down to the boat with the other victims, then take off to who knows where.

She held her breath and waited until he was inches away, and then pushed out with all her strength on the heavy steel door. Knocking him down, she burst out of the container and started running, trying to get her bearings.

She found herself in some kind of storage yard near the river. It was surrounded by a high chain-link fence.

Behind her, she heard Axel screaming.

"I don't know *why* you are making this so *hard*. I brought you back for a *reason*. I'm going to send you to a higher *place*."

But Maddy was halfway across the yard by now, zig-zagging in and out of the containers, toward the fence along the street.

Axel raced back to a container next to the one with the body bags. Inside, he'd stored one of his vehicles—an old Chevy pickup with a camper shell covering the flatbed. He quickly popped the lock on the container door and pulled it open, jumping up and over the hood of the truck which he'd backed inside.

The container had been too narrow for him to enter or exit through the door, so he went over the top of the cab and in through the door at the back of the camper shell. From there, he scrambled along the flatbed and into the window at the rear of the truck cab.

Once in the driver's seat Axel found the keys which he kept in the pickup's ignition and started the engine.

Maddy was halfway up the chain link fence when Axel roared out of the container, giving chase. She looked up and saw that the fence was covered with razor wire on top. She could hear the sound of the pick-up getting closer, so she reached into her pocket and found her cell phone; praying that the battery hadn't died. It rang once, twice and Forbes picked up.

He was in the Crown Vic, racing along Lake Shore drive by the Zoo. "Where the hell have you been?"

"No time now," she said, hyperventilating. "He's got me in some kind of freight yard. It's down by the river; full of containers" She looked up. "There's a bridge overhead."

Forbes quickly scanned a map. "Christ, there must be three dozen bridges over the river. Do you see anything else?"

From her position on the fence, Maddy couldn't see much beyond the street level. So she put the phone in her teeth and climbed to the top, just below the circle of razor wire.

"The building across the river says Merchandise Mart."

Forbes eyed the map.

"O.K. I've got you. It's the bridge at Franklin Street. Keep the line open and hold on. I'm five minutes away."

With that, Forbes pushed the pedal to the floor of the Crown Victoria, doing eighty toward the Wacker Drive exit off Lake Shore. Without Capt. Jamal's direct number he called 911 Dispatch and gave them his old FBI I.D. number, with the ten-zero-one code for "Officer Needs Help."

Back at the yard now, Axel had reached the fence in the pick up. He looked up and saw Maddy at the top holding on.

He got out of the truck and yelled up at her.

"You know I have been *incredibly* patient with you. Do you have any idea the lengths to which I've gone to keep you from sustaining any serious trauma? I could have broken your fucking neck back in Washington. I could have drilled you that night at the motel or slit your throat, back at the Park. I think, at this point, you owe me the courtesy of a little *understanding*!"

"Are you out of your fuckin *mind*?" said Maddy at the top of the fence. "No, don't even bother to answer that."

Just then, she heard sirens. She looked up at the bridge as a pair of Chicago PD units approached.

Axel raged now.

"Alright. Have it your way. You're coming off that fence, one way or another, so you might as well climb the fuck down."

He jumped back into the pickup and backed it up. Then he roared forward, slamming the front bumper into one of the twenty-foot metal posts on the chain link fence. BOOM!

The fence vibrated and Maddy lost her grip. She fell about five feet, but grabbed onto the fence and held on.

Down below Axel backed up again and roared forward. BOOM!

Maddy fell another couple of feet, holding tightly to the fence as she weighed her options. The closest container was ten feet from the fence. If she tried to jump for it, she'd never make it. She couldn't go over the razor wire at the top and the next time he hit that post, she'd be on the ground for sure.

So she looked down and just as the pickup was about to slam into the fence for the third time, she pushed off backwards and dropped onto the roof of the camper shell.

Axel screamed as he heard her hit the roof.

He slammed the truck into reverse, speeding backwards through the yard. Maddy grabbed the knife from her belt buckle and jammed it into the camper shell so she had something to hold onto.

She lay spread eagle on the roof as Axel spun the pickup into a 180 degree turn and roared toward the river.

"God*damn* it," he screamed from inside the truck. "You are fucking with history now and I have run out of PATIENCE!"

29

AXEL POUNDED THE ROOF OF THE PICKUP with his right fist as he spun the wheel with his left hand and cut in and out of the containers. He could feel the spikes of a migraine about to drive into his brain, so he flung open the glove compartment and pulled out a bottle of Dexedrine, gnawing the cap off and swallowing a handful of uppers.

Dr. Forbes was just two blocks away now. He turned the Ford right on Orleans, almost taking the corner on two wheels, as he used the massive Mart building as a guide to get him to the river. Maddy had kept the cell phone connection open and on the speaker on his own cell, Forbes could hear the psychopath screaming as he tried to knock her off the truck.

"Alright. That's it. I don't give a *fuck* what this is going to do to your skin."

And with that, he slammed on the brakes, causing Maddy to shoot forward and onto the hood of the pickup. She rolled down onto the freight yard in front of him. The shock from the fall left her stunned for a moment, while Axel gunned the engine and hit the high beams. The light was blinding.

The sirens were getting louder now as the CPD units closed in. Axel could feel the migraine cutting through his choroid plexus. He saw himself back in the closet, his bladder bursting, trying to hold back the pee pee with Raymond outside the door and the preacher's voice screaming.

"The temptress looked up at the serpent. She coveted the forbidden fruit..." Now the temptress was lying in front of him and Axel was about to slam the truck into gear to crush her, when suddenly... BOOM! The big Crown Victoria blasted through the gates of the container yard and Dr. Forbes roared in. He looked left, right, around the yard and spotted the pickup with Maddy in front of it on the ground, so he headed straight for it, slamming into the side of Axel's truck and flipping it on its side.

With the gas pedal to the floor, he used the big Town Car to push the pickup against the side of a container.

Upended now, Axel was temporarily pinned, but he kicked out the windshield of the Chevy and took off toward the river as Dr. Forbes jumped out of the Crown Victoria and rushed to Maddy's side.

He didn't even have a chance to ask her if she was alright before she was up and running, yelling at him.

"Let me have your Beretta." But Forbes was already in motion. He reached down and pulled a Walther 9 mm from an ankle holster and tossed it to her as they gave chase.

The amphetamine was coursing through Axel's bloodstream now. He made it to the Bayliner and jumped down into the cuddy cabin, grabbing Maddy's Smith and Wesson.

He hadn't come this far to leave his prize in that container yard, so he fired at Forbes, who dove down behind one of the big steel storage boxes. Maddy ducked behind another container and came up firing.

Boom! Boom! One of the Glaser Safety Slugs exploded on the Bayliner just above Axel's head, sending a hot spray of lead BB's at him.

"Goddamn it, you bitch," said the killer, jumping up and firing a round from the Smith. "I've got to look good for this too."

The two Chicago PD units raced into the yard now, as Axel traded shots with Maddy and Forbes. Just then, one of the uniforms issued a warning over the speaker in his squad car. "CHICAGO POLICE! STOP FIRING OR YOU'LL BE FIRED UPON."

But Maddy wouldn't stop. She fired another round toward the Bayliner and the two uniforms drew their weapons, exiting their units and closing in on Forbes and Maddy from behind.

Forbes realized that if he didn't do something, the two of them would be killed by friendly fire. So he stopped and held his Berretta in the air, yelling, "Don't shoot. FBI."

He pulled out his old FBI I.D. and held his thumb over the word "RETIRED" while the cops approached him cautiously.

But now, down at the river's edge, Maddy raced forward.

Axel moved away from the Bayliner and hid behind a thick concrete bridge support, plotting to grab her from behind and pull her into the boat. Then, as she passed the support, he lunged out, but she spun on him.

"You don't get *five* chances fucker,"

She fired, point blank at his head. But the Walther jammed: the slug literally stood upright in the slide as Axel smiled.

"What did I say about fate?."

One of the uniforms was moving toward them now, brandishing a shotgun. "Drop your weapons. Repeat, drop your *weapons*." He fired a warning shot and it whizzed over Maddy's head.

Just then, she managed to rack the slide on the Walther and free the round. The cop fired again, as Axel turned and dove into the river.

So Maddy fired multiple shots.

THWANG, THWANG. THWANG. She fired into the water repeatedly, then rushed to the river's edge and looked down.

The phantom killer had disappeared.

30

IF THE MEDIA FRENZY HAD BEEN INTENSE two days *earlier* when Maddy and Dr. Forbes first hit town, it was now at a fever pitch. The Parks Department container yard had become a crime scene and dozens of reporters were laying siege to the front gate of the chain link fence.

In addition to the three local stations, there were microwave trucks from all four broadcast networks, plus *CNN* and *MSNBC*. Even the *CBC* and *Telemundo* were present along with print reporters from *Time, Newsweek, The New York Times* and *The Washington Post*. With the discovery of three fresh bodies and the attempted abduction of the attractive young female deputy, the serial killer stalking Chicago was now an international sensation.

Deborah Schilling from *WBBM*, who had owned the story the day before, was now playing catch up with here colleagues from *WMAQ*, *WGN* and the two local dailies. But, with her contacts inside the P.D. she had managed to grab another exclusive. She stood outside the container yard gate doing a live standup for *WBBM*'s 11:00 a.m. newscast:

"Channel Two News has learned that the Chicago Police Department has set up a special Task Force to investigate the recent series of abductions, which culminated here last night in a shootout between police and the primary suspect. There are unconfirmed reports that the dramatic incident may have involved Deputy Maddy Bergstrom of the Snoqualmie, Washington Sheriff's Department who gave an exclusive interview to this reporter which aired just hours before the shooting. The Task Force will be headed by Chicago Homicide boss Winston Jamal, giving credence to Deputy Bergstrom's admission to us yesterday that the abductions are linked to a serial killer who goes by the name of Axel.

"A sketch of the suspect was released just moments ago and the description we received from the Deputy in a Channel 2 News exclusive, was a perfect match. Sources tell us that the FBI is heavily involved in this probe and that two police units were summoned to this location at 12:15 a.m. after a 911 call from an individual identifying himself as having links to The Bureau. The fugitive subject is a white male, in his mid twenties and I've just learned that he's known in files at the FBI's Behavioral Analysis Unit as 'Stranger 456.' The CPD's Mobile Command Center has been moved inside the yard behind me and we expect to hear any minute from Captain Jamal."

Now, as reporters jockeyed for position on the story, if there was tension *outside* the container yard, the mood *inside* the CPD's 40 foot Command Center was positively incendiary.

Not only had Maddy Bergstrom, an out-of-state uniform, done an end-run to the media, but she'd put herself at risk along with a pair of Chicago uniforms, not to mention her sidekick, the disgraced ex-serial hunter T.C. Forbes, who left The Bureau under a cloud. At least that was the spin SSA Ron Killebrew was putting on the story as he sought to dominate the investigation.

Fortunately for Forbes and Maddy, Captain Jamal was a straight shooter who had no particular fondness for The Bureau and he wasn't about to let the Feds hijack what was fast becoming the defining case of his career.

Still, there are few forces more intimidating than the FBI when it seeks to control a criminal investigation; especially one that crosses state lines. In a case like this, now associated with abductions from Washington State to Indiana, The Bureau didn't even have to *ask* permission to intervene, and because of the weight they pulled with the media it could be suicide for a local lawman like Jamal to try and buck them.

Ron Killebrew understood that dynamic unlike few SSA's before him and he was now strutting through the $326,000 Command Center as if he owned it.

"Let me run the numbers on this for you, Winston," said Killebrew. "You don't mind if I call you by your *first* name, do you, Captain?"

Jamal ground his teeth and shook his head, "no."

"You've got an inexperienced, out-of-state uniform with less than a year on the job, who happens, for reasons unknown, to be one of the prime suspect's intended *victims*. She's entered your jurisdiction armed, given an unauthorized interview with the media and put herself in harm's way, resulting in an officer-involved shootout in which she used a hand gun that's not even registered to her. On top of that, she refused *two* direct orders from your men to lay down her weapon, and for the *third* time, by my count, she allowed a predatory serial murderer to escape."

"I'm not surprised you see it like that," said the Captain. "But you have to admit—"

"What?"

"There *is* another perspective."

Captain Jamal handed Killebrew the morning *Sun Times*. It had a front page picture of Maddy from her interview with *WBBM*. The banner headline read:

HERO DEPUTY TO SK MONSTER: "TAKE ME."

"Fucking tabloid," said Killebrew sniffing. "Who cares?"

"Then how about the paper that started the Spanish-American war?"

He nodded to Sergeant Edmonds. "Can you hand me the Tribune?" She passed him a copy and Captain Jamal began to read the three column story on page one above the fold. The headline was:

WASHINGTON STATE DEPUTY SHERIFF
IN ATTEMPTED ABDUCTION AFTER LINKING
MISSING CASES TO SERIAL KILLER

"I'll just jump into the piece a few paragraphs down," said Jamal. "Let's see, blah, blah, blah… O.K. Listen to this: 'Sources close to the investigation say that Bergstrom took the job after her brother, a Marine hero, was killed in Iraq. She flew to Chicago at her own expense, when the suspect, identified as Axel, sent her a lock of hair from Ginny Kendrick, 12, a student at Chase Prep, whose father, Dr. Otto Kendrick is chief of surgery at Cooke County Hospital. 'Our family is deeply grateful to this young Deputy,' said Dr. Kendrick. 'She was willing to put herself as risk in order to further an investigation into our daughter's disappearance.'"

Jamal proffered the Tribune to Killebrew who winced at him.

"So what? You're letting the papers dictate policy?"

"Wait, wait. There's more," said Jamal who continued reading. "'Deputy Bergstrom was accompanied to Chicago by Dr. T. C. Forbes, a decorated former FBI agent who was wounded investigating the I-80 truck stop killings. Sources say that it was Dr. Forbes who made the 911 call which summoned two CPD squad cars to the freight yard where the suspect escaped after Bergstrom and Dr. Forbes closed in on him during a life-threatening shootout."

Jamal looked over at Killebrew. "I tell you Ron—If you're not careful, FBI Director Mueller's gonna be out here for a photo op giving Forbes the Hoover Medal."

"So let me get this straight," said Killebrew, playing to Troy Metzger and Rudi Gonzalves the two Chicago Field Office Agents with him. "When you're workin' a case you wet your finger, then you walk out on State Street and hold it up in the wind? Dependin' on which side of your finger dries first, that's how you call the play?"

"No, but I'll tell you what." said Jamal, getting up to face him. "I do *not* celebrate the chain of command at all costs, the way you do at The Bureau. When an officer shows some initiative and we get a break, I don't call in IAD and open up an internal affairs file on him. Until that young woman and Forbes came to this city we had *nothing* on this case. Zip. Just two missing females. Forbes and Bergstrom tied it in to I-80. They put a face to the suspect. And that young deputy with eleven months on the job? She showed more courage last night then most of the Feds I know who are six months away from their pensions."

"Fine," said Killebrew smugly. "But that I-80 lead is bullshit."

"Actually, you may be wrong about that. Forbes says he's got some new intel."

"Don't bet on it."

Just then, a phone on the Command Center console rang. Jamal picked up. "Yeah. Send them in."

Dr. Forbes and Maddy entered and crossed to Jamal, ignoring Killebrew. Forbes handed the Captain a fax.

"Ten minutes ago, the State Police lab in Tacoma got a positive DNA match tying Axel/456 to the I-80 murders."

"That's forty-four confirmed deaths," said Maddy. "Plus Kendrick and Sloane and the three last night, who make it forty-nine." She showed him the latest morgue shots of the three from the body bags.

"But a middle aged woman and a derelict? Now a baby?" said Jamal, incredulous.

"He defies any profile ever constructed," said Forbes shooting a look at Killebrew who turned away in disgust.

Maddy nodded to the homicide chief.

"It gets worse."

She opened out a map of the continental U.S.

Atop the map Forbes extended a see-through plastic overlay pinpointing the locations of all open missing person cases in the country. Each of them was marked with red and blue figures representing men and women. Missing children were represented in green.

"Excluding runaways and custody abductions there are currently more than 250 open missing person cases nationwide," said Forbes. "These are people who have been reported gone for more than thirty days."

Maddy pointed to lines on the overlay, fanning out from Chicago, connecting the missing persons cases. "Assuming the Midwest as a base, and given the timing of disappearances, we think it's *possible* that Axel's connected."

"To how many?" demanded Jamal.

Dr. Forbes and Maddy looked at each other.

"All of them."

31

KILLEBREW EXPLODED. "That is fucking outrageous."

But Maddy ignored him, brandishing a series of files. "We think he's taking them in an organized pattern."

She started tossing down Missing Person photos and reports as Dr. Forbes traced them on the map.

"August 5th," said Forbes, "Robert Dowd, a meter reader vanishes in Atlanta. Father of four. Afghan war veteran. Disappeared."

Maddy showed Jamal a blow-up of Dowd's driver's license.

"The next day, Jacqueline DeFries, a flight attendant with Delta goes missing in Nashville. Just swallowed up."

Maddy pulled out the victim's Delta I.D.

"A day later," said Forbes, "the mail truck of one Connie De Angelo, a postal worker is found abandoned in Muncie, Indiana."

Maddy produced a Muncie P.D. photo of the truck.

"Each of these abductions occurred on a straight line back to the Midwest toward Chicago," said Forbes. "We've only had time to check this one leg, but we think he's followed a similar pattern for months."

Now, even Captain Jamal, who was prone to believe them at first, looked skeptical.

"You're talking about hundreds of people vanishing. Why haven't there been any alarms sounded?"

"Yeah," said Killebrew, "Even with *alien* abductions you get those little *crop* circles."

Mocking Maddy and Forbes, he elbowed Metzger, one of his agents. But Jamal got in his face.

"Back off and let them finish." He nodded to Dr. Forbes to go on.

"There's been no urgency in investigating the disappearances because they're all *apparently* unrelated; spread across multiple jurisdictions."

"Until now," said Maddy.

"So what's he doing with the bodies," asked Killebrew.

"We don't know," said Forbes, "But for some reason he needs to keep them preserved."

"How in God's name is he doing that?" asked Jamal.

"Killebrew knows," said Maddy. "When they inventoried the van that Axel crashed up in Washington, they found a trochar."

"It's a tool used by undertakers," said Forbes. "We think he's keeping the bodies fresh by embalming them on the spot, or moving them back to some location near here."

"Jesus..." said Jamal. The veteran cop was clearly stunned by the theory. "How the hell is he financing this?"

"Robbing the victims," said Forbes. "Cash, credit cards, their jewelry..."

He showed Jamal a picture of Miriam Purloff, the wealthy woman Axel had strangled and robbed on the train.

"Thirty-six hours after 456 escaped from Snoqualmie, this woman was found murdered in an

Amtrak passenger train bound for Milwaukee. More than ten thousand dollars in jewelry was missing along with her car, a Mercedes Cabriolet."

Captain Jamal eyed the evidence. Their theory was wild but it was plausible, *if* they could unlock Axel's motive. That was the theory's weakness and Killebrew sensed it.

He finally weighed in with the fatal question.

"And what's the grand design behind this insanity?"

Dr. Forbes and Maddy shook their heads.

"We don't know."

"Of course not, 'cause there *is* none," said Killebrew, turning to Captain Jamal. "You know what you should do Winston? Go find yourself a judge and appoint a guardian ad litem for Forbes. He's certifiable."

Killebrew pointed to the artist's sketch of Axel.

"If this guy did all the 37 open missings I have, plus all these from around the country AND the I-80 deaths, you're talking about—"

"The most prolific serial killer in history," said Forbes. "A body count bigger than Chikatilo in Russia or Sobraj in Asia who killed more than two hundred."

"But we still don't know why?" said Jamal.

"Ask The Bureau," said Maddy. "Killebrew has files going back to Axel's childhood."

"These killers aren't born, they're made," said Forbes echoing the opening line of his unpublished monograph. "We need to go back and work him."

Jamal was convinced.

"O.K., so let's do it." He turned to Killebrew. "Where's the data?"

The FBI agent hesitated then leaned in and whispered to him.

"I need to speak with you privately."

"He's stalling," said Forbes. "Don't listen to him."

But Killebrew cocked his head for Jamal to follow him outside.

When they exited the big white Command Center, Killebrew nodded for agent Gonzalves to hand him a file. "I didn't want to have to show you this 'cause the sonovabitch is on his last leg, but during I-80 we found him tampering with evidence."

"Who? Forbes?" Jamal looked shocked.

"Yeah," said the FBI SSA. "He seeded three of the crime scenes with the same DNA to show a pattern. The A.G. decided to let him cash out at half pension to avoid a circus on Capitol Hill."

He opened the file and took out a letter on Department Of Justice stationery signed by Attorney General Eric Holder.

As Captain Jamal scanned it, he saw phrases like "evidence tampering" and "agent suspended," highlighted in yellow.

But before he could finish reading, Dr. Forbes burst out of the trailer, ripshit and limping. He grabbed the letter and slammed Killebrew back against the big truck.

"You cocksucker. That was a rat fuck and you know it. I was set up."

"Listen to him Captain," said Maddy backing him up.

But Killebrew just smiled. "Read his psych report. You'll find the words, 'paranoid' and 'delusional.'"

"Fuck you," said Forbes, rubbing his leg from the pain. "It's classic Bureau, Captain. "An ad hominem attack. They can't take the criticism, so they denigrate the critic."

Jamal wasn't sure who to believe now. So Killebrew moved over and put his arm on his shoulder.

"Listen Captain, I'm going to say this again." He pointed toward the front gate where the media was waiting for an announcement.

"In about five minutes when you face that mob out there, if they think this case has gotten away from you, they're gonna take off your skin. So who do you want to have standing next to you when you face the cameras? The head of the FBI's Behavioral Analysis Unit, or some goddamn washout who thinks he's Fox fuckin' Muldar?"

Dr. Forbes looked at Jamal who had backed him. The Captain had no love for the FBI, in fact, he resented the heavy handedness of the Feds. But he was reading the file on Forbes with the FBI logo.

It was stamped OFFICIAL, DECLASSIFIED.

It had the red, white and blue Bureau logo with the words *Fidelity, Bravery & Integrity* below a shield with the scales of justice.

Then he looked over at Forbes in jeans under a rumpled tweed jacket. He was rubbing his thigh as he waited for a decision.

Jamal looked at Maddy, the earnest, but rooky cop whose own exuberance had almost gotten her killed. Then he looked at Killebrew in his double breasted suit, starched white shirt and red tie. He was wearing black wing tips with the mirrored polish of an ex-Marine.

Finally, Captain Jamal turned to Dr. Forbes. He dropped his head and said, "I'm sorry."

32

THE NEXT MISSING PERSON in the serial killer case, now called "The Axel Murders," was Dr. T. C. Forbes himself. He hadn't been abducted like Maddy and the others, but he was gone nonetheless. After the rejection of his theory by Captain Jamal, Forbes didn't say a word in response. He shoved something in Maddy's windbreaker pocket and walked out through the tangle of forensic investigators working the container yard crime scene.

Maddy ran to catch up with him, but by the time she got to the edge of the media mob, Forbes was gone. She reached into her pocket and discovered that he'd given her the keys to the Crown Vic.

Even after its crash into Axel's pickup, the heavy town car was still drivable. But Maddy had to wait until the CSI techs had released it before she could exit the yard. Forbes had a thirty minute start on her and she had no idea where he'd go.

She called him multiple times on his cell and left messages, but got no response. It was 4:00 p.m., well into the afternoon rush hour, when she headed north on I-94 toward the motel in Niles. It took her forty-five minutes to get there. But their three-room "suite" at the Traveler's Inn was empty.

Forbes had already made a deep impression on the young rookie Deputy. In the days since she'd met him, Maddy had sought his counsel for insight into the psychopath who killed across every victim class and apparently without motive. A predator like Axel defied every criminal stereotype and Forbes had amassed a career's worth of empirical knowledge that he had been willing to share.

Many professionals with specialized skills hoarded what they had learned. But Forbes was generous; a natural teacher. And though Maddy's willingness to take risks had angered him, Forbes understood the hunger for vindication that a cop feels when he's been defeated by a criminal. He carried that weight with him every day.

Every time he saw another photo of an Axel victim Forbes felt shame and guilt for not having stopped him during the I-80 killing spree. Every time he took a step, Forbes was reminded how Axel had come at him from behind and jammed the knife in his leg. Every Percodan capsule he swallowed made him weaker. Every bottle he emptied was another measure of the killer's hold on him.

Dr. Forbes had chosen to bury his demons with painkillers and Maddy guessed that now he would seek refuge in a bar. Getting a prescription for Percodan filled after dark in this city, was difficult, but there were four thousand places in Chicago where liquor was sold and most of them would be open late.

Maddy decided to find him by using a technique that Forbes had taught her about homicide investigation. On the flight from Seattle, he'd talked about what to do when you hit a brick wall. When all the leads had played out and you were dead in the water, Forbes said, the best thing to do was go back to "the murder book."

That's what he called the file of the case.

Forbes kept all of his files in chronological order measured from the date when the killer took his first victim. If, for example, a body was discovered in a chain of serial deaths, he would insert the case material into the "book" at the point of abduction. Using a two-hole legal file punch, he would bind the "chapters" of the book at the top of each page with 2¾ inch Acco prong fasteners.

Once he and Maddy had been launched on their Axel hunt, Forbes had helped her assemble new "chapters," which they'd integrated into his I-80 files. After they hit Chicago, they copied the pages of Axel's Journal and worked them into the "book." Whenever he went back to the files, Forbes told her, he would reread them first in linear order and then at random, mixing up the evidence, to see if it might provoke a breakthrough or a new lead.

Maddy had kept her own "chapter" on Forbes himself. The material she'd first printed out after her Google search on him was held together with one of those Acco fasteners. And now, in the war room, she picked up the file and started going through it for some insight into Dr. Forbes and where he might be.

It took her fifteen minutes to come up with a location.

In the bio file that described Forbes' studies at the Kennedy School of Government, she learned that he'd written his doctoral thesis on John Wayne Gacy. Dubbed "The Killer Clown," Gacy got the nickname from the block parties he'd throw for children in his neighborhood. He'd lived in Norwood Park, a middle class suburb in northwest Cooke County. Gacy was a former shoe salesman who'd actually volunteered as a Democratic precinct captain. He ultimately confessed to the rape and murder of 33 young men and boys between 1972 and 1978.

Prior to his death by lethal injection, Gacy had been interviewed by Dr. Helen Morrison, a medical doctor who also examined his brain post-mortem. She had clashed with FBI profilers during testimony at Gacy's trial, insisting that his sadistic style of sexual torture defied all known patterns. Like Wayne Williams in Atlanta, Gacy had used multiple dumpsites. He'd dropped several of his victims in the Des Plaines River in addition to the 27 bodies he'd buried in a crawl space beneath his house.

Years later, after working with Killebrew, Dr. Forbes reasoned that if Ron the profiler had been working the Gacy case, The Bureau would have been looking for multiple suspects.

In the winter of 2005, Dr. Forbes had spent several weeks in Chicago interviewing Dr. Morrison who published her own Gacy memoir a year later.

Now, going to the Kennedy School website, Maddy was actually able to access Dr. Forbes's dissertation. In the section on "acknowledgements" he thanked Dr. Morrison for her "insights" and noted that they had conducted a number of interviews at "The Old Style House," a tavern three blocks away from Gacy's dumpsite home on West Summerdale Avenue.

A Mapquest search revealed that the bar was two blocks from the Norwood Park Metrarail station. It was less than 25 blocks south of their motel in Niles; practically walking distance for the disgraced FBI agent who had just been humiliated by the very SSA who had profited most by his exit from The Bureau.

When Maddy pulled up in the damaged Crown Victoria, she found a parking space on North Avondale Avenue, across from the tavern. There was no mistaking the red, white, blue and gold sign outside. The chevron-like logo for Heileman's "Old Style" beer was ubiquitous in Chicago. The regional brew. What Ranier had been to Seattle before its brewery was sold to Stroh's.

When she pushed through the heavy paneled front door Maddy didn't see him at first. The place was filled with a Happy Hour crowd; mostly lab techs and nurses from Resurrection Medical Center near the Kennedy Expressway.

But when she walked to the back, she spotted him at the very end of the bar, standing against a stool. Above him on the wall was a framed *Sun Times* front page of Gacy dressed as "Pogo The Clown." He was making balloon animals for children. The headline read:

GACY: "I RUN A CEMETERY
WITHOUT A LICENSE"

Just below that headline now, Dr. Thomas Charles Forbes was doing his best to exorcise his own demons. His denim shirt was open at the collar. His jacket was off and he was holding an empty Martini glass. His eyes were half closed and he was reciting something over and over with a grin on his face.

As Maddy came up behind him, she noticed four green plastic swords on the counter. Dr. Forbes had organized them in neat little parallel rows. The bartender had used them to skewer the olives in Dr. Forbes' cocktails.

If this was his fifth martini, thought Maddy, it meant that in the space of an hour he'd consumed more than ten ounces of gin or vodka with vermouth. Given that the Percodan was still running through his system, it was a wonder he was still standing, much less forming sentences.

Maddy leaned in from behind so that she could hear what he was saying. "I like to drink a Martini. Two at the very most. At three I'm under the table. At four, I'm under the host."

"Is that your own line?" asked Maddy.

"Hardly," said Forbes, not bothering to turn. "Dorothy Parker. Now *that* was a woman who knew how to drink." He took a sip from the empty glass. "Bartender..."

"Happy hour's over Doc," said Maddy.

"Unh uh," slurred Forbes. "The bars in Cooke County stay open until 2:00 a.m. and I'm—still not happy."

He raised his index finger to the bartender as if to say "one more," but Maddy pulled out her Sheriff's badge and shook her head to him.

"Just his tab," she said, "and some coffee."

The bartender nodded and set a cup with a shot glass full of milk down in front of them as Maddy took the next stool.

"Actually, can you make that *two* coffees?" she said, dropping her Master Card on the bar.

Forbes seemed to ignore her. He was staring straight ahead, now, looking down the bar at the Happy Hour crowd.

"Hey Doc," she said.

Forbes was silent. She tried again. Nothing. So she turned and put her hand on his forearm, as if to jostle him awake."

Finally, he looked at her and smiled.

"You found me. You worked my file. That was good."

"Thanks."

"So this trip wasn't a washout after all. The next time you come across a serial killer, you'll know what to do."

"Yeah. Here, drink some coffee." She poured a little milk in it. His hand was shaky and she wasn't sure he could sip it without burning himself. So she asked the bartender for a rock glass full of ice and poured the coffee over it. Maddy put the glass in his hand. A few seconds went by and Forbes took a sip.

"You remembered—how I take it," he said, seemingly touched that Maddy had learned that little detail about his behavior."

"Yeah, just like you Doc, very dark, with no sugar..."

33

FORBES DIDN'T SMILE AT THAT. He took another sip. He was a little steadier now, as Maddy signed the credit card receipt. After he emptied the glass, she took a sip of hot coffee and turned to him.

"So what do you want to do, Doc?"

"*Now*, or with the rest of my life?"

Maddy smiled. "Right now."

Forbes hesitated. "I know what I *don't* want to do..."

"You're tired of catching bad guys, right?

"Somethin' like that." His speech was still slightly impaired.

"Alright, then let's talk about something else. You like movies?"

"You want to take me to a film?"

"No. I want to talk about one. A real classic. *Apocalypse Now*."

Forbes seemed confused. "I don't underst—"

"You know, Brando, Martin Sheen. Vietnam, up the river? *Heart of Darkness*?"

"Yeah, what about it?"

"You remember the way it opened?"

She nodded to the bartender who filled the rock glass and poured another iced coffee for Forbes.

"Apocal—Yeah." said, Forbes, smiling again. "The Doors. Lot's of napalm..."

"After that," said Maddy. "You remember Captain Willard in the hotel room—waiting for his mission?"

Forbes was still shaky, but he nodded, thinking back.

"Fan on the ceiling. Cuts his hand on a mirror."

"That's right," she said. "Now do you remember what happened when those guys came to get him?"

Forbes stood there, bobbing for a moment, trying to focus. He narrowed his eyebrows, thinking back to the film. And then his eyes went wide and he turned to face her.

"They threw him in a shower with his clothes on..."

Ten minutes later, she dropped him into the bathtub shower in his room at the motel and turned on the cold water. "Arrrggghhh."

One of the waiters at the tavern had helped her get him into the back seat of the Crown Vic. He traveled lying down, as she roared north to the motel. From the parking lot of the Traveler's Inn she got him upstairs with the help of the night man in the lobby. She'd tipped them each five dollars.

Now, the freezing water was soaking his corduroy jacket, his denim shirt and his khakis. She hadn't even bothered to take off his loafers and socks.

She'd cleaned off the bottles on the sink ledge and she was rifling through his shaving kit now, emptying every bottle of painkiller she could find, and flushing the Perc capsules down the toilet.

A few minutes later, while he was still soaking wet, she pulled him out of the bathroom and dragged him to a chair in the war room, forcing him to face the files on the wall.

Careful to disarm him *before* he went into the tub, Maddy now grabbed his Beretta, racked the slide and slammed a round into the chamber: KAJACK!

Startled by the noise, Forbes began to come to. When he opened his eyes, he found himself staring at the pictures of Axel's victims. He tried to turn away, but Maddy took his face in her hands and forced him to look.

"You need to focus," she said.

"No. I need to *go*." He started to get up from the chair, but she slammed him down by both shoulders, then tossed him a towel to dry off with. "Leave me alone," he said.

"Sorry. I've been listening to you for a week. Now *I* get to talk."

He tried to get up one more time, but she pushed him back down. Then she started circling the chair.

"You have this knowledge and you wish you didn't." She nodded toward the grisly crime scene pictures. "You carry all of this sickness in your head—this pathology..."

"I don't want to *hear* this."

He started to get up for the third time, but she slammed him back into the chair. "Let me FINISH!"

She grabbed his Beretta and in one deft move, ejected the cartridge in the chamber, caught it with one hand, and popped the mag out. Then she continued to circle him.

"You wish you could crawl into a Perc bottle, but you can't. I mean, who's gonna stop this if you walk away?"

Now she stood in front of Axel's victim wall.

"It comes down to this, Doc: door number one or door number two." She held up an empty bottle of Percodan, then pointed to herself. "I'm gonna get him whether you help me or not and I don't have the time to pull you through rehab."

Forbes sat there silently.

"Come on, damnit. Make a decision. The green pill or the red pill?" He said nothing for another thirty seconds, just staring at the wall of victims. Finally…

"You know, it takes a cold hearted bitch to tempt a junkie with his drugs…" Forbes grabbed the Perc bottle from her. Maddy looked away, sure that she'd lost him.

Another moment went by and he went to the door of the war room as if he was about to leave. Then he stopped, jerked it open and flung the bottle out into the parking lot below.

"But that's just what I need for a partner, right now"

"What?"

"A cold hearted bitch."

34

Axel had also felt the force of cold water. After jumping into the Chicago River with Maddy's bullets slicing the water around him, he quickly surfaced in the dark to get his bearings. Knowing that he could die from hypothermia in the frigid November waters, he watched as one of the uniformed cops panned the searchlight from his squad car along the container yard dock, searching for him.

Suddenly, Axel heard the sound of a motor approaching 50 yards to the east. A huge garbage barge bore down on him. Pushed by a small tug, it was closing in at an alarming rate, so he swam with all his strength for the opposite bank. He came ashore just west of the Franklin Street bridge.

Luckily this section of riverbank was rimmed by a twenty-foot wide swath of small trees and bushes, giving him cover as he crawled out of the water. The belt of green wrapped around a parking lot that serviced the Holiday Inn at Mart Plaza, next to the Merchandise Mart. Axel was shivering uncontrollably now as he pulled himself through the bushes, up onto a path that ran along the bank.

The outside temperature in December was in the low 20's. His only hope was to get into one of the cars in the lot. So he dragged himself up and dropped down between a Honda Civic and a Subaru Outback. Both cars would have alarm systems, but they were low-end compacts. So there was a 50/50 chance that they wouldn't have motion sensors. He peered into the back of the Honda and saw an empty baby's car seat and a blanket.

Axel leaned backed against the Subaru and kicked out the driver's side window on the Civic. He held his breath, but there was no alarm. So he quickly reached in through the shattered glass and opened the door, ripping off his water-soaked jacket and pants and covering himself with the blanket. To keep out the cold, he jammed the baby seat into the empty space where the window had been and tried to stop shaking.

Ten minutes later, having staved off hypothermia, Axel ripped out the back seat of the Honda and found a woman's jogging suit in a gym bag in the trunk. He opened the ashtray in the driver's seat and found about four dollars in quarters. He changed, then tied his wet clothes into a bundle and dropped them into a trash container outside the Holiday Inn.

He walked two blocks to the Metrarail station near the corner of North Wells and West Kinzie, and took the elevated train downtown; getting off at Adams Street. It was just a four block walk west to Union Station. He kept a locker there with cash, a change of clothing and the keys to a Bronco that he'd parked in a garage on West Van Buren Street. Less than two hours after he'd gone into the river, the killer was back at the slaughterhouse, more determined than ever to capture the redhead and bring her there.

Now sober enough to drive, Dr. Forbes was at the wheel of the Crown Vic when he pulled up with

Maddy outside the legendary Drake Hotel on East Walton Place, off Michigan Avenue. Designed in Italian Renaissance style, The Drake had been a Chicago landmark since 1920. Its enormous red rooftop sign literally defined the skyline along the city's "Gold Coast." The original radio studios of *WGN* were in the Drake. At the height of Prohibition, Frank "The Enforcer" Nitti had his offices there. Over the years, the hotel played host to every luminary from Winston Churchill to Princess Diana. DiMaggio and Monroe carved their initials into the oak bar of the Cape Cod Room and Cary Grant made his way to Mount Rushmore from the Drake in *North By Northwest*.

As a Supervisory Special Agent, Ron Killebrew had an expense account for travel that would have precluded the suite of rooms that he now occupied at the Drake. Typically they rented for $800.00 a night. But the FBI maintained a number of "off site" locations for debriefing witnesses and furthering undercover investigations. As such, hotels like the Drake cut deals for The Bureau. In return for the kind of "cooperation" only the FBI could provide, they "comped" rooms to visiting officials from Bureau Headquarters in D.C. Career agents like Killebrew were expert at exploiting these perks. So on the expense report that he'd later file after returning to Quantico, his nightly room charge would be $140.00; a figure that wouldn't buy him a "standard Queen" at the Comfort Inn on East Ohio Street.

Once Forbes had changed into dry clothes and decided to continue the Axel hunt, he told Maddy that if they wanted to find Axel they had only one choice: steal Killebrew's files. She'd learned from Sgt. Edmonds that the SSA from Quantico was staying at the Drake. But as they found a parking space down the block on

East Walton, she wondered why they weren't heading to the FBI's Chicago Field Office on West Roosevelt.

"You think he'd keep paper that could wreck his career down there?" said Forbes. He exited the Crown Vic, then went to the trunk and pulled out a couple of pairs of latex gloves. When they got to the hotel's front entrance, he asked Maddy for Killebrew's room number.

"Eleven O Three," she said. The ex-FBI agent nodded and looked up at the 11th floor. An ornamental concrete ledge skirted the building just below the 11th floor windows. In his ten years in the field, Dr. Forbes had amassed a body of practical knowledge that went far beyond the rudimentary tradecraft he'd been taught at the FBI Academy. He could pick most tumbler locks. He could disarm most home security systems. And he knew how to enter and exit a location without leaving a trail of trace evidence.

Such off the books searches were legally forbidden. Any evidence seized would be inadmissible at trial. But an illegal search often provided the break an agent needed to advance an investigation.

No one in The Bureau would ever admit it, on the record, but FBI "black bag" operations were common. Still, Forbes had learned the *most* about surreptitious entry by studying the techniques of serial killers. Having started out in their teens as peeping toms, then graduating to home invasion, SK's, as they were known at Quantico, were often accomplished second story men.

For reasons of ego, a few chose to leave their signatures at a crime scene. But as Forbes soon learned, most serials sought to get in, murder their victim and get out without leaving anything behind for the forensic team. This defied the stereotype embodied by William Heirens, the 17 year old University of Chicago student who killed three women in the mid 1940's after breaking into their apartments.

One of the earliest known American serials, Heirens had used the lipstick of one of his victims to leave a message on a crime scene wall: "Catch me before I kill again. I can't control myself." In homage to Heirens, Axel had left that quote from Carmina Burana on the mirror in Maddy's bedroom and he'd painted the stomach of Miriam Purloff. But those were aberrations. Most serial killers couldn't *wait* to kill again and Dr. Forbes understood that. These hunters of humans just *lived* for a chance to take another life. The last thing they wanted to do was leave a snail's trail for the cops. So Dr. Forbes learned from these phantoms. He took note of how they worked in the shadows. How they returned to their dumpsites to ritualize or have sex with a body before the cops could discover it.

Back on the I-80 case, he thought he might get ahead of the killer by staking out the place where he'd just begun to dump bodies. But the genius who had taken dozens of hookers along Interstate 80 defied his own previous pattern and, instead, lay in wait for Dr. Forbes.

Now the file on that killer was hidden away somewhere on the 11th floor of the Drake Hotel and the wounded Ph.D. from Seattle was going to utilize every trick that he knew to find it.

35

Dr. Forbes picked up a house phone off the lobby and dialed the 7 prefix and the number 1103. Inside Killebrew's empty suite, the phone rang four times before Forbes hung up, sure that the SSA from Quantico was out.

Next, Forbes dialed room service.

"Yes Good evening. This is Mr. Killebrew in 1103. I came down to the lobby to buy a couple of small bottles of vodka, but the gift shop's closed. Do you think you could send somebody up to restock my mini-bar?"

There was a pause as Maddy strained to hear the other side of the conversation.

"Vodka. Yeah. You'll send somebody up right away? Great."

On the off chance they might run into Killebrew on his way back, Forbes and Maddy took the service elevator to eleven. They walked past his suite, then hid around opposite corners of the corridor until the mini-bar cart arrived.

The Drake was designed with a footprint in the shape of an "H." The vertical sides of the "H" ran parallel, North to South between Lake Michigan and Michigan Avenue.

The horizontal "cross" of the "H" contained suites on the north side facing Lake Shore Drive. Suite 1103 was located in the middle of that horizontal corridor, overlooking the park.

Forbes told Maddy that this form of illegal entry was a variation on the "brush pass" used by pickpockets. While one of them distracted the mark, another would move behind him to execute "the pull."

She waited around one corner of the "H" until the mini bar Porter knocked on the door to 1103. No response, so he used his electronic key card to enter the room.

He bent down and placed two tiny blue bottles of SKYY Vodka on the small refrigerator. Then, as he opened the mini-bar door with his master key, he looked confused. It was fully stocked.

But the Porter decided to leave the bottles atop the bar anyway. No sense risking a complaining phone call from a dissatisfied guest later on. Now, as he was starting to exit 1103, Maddy appeared.

"Excuse me sir," she said. "I'm supposed to meet a friend in Room 1125. Can you show me the way?" Room 1125 was around a corner of the "H" shaped floor to the right.

In order to guide her, the Porter had to leave his cart for a moment. When he did, Dr. Forbes moved up behind him and caught the door to 1103 before it closed.

Moments later, after the Porter left with the cart, Maddy returned and knocked on the door. Forbes let her in.

They had now committed a felony. As Maddy commenced the search for the files, she hoped it was worth it.

She looked in all of the obvious places: under the bed, under the mattress, inside the box spring, then in the closet and through his luggage. He had conveniently left his TSA locks open. She checked the dressers and drawers, behind the flat panel T.V. and behind the credenza which held the mini bar.

She checked inside the toilet housing. Nothing. There were no other hiding places in the marble-walled bathroom. The ceiling was white painted plaster. No hanging panels to hide something above.

She went around the perimeter of both rooms, checking the carpet to see if he might have pulled it up and slipped the files under it. Zero. She pulled off the face plate to the air duct, but there was nothing inside.

While all of this was going on, Forbes casually moved the curtain back and looked out the bedroom window.

Finally, Maddy walked into the living room, frustrated.

"The place is clean," she said.

Forbes eyed her and smiled. "Are you sure?"

"Positive. I've been over every square inch. He must have the files with him. Come on, let's go before he gets back."

But Dr. Forbes just stood there grinning.

"What's so funny," asked Maddy.

"Remember what your father told you about 'the road to hell?'"

"You're quoting my *father* now?"

"Just what you *told* me..."

He walked over to the window and opened it. There was a chill off the Lake as he leaned out and reached down. Taped to that ornamental concrete ledge below the window, he found a waterproof plastic folder.

Inside were Killebrew's Axel files.

"O.K." said Maddy. "I'm impressed. How did you—?"

"DEA stash manual. Before he came to Quantico, Killebrew worked drug enforcement."

He nodded for her to exit. As they walked out the door, he picked up the two bottles of SKYY vodka.

"Never bring anything *into* a crime scene or leave

anything behind when you go," he said. "Especially if it comes in a bottle."

36

IT WAS ALMOST ELEVEN P.M., when they got back to the war room at the Traveler's Inn. All of Killebrew's Axel files were now spread out on the bed and they were working quickly to evaluate them. Dr. Forbes checked his watch.

"Six hours. As soon as he leaves in the morning, these go back."

"What if he checks tonight?"

He eyed her and grinned.

"A dozen FBI bulls bash down the door and arrest us for B&E, theft, and obstruction. Then, after you get paroled, you can rejoin the Nomads."

Maddy smiled, but swallowed hard. "Right..."

Dr. Forbes picked up a page from a report by The Illinois Department of Child and Family Services. It had a picture of seven year-old Axel attached.

"Says here his real name is Bobby. Bobby Leroy Cole."

Maddy examined the crime scene photos from the fire that killed his foster parents. Their two bodies were charred beyond recognition.

"Killebrew told me that he stabbed them, then started the fire to cover it up. What child could even conceive of doing something like that at age seven?"

"A child with a 160 I.Q.," said Forbes handing her another report.

"Three more foster homes before he was ten. The longest stretch was two years. He got sent to an orphanage down in Joliet and then dropped off the radar 'til 2006.

Just then, Dr. Forbes found an Interpol report.

"This is strange."

"What is it?"

"A flash alert from Rome station. They sent The Bureau a video still of 456/Axel going through a metal detector in Vatican City."

Forbes handed her a copy of the still.

"That's him alright."

"It seems he'd gone in and out of St. Peter's dozens of times. His passport showed a series of trips to the middle east so, post 9/11, Interpol put him on a watch list."

Maddy opened a file and shook her head.

"How's this for balls? In 2010, he filed an application with The *Bureau.*" There was a copy of a handwritten note from Axel. Maddy read it to Forbes.

"'I believe I am uniquely qualified to assist in crime scene analysis. The I-80 offender fascinates me.'"

"Why'd he call him an offender?"

"It's a profiling term. The BAU uses it versus *suspect.* This guy's a junkie for investigative protocol. He can't get enough of it."

"There's a whole sub section in Killebrew's files on I-80."

Dr. Forbes started flipping through it quickly, then stopped.

"Oh fuck..."

He handed her an FBI Lab Workup Form.

"Killebrew requested a DNA scan comparing saliva on the envelope from Axel's Bureau application to the fibers we pulled from the I-80 dump site. That was two years ago."

Maddy examined the results and turned to him, shocked.

"It was a match. Axel was Suspect Number One for I-80. Killebrew *knew* it and let you burn.

Dr. Forbes got up and started to gather the files.

"We'll deal with him later. Let's go."

"Where?"

"A 24-hour Kinko's to copy these. We get some sleep, then hit the Drake in the morning to put back the files when he leaves."

"What's our next move after that?"

Forbes was already halfway out the door.

"Axel was fixated on The Vatican, right?"

"Yeah?

"That orphanage he was in down in Joliet—St. Timothy's…"

"What about it?"

"It's run by The Catholic Church."

37

THE NEXT MORNING, Axel was up at six a.m. back atop the scaffolding. Naked except for a small black pair of briefs, he was painting the face of Christie Sloane on the upper wall of the big space. Though it wasn't even dawn yet, he had Rammstein's German metal hit *Du Hast* blasting from the speakers down below. He popped open a bottle of Benzedrine, and swallowed some capsules, working against his deadline. Then, in haste, Axel made a mistake with a brush stroke on Christie's blood red lips. Raging, he splattered red paint across her face… "Goddamn—you fat fucking slut."

He grabbed the rope and slid down from the scaffold, eyeing a series of sketches on a nearby worktable. They were line drawings of an old man, a heavy set woman and a cherub—the three "subjects" he'd been forced to leave on the river bank in Chicago when he'd made his escape. Axel stormed into his office and checked the calendar on his missings wall. The days counting down until December 15th had been marked off. He now had less than a week.

He needed more bodies to serve as models for his master work. With the time he had left, he could surely find an old wino again and heavy set, middle-aged women were easy prey, especially if he trolled the homeless shelters. But children were much more difficult. Now that the media had gotten word that a baby had been taken, every parent from Winnetka to Gary would have a leash on their kid. As the clock ticked against him, Axel was growing meaner and more bitter. Outside forces were preventing him from realizing his life's work. All artists are possessed with some sense of entitlement. But few painters in history had been more presumptive of their importance than the man born Bobby Leroy Cole.

He worked in oils, but the extraordinary series of murals that he was executing might as well have been painted in blood. Until his search had put the redhead in his path, Axel had felt lifted up; buoyed by the legacy of the master to whom he paid homage.

But ever since he'd found her Polaroid in that tattoo parlor and traveled more than two thousand miles to take her, his luck had changed. The forces were turning against him and now they threatened to undermine this project to which he'd devoted so many years.

Then suddenly, the alarm sounded on his computer and Axel was given a gift. He went to his laptop and there they were: the pictures of all three "victims" on the front page of the *Sun Times*. There was even video of the toddler, Eric Kovecki whom he'd snatched from a day care center on Sheridan Road after pulling a fire alarm and sending the staff into a panic. Axel took video stills from the online coverage and improvised, painting the bodies of the adults from memory. He was breaking his own exacting protocol now, but time was of the essence.

He painted without stopping for the next three hours and fell asleep exhausted, at the top of the scaffold. When he awoke, he climbed down and lay on the faux marble floor, arms out, legs out, staring up at his masterpiece. He should have felt joy. But as he looked up at the ceiling of his lair he was reminded that he was still missing the centerpiece. The red headed bitch from the Garden of Eden who would turn this work into one for the ages. He wondered where she was right now. He was sure she was thinking of him. He went into his bedroom and smelled the pillowcase where he'd kept her panties. Her scent was still on it. Next to the mattress he slept on, he kept a color copy of the Polaroid that he'd lost that night on the mountain—the night in the storm when he'd first held her—the defiant biker bitch in the black leather halter and chaps.

He wished he could paint her like that and maybe he would, once he got her down here. Once he'd finished posing her for his masterpiece, maybe he'd dress her up in leather and platform spikes with a studded dog collar and force her to suck him before he broke her neck.

His mother had been a redhead, though he was certain her hair was dyed. He never knew who his birth mother was until that awful man came to see him at the orphanage. The nuns had told him that the man was his uncle. They said that he'd come to talk to little "Bobby" about leaving St. Tim's and living with him. The man said his name was Walter. "Uncle Walter."

He had yellowed fingers and he reeked of cigarette smoke. He showed little Bobby a picture of a woman he said was his sister; Axel's mother. She was smiling in the picture. She was wearing a red bra with panties and red heels. She was leaning over a platform or a stage and there were men around her. They had money in their hands. Uncle Walter told little "Bobby" that his mother was a dancer. She had wanted him to come and live with her, but it wasn't possible. Axel asked him why not and the smelly man said that she'd taken some medicine and she'd gone to sleep.

Well, why couldn't she come to take him after she woke *up*, asked little Axel. But the man had said that she would never wake up. That she had "gone up to God" and now Bobby had to come and live with him. But Axel refused.

Uncle Walter had looked at him the way the boys did in the DCFS holding facility before they tied him down to his bed and raped him. The smelly old man put his hand on Axel's leg as he sat on the edge of his bed. He started to move his yellowed hand up toward Axel's pee pee, so the little boy looked around and found a pencil on the table beside his bed.

He grabbed it and jammed the lead point into the man's hand. There was blood everywhere and the man started screaming. That was the first time in his life when Axel felt himself getting hard. Seeing this awful man, writhing on the floor as the red blood spurted out of his hand, gave little Axel a sense of satisfaction that he'd never known. The nuns had come running in and they took the man away. He had never come back. All little Axel was left with was that picture of his mother in the red bra and panties. There was blood on it and little Axel rubbed it across her face.

From that moment on he had a visual image of the woman who had brought him into the world and then abandoned him. The whore who had left him alone, while she danced for money with men who smoked cigarettes.

All those years before, growing up in the foster homes, he'd prayed that she would come and rescue him; that she'd take him out of those horrible places. But she never did. At that point he knew for sure that he would spend the rest of his life alone. Then Sister Veronica had shown him the picture. The beautiful picture of all those people up on that ceiling.

Hundreds of them surrounding a woman in a garden, getting an apple from a snake. The woman was a redhead. She reminded him of his mother and he knew that one day he would draw her. Even though his own mother was gone. He would find someone else. Another woman who would pose for him.

Now as Axel lay spread eagle on the fake marble floor and stared up at his reproduction of that work, he felt the spikes jamming into his brain. Try as he could, the forces that had brought him to this place were conspiring against him. They had brought him up to the ceiling and now he was down on the floor.

He'd been so close to capturing the redhead and bringing her here. Twice in Washington, she'd been in his hands. In the bedroom she'd been close enough for him to lick her and leave his saliva on her skin. Then again in Chicago, after he'd drawn her to him, he'd touched the nape of her neck where he was going to brand her and felt the surge of blood through his cock. But again, she'd escaped. No matter how hard he'd tried, this defiant redheaded bitch had eluded him.

So now, for the good of his masterwork, he would have to find a substitute; another redhead to pose for him so that he could bring the project to its end. Days away from the wrecking ball, he would finish it, except for her face. And then, no matter how great the risk, he would find her again. He would capture her one last time and bring her here so that she'd understand exactly why she'd been chosen.

38

AT THE TURN OF THE TWENTIETH CENTURY, almost fifty thousand children were housed in orphanages across the United States, and of that number, nearly half were under the care of the Roman Catholic Church.

More than two dozen of the "orphan asylums" were run by The Sisters of Charity of the Nazarene, an order dedicated to "the guidance and welfare of children abandoned by circumstance."

The Church's role as caretaker to so many children, was not simply a function of its anti-abortion position. It was grounded in ecclesiastical history. As far back as the 4th century, the Apostolic Constitutions—a collection of eight books on early Christian doctrine—decreed that "bishops should have orphans brought up at the expense of the church," and that boys, in particular, "should learn some art or handicraft and then be provided with tools and placed in a condition to earn their own living."

In 1894, the Diocese of Joliet approved the expenditure of $950,000 for the construction of "a free home for well-behaved orphans in destitute circumstances, physically and mentally sound, from the age of five years."

The prominent Chicago architect Edmund Sewell Langdon, who had been a protégé of H.H. Richardson's, was commissioned to design "a facility of some 200 beds."

The *orphan inmates* as they were known back then, were to be "under the care of the asylum trustees until fifteen years of age."

A wealthy Catholic industrialist named Timothy Dornan donated 12 acres of farmland for the site and Langdon designed an institution inspired by Richardson's famous Asylum for the Insane in Buffalo, New York.

It was a Romanesque facility constructed of large Medina red sandstone and brick. There were two segregated pavilions marked by towers with steeply pitched mansard roofs. 96 boys and 96 girls were housed in wards of 24 each on the four floors of the east and west pavilions.

There was a four-story administration building, a school on the north side of the grounds and a convent for the orphanage's 20 nuns which adjoined a church to the south.

Named for the benefactor of the grounds, St. Timothy's was a dark and foreboding place. It had tiny windows and thick cement walls. A twelve-foot high, black cast iron fence surrounded the perimeter, keeping the children in and unwanted visitors out.

Virtually all of the children here were born to parents who had "disgraced" their lives in some way through alcohol, prostitution or other crimes. The unyielding staff was convinced that their charges had come to them as a result of "God's will."

So they saw their role as both educational and penal. To the black-robed nuns who prowled its dimly lit corridors, St. Timothy's was a kind of transitional purgatory. While they lived up to the orphanage charter of teaching each child a trade, they also considered themselves enforcers, making sure that no child left the institution with any "infirmity."

Axel had first passed through St. Tim's gates at the age of seven.

The last of his five foster homes had been in Metamora, Illinois, a tiny suburb of Peoria that sits in Woodford County at the midpoint of the state. The median income in Metamora was $45,000.

Axel had been assigned by the DCFS to Albert and Marion Granger, a late 50's couple with three other foster children. They were considered "parents of last resort." The DCFS sent them only "hardened juveniles."

After being sodomized in Kankakee, Axel at first saw his move to the idyllic "village" where Granger ran a small hardware store, as a kind of deliverance. But he soon found the couple even more sadistic than the Tingleys.

They would routinely shackle their wards to a concrete wall in the hardware store basement which adjoined their four bedroom house. Mrs. Granger would administer regular beatings to the buttocks of the children with a "switch" that she'd cut from a lilac tree in the backyard. The punishment for bed wetting was "two cuts" of the flexible switch which felt like a bullwhip made of wire.

She'd only succeeded in punishing Axel once, before he'd stolen a pair of bolt cutters from the store, freed the other kids and then murdered the couple as they slept. He slit their carotid arteries with the blade of a knife that he'd received from his Cub Scout master after obtaining his Bobcat Badge. Then he used the corkscrew to pop open a two gallon container of kerosene.

After pouring half the contents over his foster parent's bed, Axel spilled the rest in front of him as he backed along the second floor hallway, down the wooden stairway and out the front door.

He soaked his yellow scout handkerchief in the volatile liquid and used it as an improvised fuse to set the empty can on fire with a box of safety matches. By the time the volunteer firefighters had arrived, the house/store was a blazing inferno. They found Axel sitting on the curb across the street with a lilac switch in his hand.

When the local police chief, a member of the Catholic Knights of Columbus, found the shackles in the Granger's fire-charred basement, he decided not to charge the seven year-old boy. Instead, through the local parish, he arranged for Axel to be sent to St. Tim's, as it was then known in rural Illinois.

That was 1990. The orphanage was closed nine years later after the Catholic Church child abuse scandal resulted in an investigation of St. Timothy's pastor, father Frederick Dozier. While most of the orphans had been physically abused by the nuns, the pedophile priest had raped or sodomized a dozen young girls over the years.

By 1999 the Archbishop of Joliet signed a consent degree and St. Tim's was shuttered. Most of the nuns were transferred to other facilities and Father Dozier was indicted on criminal charges.

Now the convent housed only six remaining elderly nuns who stayed on, pending a sale to help pay off the multi-million dollar class action settlement.

When Maddy and Dr. Forbes arrived, they were greeted by a caretaker named Johnston in a tiny stone house at the front gate. Maddy flashed her Sheriff's badge and Dr. Forbes showed his FBI I.D., careful, again, to obscure his "retired" status.

Maddy presented Johnston with a copy of a DCFS file on Axel. It noted that he'd lived in a ward called "Four East."

Unable to leave his post at the gate, Johnston gave them a key and a flashlight. He told them that when they got to the East Pavilion, they'd have to walk to the fourth floor on their own since the elevator was no longer operational.

It was almost noon when they climbed the stairs and unlocked the door to Four East. The sun was out, but even at midday, the long abandoned ward seemed dark.

Tall, yellowed shades covered the windows. There were two rows of cast iron beds on each side of the 100 foot room. Each bed had a small two-inch mattress. Most were mildewed. Some were covered with blood stains.

Maddy asked Dr. Forbes for the flashlight and checked a DCFS file page. Axel had been in #24 at the end of the ward.

As they approached the bed and panned the light, they could see that the mattress was stained yellow. It still had the stench of urine. At the head and foot of the bed, secured to the metal rails, there were hand and leg restraints.

Maddy winced at the smell.

"Christ, no wonder these kids turn into—"

"Made, not born," said Forbes, reciting his mantra. He looked up above the head board. "Wait, what's that?"

He gestured for Maddy to hand him the flashlight and noticed that above the bed on the wall, there was a yellowed rectangle of Scotch tape. It was about a foot wide and ten inches from top to bottom.

"Something was taped here," he said.

"A medical chart maybe?"

But Forbes panned the light to the wall above other beds.

"No. See? The walls above the other beds are clean. Who ran the ward here?" Maddy studied the file.

"A Sister Veronica. It says she was also the art teacher."

"Call the caretaker," said Forbes. "Let's see if she's still on the grounds."

39

Sister Veronica Vincent had found her vocation early in life. She had grown up the youngest of twelve children in the North End of Boston. Her father Vincenzo had emigrated from Radda in the Chianti region of Italy and her mother Ronnie had come through Ellis Island after arriving in steerage from County Mayo.

The young Irish immigrant found her way to South Boston, where she worked as a chambermaid in the rectory of Our Lady of Sorrows, Roman Catholic Church. Good looking, dark-haired Vinnie was the janitor.

Although it was never discussed, Sister Veronica's oldest sibling Terrance was born eight months after her parent's marriage in the church's downstairs chapel.

At an early age, Veronica had shown a talent for drawing. She won a twenty-five dollar Savings Bond in a contest sponsored by The Suffolk-Franklin bank. She was the first in her line to even consider higher education, and when she graduated from St. Augustin's high school at the age of sixteen—after skipping two grades—Veronica got a scholarship to the exclusive Rhode Island School of Design.

Though Providence was only fifty miles south of where she grew up, she might as well have been in Europe. After taking the last chair her whole life at a table with eleven other children, Veronica thanked God for giving her a chance to rise above her station and embrace a cultured life.

But two weeks after arriving on College Hill, she was walking home alone one night when she was attacked by a pair of sailors on liberty from the Naval Base in Newport. After waking up in an ambulance, Veronica soon learned that they'd not only beaten her senseless, they'd taken her most precious gift: her virginity. She later found out that she was pregnant by one of the men.

Abortion was not only illegal back then, it was forbidden by her faith. So Veronica was forced to drop out of RISD, give up the scholarship and travel to Worcester, Massachusetts in disgrace. There, she was taken in by The Sisters of Charity where the child—a son—was born. The Nazarene Sisters were an order that specialized in running orphanages.

After she'd given up the child for adoption, Veronica was convinced by the Mother Superior at the convent that the attack had been God's way of directing her to the sisterhood. She took her vows at the age of eighteen and continued her studies in art history. But from the day she put on the habit, something inside of Veronica died.

It wasn't just her girlhood or the hope that she might someday be a bride, a wife and a mother—the dream of most girls her age. But the long black robe over the tight fitting head dress that wrapped around her chin, became a cover that hid the utter hatred in her heart.

She knew it was a sin to hold such a grudge and each day at Mass she asked God to forgive her. But Veronica lacked the capacity for forgiveness.

She secretly prayed for the ruination of the drunken sailors who had changed her life in single night. Like little Axel, who lived to punish every foster parent who had ever abused him, she devoted herself to the re-education of any young male who might consider taking advantage of a helpless girl.

In the early 1960's, sister V.V., as she was called, was transferred to St. Timothy's. There she spent the next thirty years introducing her students to the beauty of art, while dispensing a level of corporal punishment that would have been illegal in public schools.

Behind the 12 foot iron gates of St. Tim's, she used a wooden yardstick with a metal strip along its edge, to correct whatever defects she could find in the orphan boys of the East Pavilion.

She was now one of the half dozen remaining nuns on the orphanage grounds, restricted to her room after a paralyzing stroke in 2009 that took her speech and her motor skills. As she sat locked in a wheelchair, staring down from her fourth story window each day, she knew that this was God's punishment on earth. He'd taken away her ability to do the one thing that gave her pleasure: painting.

When Maddy and Dr. Forbes went back to the caretaker's office, Johnston didn't warn them of her affliction. He simply called the convent and informed the orderly that they were coming over.

The orderly's name was Guzman. He was a heavy set man in his late thirties, who had been a paramedic in El Salvador. After working for a Nazarene mission in San Miguel he'd obtained his Green Card. Now he took care of the six remaining nuns.

Even though it was early afternoon, the blinds were partly drawn and Sister V.V.'s room was half in shadow. Guzman gestured for quiet, as he led Maddy and Dr. Forbes inside.

There were vigil lights atop her dresser, giving the room an eerie church-like feeling. The walls were covered with framed reproductions of classic paintings by the Italian masters. There was Caravaggio's *David With Head of Goliath*, Raphael's *Deposition of Christ* and DaVinci's *Annunciation.* A table along the wall, opposite the bed, was covered with thick art books.

As they entered, the old nun was seated with her back to them facing the window. Her black robe covered the back of the wheelchair into which she had to be strapped each morning so that she could sit upright.

Dr. Forbes turned to Guzman and whispered. "Will she talk to us?"

Guzman shook his head, motioning for them to wait as he moved up behind her and turned her wheelchair around. Sister Veronica's eyes flickered up to them but the harsh light from the corridor seemed to blind her for a moment, so she winced. Guzman quickly shut the door to the room making it even darker. He walked back to her and knelt down in front of her.

"You have visitors, Sister," he said, as he took a handkerchief from his pocket and wiped drool from the old nun's mouth. Then he turned to them.

"She had a stroke three years back. Hasn't said a word since. The only person she talks to is God now and she does it up here." He pointed to his temple.

Maddy traded a look with Dr. Forbes. It was a dead end.

A few minutes later Forbes and Maddy were exiting the convent, walking toward the Crown Vic. They were both really down.

"Square one," said Maddy.

"No. It's worse," said Forbes. "We're not even on the board." He began rubbing his leg again. "I need something for this pain."

He started to get into the car, but Maddy stopped him.

"We'll just go back and work his files again. There's got to be something else that we missed." But Forbes stopped her.

"*Listen* to me. The killer's escalating. There were three more abductions the same day he grabbed you and we still don't know why. We took a shot down here and we missed. You just have to face it—"

Suddenly Maddy cut him off. She was staring at something in front of the abandoned church which was adjacent to the convent.

"Quick. Give me the car keys?"

"Why? What's going on?"

Maddy took the keys and ran to the back of the car, popping open the trunk. She pulled out Axel's journal and ran to the front of the church. Flipping through the book, she looked up at old sign in front of the long-shuttered chapel.

"This is it!"

She pointed to the mysterious series of letters and numbers in Axel's journal. M 23:12-24; J 11:5-12 etc. Then she nodded up to the sign which still carried the schedule of Sunday masses. There was a series of biblical citations noting the readings for the last mass held at the church before it was closed.

"Don't you see it? Matthew, Book 4 Verses 20-28; Luke, Book 2:11-34. He's using scripture to mark his victims."

Forbes limped over to her and examined the sign. Then he looked at a page of Axel's journal. Finally, he allowed himself a smile. Stoked at their first big break,

Maddy threw her arms around him. There was an awkward moment as he hesitated, then hugged her back.

Up above in Sister Veronica's room, Guzman the orderly, looked down at them. He pulled a cell phone out of his pocket and dialed a number. The phone rang once, then again.

Axel was in a stolen Air Nautique 211 ski boat roaring across Lake Michigan along the coast by Gary, Indiana. The lake was shrouded in fog. Visibility was under 100 feet.

In the open cuddy cabin at the bow of the boat there was another body bag. The killer had one hand on the wheel and another on the handle of a search light mounted on the bow. He had to release his hand from the light to answer the phone.

"What the fuck's wrong?" he said, shouting over the sound of the engine.

"You said to call if anybody came to see the Sister," said Guzman.

"Yeah? So?"

"Somebody just came."

Axel hung up seething, distracted for a moment, when suddenly, from the fog, a ten foot high metal lake buoy appeared out of nowhere. The Nautique was doing thirty knots, bearing down on it, head on, when Axel quickly spun the wheel to avoid it.

The last thing he heard was the sound of the crash.

40

FORBES WAS IN THE DRIVER'S SEAT of the Crown Vic heading north toward The Loop on I-94, the Dan Ryan Expressway. Maddy was in the shotgun seat with Axel's journal open. She was excited; running through his numbers.

"J must be John or maybe James…"

Just then, they passed a sign for The University of Chicago and Forbes exited on East 63rd Street.

"Where are you going?"

"The Divinity School at the University. We need to talk to somebody who can take us through that."

As he pulled onto the local street, the rush hour traffic was bumper to bumper. Anxious, Maddy checked the dash clock.

"It's after five. By the time we get there, they may be closed."

"What do you want me to do, we're driving a tank."

"I thought you were the one who ran red lights."

Dr. Forbes picked up speed, but he was rubbing his leg, really in pain. "O.K. I get it," said Maddy. "You want me to drive."

"No. I can handle it."

"You haven't had a Percodan in what?

"Seven hours."

"How bad's the pain?

"It's a three."

"I don't get it."

"When I'm off the Perc, I rate the pain by the number of martinis it'll take to feel better."

Maddy smiled. "So you've been off it before?"

Forbes nodded. "Every so often an attractive young teaching assistant enters my life and—"

"Oh I get it. Diminished libido."

He nodded sheepishly. Maddy thought about it for a moment and smiled. "Tell me you didn't kick to have sex."

"With you? Not a chance." Forbes looked indignant. "I haven't slept with a partner yet."

"That's 'cause you've never worked with a woman. And while we're on it, how come you've never done the deed?"

She held up her ring finger.

"Marriage? Right..." He started acting out the kind of speech he'd give to his wife after a hard day of work.

"Hi honey, I'm home. You won't believe the dump site I processed today. We found two partially decomposed corpses and a bird's nest with human hair."

Maddy felt foolish now. "That really happened?"

Dr. Forbes nodded and turned away from her.

"Tama Jean Ottinger. Twenty two. A waitress at Stucky's in Dayton. The Ohio River murders in '07."

"You remember every one?"

Forbes turned to face her. "Wouldn't you?"

Half an hour later, it was just getting dark when a Police Boat from Gary, Indiana sounded its horn. A searchlight from the boat cut through the fog. There was a bell from a lake buoy striking in the distance.

As the boat came out of the fog, a uniformed cop standing next to the boat captain shined a hand-held search light toward the buoy. Next to it, in the fog, was the Nautique that Axel had been riding in. The boat was half submerged and sinking.

The pain in Dr. Forbes' leg was getting more intense as he drove up to the Divinity School on East 58th Street.

"Listen," said Maddy. "Do you want to stop at a drug store and maybe get something for that over the counter?"

"You said it yourself, we don't have time."

He stopped the car. "How about talking to one of those security guards to find out if any of the professors have night classes?"

Maddy nodded. She was about to exit the car, when Dr. Forbes' cell phone rang. He answered it and listened for a moment. He looked shocked.

"When? Where?" He listened to the response and then hung up the phone, staring straight ahead, not saying a word. Finally, Maddy turned and shook him.

"What is it? What did they say?"

"It was Captain Jamal. He said they just found a boat on the lake with another body… Apparently, Axel's dead."

PART THREE

41

When Maddy and Dr. Forbes walked into the Homicide bullpen, the squad of detectives and uniforms was gathered around a large flat panel T.V. On the CBS 2 News at 11 a.m. the anchor was leading the program with the latest Axel discovery.

"Panic sets in across Chicagoland, as police confirm yet another Axel murder. This time the victim is believed to be a female student from the University of Wisconsin. The Chicago P.D. has withheld her name and picture pending notification to next of kin. The grisly discovery was made in the fog shrouded waters of Lake Michigan off Gary, Indiana."

Just then, Captain Jamal walked out of his office.

"Shut that thing off."

Maddy rushed over to him with Axel's journal.

"We know how he's marking his victims," she said.

"Hopefully it won't matter now," said Jamal. "Gary P.D. found a half sunken outboard on the lake. There was a body bag inside."

He handed Dr. Forbes a crime scene photo of the corpse, a young redhead who was about Maddy's size and build.

"What's this about him being dead?" asked Forbes.

"Gary forensics found a right incisor with traces of blood in the cockpit of the boat."

Jamal showed them an evidence picture of the tooth. "The DNA matches Axel's. We're waiting for an ID on the tooth against childhood dental X-rays from the DCFS."

"We just got it," said Killebrew, storming in with Metzger and Gonzalves, his two field agents. He brandished a DCFS report. "Positive I.D."

"Thank God," said Jamal." He turned to Sgt. Edmonds. "Call the Mayor's office."

"Better hold off 'til you have his body," said Forbes. "It may be, he's just wounded."

"He's right Captain," said Maddy. "This guy has epic survival skills."

"What about *yours*?" said Killebrew. "You're gonna need 'em after stealin' my files."

He turned to his two FBI bulls. "Arrest the two of 'em."

Special Agent Metzger pulled out a pair of hand cuffs and started to move on Forbes, when Captain Jamal intervened.

"Wait a second. What's the charge?"

"Breakin' and enterin,' theft of FBI files and obstruction," said Killebrew, nodding to Maddy. "A room service Porter at the Drake spotted her outside my room and *these* were missin'."

He held up his Axel files in a see-through Evidence envelope. One of the agents started to read Dr. Forbes his rights, while the second one tried to cuff him from behind.

Suddenly, Maddy grabbed Killebrew by the lapel and pulled him inside Jamal's office. Slamming the door, she leaned into him with her teeth clenched. "Listen you wing-tipped asshole. We *know* you cooked the books on I-80."

"Bullshit."

"No. You had Axel two goddamn *years* ago but you let Forbes take a knife in his thigh so you could get him out of the BAU and run the show."

"Prove it."

"It's all in your files. We made copies."

At that revelation, Killebrew rocked back. But Maddy kept going.

"You might want to explain to the Captain why you withheld crucial evidence on the psycho who killed half a dozen people in Cooke County."

Killebrew tried to pull away, but she wouldn't stop. "How many more has Axel killed since I-80? Huh? Talk about obstruction..."

She gestured outside the office toward Forbes. "If you don't take the cuffs off him right *now*, I'll call Channel Two and you'll be dodging punk dates from a cell down in Leavenworth."

Killebrew wanted to clock her, but he was too smart to run the risk of an investigation by the CPD. Burning a look into Maddy, he decided to settle the score later. He took another moment to compose himself and then, opened the door out to the bullpen.

"Alright, cut him loose."

But as soon as Agent Metzger popped the cuffs, Dr. Forbes lunged at him. "You sonovabitch, this ends now."

"Damn *right* it does," said Captain Jamal, coming between them. He turned to Killebrew.

"The Doc is right. We need positive confirmation that Axel's bought it. I suggest you get the Feds up to Gary to help drag that lake. The currents being what they were at the time the boat crashed, he should've washed in."

"You want a body? You'll get one," said Killebrew.

He started to exit with the blue-jacketed agents. Then he stopped and pointed his index finger at Forbes.

"You are *finished* man. You will never walk onto another crime scene."

"Who the hell are you to make threats," said Forbes. "You can't even hold onto your files." He flipped Killebrew the under-the-chin Italian hand gesture for "fuck you" and the trio of Feds took off.

Forbes waited until they were gone, then picked up a crime scene photo of the Wisconsin co-ed that the cops had just pulled out of Axel's boat. He held it up to Maddy. "We have to talk."

Back in the motel "war room," Dr. Forbes was pacing and his limp was getting worse. Maddy was seated in one of the chairs staring at the photo of the redhead. "It's time for you to tell me *everything,*" he said.

She got defensive. "What do you mean?"

Forbes exploded and grabbed the picture. "This woman is a substitute for *you*. Same build. Same complexion. Red hair. No freckles. Perfect white skin."

"I didn't know you *cared,* Doc." She turned away.

But Forbes grabbed her by both shoulders. "Don't play *games* with me." He pointed to the artist's sketch of Axel on the wall. "This guy drives twenty-one hundred miles across country to find *you*. He's obsessed with capturing you. I want to know why."

"I told you, I don't know!"

"LISTEN to me! I want you to think back to what he said to you when he had you on the bed..."

"He ripped my robe open..."

"To rape you?"

"No." She was trembling now, remembering Axel's assault in her bedroom.

"Then for what? Let me see. Take your sweater off."

Maddy hesitated.

"Do it *now*, or I walk out that door."

Finally, Maddy reached up and pulled the sweater down over her right shoulder. She showed him the scar.

"What was that? A tattoo?"

Maddy nodded. "Yeah. The Angel of Death. I got it when I ran with the Nomads. Somehow he knew about it."

Forbes understood right away. "Christ, he's trolling tattoo parlors. Selecting his victims from shots of the ink work."

"That doesn't explain Ginny Kendrick."

"No. But it's the first lead we've had on his victim selection. Call Jamal. He needs to send copies of Axel's picture to every tattoo joint from Ann Arbor to Bloomington."

Maddy picked up her cell and started to dial. But Forbes was already out the door.

"You can do it on the way."

"Where are we going?"

"The Divinity School." He nodded to Axel's journal. "If we find out how those letters and numbers link to his victims, maybe we can locate his dumpsite."

"O.K. But what makes you so sure he's still out there?"

Forbes held up the shot of the Wisconsin redhead.

"He doesn't have *you* yet."

42

AXEL WAS NOW SURE that monstrous, empty fate had turned against him. The crash into the lake buoy had sent him into the water for the second time in 24 hours. But in truth, he should have been grateful for surviving. The 19 year-old freshman he'd taken off the jogging path up in Madison had saved his life.

When the Nautique with its 343 horsepower Excalibur engine smashed into the steel buoy, the body bag had been thrown into the cockpit and Axel was cushioned from the full impact of the crash. His head had slammed against the neoprene gunwale and he lost a tooth and some blood. But he was able to grab one of the lifejackets stowed in a rear cargo bin, as the boat started to take on water. With the gaping hole in the bow, it would have sunk like a stone, but the bowline got fouled up on one of the chains anchoring the buoy to the lake floor and by the time the police patrol boat came by, the stern of the Nautique was still visible.

As the cops shined their searchlights through the fog, the body of Andrea McMartin, the second year accounting major, was still wrapped in the black plastic morgue bag. The handles of the bag had hung up on the prop and it was bobbing alongside the boat.

Driven half mad by the migraines and downing every capsule of Dex that he had in his water-soaked cargo pants, Axel was overcome with rage. He swam a hundred yards from the buoy and came ashore near Marquette Park, just west of the Indian Dunes National Seashore.

There, he found a pair of coveralls and an old Honda 500 dirt bike in a maintenance shed. Kick starting the bike, he headed due West on East Dunes Highway until he connected to the I-90 West at Clay St.

At Gary/Chicago Airport Axel rented a Ford Taurus using the credit card and license of William Hennessey, a 30 year-old-lineman from Macon Georgia whom he'd murdered during a harvesting trip to the South two months earlier.

Axel resembled the blue-eyed Hennessey and he'd subsequently used him to pose for one of Noah's sons in a panel of his epic mural. The killer knew that if he paid cash for the one day rental, promising to return the Ford to the airport, the card wouldn't be run until after midnight. Hertz would merely use it to secure the vehicle. By then, he'd be back in the slaughterhouse. So once in the car, Axel headed West on I-94 out of the airport.

He picked up the junction of 57 South to Kankakee in the South Chicago suburb of Evergreen Park.

As soon as he got home and changed that night, Axel decided to pay a visit to his mentor—the woman most responsible for turning him into the man he was.

For the trip to Joliet, he took along his Nikon D3 with the 50 MM Nikkor f/1.4 D lens. At 12.1 mega pixels he wanted to make sure that he got every line in the old nun's face. She was about to play a crucial role in his final work. Axel decided to dress up for the meeting.

He'd been saving a double breasted blue pinstriped suit that he'd taken off Bobby Schein, a commodities broker from the Chicago Board of Trade. Schein was his precise height: six foot two and weight: 190. They even had the same shoe size: ten and a half regular and the same sleeve length: 33.

Now, as he dressed for the visit to the orphanage, Axel took pains to polish the broker's dark brown Cole Haan loafers. He snapped his silk braces onto the buttons at the top of the freshly pressed trousers and he put a modified Windsor knot into the red paisley Ralph Lauren tie.

That piece of clothing had been problematic. Axel had used it to snap the hyoid bone at the base of Schein's throat. Since it was a murder weapon, he couldn't risk having it dry cleaned. So he spent five minutes with an iron pressing it before he put the tie around his own neck.

Axel used a straight razor to shave, sharpening it on a strop that he'd bought at the auction of a farm estate down in Mattoon. The couple that had lived in the five-room farm house had died tragically after being side-swiped in their car driving home from an A.A. meeting.

The hit-and-run driver was never found. No one had any idea, that it was the little boy they'd locked in the closet so many year ago. And Axel made sure to check the local classifieds in the Mattoon Journal Gazette for the public auction notice. Now, he used the strop that Roger Tingley had beat him with to hone the blade of his foster father's straight razor. That way, when he kissed the old nun, she would touch the soft skin of his face without a trace of stubble.

Axel made the trip to St. Tim's in a nondescript brown Chevy Impala. It was the kind of car that he could park on a nearby street a few blocks from the 12 foot gates and not attract any attention. He scaled the fence on the north side furthest from the stone caretaker's building and used a passkey he'd stolen as a teenager to enter the rear door of the convent.

Before he gained entry, Axel walked around to the Orderly's room and made sure that he was asleep. He planned to interrogate him *after* he'd finished with the sister, so he didn't kill him first.

As soon as he entered the convent, Axel felt nauseous. The strange combination of smells made him sick. He picked up the odor of burnt candle wax and the smell of turpentine. They'd used it to wax the convent floors. It had been a job the nuns had forced the children to do each week and as he remembered all those hours of forced servitude Axel wanted to wretch.

He'd intended to make this visit on the night that he finished the masterwork. He'd planned to take a picture of the final piece to show Sister V.V. just before he snuffed out her life. But the rapid events of the past few days, including the visit here by the redhead, had forced him to alter his timetable.

Removing the leather-soled loafers just inside the door, Axel walked with stealth along the fourth floor corridor. As he used the key on the door of her room, Axel could see the votive lights flickering. She was in her bed, strapped down so as not to fall out in the night. Leaning over her, Axel opened the pearl handled straight razor and shook her gently. He wanted to see the look in her eyes as the blade glistened in the candle light.

43

"GOOD EVENING, SISTER," he said, putting his hand over her mouth to stop her breath for an instant and force her awake. The old woman snorted and her eyes went wide as she saw her former student standing over her.

Axel just smiled and quickly cut the restraints on her bed. She was trembling with fear as he reached under the covers and picked her up. Her bones had thinned in the years since he'd last seen her. She was light; almost birdlike now. He remembered her as a thick woman, towering over him as he lay shivering in his bed each night. He could almost smell the urine that soaked his "feety" pajamas.

Axel moved the nun to the wheelchair and set her down. He used the restraints to sit her upright, tightening them just enough to allow her to breathe. Then he went to the door and locked it from the inside. From her table with the art books he picked up the wooden yardstick that she'd used on him night after night.

The back of the 36 inch ruler contained row after row of tiny initials; little BLC's, standing for Bobby Leroy Cole. They ran up and down the measuring stick on either side.

Every time he'd wet the bed and she'd punished him, Sister V.V. had insisted that he sign her ruler. It didn't happen every night. But in the course of seven years at St. Timothy's, his bladder had failed him once or twice a week, so there were hundreds of initials.

Years later, when he got the W.A.R. ink on the bottom of his foot, the tattoo artist had asked him what had caused all of the tiny slice marks on the backs of his legs? Had he been into some kind of S&M, the artist wondered?

Axel had told him "Yeah. This bitch in a black robe used to hurt me," leaving the artist with visions of some dominatrix in black leather and thigh-high boots.

But the sick, sadistic person, who had beaten this helpless young boy, was actually a woman of God; a bride of Christ. Bent on exacting her revenge for the cruel way that those sailors had left her, Sister V.V. had tortured him at night, while inspiring him during the day.

In a few moments she would sit in final judgment before God. But first, she would sit for Axel in this room. He tapped the yard stick in his hand like a military crop as he circled the wheelchair. Drool was running down the old woman's mouth.

"I'm sorry I didn't come sooner." She was trembling with fear. But Axel kept his voice soft. "I know it's been awhile and I haven't been good about keeping in touch. You always said that I was an irresponsible little fuck who wouldn't amount to jack *shit!*"

He slammed the yardstick on the bed rail and her eyes flashed fear. Then, he got down on his knees in front of her and smiled. She could see that his right incisor was missing.

"Unnnhhh… Unnhhh," moaned the nun, unable to form any words. She was struggling to cry out for help, but the Orderly was sleeping four floors below and she was the only resident on the fourth floor. Axel got up again and started pacing, pointing to the prints of the Italian masters on her wall.

"Oh don't get me wrong, Sister. "I'm grateful for everything you exposed me to..."

"You opened up my miserable little life; introduced me to Raphael, Caravaggio and my mentor..." Axel stopped. Suddenly his mood swung radically and he began to weep. "You gave me sooo many gifts, along with the ice water enemas and the twice weekly visits with our *friend* here."

He slammed down the yardstick on the bed, viciously.

"Unhhhh! UNHHHHHHH!!!!" The old woman was almost apoplectic with fear, begging God now for the strength to cry out as Axel continued.

"But I never understood the contradiction." He nodded to the paintings and the art books. "How is it that with all of this beauty, you allowed yourself to vilify the human flesh the way you did." Another slam with the stick. "You used this stick on me week after week and shoved those awful things up my ass when I wet my bed." He nodded to a cross of Jesus hanging on her wall.

"What kind of a God brings little angels into this world only to subject them to that kind of pain? Why would He create something as perfect as the human body only to corrupt it by age and death?" He opened one of the art books to a series of plates by Michelangelo. "The masters knew. They devoted their lives to the preservation of beauty. They took snapshots in time with their brushes. Every soul in their work lived forever."

He moved closer to the bed. It was a miracle that the old woman's heart hadn't ruptured from the terror. Axel leaned down and whispered to her softly.

"It's time now for you to meet them." With that, he took the Nikon from a strap around his neck and started shooting her from every angle. He banged off a half dozen shots and then set the camera on the bed. Finally, he pulled out the straight razor and cut her restraints from the chair. He stabbed the razor into the mattress of her bed and picked her up, moving toward the fourth floor window.

Then he hauled back and threw her body against the glass.

"Night, night, Sister V.V."

The window broke outward and the nun fell more than forty feet to the pavement below. She fractured her skull and broke her neck along with her arms and legs. But she lived long enough to see the inscription on the statue of Jesus at the convent entrance:

> *Suffer the little children who come unto me;*
> *for such is the kingdom of heaven.*
>
> —Matthew 19:14.

Up above at the window Axel looked at the tattoo on the inside of his wrist, noting another citation from Matthew.

Then he grabbed the straight razor and the camera from the bed. He exited the room, running down the corridor, so that he could deal with the Orderly.

But when he got to the wily Salvadoran's room, he could hear him double locking his door. Inside, Guzman was on his cell phone calling 911.

Axel knew that he only had 48 hours left now, so he took the path of least resistance and exited down into the convent basement and out a crawl space into the yard.

He was up over the fence and into the brown Impala when he heard the sirens approaching.

He had closed the books on one account tonight and when he got the redhead up on that ceiling with that sadistic old bitch, he would close another.

44

NEWS OF SISTER VERONICA VINCENT'S DEATH reached Dr. Forbes and Maddy when they were just minutes away from the University of Chicago campus. Ironically, the link between the nun and the Axel murders was the result of a series of events set in motion by SSA Ron Killebrew. The call to the Crown Vic had come from Sgt. Edmonds after CPD dispatch received an alert from the Joliet P.D.

The detective first on the scene after Sister V.V. went out the window, was Lieutenant Ted Gilliam, an African American who'd met Captain Jamal through the Black Officer's Association.

That very morning, Lt. Gilliam had read a Chicago Tribune story noting that Killebrew was working with the CPD homicide squad on the Axel task force.

Curiously, just after Maddy and Forbes had left the orphanage, Johnston, the caretaker, had received a call from the FBI's Field Office informing him that agents were interested in talking to the old nun.

When he told them that she was unable to speak, they'd cancelled the request for the visit. Now with Sister Veronica's death, Johnston told Gilliam of the sudden Bureau interest and the detective had reached out to Jamal.

As soon as Forbes got the phone call from Sgt. Edmonds, he pulled the Crown Vic to the side of the road and got out.

"What is it?" asked Maddy.

"The nun's dead," said Forbes. "But right now, harsh as it may sound, that's not my immediate concern."

"What are you worried about?"

"Killebrew's already onto to her and we need to know why."

He went to the trunk of the Crown Vic and pulled out a flashlight. Then he popped the hood of the town car and started examining it. Maddy got out. "What are we looking for?"

" A transponder. Somehow The Bureau knew we'd been down to the orphanage."

He asked her to call Avis at O'Hare. Maddy had rented the Crown Victoria in her name. She'd presented her Sheriff's badge along with her Washington license for ID.

"See if the car has a Lojack system," he said.

When Maddy made the call and confirmed that it did, Forbes asked her to find out where it was installed. Maddy made it clear to the Avis staffer on the phone that this was a police matter. She asked her to pull up the rental contract. It would show that she was a law enforcement officer working a case. The presence of the transponder, she said, could put her and her partner in jeopardy.

At that point, the staffer put her on hold and a few minutes later, a Supervisor from the Avis O'Hare rental office came on.

For privacy purposes, he asked Maddy the number of her Washington State license, her DOB, the last four digits of her Social and the three digit I.D. on the back of her Master Card.

Satisfied that he was talking to Sheriff Madeline Bergstrom, he informed her that the Lojack system was installed in a hollow cavity inside the wheel well.

She thanked him and hung up.

"That means they've been tracking us since the day we landed," said Dr. Forbes. He located the Lojack transponder and ripped it out.

"I don't get it," said Maddy. "How'd they get the transponder number?"

"Easy. Once they had our plate number, they could access Illinois DMV records for the VIN. All the major car rental companies provide The Bureau with a VIN number database to stop interstate auto theft. The VIN would indicate whether the car was carrying Lojack. Once they had the Lojack 'chirping number' all they had to do was go into the NCIC and they could track us to within twenty yards."

"So Killebrew knew we went down to see the nun."

"Yeah and my guess is he's already down there."

45

LT. GILLIAM AND HIS FORENSICS UNIT had cordoned off two crime scenes; one in a twenty foot perimeter around the nun's body outside the convent and a second in her fourth floor room. But by the time Forbes and Maddy arrived, Killebrew was dominating the scene, dictating orders to the local detective. "I want audio and video of the autopsy and a full toxicology work up for the drugs in her system."

"That's gonna take some time," said Gilliam. "We're short staffed down here."

"Fine, then I'll tell your buddy Winston that you don't consider this breakthrough in the Axel case a priority."

"I didn't *say* that," said Gilliam.

"Look, it's clearly a suicide," said Killebrew. "It's not gonna affect your murder stats. Just wrap it up for us. O.K., brother?"

"I already *have* a brother," said Gilliam "And he's got enough sense not to throw his weight around in another man's crime scene."

"That's O.K.," said Dr. Forbes, pushing in. "You've got to cut Ronnie here some slack. This man is a legend. The model for Jack Crawford in *The Silence of the Lambs*. I mean, Ron and Tony Hopkins are like this." He crossed his fingers. "You know that fava beans line? That was Killebrew's."

Gilliam was a hip enough cop to pick up on Dr. Forbes' ridicule of his ex-FBI partner. "I hear you," said Gilliam smiling.

"Good," said Forbes. "Because I want to make sure you're not gonna swallow that horseshit about suicide."

"What the hell *else*, was it," snapped Killebrew. "The woman had zero contacts for six years. Then, you two show up and start grilling her."

"And how does she end up down here," asks Maddy, grinning.

"Simple. She gets the shocking news from you that some kid she taught has turned into the *Lord of the Flies*. She feels guilty. Distraught. So she ends it." He looked up at the broken fourth floor window.

Forbes just smiled. He glanced up at the window and down at the nun's body. "That's good Ronnie. It defies the laws of physics, but it's good."

"Why don't you just run along and get some quack to write you a prescription," said Killebrew. He turned to Lt. Gilliam. "You know this guy's an addict, right?"

"I'd still like to hear what he has to say," said Gilliam. "From what I understand he and the Deputy were the last to see the sister alive."

"Second to last," said Maddy. Forbes squatted down and examined the nun's body. He pointed to the silver cross around her broken neck. "First of all, in the Catholic Church suicide is a one-way ticket to hell. If this woman killed herself she'd have given up everything she had lived for. Second, she's a bed-bound quadriplegic. You tell me how a paralyzed stroke victim gets herself up, crosses the floor and goes out the window?"

Just then, Maddy spotted, the Orderly, Guzman. He was standing at the edge of the crime scene, shaking his head.

"So you're saying she was pushed?" asked Lt. Gilliam.

"Absolutely, she was pushed," said Forbes.

"By who," demanded Killebrew.

"You *know* or you wouldn't even be down here," said Forbes. "You'd be on the G-5 back to Quantico, sucking The Director's dick."

"That's it." Killebrew took out his gun and tossed it to Agent Gonzalves. He pulled off his jacket, ready to rumble.

"Come on, you gimp," he said, nodding to Dr. Forbes' leg. Killebrew put his fists up. "I'll let you take the first punch." He was dancing around now, throwing mock sticks and jabs. "Come on Tommy. You're nothin' but a doped out, pussy whipped, chicken shit."

Forbes practically lunged at him, but, Maddy pulled him back. She whispered, "Behind me. Right shoulder." Forbes looked over and eyed Guzman, ducking into the shadows. "You do this *now* and we'll lose him," she whispered.

"Come on, Forbes," said Killebrew taunting him. "Let's get this over with."

Forbes had his fists up now, ready to fight. But Maddy pulled him aside. "You can take him down later," she said. "Please." There was a long pause as Forbes gritted his teeth. If it were up to him he would have gone down swinging. But Maddy put her arm on his shoulder and finally, he pulled back.

"Another time."

"Oh yeah, yeah, right," said Killebrew, high-fiving the two Special Agents from Chicago. "I told you this guy had no balls."

Minutes later, Maddy and Forbes were behind the convent. The Orderly was pacing nervously and smoking. "Somebody killed her," said Forbes, "and clearly it wasn't you."

"We can testify to that," said Maddy. "We saw how dedicated you were to that nun."

Guzman hesitated. "Listen, I got a wife and three kids. I'm just about to get my U.S. citizenship. They pay my health insurance. I can't lose this job."

"You don't have to worry," said Forbes. "We'll back you a hundred per cent. Now tell us. Did Axel ever come down here?"

Guzman threw down the cigarette and shook his head. "No. I took the cabron's money, but he never told me he was gonna hurt that old girl..."

Maddy saw a crime scene tech coming, so she pulled Guzman around a corner. "How did he approach you?" asked Forbes.

"It was like three years ago," he said. "Just after the Sister went down with the stroke, I started findin' envelopes in my locker. First of each month. A C-note each time. I couldn't figure it out 'til this guy called and told me to watch her. You know... Let him know who came to see her."

"What kind of visitors did she have?" asked Forbes.

"None, 'til you people. I called him after you left. Next thing I know, the nun's dead." Guzman covered his face in his hands. There were tears in his eyes. Maddy moved over and put her hand on his shoulder. "Can you show me the phone number?" Guzman hesitated again. Then he pulled out his cell phone and punched the Recent Calls button. He was about to show her the number when they heard a commotion inside.

Forbes opened the back door a crack and spotted agents Metzger and Gonzalves walking out with banker's boxes full of books and pictures from the dead nun's room. One of the boxes contained a yardstick. Maddy walked up beside him.

"They're wiping the crime scene," said Forbes. "There won't be a piece of evidence left." When they turned back, Guzman was gone.

46

MADDY WAS DRIVING NOW as the Crown Vic roared north from Joliet. Dr. Forbes was slumped down in the shotgun seat, rubbing his leg and shivering.

"Why don't we just find out from the caretaker where Guzman lives and go find him," said Maddy. "If he's got Axel's number, we can draw him out again."

"I don't want to take the chance that Killebrew might find him. Besides, I've got another priority right now."

"What's that?"

"Vomiting."

"You really feel that bad?"

He nodded. "Try kicking barbiturates."

Maddy looked away and smiled. "So he was right."

"Who?"

"Killebrew. You're a doped-out, pussy whipped chickenshit."

"You had to beg me to drive, didn't you?"

"Yeah. So?"

"That proves I'm not pussy whipped."

Maddy smiled. "O.K. Two out of three."

Forbes turned away, but Maddy shot him a look.

"Just let me know ahead of time. O.K.?"

"About what? When I'm gonna puke?"

"No. When we're gonna sleep together. Now that you're off the Perc. I just want to prepare for it—mentally." Dr. Forbes tried to smile, but suddenly he felt it coming. He looked out and spotted a truck stop.

"Pull over."

Maddy screeched right and just made the exit in time.

Minutes later, she was outside the truck stop men's room listening as Dr. Forbes threw up his lunch. Figuring he might need some privacy, she went around a corner to a convenience store. A truck was just pulling up with a bundle of *Sun Times*. The tabloid headline read:

FLYING NUN: AXEL'S TEACHER A SUICIDE

Maddy shook her head at Killebrew's media victory. "Bastard."

She went to the counter to buy gum. There was a television on the wall above the attendant. *WGN*'s 5:00 p.m. news was on but the sound was turned down. Next to the anchor's head there was a graphic of the redhead Axel had in the boat.

"Can you please turn that up," Maddy asked. The attendant found a remote and increased the volume.

"Police have now identified the final victim in the string of grisly abduction-murders that's shocked Chicago. Andrea McMartin, nineteen, was a second year student at the University of Wisconsin."

Just then, Dr. Forbes came up behind her. He eyed the picture of the red-headed coed.

"Dead ringer for you. That means he's got to find another one.

"Yeah, unless he finds me first."

They walked out to the car now and Forbes took the disconnected Lojack transceiver out of his pocket.

"Not likely since they don't know where we are."

Maddy stopped in her tracks.

"Wait a second. Are you suggesting that *Killebrew* is actually *working* with this maniac."

"I wasn't sure until I looked at his files," said Forbes. "Killebrew had enough evidence during I-80 for a positive I.D. and a nationwide BOLO, but he let him keep going. Then there's what happened to me."

He rubbed his leg again.

"What do you mean?"

"I'd discovered his dumpsite. Nobody in the media knew about it. So I decided to stake it out. All of a sudden, the fucker shows up and catches me from behind."

Forbes stabbed down with his hand toward his leg, indicating the path of Axel's knife.

"But what's that go to do with—"

"Killebrew? He was the only other person who knew I was going to be there that night."

"Christ, are you saying he tipped him *off*?"

Forbes nodded.

"A senior FBI agent has been letting a psychopath get away with *murder*?"

"What better way to enhance his position at the BAU," said Forbes. "Once I was out, serial murder became a growth industry and it was all on Killebrew's watch."

"You think he's still running interference for him?"

"I wouldn't doubt it. But if he is, we don't have much time. Axel's getting careless. Whatever he's doing, he's under some kind of time pressure. He missed you. He crashed the boat before he could use that McMartin girl. So he's got to be trolling for a substitute. I guarantee he's out there right now, looking for another 'Maddy.'"

47

STAGES WAS A LOW RENT STRIP CLUB on South East Avenue in Kankakee. It was almost 2:00 a.m. and they'd just announced last call. The final dancer of the night was on stage, grinding around a chrome pole. Axel watched from a booth in the shadows as she strutted around in a white vinyl nurse's costume with white fishnet stockings and six inch platform spikes.

The "nurse" was a stunning redhead with tits spilling out of a white silk bra and an ass that was forced upward by the angle of her feet in the stiletto heels. She had a stethoscope around her neck that she dropped to the stage as she peeled off the outfit. Pretty soon she'd stripped down to the heels and a g-string. There was a white vinyl choker around her neck with a Red Cross in the middle of it.

Axel moved over to the edge of the stage. Some of the patrons in the club were laying singles and fives down in front of her. But Axel put down a twenty. That caused the "nurse" to crawl over. She lifted her legs in a "V" and dropped her head over the edge of the stage at crotch level. Axel eyed her enormous breasts. Then, she came off the stage and started grinding against him.

As he stared at the redheaded stripper, Axel thought about his mother. How many times had she opened her legs in a place like this? How could she expose herself to such men; degrading herself for money? How could she work amid such filth, knowing she had a helpless little boy who needed her?

He stared at the stripper wide-eyed as she rubbed her ass against his cock. When she leaned back against him, he could smell the perfume in her long red hair. Then he remembered where he was.

"I've got fifty for a blow job, when you're done."

"Make it a hundred and I'll give you half and half."

Moments later, as the neon sign outside the club went dark, the stripper, in a black leather trench coat and boots, followed Axel out toward his van.

This time she was wearing a spandex mini-skirt and spike heels with a fishnet top. The nails on both of her hands were long and covered with glitter polish. There was a black studded dog collar around her neck. Axel opened the side door and gestured for her to slip inside.

The stripper held out her hand. "Money, honey," she said.

For the first time, without the music competing against her, Axel thought that her voice was really low.

He handed her five more twenties.

She stuck them in her stockings and eyed him suspiciously.

"You're not a cop right?"

Axel smiled. He reached over and took her hand. He unzipped his fly and pulled his cock out so she could touch it. Undercover vice cops were forbidden to expose themselves this way, so the stripper/hooker knew that she had a real john.

When she got into the van, she saw that Axel had a mattress laid out in the back. He turned on the engine so that the heat would come up as she knelt down.

The killer got inside and rolled the door shut. The windows had been covered with silver Mylar so that nobody could see in.

The young woman was the same height and build as Maddy and her hair color was close. As she started to go down on him, Axel touched the back of her head.

As soon as he felt her hair, he went limp. He grabbed a fist full and realized that it was a wig. So he ripped it off. Underneath, she had tightly cropped hair like a man's.

"What the fuck are you doin'?"

The hooker struggled to get the wig back on, but Axel had grabbed her by the collar. He started twisting and it snapped off, revealing, an Adam's Apple. He'd just paid a hundred dollars for a blow job from a transsexual.

"You're a goddamn disgrace."

"Fuck you."

The hooker threw a punch at Axel. But he pulled the stun gun and zapped her. As soon as she was unconscious, he took off her panties and twisted them around her neck until she stopped breathing.

Ten minutes later Axel pulled off I-57 and took the exit for Rural Route 50. There was farmland on either side of the road for miles.

He spotted a drainage ditch with a culvert. So he skidded the van to a stop and dragged the body down and into the ditch.

Finally, he shoved it up into the four foot-wide corrugated metal pipe that fed the ditch. It would be days before somebody found it. As he got into the van, Axel heard a dog barking in the distance.

Four hours after that, a Kankakee County Sheriff's unit was moving down Rural Route 50. Suddenly, the unit stopped. There was something in the road ahead.

As the unit got closer, the Deputy inside hit his high beams. He saw that two dogs were fighting over something in the road. He couldn't tell what it was, so he got out. He grabbed a small handheld flashlight and approached the dogs slowly. They were growling, almost rabid, so he drew his weapon.

"Hey, get away now. Come on, get..." He tried to call the dogs off, but they wouldn't go, so he fired a single shot into the air.

BOOM! The dogs scattered. The Deputy walked closer now and shined the light. In the middle of the road there was a single human finger. Its nail was covered in glitter polish.

Reeling for a second at the sight, the Deputy panned the beam of the light down along the trail of blood that led to the drainage ditch. When he got there, he found the body of the dead transsexual. The fingers of the left hand had been eaten off.

48

ON THEIR WAY BACK to the Divinity School, Maddy had consulted the University of Chicago's website for a list of faculty profiles. Forbes' initial thought was to seek out a Roman Catholic theologian who might help them interpret Axel's citations.

But the professor whose name came up on two searches for *New Testament + University of Chicago Divinity School + citations,* was Rabbi Asher Weitzman.

On loan from Brandeis University where he was the Rose Melman Professor of Jewish Studies, Dr. Weitzman had received his second Ph.D. at the Catholic University of Louvaine in Brussels.

He was considered an international scholar on the New Testament as it related to Old Testament prophecies. He was also an avid mystery reader, so he was all too happy to accommodate the ex-FBI agent and the attractive young Deputy when they knocked on the door of his office.

The rabbi took almost half an hour to page through Axel's journal, occasionally interrupting the notes he was taking with the words "incredible" and "extraordinary."

When he was done, he looked up at them and smiled. "Clearly the mind of a disturbed individual," he said, "Albeit a brilliant one."

"So were we right?" asked Maddy. "Do his letters and numbers correspond to biblical citations?"

"Most assuredly," he said, stroking his goatee. "As you can see, his primary replicate letters each relate to one of the prophets. See here..." He turned the journal around to show them. "I for Isaiah, E for Ezekiel, D for Daniel, etcetera. In other instances he cites the Evangelists: Matthew, Mark, Luke and John."

"What about H 20:14-18?" asked Forbes. "He repeats that one over and over."

"It's Jeremiah, chapter twenty," said Weitzman.

He opened a nearby bible that he'd marked with a Post-it and showed them the passage. Maddy read it aloud. "Cursed be the day I was born. Let not the day my mother bore me be blessed. Let him hear the cry when I came forth out of the womb."

She nodded to Dr. Forbes. "That's our boy."

"Clearly, a tormented young man," said the rabbi.

But Dr. Forbes was confused: "You said Jeremiah, but the citation's written with an 'H.'"

"Yes. That passage confused me at first, then I made the connection to the Renaissance painters."

"Meaning?"

"In 15th century Italy, the masters represented the letter "J" in their work as an "H." He eyed them both. "But you must have *known* that, considering where the prophecies are found."

Maddy looked at Dr. Forbes, confused.

"No," said Forbes. "We have no idea. That's why we came to you."

The rabbi shook his head. He got up and crossed the room. From a wall full of books he pulled out a large volume and opened it.

"These twelve prophets were celebrated by Michelangelo as cornerstones to his work in the Sistine Chapel."

He paged through the book until he came to a section of color plates.

"The frescos on the walls were executed by a series of artists including Perugino, Botticelli and Ghirlandaio. But the crowning achievement was in the ceiling."

"It's Michelangelo's magnum opus. The greatest work of art executed by a single hand in Western history. For Christians, it tells the story of creation from Genesis up to what they believe to be the Ascension of Jesus."

Dr. Forbes and Maddy traded looks.

"The Vatican."

"How big is the original in Rome?" asked Forbes.

"Over 12,000 square feet. It took Michelangelo four years painting from scaffolding 40 feet high to complete it. The legend was that he painted each night on his back, but that's actually incorrect. The scaffolding that he built himself allowed him to stand while working on the fresco." Just then, a chill went up Maddy's spine.

"As you can see, the prophets are surrounded by naked figures called Ignudi. The other figures represent the saints, various angels and other biblical characters. Each has its own scriptural reference."

He wrote down one of Axel's many numbers. I 12:32-44.

"See here, in the corner: Isaiah twelve." The rabbi looked up at them, as Maddy and Forbes gazed at the giant mural. "Forgive me, but I don't understand. Why does this interest the police?"

Dr. Forbes eyed the dozens of figures in the plates of the chapel ceiling and walls: old men, young girls, angels and mothers.

"How many figures are in the fresco?"

"Three hundred, exactly. Why?"

Maddy scanned Axel's journal with hundreds of numbers and turned to Forbes. "The I-80 killings, the missing women out west. All the other missings from around the country..."

"And the last six in Chicago," said Forbes. "Two hundred and ninety—"

"Eight," said Maddy. "Nine if you count the nun."

"He's almost finished."

Finally, Forbes and Maddy understood Axel's horrible plan. They thanked the rabbi, asked for a copy of his notes and raced out of his office.

49

ON THE CHAIN-LINK FENCE surrounding the old Armour Plant on Highway 17 in Kankakee, the orange metal sign said:

ROUTE 17 SPUR DEMOLITION
TO BEGIN DECEMBER 15TH
USE ALTERNATE ROUTES

Inside his office, Axel had used his black Sharpie to put a big X on every page of his calendar counting down to the fifteenth. There were two more days left before the wrecking ball threatened to take down his masterpiece. So now, up at the top of the scaffolding, stripped to his underwear, he painted feverishly, putting the finishing touches on his homage to Michelangelo. Considering how he had selected his subjects, it was the ultimate coalescence of the scared and the profane.

This time, instead of metal music, Pavarotti's version of *Nessun Dorma* played in the background.

Each one of the figures on the ceiling and walls corresponded to a missing person in the pictures on his office wall.

Twelve-year-old Ginny Kendrick was an angel. The old wino that Axel had left in the container yard was the prophet Jeremiah. Black haired Christie Sloane was in a panel depicting the Last Judgment.

But the centerpiece of the work was *The Garden of Eden*. A green serpent wrapped itself around the tree of forbidden fruit. As Axel finished painting it, he referred to a series of digital photos he'd just taken.

The face of the snake would be that of the vicious Sister Veronica. The figure representing Adam had Axel's face. But there was something missing. The last blank space on the enormous fresco was reserved for the face of Eve.

Taped to the scaffold as a reference was a yellowed color plate of the entire chapel ceiling. It was rectangular. Its border was covered with old, hardened Scotch tape. This was the picture that had hung above poor little Axel's bed as he was strapped down and tortured at St. Timothy's.

Night after night, he'd stare up at this painting with the three hundred faces and one night he'd contrived his own hideous version of the masterpiece.

He'd been working on it now in one way or another for the last thirteen years; sharpening his classical painting technique, as he honed his skills as a home invader, auto thief, kidnapper, cosmetologist, undertaker, and serial murderer.

As they headed back to the motel "war room," Dr. Forbes didn't want to admit what he knew to be true: that the only way they could stop the killer at this point was to draw him back toward Maddy one last time.

She had been right. They needed to get his cell phone number from Guzman.

In fact, she'd been right to try and draw him out the first time in Lincoln Park. Her only mistake had been in underestimating Axel's strength and his capacity for treachery.

For a rookie Deputy, Maddy Bergstrom had remarkable investigative instincts, and Forbes was depending on her now to help stop this fiend.

Detective work was a crap shoot—especially in a serial murder investigation. After a given homicide, there might be five roads to go down and if you picked wrong, the trail would grow cold until you doubled back and took the right one.

With an aggressive killer speeding on meth like Axel, every time you had to retrace your steps valuable time would be lost and people would die in the interim.

On television and in popular literature, the new exploding science of crime scene investigation was all the rage. But despite what went down on CBS three times a week, real cases got made, more often than not, by guessing right on the killer's trajectory.

That's where empiricism, or inductive reasoning failed. More often than not it was rationalism, or deductive reasoning that broke the case: the ability to sit at your desk and "feel" the killer's intent.

The colloquial term for this non-linear form of thinking was "gut instinct," or as it was more appropriately called, "intuition."

As an undergraduate at Northeastern University in Boston, Dr. Forbes had taken a philosophy course with a remarkable professor named Mica Salas. She'd spent an entire semester discussing the two parallel schools of western thought: rationalism and empiricism.

They derived, she said, from the time when homo sapiens still lived in caves. Metaphorically speaking, the males were the hunters—the empiricists. The women were the rationalists.

Like modern day detectives, scientists and investigative reporters, they would venture out from their caves and *induce* knowledge through their senses. In pursuit of food, they would ford streams, get struck by lightning or attacked by predators.

By experiencing life in the field, they derived certain truths. They learned that it was dangerous to cross open water during a storm; it was safer to capture a tiger in a trap than with spears; and that the stars could serve as beacons for navigation.

Having *induced* this body of knowledge, the males would return to their caves to impart what they'd learned to their wives and daughters who had remained behind, tending the hearth.

As Dr. Salas put it, during those Philosophy 101 classes, "The men would come home and say, 'Gee honey you wouldn't believe what I *learned* today.' And the women would say, 'I already *know* what you learned. I could *feel* it…'"

Bound by the hearth and unable to move the way men did, woman cultivated another form of reasoning called rationalism. The truth wasn't so much *experienced* as *deduced*. Several millennia later, the French philosopher Rene Descartes summed up the process in a single phrase:

Cogito Ergo Sum – I think, therefore I am.

In the years that had passed since college, as he began to hone his skills as a criminal investigator, Dr. Forbes relied more and more on this deductive form of thinking which had come to be known as "female intuition."

That's why, during his years at the FBI, he regularly consulted women. And that's why, at this critical moment in the Axel murder case, he would listen to Maddy. Though it was an extraordinary risk, they'd have to try and draw the killer back to her one more time.

So Maddy called Guzman. It didn't take much coaxing for him to give up the cell number. Not after he'd gone back, as she'd suggested, and read the newspaper coverage of Axel's earlier murder spree.

They were back at the motel in Niles when she made the call.

Axel heard his cell phone ring once; then twice. It was down in his office and the opera had ended. So he grabbed onto the rope, slid down and answered it on the fourth ring.

He assumed it was the Orderly. Guzman was the only living person who had the number to the throwaway "Go phone" he'd bought. But it was the redhead. "Hello Axel…" she said.

She'd caught him off guard. The killer's heart rate began to increase. "How did you get this number?"

"I'm a cop, remember?"

Sensing Dr. Forbes on the line, Axel flared. "Tell the gimp to hang up." Maddy shot a look at Forbes who complied, but Axel kept pressing. "What do you see in that cripple?"

Maddy eyed Forbes who moved up close to her so he could listen. "He tells me the truth. To a woman, that's sexy."

"Funny, the women I've known all want to be lied to."

"Not this girl… So tell me, when can I see your masterpiece?"

Axel rocked back at the realization that she'd discovered his plan. "How do you know about that?"

"What did you expect? You left your journal in the

van." She sighed like she was giving phone sex. "So can I, Axel? Can I see it?"

"What? My painting or my cock?"

"First things first." She looked at Forbes and winced, almost gagging. "Now where can I find you?"

There was a pause as he thought it over. Then he walked to a wall in his office and eyed a map of Chicago.

"I'll find you…"

"Where?"

"The Michigan Avenue Bridge. Midnight. Bring climbing gear and come alone."

50

AFTER THE KILLER HUNG UP, Maddy threw her arms around Dr. Forbes. She was ecstatic.

"He went for it," she said.

"Yeah. Now call your father."

Maddy pulled away. "What? So he can take me home?"

"No. So he can watch your back." He checked his watch. "If he catches a flight from SEA-TAC before six, he can be in Chicago by eleven.

"Why?"

"Air support. You're not going *near* that maniac unless you're covered. We can't trust The Bureau, and we can't rely on Chicago P.D." Touched that he was so worried about her, Maddy inched toward him.

"And I don't have a choice?"

"Unh uh."

She moved closer.

"You're being strictly professional, right? It's a threat assessment without regard to your feelings toward—"

"Maddy…"

"What?"

He pulled her close and kissed her hard. She threw her arms around him and kissed him on the neck. Without another word he grabbed her, picked her up and carried her to the bed in his room.

Closing the door to the war room behind them, the ex-FBI serial hunter made love to her like it was their last night on earth.

For Maddy it was a moment years overdue. The sudden death of her mother and her father's stern, Marine-like response had robbed her of what she needed most at the time—a man who could appreciate the aching sense of loss that she felt.

Her brother's competitive need to fill the void for their father pushed her further away, to the point where she'd had to escape. Unfortunately, Maddy's withdrawal had sent her into the hands of an outlaw gang of men who confused brutality with strength and used her as chattel.

By the time she got out of rehab and crawled back home, the local boys who pursued her seemed naïve and weak. There wasn't a single male in Snoqualmie who had seen what she'd seen, or done what she'd done.

For months after that, she'd simply stopped dating. She wore the uniform, trying to please her father, trying to pick up her brother's mantle, but she didn't have a clue who she was or who she was expected to be. Until she met this bitter, wounded ex-agent; this brilliant investigator who had spent his career hunting demons.

He'd fallen, just like she had, but in a different way. And just like her, he'd been hiding.

Because he'd spent so much time in the presence of true evil, Dr. Forbes had built a wall around his emotions. With every crime scene he processed, every dumpsite he walked through, he became more isolated; less able to articulate what he knew.

Marriage and fatherhood were out of the question. How could he possibly share this awful work with a woman? With all the death he'd seen, how could he ever bring children into this world?

Professionally, Dr. Forbes lost the battle with Killebrew. Though his understanding of the serial mindset was dead on—it defied the mythology on which the Behavioral Analysis Unit was based. So he had to go.

Axel's attack at the dump site and his subsequent addiction to Percodan were the precipitating events—but Forbes had been isolated long before that. In the years since his withdrawal, as he retreated to teaching, his occasional affairs involved no commitment and little emotional depth.

And then he met this brave young woman who was putting herself at risk; trying to make up for the fact that she'd unleashed a madman.

In the week that they'd been together, she'd surprised him time and time again with her intelligence and her grit. But more importantly, her capacity to grasp a concept that had taken him two decades to learn: that these predators would keep on killing until they were stopped.

For the first few days as they worked the case, Forbes had forced himself to look at Maddy as a partner—not a woman. But that night in the container yard, when she'd shown so much courage, he saw her a different way. She was sitting on the riverbank shivering. She was vulnerable. The stench of the killer was still on her and yet she had the strength of will to go after him again. Suddenly, he was overwhelmed with a desire to stay with her and protect her.

So now, as they lay in his bed in the motel room with the pictures of Axel's victims locked off in the next room, the veteran investigator and the rookie cop saw each other for the first time as a man and woman;

knowing that depending on what happened that night on the river, this might be the beginning of their commitment to each other or the end.

As the light went out in Dr. Forbes' bedroom, a dark figure looked up from the parking lot of the Traveler's Inn. It wasn't the killer. It was Troy Metzger, one of the Chicago field agents working for Killebrew. He scanned the lot and saw the Crown Vic with the damaged front bumper, parked face-in along the downstairs row of rooms.

The Special Agent took a Ford master key out of a small black pouch on his belt and opened the trunk. He put a nine-volt battery linked to a transponder into the wheel well then covered it. He checked a receiver to make sure it was "chirping," then locked the trunk, walked around a corner and got into the black Suburban.

His partner, Rudi Gonzalves, was at the wheel. Metzger took the shotgun seat and turned to give the "thumbs up" to SSA Ron Killebrew who was in the back. As they took off down North Waukegan Road, Killebrew looked up at the second floor set of rooms.

He knew by now just how important the deputy was to Axel. Killebrew had let him run rampant for years; using the killer to advance himself in The Bureau. But at this point, the kid had outlived his usefulness. He was off the leash and he had to be brought back in.

Axel's takedown would be the crowning event in Killebrew's long career. He would "harvest" the psychopath whom he'd nurtured for almost a decade. The girl would be the tethered goat who'd attract him.

Follow her and she would lead him to 456. It was up to Killebrew to make sure that neither of them got out alive.

51

MADDY WAITED JUST OUTSIDE the passenger exit in the B Concourse of United's Terminal One at O'Hare. When she spotted her father, carrying a small overnight bag, she ran up and hugged him.

"Daddy..."

Sheriff Bergstrom embraced her coldly then pulled back. The ex-Marine pilot was armed for bear.

"You want to have this out now or later?"

Maddy backed away, disappointed, as Dr. Forbes came up behind her and held his hand out to shake.

"Thanks for coming Sheriff. I'm Tom Forbes."

Sheriff Bergstrom greeted him politely then nodded to his daughter. "Do you mind excusing us?"

"No. But you and I need to talk first." He gestured out the window as a Sikorsky S-76 helicopter landed across the tarmac at the General Aviation Terminal.

"It rents by the hour," said Forbes.

"What's that got to do with me? I came here to pick up my daughter."

"O.K. I understand that, but just hear me out."

The Sheriff hesitated, then nodded. Dr. Forbes motioned for him to step away so that they could have some privacy.

When they were out of Maddy's earshot, Forbes handed him a folded copy of the *Sun Times*. Above the fold in 72 point type the headline read:

HERO DEPUTY

"I've read the story," said the Sheriff. "I've been following it online. But you're only giving me half of it." He unfolded the paper. The bottom half of the headline read:

TO SK MONSTER: "TAKE ME."

"That's just what I wanted to talk about," said Forbes. "In all the years I've been doing this, I've never worked with an officer who has more tenacity and more heart."

He nodded toward Maddy who was waiting about 10 yards away. "Right now, she's about to go into harm's way against a man who *kills* the way most people *breathe*."

"And this is supposed to make me feel *comfortable*?"

"No, but she's willing to risk it because of you. She feels like she let you down."

"Look, I appreciate what she's done. But you said it yourself: the man's a killing machine. She's no match for—"

"Right, which is why I asked her to call you."

"I still don't follow..."

Forbes gestured out toward the Sikorsky.

"I need you to gas up that chopper and be ready to fly in fifteen minutes. Off the books. No flight plan. Right into downtown Chicago."

"And wreck a career I've spent thirty years building?"

"Maybe... But you'd be helping your daughter stop a psychopath."

Sheriff Bergstrom hesitated then he shook his head.

"Sorry."

He started to back away but Forbes stopped him.

"Come on, Sheriff. You didn't go into police work to pull skiers off mountains." He handed him the sketch of Axel. "I'm talking about a man who's killed almost three hundred people. And if you don't do this, she'll be next." He nodded toward Maddy.

The Sheriff just stared at him unmoved; so Forbes pressed him.

"She is not going back, O.K.? When I even suggested that to her, she used one of your phrases."

"Which one?"

"Retreat is not an option."

"She said that?"

"Yeah," said Forbes. "She's more your daughter than you think."

Bergstrom gritted his teeth. He looked over at Maddy pacing, ready to do battle. She was carrying herself with a confidence and weight he'd never seen. Finally, he gestured for her to come toward them.

"Yeah Dad. So what's it gonna be?"

She eyed him, expecting to be disappointed again. But he nodded.

"I'll do it."

Maddy threw her arms out to hug him.

"On one condition."

"What?"

She was afraid he was going to undercut her again, like he'd done in the hospital. "You have to bring me an Apple Fritter every day for the rest of my life."

Maddy burst into tears as the Sheriff hugged her for dear life.

Moments later, SSA Ron FBI Killebrew was in the Operations Center of The Bureau's Field Office with SA's Metzger and Gonzalves. There was a wall of flat panel monitors behind a console with an active GPS map of Chicago.

The blip from the transponder on the Crown Victoria indicated that the town car was at O'Hare.

"You think she's skipping town?" asked Gonzalves.

"Unlikely," said Metzger. Her old man phoned us earlier to say he was coming in. Wanted to link with us at some point." Killebrew opened a file on the Sheriff. "Guy's a fuckin' Eagle Scout. Strictly by the book. His profile says 'chain of command.' He'll do whatever we tell him."

Just then, Gonzalves pointed up at the board. The transponder was moving, heading in town along the Kennedy Expressway. "Look's like she's decided to stay," he said. "You think she's got the old man with her?"

"Doesn't matter," said Killebrew, turning to Metzger. "How long before we can get airborne."

"Yeah, well that's a problem, sir."

"What do you mean?"

"The two choppers assigned to the Field office are down. One's in Champaign-Urbana on a bank robbery. The other's in overhaul."

"And I'm finding out about this *now?*"

"Sir, we thought Chopper One would be free, but—"

"O.K. gentleman. I take it you want to get assigned to Headquarters at some point—move up the food chain?"

"Yeah," said Gonzalves.

"No question," said Metzger.

"Then here's what you do," said the SSA. "Call DEA. Tell them we picked up a wiretap lead on a drug transaction. They can scramble a bird. Pick us up on the roof."

"What happens when we get airborne?" asked Metzger.

"Yeah," said Gonzalves. "When they realize it's a false requisition?"

"Let me worry about that," said Killebrew. He eyed the screen as the blip from Maddy's Crown Vic got closer and closer to The Loop.

"Just make it happen…"

52

IT WAS THREE MINUTES BEFORE MIDNIGHT when Axel snaked along Navy Pier in a stolen Boston Whaler with twin 500 HP Merc outboards. He headed due west under the overpass for Lake Shore Drive, along East Wacker Drive and under North Columbus, heading for the bridge at Michigan Avenue.

This was the celebrated span that separated the downtown Chicago Loop from the Near North Side. Located at the foot of what Chicagoans called "The Magnificent Mile," it was anchored on the north by two of the city's most historic landmarks, The Wrigley Building and the Chicago Tribune Tower.

Maddy parked the Crown Vic on Lower Wacker drive and pulled out a rappelling harness with 100 feet of line. She walked up the steps of the bridge by the McCormick Tribune bridge house and onto Michigan Avenue.

At this time of night there were just a few cars on The Magnificent Mile and no police presence that she could see.

Cautiously, Maddy walked to the midpoint of the bridge. Taped to the railing, she spotted a Sprint cell phone.

The Bell Jet Ranger that Killebrew had just requisitioned from the DEA was a 407, a much newer model than Sheriff Bergstrom's 206L "LongRanger." At 12:02

a.m. it lifted off from the small helipad atop the FBI's Chicago Field Office on West Roosevelt Road. A DEA pilot was at the controls. Killebrew rode shotgun and an FBI Sniper was in the back seat.

On the ground, SAs Troy Metzger and Rudi Gonzalves where in twin black Suburbans, heading toward opposite ends of the bridge.

Metzger had a small laptop in front of him with a map of downtown. The GPS transponder blip pinpointed the location of the Crown Vic which had stopped on Lower Wacker Drive.

He radioed back to Killebrew who was airborne.

"Looks like she parked. We're moving into place on either side of the bridge."

"Make sure you don't lose her," said Killebrew. He nodded to the pilot and instructed him to head toward The Wrigley Building. Then he turned to the FBI sniper behind him who was rolling open the chopper door.

"Case of Johnny Walker Black if you make it a head shot."

"Sir, what happens if the Deputy gets too close to the subject," asked the sniper.

"I'm sure she's wearing a vest."

"But what if—"

Killebrew cut him off. "When he's in the crosshairs it's your call. But in no event are you to let this man escape." The sniper shook his head, wondering what he'd gotten himself into.

As the Sikorsky took off from O'Hare, Dr. Forbes communicated with Sheriff Bergstrom via their helmet radios.

"Which way do you think he'll break?" asked the Sheriff.

"If he's true to form, it'll be a Lake escape."

He dialed Maddy's cell. She answered from the midpoint of the bridge via a Bluetooth head set.

"Two minutes and closing," said Forbes, eyeing a map.

"Why don't you stay wide until I've made contact," she advised. "Otherwise you're gonna spook him."

"Roger that," said her father.

At the top of the bridge, Maddy smiled. She couldn't remember the last time that her father had followed her lead.

"Just keep the line open," he said. "You're gonna be fine."

Maddy swallowed hard. "From your lips to God's whatever, Dad."

Now in the Boston Whaler, Axel was under the bridge. He looked up and spotted Maddy, so he hit her with two short blasts on the Sprint's walkie-talkie.

"Get up on the west side railing. Thirty seconds."

Another two blasts and Maddy gritted her teeth. She checked the .380 Beretta that her father had given her. It was in a paddle holster at the small of her back.

"Right," she said, responding on the Sprint. "Let's do this."

She looked down through the grate in the bridge roadway as Axel eased the Whaler forward. Then she climbed up onto the railing, teetering forty feet above the water.

Suddenly, the black Suburbans driven by Metzger and Gonzalves pulled to a stop at either side of the bridge.

Down below, Axel erupted.

"What the fuck is that? I said come alone."

"It's The Bureau," said Maddy. "An end-run."

"Then get the fuck down here," said Axel, making tight circles below the bridge with the Whaler.

The two agents exited their Suburbans with guns drawn and started running toward the middle of the bridge.

As soon as she saw them, Maddy went over on the rappelling line, dropping four stories to the waterline and into the killer's boat.

Just then, Axel slashed the line and hid back under the bridge as the agents up above drew down on him.

"Where's your boyfriend?"

"I told you, I came alone. Those are Killebrew's men."

Axel turned back toward the wheel. Maddy was about to pull her .380, when he slammed the throttle forward and she fell back. Quickly, Axel pounced on her with his Taser. Maddy tried to side step him, but he kissed her with one of the contacts and she collapsed. He grabbed the Bluetooth headset from her ear and tossed it into the river. Then he covered her with a tarp just as...

VAROOOM... The Sikorsky roared by overhead.

Dr. Forbes looked down with a night scope and spotted them.

"Under the bridge. Watch for him to break for the Lake."

Sheriff Bergstrom put the chopper into a circle over the bridge, but then...

The DEA Bell Jet Ranger bore down on them.

Killebrew jumped on the radio.

"This is a no fly zone. You are interdicting a joint FBI/DEA operation. Vacate the air space forthwith. Repeat, vacate—"

Sheriff Bergstrom pulled back on the stick and banked hard to the East over the Lake when suddenly, down below...

The Boston Whaler took off in the *opposite* direction.

In the Sikorsky, Sheriff Bergstrom pointed downward.

"Wrong call. He's heading into the river."

Dr. Forbes quickly checked the map.

"Jesus. It goes south, southwest into The Des Plaines River. There's an Illinois and Ohio Canal below that, running 50 miles south. That's how he's been getting in and out of the city."

"Don't tell me he's smart. Just tell me my daughter's *alive*."

Through the night scope Dr. Forbes struggled to keep the Whaler in sight as it began to snake west, then south.

"Yeah. There's a tarp behind him. Something moved underneath."

The Sheriff gritted his teeth. His fighter pilot training kicked in.

"Hold onto your balls." He pulled forward on the stick and roared down to a point... 50 feet above the River.

Metzger and Gonzalves ran back to their Chevy's.

The DEA chopper followed and, on either side of the River, the two FBI Suburbans gave chase along the ground, commencing the greatest night time, air, water, land chase in FBI history.

53

After receiving the phone call from Maddy, Axel prepared himself for an epic chase. He knew that once he put himself out on the river, the cops would come at him with everything they had. Such a race deserved a proper sound track. So he'd taped a Sony ZSS21P boom box to the upright console of the Whaler. Now, as he throttled down, and the twin Mercs roared behind him, he slammed an iPod into the Sony and the river erupted with *Master of Puppets* by Metallica.

> *End of passion play, crumbling away.*
> *I'm your source of self-destruction…*

The music was so loud that Metzger and Gonzalves could hear it from the river banks on either side. Except for the few opera pieces that soothed him when the spikes began to invade his skull, metal was the musical substrata that drove Axel.

He'd been a *head banger* and a *metal head,* since the night he'd escaped from St. Timothy's on the eve of his 15th birthday.

The orphanage had a policy that any child not adopted by the age of 15 would be sent back into the foster care system until they were "emancipated" on their 18th birthday. So fearing that he would end up in another household of Tingleys or Grangers, Axel had planned his escape in the months before his exit date.

The East Pavilion at the orphanage was a virtual fortress. It was locked down day and night. Dogs patrolled the grounds after dark and it would be impossible to break a window and make a run for the fence.

But Axel had contrived an escape route.

Once, during one of the weekly floor polishing sessions in the convent, he was sent down to the basement to retrieve a can of turpentine. While down there, Axel discovered an old coal chute that had been boarded up for decades, ever since St. Tim's had made the conversion to oil heat. There was a ray of light coming out from behind the sheet of plywood that covered the old chute.

So Axel pulled it away and crawled up to the ground floor entry door where delivery trucks would dump the coal into the chute. The door was on a hinge held in place with a metal slide. When Axel opened it, he saw that the chute was only twenty feet from the twelve foot fence.

He figured that if he could get down to the convent basement at night, he could go up the chute and run to the fence before the dogs would be on him. He'd have to construct some kind of replica of himself to fool the nuns when they made their nightly bed rounds, but, for the young artist, that was a simple prospect.

For weeks now, he'd been stealing buffing rags from the floor cleaning sessions. With a knife he'd pilfered from the dining hall, he cut a slit in his mattress and he'd been hiding the rags inside. By the night of his escape, he had enough rags to stuff into a pillow case. He used paints requisitioned from art class to create a "head" for the dummy.

After lights-out at eight, the nuns checked the ward every three hours. So he'd have a couple of hours head start if he could get down to the convent. That proved to be the most difficult part of his escape, since he was four floors up. But Axel found a set of blueprints for St. Timothy's in the school library.

The mansard roofs of the Towers that anchored each pavilion had four-inch copper rain gutters and eight-inch ceramic drainpipes that ran up and down the Towers.

The pipes were anchored to the Medina stone of the Tower walls by metal "V" braces that were spaced every three feet from top to bottom. Since his 14th birthday, Axel had shot up to five-foot-eight, so his legs were long enough to reach each brace as he climbed down.

The tricky part, and the most dangerous, would be hanging from the rain gutters along the edge of the pavilion roof until he got to the East Tower. But nothing could keep him in this place. The fear of ending up in another sadist's dungeon overcame any worry he might have had. So the night before his birthday, as soon as Sister V.V. had made her rounds, Axel got up, assembled the facsimile of himself and put it under the blanket. He waited another 10 minutes until he could be sure the other 23 boys on the ward were asleep, then he opened the trunk at the foot of his bed where his school uniform was stored.

He pulled on the navy blue pants and the light blue Oxford cloth shirt. The black shoes had slippery leather soles, so he tied their strings together and put the shoes around his neck, stepping into his old flannel slippers. Then he climbed up onto the sill and opened the window which swung outward on a right opening hinge. The windows on the lower floors were always locked, but because of the height, the nuns saw no reason to secure the windows on the 4th floor.

Axel had already promised himself that he wouldn't look down, but as soon as the cold air hit his face, he couldn't help but gaze into the stone courtyard below. With his heart pounding, he stepped out onto the ledge. The window was only two feet wide, by four feet high, so he had to go out facing the courtyard. He grabbed onto the sill and pulled himself up reaching for the overhanging gutter. Then, once he felt steady, he turned himself around and closed the window with his foot as he edged himself toward the Tower.

It was a clear night. But there had been rain that morning and the gutters were slick. When he reached the Tower and climbed out onto the drainpipe, he almost slipped at the first "V" brace he stepped onto. Just then, he heard one of the German Shepherds in the yard start to bark.

A light came on in the West Pavilion across the courtyard, so he hugged the drainpipe, thankful that there was no moon that night.

Finally, Axel climbed down to the bottom of the courtyard. He clung closely to the wall and walked around the quadrangle until he came to a basement window in the convent.

This was the most dangerous part of his escape, because inside that building there were 20 nuns who always seemed to have eyes in the backs of their black hooded heads. They never seemed to sleep. They were nocturnal, like bats. That's how he always thought of them as they roamed the dark corridors, punishing the children.

The window was locked shut. But he'd brought the knife he'd stolen from the dining hall and he used it to cut the putty away that was holding the glass in place.

When he'd done that, Axel was able to reach in and unlock the window from the top. It opened inward and down. He held his breath as he took off his slippers and laid the pane of glass on them, careful not to let it hit the stone of the courtyard. Then he went through the window and into the basement.

Now down below, he put his shoes on and tied them. Behind the plywood cover on the chute he'd hidden an old leather bomber jacket that he'd stolen from the locker of one of the custodians. He put it on and zipped it up quietly.

Then he crawled up the chute and opened the door into the back yard. He paused to listen for the dogs and when he didn't hear them, he ran toward the fence and climbed up and over it.

At the top, one of the black cast iron points ripped his pant leg and he got hung up for a moment, but he pulled himself free and jumped down. The young man who had spent most of his life as an inmate, had now liberated himself from his prison.

The most uncertain part of his escape lay ahead.

54

AXEL HAD STARTED RUNNING TRACK the year before. He began with the 220 and then graduated to the 440, the 880 and finally the mile.

So he ran and he ran that night, moving quickly through the back streets of Joliet. He used the trees and the parked cars along the sidewalks to hide himself as much as he could. And then finally, he got to the entry ramp for I-80.

He'd found a map of the town in the library and studied it until he'd learned where the exit was for the Interstate. It was February 17th, the next day would be his 15th birthday and he'd already decided to go West to California.

At the bottom of the ramp, headlights flashed and blinded him for a second. Then a van pulled up. It was black. There were Iron Crosses painted on the side with skulls and crossbones.

A side door swung open. Immediately he sensed a strange smelling smoke coming from inside. A figure dressed in black leather with an arm full of tattoos leaned out of the van. He was big, blonde and muscular.

"Where you going kid?" asked the figure.

"Ca—California," said Axel, whose name at that point in his life was still Bobby Cole.

"What kind of music you listen to?"

Axel didn't know how to answer him. The nuns had forbidden the children to watch television, or even listen to the radio. He had no idea what popular music sounded like.

"I don't know."

"O.K. then answer this: What's your favorite *color*?" Axel, the 15 year old boy with the 160 I.Q. eyed the van and the man whose fingers were covered with rings shaped liked skulls.

"Black," he said.

"Right answer, kid. Get in."

And from that moment on, Axel became a head banger.

The van that had picked him up was full of roadies—the advance crew that helped set up and break down every concert for one of the grittiest metal bands in history: Guns N' Roses.

For the next three years, he traveled with them, working on the road crew, getting a world class education in the blown-out nihilistic sub-genre that was spawned in the 60's and early 70's as a fusion of blues rock and psychedelic.

The figure in the van was named Jimmy—the lead roadie. When Axel first got inside and got a look at him, the man reminded him of the Vikings that he'd studied in world history.

Jimmy was tall, over six foot five. He had piercing blue eyes like Axel's and a full head of blonde hair that ran down below his shoulders. Most of the time he kept it back in a ponytail so that the epic tattoo that covered his back was clearly visible. Even in winter, Jimmy was usually naked above his jack boots, his black leather pants and his studded belt. The tat that ran from the small of his back to his neck was a cross—a full color rendering from GNR's first album cover *Appetite for Destruction.*

The cross was suspended between orange and red ribbons containing the names of the band and the album. On each point of the cross was a skull's head representing one of the band members: Izzy Stradlin, Duff McKagan, Steven Adler and Slash. The skull in the middle represented Axl Rose. The image had been designed by an artist named William White after their record company had refused to ship the original album cover based on a painting by Robert Williams depicting a metal avenger about to punish a robot rapist.

"Jimmy The Viking," as Axel soon called him, had the image drawn on his back over a 13 month period as the road crew moved from city to city on GNR's first cross-country tour. Now, as he took a hit on a bong constructed out of a foot square Plexiglas box, Jimmy decided he'd take the fugitive orphan under his wing.

In the three years Axel stayed with the band, Jimmy never laid a hand on him. He treated him like a little brother and called him "kid" until he reached his 18th birthday. That was the night, after the show, when Jimmy took the young man, still known as Bobby Cole, to a tat parlor in Anaheim and christened him with his new name.

Jimmy had gotten permission from Rose himself to allow Bobby to mark himself with his initials W.A.R. and Axl, ever generous and always searching for the dark underside of life, told "the kid" to put it on the bottom of his foot. That way, someday, if Bobby had to infiltrate the straight culture he would always know that he was hardcore underneath.

Until the night of his escape, Axel had received his first formal education from the clergy of the Catholic Church. For the next three years he would study under a different order. But they also dressed in black.

Though Axl Rose was the high priest, Jimmy the Viking was one of his main acolytes. And he saw it as his personal mission to school the young runaway by exposing him to a collection of heavy metal CD's that was second to none.

As they criss-crossed the country the "kid," reborn as Axel, listened first to the "fathers" of metal: Black Sabbath, Led Zeppelin, Deep Purple and Judas Priest, then the Brit bands like Iron Maiden and Motörhead; and finally the mid 80's glam groups like Mötley Crue and the thrash bands like Metallica and Slayer.

Now on the Chicago river, Axel pulled back the tarp covering Maddy. He set the wheel with a piece of shock cord and in two deft moves, tied her arms behind her and her legs together with flex-ties.

Then he pulled a ski mask over her head with the eye sockets behind her so that she couldn't see. He turned back and cranked up the music, screaming out the lyrics so that she knew they were meant for her.

He throttled down on the twin Mercs, zig-zagging in an out of oil barges; and under the bridges while…

On both sides of the river along the perimeter roads, The FBI Suburbans gave chase and…

Up above in the Sikorsky Dr. Forbes tracked the boat with the searchlight as Sheriff Bergstrom dodged the power lines and…

SSA Ron Killebrew followed them in the DEA chopper, promising himself that before the night was over, Axel would be dead.

55

MADDY'S CELL PHONE WAS STILL ON in her windbreaker, so up in the Sikorsky Dr. Forbes could hear the thundering heavy metal music from the boom box down below.

I just heard him sing to her," said Forbes to the Sheriff. "She must be alive."

The Sheriff motioned for Forbes to hand him the cell phone.

"I don't believe it. We're bearing down on him and he's giving himself a soundtrack."

Dr. Forbes nodded.

"This guy is way beyond certifiable."

Just then, the DEA chopper passed under them and got buffeted by the Sikorsky's rotor downdraft.

From the Bell Jet Ranger, Killebrew switched on a loud speaker.

"Cease and desist or we'll fire."

There was no response from Sheriff Bergstrom, so Killebrew nodded to the sniper

"Put one across his bow."

"Sir, I need to know who the target is?"

"No, you need to follow orders."

Just then, the pilot jumped in. "Listen, we were told this was some kind of drug interdiction. Is the bad guy in the boat or in the chopper?"

"He's where I say he is," said Killebrew, turning to the sniper. "You're FBI. You're under my authority.

Now that chopper is interfering with the pursuit of a killer. I want you to fire a warning shot."

The sniper hesitated.

"How close?"

"Enough to dissuade them from pursuing this chase."

And with that, the sniper fired a round from his M-40.

Zwammm. The bullet roared through the top of the cockpit, between Bergstrom and Dr. Forbes, cracking the window on the Sikorsky's passenger side door, causing...

Sheriff Bergstrom to bank the bird radically left.

"I don't believe this," said Bergstrom.

"So much for your Semper Fi, buddy," said Forbes.

"It's goddamn Desert Storm all over again..."

"Can you still escape and evade?"

"I guess, we'll see."

VAROOOOM. He put the Sikorsky into another steep dive while...

Down on the river Axel throttled down on the Boston Whaler cutting in and out of river barges. The channel was getting narrower now and on either side, the Suburbans were starting to catch up.

The right bank Suburban pulled neck and neck with the Whaler. So Metzger radioed up to the DEA Chopper.

"I've got a visual. You want us to take the shot?

"Do you have to *ask*?" said Killebrew from up above.

Now, through the moon roof in the Suburban, another FBI sniper came up and steadied his rifle on the roof.

They were doing sixty on the perimeter road as he drew down on the Whaler's Mercury engines in his night scope. His finger touched the trigger to squeeze off a shot when, suddenly . . .

A container truck began backing out of a freight yard ahead and the Suburban driver had to hit the brakes and swing wide, causing . . .

Zwmmm. The shot to go wide. It screamed across the river and missed the Whaler, hitting a gas storage tank, which exploded in a fireball.

Suddenly, the right bank Suburban swerved to avoid the container truck and ran up onto a sidewalk, crashing into a wall of wooden pallets.

Axel let out a war whoop, echoing the semi-truck driver he'd almost plowed into on the mountain road . . .

"Fuck you, you fucking fucks . . ."

Up above, Killebrew was now getting worried.

"Metzger," he screamed into the radio. "What's your twenty?"

"Sir," we're down. Looks like the right rear tire got punctured."

"What about Gonzalves? Do you copy? Are you still in this?"

The other Special Agent in the left bank Suburban eyed a map.

"Sir. We don't pick up the river again 'til a quarter mile down.

"Then get the fuck down there."

Now, on the river, the Boston Whaler was alone except for the pursuing choppers. So Axel reached back and pulled the tarp away. Maddy was starting to stir. Looking ahead about 50 yards, he spotted an oil barge docked along the bank, so he spun the wheel and cut in between the barge and the bank, slowing to a virtual stall while . . .

In the Sikorsky up above, Dr. Forbes panned the light left and right across the river, searching for him.

"Lost him behind that barge. Keep the circle tight."

"Roger"

The Sheriff spun the chopper into a narrow arc as...

Killebrew spotted them circling and nodded to his pilot.

"Start to close on them."

He looked down, searching for the Whaler.

"Shit. The prick must have banked it."

He radioed down now to Gonzalves in the left bank Suburban.

"How soon can you get across man? We are losing this bastard."

"Another minute," said Gonzalves. "Bridge up ahead. We'll double back and close in."

Now behind the barge, Axel pulled the Whaler to a stop. He came up to a ladder and tied the bowline onto one of the lower rungs. Then he jumped up and looked around to see if he was being pursued on the ground.

No Suburbans in sight, so he climbed onto the dock and ran to a container parked nearby. It was another one of his stash points.

He popped open a padlock and pulled back the doors to reveal: a black Jeep Wrangler inside. The killer ran back to the Whaler. Maddy was starting to yell, so he grabbed some duct tape and covered her mouth.

Up above in the Sikorsky, Dr. Forbes put the cell phone to his ear. "Wait. I just heard her. She started to say something, but he shut her up."

"You don't think—?"

"Not at this point," said Forbes. "He wouldn't have gone to all this trouble, if he didn't want to keep her alive."

"Alright, just try and find them, will you?"

Forbes shined the light along the edge of the oil barge, but there was an overhang and he couldn't see.

"Can you get us any lower?"

The Sheriff nodded and he brought the Sikorsky down to a point about thirty feet over the water.

Just then, Axel picked up Maddy and threw her over his shoulder. He grabbed her rappelling gear and climbed the ladder onto the dock.

"We've got power lines on both sides," said the Sheriff. "I can't keep her here for long."

Forbes panned the light, left, then right…

Down below, as Axel dropped Maddy into the back of the Jeep he spotted the .380 in the paddle holster at her back. So he disarmed her and put the gun into the glove box. He did a quick search and found the cell phone which was still active. So he turned it off and tossed it into the river.

Up above in the Sikorsky, Forbes realized that the call had ended. He panned the searchlight quickly along the edge of the dock by the barge and suddenly, caught sight of the Wrangler.

"I've got him," said Forbes. "There's a black Jeep backing out of a container at three o'clock. Hold her steady."

But just then, the DEA chopper roared down on them and Sheriff Bergstrom had to push forward on the stick.

In the Bell Jet Ranger, Killebrew yelled to the pilot. "Pull alongside him."

"Negative," said the pilot. "We are low on fuel. Repeat, the needle's kissin' empty."

"How the fuck did *that* happen?"

"We were just coming in from a run when you grabbed us. Another two minutes, we'll have to set down."

Killebrew turned to the Sniper behind him.

"O.K. I'm not gonna say this twice: put that bird in your crosshairs."

The sniper shook his head.

"Sir, if you're going to ask me to fire on that chopper again, I'm gonna need authorization from the ASAC in the Field Office.

Just then, Sheriff Bergstrom used the loudspeaker in the Sikorsky.

"To the Bell Jet, tail number: N652M… I'm a sworn law enforcement officer in pursuit of a suspect who fled my jurisdiction. I have a warrant for his arrest, signed by a magistrate."

The two helicopters were hovering over the river now, maybe thirty yards apart. Dr. Forbes pulled his Beretta and steadied it against the broken window frame as he drew down on Killebrew.

"We've been fired on once" said the Sheriff. "Engage us again and we'll return fire."

Dr. Forbes keyed the loudspeaker mike in his helmet.

"Is that what you want Ronnie? Dog fight over Chicago? I can see that on CNN. We're closing in on the world's most vicious serial killer and you let him escape with a Sheriff's Deputy."

"Call it *now* or we're goin' in," said the Sheriff.

Killebrew gritted his teeth. Another second went by and then he tapped the pilot. "Back the fuck off—" The DEA chopper pilot pulled up and away. Killebrew had barely gotten the words out when…

The Sikorsky roared downward as Axel pulled out of the container and started to take off with Maddy, cutting under an overpass, out of sight for a moment, while…

The DEA Ranger landed on the bank nearby. Killebrew jumped out, studying a map. He was on the radio with SA Gonzalves in the left bank Suburban. "Do you see him yet? Repeat, do you—"

"Yeah, said Gonzalves, crossing a bridge up above the container.

"He's in a black Jeep Wrangler. I see him—Wait..."

"Well do you or *don't* you," bellowed Killebrew.

"I had him for a second. Now he's gone."

"Christ, give me some fucking options." As the Suburban headed down to the dock area from where Axel had exited, Gonzalves looked at a GPS screen. "He's got two ways out: Route 12 East or I-57 South."

Killebrew was pacing, going ballistic...

"So which is it? We're losing seconds..."

Just then, the Suburban screeched to a stop right next to the DEA chopper. Gonzalves jumped out and crossed quickly to Killebrew.

"I'm thinking 12," he said. "It's got twice the number of exits than the Interstate."

"You better have your pension vested if you're wrong," said Killebrew. "Do *not* lose him, do you hear me?" Gonzalves nodded sheepishly.

"I'm heading back to the OP Center, so we can pull in more assets. I want minute by minute reports."

"No problem, sir. We'll find him..."

Killebrew got back in the Bell Jet Ranger and cocked his head to the pilot. "You got enough gas to get me to the Field Office?"

Without even responding, the pilot lifted off.

56

But as soon as Killebrew was deposited back on the rooftop of the FBI's Chicago Field Office, he didn't go to the Operations Center. After failing to stop Axel's escape, he realized now that he would have to move quickly toward a containment mode.

The female Sheriff's Deputy had been correct when she'd pulled him into Jamal's office: the files that he'd secretly kept on Bobby Leroy Cole wouldn't just cost him his position as the FBI's leading serial hunter, they could land him in prison. He had to find the copies she'd made with Forbes and destroy them at all costs. Killebrew had invested twenty-five years of his life in The Bureau and he'd navigated mine fields like this before—but none more dangerous.

Having started out in his first years as a special agent, devoting a hundred per cent of his attention to fighting crime, he was, by now, a quarter of a century later, a purely political animal. The only game that he played these days was defense and he utilized all of his skills to protect his position. He'd become the living embodiment of a pathology that had infected The Bureau since the earliest days of its first boss J. Edgar Hoover.

For 48 years, "The Director" as he was known, had run the FBI and its predecessor agency with an iron hand. He'd intimidated Presidents and threatened members of Congress with a management style that he'd built on fear mongering and blackmail.

From Prohibition through the Great Depression, World War II and the Cold War up through the civil rights movement, Hoover had used his agents to collect dirt on his political enemies.

As the country grew, so did the crime rate. When America went to war in 1941, the danger of foreign espionage increased. Post war, there was the Red Scare; real or imagined. And with each potential threat, Hoover exploited the public's fear by extorting ever-increasing budgets and ever-expanding powers from the lawmakers on Capitol Hill.

A shameless self promoter, he rewrote the rule book on Machiavellian strategy, carefully eliminating any agents whom the press regarded as too "special." One of the earliest G-men to threaten Hoover's place in the spotlight was Melvin Purvis, the agent who brought down the notorious bank robber John Dillinger. The Bureau's first "Public Enemy Number One," Dillinger had become something of a folk hero for robbing the same Depression-era banks that had foreclosed on so many Midwestern farmers.

With each succeeding escape, Dillinger seemed to mock The Bureau and its young Director, so Hoover put Purvis, his best agent, on the manhunt. It ended on the night of July 22, 1934 outside the Biograph Theater in Chicago, just blocks from the place where Axel had mailed Ginny Kendrick's pigtail to Maddy.

According to press accounts, Dillinger died in a hail of bullets after Purvis faced him down with the immortal words "Stick 'em up Johnny." The ensuing page-one headlines touting Purvis as a national hero rivaled those of any matinee idol of the day.

So Hoover targeted Purvis for elimination. Within a year he resigned under pressure and the media focus went back to The Director. Decades later, Purvis died from what was described by Bureau agents as a self-inflicted gunshot wound. But the truth was, that he'd "died" long before that at the hands of his vindictive boss.

Hoover's threatening management style sunk to new depths in the early 1960's with the formation of The Counter Intelligence Program, aka COINTELPRO, a secret operation within The Bureau designed to wipe out "subversive" elements in the country.

Its initial target was the Ku Klux Klan, whose murder of three civil rights workers in 1964 had sorely embarrassed Hoover as dozens of hapless agents dispatched to Mississippi were unable to locate their bodies. Years later, it was revealed that Hoover had actually reached out to the Mafia—an organization that, for decades, he'd refused to acknowledge—and cracked the case by recruiting a young homicidal hit man named Gregory Scarpa.

A Bensonhurst killer who later became known as "The Grim Reaper," Scarpa was flown by the FBI to Mississippi. In the town of Laurel he kidnapped a local politician with Klan ties and threatened to cut off his genitals if he didn't give up the burial site of Goodman, Schwerner and Chaney, whose station wagon had been found burned and abandoned.

Within seconds of eyeing Scarpa's razor blade, the terrified politician disclosed that the three bodies had been buried by Klansmen beneath the red clay of a nearby earthen dam. Bobby Kennedy, then the Attorney General, was appeased and Hoover scored another victory that only enhanced his power.

But few outside The Bureau knew at the time that the breakthrough in the MISSBURN case had been achieved after an unconstitutional kidnapping and interrogation executed by a blood thirsty mob killer.

Scarpa, as it turned out, was also a Top Echelon Criminal Informant for The Bureau. In a forty-two year career of murder, racketeering and mayhem, in which he advanced in the ranks of the Colombo Crime Family, he only served 30 days in jail. An FBI internal affairs probe would later suggest that Scarpa was aided and abetted by his Bureau "control" agent who allegedly slipped him intelligence on his enemies so that he could take them out one by one. Years later, testifying at a murder trial in Brooklyn, Scarpa's protégé revealed that Greg had "stopped counting" after "fifty" homicides—making him the most prolific killer in the history of "La Cosa Nostra."

The Judge in that trial described this unholy alliance between the hit man and the G-men as a "deal with the devil."

It was a kind of ends-justify-the-means relationship in which the FBI had conspired with an arch criminal to stop crime. By any measure, Greg Scarpa was a serial killer, but for decades, nobody outside the Justice Department had any hint that his violent tactics had apparently been winked at by senior Bureau officials.

It was in that pathological environment that Ron Killebrew came of age. Like all rookie agents, he'd left the Academy in Quantico as a bright-eyed, enthusiastic young crime fighter whose principal goal was to put bad guys away. But as he took his first posting in the FBI's New York Office, Killebrew soon came to realize that the only way to advance in The Bureau was to spend increasing amounts of his time looking over his shoulder.

The Director was incredibly punitive. He would suspend an agent who came to work with his shoes unpolished or his tie askew. Under Hoover, for the most minor of infractions, a special agent could have an OPR (internal affairs investigation) opened by the FBI's Office of Professional Responsibility. The upshot was that young agents like Killebrew spent less and less time *working* cases and more and more time studying the Director's playbook.

One of the most telling examples of the fear they lived under was the infamous "KMA date," or "Kiss My Ass date;" the first day after their twentieth year when they were eligible for retirement with a full pension. As one veteran SA later told it, that was the day when, "if D.C. decided to open an OPR on me, I could put in my papers and retire before they commenced an investigation."

It was management by intimidation and there wasn't a street or "brick" agent who didn't come to work each day in constant fear of the Supervisors or SACs above them. As a result, many of the most talented agents like Purvis got out early. The agents who stayed, tended to fall into two categories: those who decided to keep their heads down and get through their "twenty" with a minimum of collateral damage, and those, like Killebrew, who used the Director's tactics to advance.

Early on, Killebrew had become enamored with COINTELPRO. After all, the program had started out with a reasonable goal: rooting out the KKK's "Invisible Empire." But it soon turned into Hoover's personal black bag operation.

By the late 1960's, The Director began using the program as a domestic spying operation to harass members of the antiwar movement. In April, 1967, after the Reverend Dr. Martin Luther King, Jr., turned against the Vietnam war, he became Hoover's obsession and prime target.

One letter sent by The Bureau to King described him as "an evil beast." Later an FBI surveillance tape of a man in the civil rights leader's Washington hotel suite having sex with a woman was sent to King's home with a note encouraging the Nobel Prize winner to take his own life. "You are done King," the note said. "There is one way out for you. You better take it before your filthy fraudulent self is bared to the nation."

Other public figures, with less strength than King, did just that. After COINTELPRO agents leaked the false word that she was pregnant with the child of a black man, the blonde actress Jean Seberg, who'd lent her high profile support to the NAACP, killed herself with an overdose of barbiturates.

Illegal spying and wiretapping, extortion, intimidation and shameless self-promotion—these were the qualities in J. Edgar Hoover that Special Agent Ron Killebrew learned to emulate.

Just as Hoover had used the hitman Scarpa and Bureau agents had allowed him to remain at large, Killebrew decided that rather than bringing down the fugitive Axel, he would actually *help* him continue his murder spree.

The more unsolved serial killer cases, the greater the apparent need for the "expertise" of the Behavioral Analysis Unit. Budgets began to increase. Killebrew took on expanded responsibilities.

When his blind devotion to the FBI's faulty profiling methods were exposed by T.C. Forbes, Killebrew decided to eliminate him.

Inspired by COINTELPRO, the SSA planted DNA evidence at the I-80 crime scenes; framing Forbes for it.

When Forbes began to connect the dots on the truck stop killer, Killebrew tipped the young psychopath to Forbes' dumpsite stakeout. The brush with death sent Forbes into a downward spiral that left him discredited and addicted to painkillers.

He was safely off in academia and no one would have been the wiser, when this fiend, whom Killebrew had aided and abetted, amped up his murder scheme to epic new levels and made the move on the female Deputy.

As soon as he got word of Axel's escape from Snoqualmie, Killebrew was on the next G-5 out of Quantico; hoping to humiliate the girl so that she'd back off. But he'd underestimated her just as he'd been outflanked by Forbes, and now their copy of his secret Axel files threatened to take him down.

Minutes after the DEA chopper put him back on the roof of the Field Office, Killebrew got the keys to a Suburban in the Field Office garage and headed north toward Niles. Along the way, he stopped at an Exxon station and paid cash for a red plastic two-gallon can which he filled with high octane gasoline. By the time he was finished, the fire at the motel wouldn't just destroy *his* files, but every record that Forbes and the girl had on Axel as well.

57

NOW, STILL AIRBORNE in the Sikorsky, Sheriff Bergstrom and Dr. Forbes were worried. In the standoff with Killebrew, they too had lost sight of Axel's Jeep. Sheriff Bergstrom swept the chopper left and right across the river in ever widening arcs as Forbes shined the spotlight down along both perimeter roads.

Just then, the Sheriff spotted the blue flashing rooftop lights of Agent Gonzalves' Suburban.

"Down there at two o'clock," he said, pointing. "What's that?"

"One of Killebrew's chase cars," said Forbes. "He's going South on Route 12."

"You think they're on him?

"There's a fifty-fifty chance. By the time he took off in the Jeep, the Feds hadn't reached the container."

He studied the map.

"There's more traffic to hide in on 57, but more exits on 12."

"What's down there?" asked the Sheriff.

"A lot of farmland 'til Kansas."

"We can't afford to guess wrong."

The two men looked down as the two routes diverged below them and for the first time since Forbes met Sheriff Bergstrom, the ex-Marine got impatient. His daughter was in that Jeep and he was worried.

"Come *on*, Doc. Which way? Left or right?"

Forbes shook his head. He couldn't decide. He thought to himself that if Maddy was with them, she'd make the right intuitive choice. But she wasn't there. She was in the back of that Wrangler and a mass murdering psycho was taking her somewhere to kill her.

Just then, his cell phone rang.

Back in the CPD Homicide bullpen, Captain Jamal was close to losing it. "*When* were you gonna fill me in?"

"On what?" asked Forbes, feigning innocence.

"The FAA picked up two unknown aircraft over The Loop. We've got reports of shots fired. What the fuck's going on?"

"He's *alive*, Captain."

"We *know* that. The DeKalb County Sheriff found a body late last night on rural route 50. Transsexual, strangled and marked with a stun gun."

"Forbes leaned forward over the map.

"Can you give me a precise twenty on the dumpsite?"

Capt. Jamal checked a map.

"About thirty miles south toward Kankakee off I-57. Why?"

Suddenly, Dr. Forbes put his hand over the cell phone mouthpiece and grabbed the Sheriff's arm.

"Go left. Left. 57 South."

Captain Jamal heard the muffled sound.

"Who the hell are you *talking* to," he demanded. "What did you tell him?"

Just then, the Sikorsky banked hard to the left toward Interstate 57 south.

"Captain, listen to me," said Forbes. "Deputy Bergstrom's been abducted again. We've been tracking the killer. But for reasons I can't get into on an open line, we can't disclose our location right now."

"Who the fuck is 'we,'" he demanded. "Are you with The Bureau on this?"

"Negative Captain. Listen, I've got to ask you to trust me. As soon as we get a fix on his destination, I'll let you know."

And with that, he hung up, leaving Jamal back at the bullpen, ripshit with anger. He yelled across to his aide, Sgt Edmonds.

"Find Killebrew and call SFG. I need SWAT and both choppers. A full CQB loadout."

"How soon?" asked Edmonds.

"Yesterday."

Jamal crossed to the glass wall of the control room where pictures of Axel's carnage hung on the wall. He eyed them and shook his head.

Twenty minutes later, as I-57 snaked south away from Chicago into rural Illinois, Axel's Jeep was one of the few vehicles left on the road.

The killer looked back. Maddy was wide-eyed and awake on the floor. Lying flat, she could see her rappelling harness and gear which Axel had shoved under the front seat when they took off.

Ever since he'd thrown her into the Wrangler, she'd been trying to break the flex ties binding her wrists behind her. This time she couldn't get to the knife on her belt buckle and her gun was now in the glove box.

Since the Jeep was open in back, she tried to look up and get some sense of a passing landmark, some way to describe her location, in case she was able to break free and get through to her father and Forbes. But Axel was moving too fast.

Her instinct would have been to engage him as he roared to their destination. Try and psyche him out and pick up some clue to the location. But he'd taped her mouth, so she was silent. The metal tracks that secured the back seats had round edges, so there was nothing sharp she could lean against to try and break the plastic ties.

By the time he pulled onto what seemed like an interstate, she decided to conserve her strength. She would try and overpower him when they got to his lair.

Maddy was sure of one thing by now. He was going to use her somehow to finish his chapel ceiling. She would be one of the 300. And there was no consolation in knowing that she'd be the last.

It was just after 1:15 a.m., an hour and a quarter after he'd captured Maddy when Axel took the exit for Highway 17 West of I-57.

The Sikorsky had been following him from a safe distance back and above since they'd finally made him in the night scope as the traffic thinned on the Interstate.

The S-76 was equipped with a "hush kit" to minimize the sound of the rotor blades and the ambient noise from the big six-lane highway had prevented Axel from detecting their presence above him and to the north.

But now that he was turning onto a deserted local farm road, the Sheriff was concerned that the engine noise might spook him, so he drifted back even further in the night sky.

There was a three quarter moon at that point in mid December, but the cloud cover had been intermittent since they'd entered Kankakee County. The ceiling was relatively low: about six hundred feet, so he was counting on the weather to give them additional protection.

Still, Dr. Forbes felt that they needed even more in the way of stealth.

"Can you kill the running lights?"

"Why not? FAA's gonna pull my ticket anyway."

He cut the blinking running lights and the S-76 became a black ghost moving across the cloudy moonlit sky while...

Down below, Axel turned off Route 17 onto the solitary two lane country road.

Dr. Forbes strained to track the Jeep's tail lights in the night scope.

Then, about four miles ahead, Forbes spotted some kind of structure. There was a large, dark building about four stories high with an enormous smokestack next to it. The entire facility was surrounded by some kind of fence.

As the Jeep pulled up to the chain link gate with the orange sign for the demolition, Axel passed a line of caterpillars, bulldozers and other heavy construction equipment. They'd been moved into place for the demolition that was to begin in another thirty hours.

When he stopped the Wrangler, Maddy became hyper-alert. Before he got out, Axel grabbed a flashlight from the glove box and shined it in her eyes.

"Almost home, baby." He got out and opened the padlock that held a chain in place across the gate. Just then, his ears pricked up like a predatory animal catching a scent. For a moment Axel thought he heard the sound of an aircraft. So he quickly shut off the Jeep's engine. But when he listened again, it was gone.

What the killer didn't know was that the Sheriff had already landed the Sikorsky about two miles to the north in an open field.

He got out with Forbes and they checked their weapons. Bergstrom had a Remington pump and his Sig. Forbes slammed a mag full of Glasers into his Beretta. They tried to get their bearings.

"Which way?" asked the Sheriff, turning around to orient himself. They were at a junction point on the country road. From the direction the Jeep had been traveling, Axel could have gone left or right.

"You tell me," said Forbes.

The Sheriff cocked his head to the right and they started off down that road, but then, Dr. Forbes grabbed his arm and stopped him. In the distance behind them, they could hear the pulsating beat of heavy metal music. So they turned and took off to the left, running.

Moments earlier Axel had driven into the plant and locked the gate behind him. He'd pulled the Jeep up to the loading dock and run inside.

Before he brought Maddy in, he wanted to set the stage for her.

So he turned on the halogen lights that illuminated the walls and the ceiling. He put his iPad into a dock and blasted *Symphony of Destruction* by Megadeth.

When he ran back out onto the loading dock, he went over to the furnace and hit a switch, igniting the huge gas-burning fire inside.

While he was gone, Maddy had pulled herself up from the floor of the back seat so that she could see over the door line.

It was dark at first, and then, as the moon moved from behind the clouds, she saw the enormous meat packing plant and its slaughterhouse. Now as Axel flung open the doors of the furnace, her eyes went wide.

She gazed up at the 19 story brick smokestack beside it. It was surrounded by a rusty circular stairway that went all the way to the top. Maddy could barely move now. She was still flex-tied, with her hands behind her; her legs still bound at the ankles.

Suddenly, Axel loomed over her. He grabbed her by the shoulders and pulled her out of the jeep, picking her up and holding her in his arms as he carried her up onto the loading dock.

"I don't want you to say anything until we get inside," he said.

"Hmmm" said Maddy under the duct tape. As if she could.

And then, as he approached the stairs next to the furnace, she almost choked from the fear that gripped her.

Next to the furnace was a twenty by twenty foot pit; a container of ashes from the furnace afterburn. As the flames flickered out, she could just make out the shape of a partial rib cage. When she got closer, she saw a jawbone.

It was Axel's killing field—the repository from his crematorium.

58

Captain Winston Jamal was pacing back and forth across the control room that had been set up for the Axel murders task force.

The Mayor's Office had trusted him with this spiraling "red ball" of a case when it merely involved two missing females and now that it had morphed dangerously into a national media story involving the most audacious serial killer since Gacy, the hot light of scrutiny was on him twenty-four/seven.

Like any senior police official he was worried about the political fallout from the killer's latest abduction. He was worried about his career and the reputation of his unit. But most of all, he was concerned for the life of Deputy Bergstrom.

The Captain was a rare breed in law enforcement: a truly dedicated detective who refused to allow himself to get jaded or cynical about the job. While always alert to the wind direction from City Hall, he was entirely devoted to reducing the murder rate in Chicago and solving every open case in his files.

In that sense, he was the antithesis of SSA Ronald Killebrew—a "public servant" who served only himself.

Jamal was the product of two devoutly religious cultures: Christianity and Islam. He'd come of age in such a conflicted household that he'd learned early on to think for himself and take responsibility for his own actions.

He knew very little about the background of either Maddy or Dr. Forbes, but he shared one thing in common with them: he'd been up and he'd been brought very low and on his long road to redemption, he'd developed a credo that he liked to call "the blank slate method."

He came to every case, every crime and every person he met, on either side of the law with an open mind. He did his best to jettison whatever prejudice or bias he might have, and take a purely empirical approach toward problem solving.

Jamal was more concerned about the truth than the *perception* of the truth. That set him apart from 90 per cent of the senior law enforcement officials he'd come to know, but it had been the key to his success until now.

His father, Winston Bradley, had emigrated from Jamaica in the late 1960's. The son of a Kingston surgeon educated in England, Winston Jr. had enjoyed a privileged life.

He'd grown up in St. Andrew Parish where he played cricket as a child. After attending "public schools" modeled on the British preparatory system, he graduated from The American International School, a coed interracial academy where diplomats sent their children.

Accepted to Northwestern in Evanston, Illinois on a full scholarship, Winston began his freshman year as an accounting major. At a Greek World "mixer" he met Genevieve Holmes, the daughter of a strict black Baptist Minister from Chicago's south side. They dated briefly and had only one intimate encounter. But Genny soon left school after learning that she was pregnant.

Winston took on a series of work study jobs at school, vowing to help raise the child, whom they learned would be a son. Genny's father married them in a simple ceremony, but he forbade the Jamaican immigrant from ever seeing his daughter or his new son again.

The year was 1968 and following the turbulent Democratic National Convention, Chicago was exploding with the "days of rage," staged by the radical Weather Underground.

After growing up as a privileged Commonwealth subject in Kingston, Winston began to realize that in the all white suburb of Evanston, he was just another "black man."

So he started to educate himself. He studied the writings of his fellow countryman Marcus Garvey. He read Richard Wright, Ralph Ellison, James Baldwin and the Autobiography of Malcolm X.

Winston joined the Student Nonviolent Coordinating Committee led by the fiery young immigrant from Trinidad, Stokely Carmichael and soon began to find a new identity in the militancy that was sweeping the civil rights movement.

By 1969, Carmichael had begun a campaign to merge "Snick" as it was known, with the Black Panther Party and Winston became one of its first crossover members.

With their full Afros, black leather jackets, and black berets, the BPP spoke to him in a way that the NAACP, CORE and other more placid groups could not.

In mid October, he dropped out of Northwestern and moved into an apartment on Monroe Street near the Panther Party's Chicago office. By November, Winston was working as a community organizer under Fred Hampton, the charismatic leader who took over the Chicago BPP Chapter.

In the months before that, Hampton had drawn together the Panthers with a street gang called the Blackstone Rangers, the all white Students for a Democratic Society (SDS) and the Hispanic Young Lords. It was Hampton who first coined the phrase "Rainbow Coalition," later used by the Reverend Jesse Jackson.

While other Panther "ministers" like Eldridge Cleaver and H. Rap Brown seemed more enamored with the media, Hampton set up a breakfast program for inner city children, and Winston became his right hand.

But the FBI's COINTEL program soon fomented a split between Bob Brown, the Panther Party's founder in Illinois, and Stokely Carmichael's SNCC. The schism sent Hampton to the top ranks of the Black Panther's national organization and Winston rose with him.

If J. Edgar Hoover mistrusted Dr. Martin Luther King, who had modeled his non-violent tactics after Gandhi, he *loathed* the militant Panthers and Fred Hampton soon became a target. By May of 1969, his name was placed in The Bureau's "Agitator Index" along with that of his "subversive cohort" Winston Bradley Jr.

Using wiretaps, anonymous letters and other tactics, COINTELPRO agents did everything they could to follow Hoover's orders and "destroy what the Black Panther Party stands for."

In addition to dirty tricks, like sending out racist cartoons mocking whites with the Black Panther logo, Hoover instructed his agents to disrupt the BPP's grass roots organizing efforts and "eradicate its 'serve the people' programs."

The Chicago PD under Mayor Richard Daley, became an enthusiastic Bureau ally, staging raids and ransacking the Party's Monroe Street Office.

Hampton was prosecuted for the crime of stealing $71.00 in Good Humor ice cream bars and incredibly, the judge imposed a sentence of two to five years. But he'd been released on bond pending his appeal.

Then, in late 1969 after two Chicago police officers were ambushed and murdered, the CPD stormed the apartment where Hampton was living with other Party members.

Multiple shots were fired and Hampton was wounded in the shoulder. But moments later, as a Panther eyewitness later claimed, rather than taking him alive, the cops shot Hampton in the head, effectively executing him in cold blood.

Winston Bradley, who had nothing to do with the shooting, was arrested and convicted of felony murder as a result of his presence in the apartment. He did six years of hard time in Joliet State Penitentiary. But during that stretch he joined The Nation of Islam.

Paroled, after forensic evidence proved that he had taken no part in the gun battle, Winston came home to find that Genevieve had filed for divorce. Working as a community organizer he got joint custody of their five-year old son, Winston III, whom he renamed with his Muslim surname "Jamal."

Young Winston III was brought up attending Friday prayers at the Nation of Islam's flagship "Mosque No. 2." Like his father, he wore severe black suits, white shirts and thin black bow ties. He shaved his head, ate no pork and preached the word of "The Prophet," Elijah Mohammed.

Meanwhile, on Sundays, his mother would come and "rescue" him and force him to sit through hours of revival services at his grandfather's Baptist church.

The tug of war between his parents drove Winston III into the streets.

At the age of 13, he started hanging around the "corners" where the Chicago's deadliest street gang, the Black P. Stones slung drugs. The gang had its roots in the old Blackstone Rangers that had formed the brief coalition with the Panthers.

By his fifteenth birthday, Winston III was living on his own and earning $5,000.00 a week in cash selling crack. Two years later he was driving a tricked out BMW and living in a condo on the near North Side that he'd paid for in cash.

But at that point Winston III began using and he got careless. Busted by undercover narcotics officers with "felony weight," he ended up in the notorious Cooke County Jail where he got his jaw broken resisting a rape attempt.

At the time of his arraignment there was a pilot project that allowed first time offenders to opt for military service rather than prison. The judge told him that if he could make it through basic training and stay clean for his two-year hitch, his criminal record would be expunged.

Winston's father and mother both showed up in court and begged their son to take the deal. If he didn't, they rightfully feared, he would end up in prison or dead.

Twenty-four hours later, he was on a bus to Fort Jackson, South Carolina. Just prior to his nine week Basic Combat Training, Winston III took a Dale Carnegie Course on "The Power of Positive Thinking."

The Army offered the top recruit in each BCT platoon a shot at Officer Candidate School. So Winston spent his off hours bulking up, working out and studying long into the night. He finished first in his Platoon and won the O.C. position. A week later, he was enrolled in the 12 week OCS course at Fort Benning, Georgia.

Winston Bradley Jamal was the product of two "true believer" mindsets: evangelical Christianity and Islam as interpreted by Elijah Mohammed. He now decided to believe in the U.S. Army. He graduated fourth in his class, the only O.C. in his rotation without a college degree. After getting his Second Lieutenant's bars he never looked back, deciding that henceforth, he would honor a code that he would write for himself.

After Benning, Winston had the pick of assignments and chose the U.S. Army Garrison in Stuttgart, Germany where he distinguished himself as an M.P.

Given his father's brush with death at the hands of the Chicago P.D. and his own arrest, law enforcement should have been last career choice on 2nd Lt. Jamal's mind.

So both of his parents were shocked went he wrote home that he'd secured a position in the 18th Military Police Brigade assigned to EUCOM at V Corps Headquarters in Heidelberg.

Then in 1990, at the age of 21, he had an experience that redefined his life. Attached to a special V Corps investigative unit probing possible war crimes by Serbian nationalists, he walked onto the huge unmarked grave that was the site of the Srebrenica Massacre.

In a campaign of genocide and "ethnic cleansing" meant to wipe out the former Yugoslavia's Muslim population, more than 8,000 men and boys had been killed there by the Scorpions, a unit under the command of General Ratko Mladic.

At that point in his life, the young, tight, black "Second Louey" from Chicago thought that he'd seen everything. But soon, he became weak in the knees as he worked with a team of U.N. pathologists who unearthed the skeletal remains of thousands in the mass grave created by Mladic's shock troops.

The day he ended that tour of duty was the day that Winston Jamal decided who he was.

He was a man who hated bullies—those who presumed—those who felt that they had an option on truth—those who used force to impose their own will on others. His time at the mass grave in Bosnia had convinced him that the ultimate act of a bully was homicide: the presumption that one person had the right to take another person's life, for whatever reason: politics, God or greed. It didn't matter. The consequence was that the bully stayed alive and his victim was dead.

So after re-upping for another tour, Winston returned to Chicago determined that he would spend the rest of his career investigating violent death.

Through intelligence, drive and an innate ability to earn the trust of his subordinates, he rose quickly through the ranks. He got his homicide detective's shield after three years in uniform.

Now, approaching his forty-third birthday, he was the head of the Squad and facing the most important multiple death case of his U.S. law enforcement career.

Naturally, his father's history with the Panthers and the FBI's role in Hampton's death made him suspicious of The Bureau. But long ago, he'd promised to bring a fresh pair of eyes to every case. So initially he'd given Killebrew his due.

Now, at that moment, as word filtered in though his contacts at DEA that Axel had led two helicopters and a pair of FBI Suburbans down the Chicago River with Deputy Bergstrom in the back of a boat, he was on a heightened state of readiness.

The CPD had two Bell Jet Rangers and he would have them prepped and ready to fly as soon as he got word back from Forbes.

There was little he could do in the meantime but wait.

But as he stared at the wall of victims in that control room, the Captain said two prayers: one to the carpenter from Nazareth whom his mother worshiped and the other one to Allah. He prayed that they would stop the bully Axel that night before he took another life.

59

Axel carried Maddy in through his office.

On one wall she spotted the calendar with the X's marking down the days. Below it was the newspaper headline with the word DEMOLITION highlighted. On the opposite door she saw the pictures of his subjects: the driver's licenses, the tattoo Polaroid's and the Facebook printouts. It was quickly beginning to make sense to her now. But it wasn't until he moved past his autopsy table and out into the "nave" of his "church" that she truly understood.

"My God…" she said to herself. Gazing upward she saw the 299 faces on the walls and the ceiling. And for the first time, for sure, she knew that he intended to make her the 300th.

Her father and Dr. Forbes had just reached the perimeter fence now. They looked up as a small plume of smoke emerged from the 19 story brick stack.

Sheriff Bergstrom shook the padlock securing the chain that kept the gate closed, but by then, Forbes had begun to work his way down along the rusty chain link fence and he found an opening. They communicated with each other using the hand signals employed by all tactical teams making surreptitious entry. Forbes held the bottom of the fence out while the Sheriff rolled under it. When he'd gotten inside, he used his leg to prop the fence open for Forbes.

Now, maybe 100 feet from the slaughterhouse, Bergstrom racked the Remington pump and Forbes racked the slide on his Beretta putting a Glaser into the chamber.

Inside the lair, Axel laid Maddy out of the faux marble floor, directly beneath the elaborately painted ceiling. He dropped down and ripped the duct tape away from her mouth.

Still half in shock, she looked up at the mural and began to recognize the faces of Axel's victims: 12-year-old Ginny and the tattooed store clerk Christie Sloane.

The killer grabbed a remote and cranked up the volume on his iPad. He walked back and knelt down over Maddy.

"It's O.K. You can scream now."

Her heart was pounding, but Maddy realized that staying calm was the only way she'd survive.

She struggled for a moment with the flex-ties on her hands and feet and noticed that Axel was rubbing himself. The fact that he had her trussed up like this was giving him an erection.

So Maddy decided to use that.

"Now I understand," she said, making herself look as vulnerable as she could. "What you talked about, you know, taking me to a better place."

"Bullshit," said Axel. He moved forward and touched her neck with his index and middle fingers, the way she'd checked his vitals in the helicopter the night of the rescue.

"Your pulse is racing so fast your heart's gonna arrest."

"That's not true, I'm just—"

"Don't fucking lie to me…"

He got up and went over to his autopsy table. He found a dark brown bottle of liquid and a white rag and came back to her.

"What's that?" she asked, trying to hide her fear.

"Chloral Hydrate. This is not going to happen if you struggle."

"No. Wait," she said. "I'll relax. Just tell me what to do."

Axel hesitated, knowing he couldn't trust her. But Maddy looked around. She saw a digital camera. Up on the scaffold nearby there were pictures he'd taken of his other victims.

"Look," she said. "You brought me here so I could pose for you, right?" He didn't answer. "I mean, how lifelike can I be if you knock me out?"

"Oh, so all of a sudden you want to be *part* of this now? As if you *would* have come here on your own."

"Oh no," said Maddy looking up at the ceiling. "I would have… Knowing that you wanted to paint me and make me a part of this work? I mean, I wouldn't have wanted to *die* if that was the price and I still don't, but considering the importance of this, of course I would have come. It was the *force* I didn't like. The deception. I told you on the phone… Honesty in a man turns me on…"

She was using the most seductive voice she could manage.

Axel stared at her for a moment wanting to believe her, but his 160 IQ and his survival instinct kicked in.

"Baby, you are good." He laughed. "I mean, you almost *had* me for a second. Wow. What better casting for the bitch in the Garden. Imagine what that redheaded cunt told Adam to get him to bite into that apple." He moved toward the autopsy table and found a scalpel.

"No," she said, fighting for her life now. "You've got it all wrong."

Axel squatted down and loomed over her.

"You're being judgmental and I *hate* being judged."

The blade of the scalpel flashed in the halogen lights.

"Then, let me put it another way," she said, trying to find the right words while her pulse rate increased. "I know the pressure you're under. They're going to tear this place down. No wonder you were on such a deadline to get it finished."

"That's not going to be a problem, after I'm done with you."

"What do you mean?" said Maddy, getting more worried.

Axel stood up and gestured to his flawless reproduction of the Sistine Chapel. "When you're up on that ceiling—when it's finished—this becomes the second greatest singular work of art in history. Forget The Trade Center. Forget Auschwitz. The mass graves of Bosnia... All of that was committee work. But this is *mine*. The crime scene of all crime scenes. They'll run tours through the place. It'll end up in the fucking Smithsonian." He gestured toward his office.

"I've kept meticulous records. Names, dates. Enough to clear 300 homicides." He crossed to a wall of books on forensics, pulling off volumes, opening them to pictures and tossing them down in front of Maddy. She could see grisly photos of Bundy's carnage. Ed Gein's pit. The Son of Sam's victims...

"All of the others killing, and for what?" said Axel. "A tabloid headline? A T.V. movie?" She saw pictures of Dahmer's victims. "They were *footnotes* to what I've become. They'll be writing books about me into the next century. The Hillside Strangler? Carrion. Jack the Ripper? A Victorian amateur. You're looking at the Michelangelo of homicide. I was born to a crack whore in Kankakee and tonight I'm going to make history."

Quietly Maddy sucked in hard. She realized that she was going to die alone here in this stinking packing plant and no one would know until they found her bones in that ash pit outside.

Her father had been right. She wasn't her brother. She wasn't even a real cop. She never should have taken this on. Slowly now, she began to weep. But suddenly, Axel lunged forward and grabbed her by the hair. "No. Wrong emotion. You're *Eve*!"

He pointed to the ceiling where the blank space for her face was. "Up there, reaching for the apple, full of hope. That's what I want."

Maddy thought about it for a second and started to recover.

"Alright. But how can I strike the right pose with my hands tied?"

Axel smiled. He cut the flex-ties binding her feet with the scalpel. Then he pulled out the Taser and placed it against her neck. Pulling her up, he walked her over to a faux backdrop of Eden from the fresco above. With the stun gun against her carotid artery, he sat her down on a faux piece of stone and slit the Flex-ties on her wrists behind her. He grabbed her left arm and flex-tied it up on the second stage of the scaffold so that Maddy appeared as Eve did in the mural, to be reaching up to accept the apple from the serpent on the tree.

At that point, he bent her knees and flex-tied her right ankle to a bolt in the floor at the edge of the faux piece of stone. In order to keep her balance, she had to put her right arm behind her.

"Look up," he said. "And you'll see how she's positioned,"

Maddy eyed the drawing above her. "But she's so..."

"What?" snapped Axel."

"So much more... *muscular* than me."

"It's an *interpretation,*" he responded angrily. "Not a reproduction. The face is yours. The body's my *mother's*. What about it?"

"O.K." said Maddy, hoping to delay the inevitable. She looked across the nave and spotted the beautician's chair and the red basin. She remembered how he'd used lipstick on the mirror in her room. The crime report from the police in Milwaukee had said that the woman on the train had been found dead with heavy makeup.

"Don't you want to make me up first? From what I can see, you did that for all the others. If I'm to be the final piece, why not take the time to—"

"We're way past that now," snapped Axel. "Maybe if you'd come with me that night in the Park... But now it's too late. I have to get finished by morning." He pointed upward, "Finished with that and... finished with you."

60

Now, with Maddy incapacitated, Axel approached her with the scalpel. Ever so slowly, he proceeded to cut her clothing away, stripping her so that he could paint her naked for the mural.

She had been wearing a windbreaker over jeans, so he cut that off first, starting at the midpoint of her waist and slitting upward with the razor sharp surgical knife.

"If you try and resist me, I will slash your face," he said.

"Don't worry. Resisting you is the last thing on my mind…"

She was lying and he knew it.

Maddy's only hope was to use her right hand to pop off the buckle knife, still hidden under two more layers of clothing. Before the killer exposed her belt, he would have to cut through the windbreaker, a sweater and a black nylon thermal tee-shirt that she'd worn to protect herself from the cold on the river.

When he got to her belt, he would spot the knife. So she would have only one chance and it would have to be a neck strike. If she could slit the artery on either side of his neck, he would drop.

Maddy had never spilled that kind of blood before and she prayed that she'd have the stomach to inflict the wound.

At that moment, seventy-three miles to the North, SSA Ron Killebrew was passing the parking lot of the Travelers Inn in Niles. He was on a virtual straight line up I-57 and I-94 from the slaughterhouse.

Since he was out to commit an act of arson, Killebrew pulled the Suburban around to the back of the motel. He got out and looked up and down the alley to see if he could spot any surveillance cameras. When he was satisfied that the place was deserted, he parked between a dumpster and a panel truck.

There was a dark blue FBI duffle bag in the back of the Chevy containing a forensics kit—standard issue on all vehicles assigned to the Chicago Field Office. So he unzipped it and emptied the contents; putting the gasoline can and the other components of the device he was about to build inside.

It was now almost 2:30 in the morning. As he'd passed the motel, there were just three vehicles in the parking lot.

One had to belong to the all-night attendant who was surely asleep behind the office. There was a brand new Saturn from Avis—probably rented by a businessman—and an old Lance RV camper atop a mid 90's pickup truck. He guessed that it belong to a retired couple who decided to treat themselves to a night of luxury at the "Inn."

All three vehicles were parked in front of ground floor rooms, so Killebrew didn't expect to encounter any resistance as he climbed the back steps of the motel which led to the second floor.

When he came to the three room "suite" he tried the locks on the Deputy's room and the opposite room that Forbes occupied. Both were secure.

He bent down with a penlight flash and spotted the shivs beneath each door. But the middle "war room" door was free of any blockage. They must have taken off from that room in a hurry.

Killebrew used a High Output electric pick on the lock and had it opened in under thirty seconds.

Once inside, he moved through all three rooms making sure the blinds were tightly closed, then he switched on the penlight flash.

His men had already been all over the Crown Victoria which Maddy had parked by the bridge and it was empty of any files.

He now followed the DEA stash manual protocol and swept all three rooms.

It took him less than five minutes to locate the copy of his Axel files. They'd been integrated into Forbes' I-80 files in a series of binders, clipped at the top with two prong legal fasteners. Forbes had hidden them behind the small refrigerator in the cabinet of the washbasin in his bathroom.

Sloppy work, but it was what he'd come to expect from Forbes ever since he'd turned into a cripple and an addict.

By organizing his files into the I-80 material the ex-agent had done him a favor. He could now concentrate on the fire's point of origin.

So he put the collected files in the middle of the bed in the center room. He soaked them with gasoline and began to construct an IID: an improvised incendiary device that would give him time to escape and establish an alibi.

After leaving the Exxon station, Killebrew had gone to an all-night Walgreen's Drug store on North Western Avenue.

There he'd paid cash for an electrical extension cord, a package of Hefty garbage bags, a package of light bulbs and a GE outdoor light timer. It was the kind people used to control their holiday lights.

All of the items were innocuous and drew no attention from the man at the checkout counter.

Now, working quickly in the motel, Killebrew took the lamp from the desk and replaced the fluorescent bulb with one of the Phillips 60 watt incandescent bulbs that he'd bought. With the butt of his gun, he gently tapped the bulb, breaking the outer glass, but leaving the filament intact. He picked up the small metal wastepaper basket from below the desk and placed the lamp inside, plugging the lamp's power cord into the timer. He then used the extension cord to plug the timer into the wall sock next to the bed.

Finally, he put the waste basket with the lamp and the broken bulb initiator on the bed in the middle of Forbes' gasoline soaked Axel files.

He poured the remaining gasoline into the waste basket, filling it so that the top level of the volatile fluid was just below the broken bulb filament. Then he used one of the Hefty bags to cover the improvised detonator so that the gasoline vapors would have time to build up inside the plastic bag. He set the timer for an hour ahead.

At that point, he'd be back in the 24 hour Operations Center of the Field Office on West Roosevelt in front of a half dozen witnesses.

When the timer went off, it would send a surge of electricity through the cord, causing the bulb filament to flash, igniting the highly flammable gasoline vapors, thus setting the bed and its contents ablaze.

Before he left the room, Killebrew stood up on a chair and covered the ceiling sprinkler with electrical tape so that it wouldn't engage and douse the flames. The fire would burn hot and bright, immediately incinerating the paper files on the bed along with the bed clothes, mattress and box spring. By the time the

Chicago Bomb and Arson Squad sifted through the debris, they would recover the wire and what was left of the timer and put if off on Axel, the manic who had committed the crime of arson before. It fit his profile.

If the night manager, the businessman and the elderly couple happened to get caught in the blaze, Killebrew would write them off as unfortunate but necessary casualties. Collateral damage.

The hardened SSA lived in a world in which every legal end he pursued justified the means he used to achieve his goal.

In the four years since T.C. Forbes had been discredited and removed from the BAU, the Unit had prospered under Killebrew.

With an exponential increase nationwide in serial homicides, Director Robert Mueller was able to go up to the Hill and argue each year for BAU budget increases that were three times the rate of inflation.

Giving Axel a long leash had been good for business. Serial murder had become a growth industry and the increases in manpower, equipment and case load had put Killebrew within striking distance of the FBI job he'd coveted for years: ADIC or Assistant Director in Charge of the New York Office—the legendary NYO. This wasn't just the flagship office in The Bureau, it was located in the media capital of the world; the city with the highest profile investigations.

James Kallstrom, the ADIC who got so much media time during the investigation into the crash of TWA Flight 800 had gone on to hit the jackpot as an Executive Vice President of MBNA in Delaware—the world's largest credit card issuer.

The bank also proved to be an attractive corporate home for Louis Freeh who became a board member and MBNA's general counsel after retiring as FBI

Director in 2001. Killebrew was certain that once he tied up the loose ends in the Axel case and got the ADIC's job in New York, he could cash out as they had, once he retired.

But before he left the motel suite he did one more thing to insure that whatever happened to the female Sheriff's Deputy, T.C. Forbes would remain in disgrace.

He could find no bottles of Percodan or Percocet in Forbes' shaving kit, so he loaded it with three vials of Oxycodon Hydrochloride and a pair of syringes. This was the highest concentration of generic Percodan. It was typically administered to patients in hospitals via IV.

To insure that the shaving kit would survive the fire, Killebrew left the sprinkler head open in Forbes' bathroom, then filled the bathtub with cold water and sunk the shaving kit to the bottom.

When the Bomb and Arson Squad examined the fire's aftermath they would recover it intact. The impression left would be that Forbes had remained so addicted to the painkillers that he was now shooting it like a junky.

As he pulled out of the alley in the Suburban and headed south, Killebrew smiled. That last touch was right out of Hoover's COINTELPRO manual.

PART FOUR

61

INSIDE THE LAIR Axel pulled up Maddy's sweater and the tee-shirt and found the belt buckle knife, which he snapped off and tossed into a corner.

Outside in the dark, The Sheriff and Dr. Forbes moved up to the edge of the meatpacking plant. Maddy's father looked up and saw an old sign with an arrow inside. It said: SLAUGHTERHOUSE. He shook his head, but signaled for Forbes to keep moving. Then at the edge of the smokestack, the Sheriff looked down and saw the ash pit with the human remains.

"Good God," he said, suddenly overcome with fear for his daughter's safety, so he broke protocol and started to run.

With Forbes behind him, Bergstrom took off across the yard and jumped onto the loading dock steps, taking them two at a time until he got to the top step and tripped, causing the shotgun to discharge: BAM!

Inside, Axel pricked up his ears at the noise.

Quickly, he backed away from Maddy and grabbed the remote, cutting the music and listening for any sound of the threat from outside. He heard nothing more, so he ran into his office and flung open a file drawer. He pulled out a Tech 9 machine pistol with a 26 shot mag. Then he moved to an electrical panel and killed the power. All the lights went out except for two emergency spotlights. The lights began to sweep across the huge space like eerie beacons, criss- crossing Axel's bizarre reproduction of The Sistine Chapel.

Outside, the Sheriff was just about to kick through the door from the loading dock when Forbes stopped him.

"He'll be right inside," he whispered, "we need to find another way in." Forbes was right and the Sheriff knew it. They'd lost the element of surprise, so he nodded for the ex-FBI agent to take the lead.

Forbes signaled for them to exit the loading dock. They walked around the perimeter of the big smokestack until they came to a window around back. It led to a hallway outside Axel's office.

Inside the "nave" there were two sets of four-story scaffolds on either side. Axel had built them from interlocking aluminum pipes. Each of the four "floors" of the staging were constructed of 4 X 8 foot sheets of three-quarter inch plywood that fit into angle brackets bolted to the pipes.

From the top of either scaffold Axel could dominate the "nave" below. There were two doors into the "nave," one closest to the loading dock on the right side and another on the left side by the office. Maddy was tied to the scaffold on that side of the huge space.

Once inside the office, Bergstrom took the lead. From the left side entry he peered out into the nave with its criss-crossing lights. As he adjusted his eyes to the dark, he noticed the mural and some kind of fake marble floor. Then he saw her. His daughter was flex-tied to the first stage of the scaffold but he was behind her so he couldn't determine her condition.

"Maddy. Are you alright?"

"Dad? Is that you? Yeah. So far he hasn't—"

Just then, Axel fired a burst of three shots into the faux marble floor, inches away from her foot.

BOOM, BOOM, BOOM... He was on the top stage of the right side scaffolding.

"Hey Daddee," he yelled, "Your daughter turned out to be a little bit more of a cop than you thought, huh? Come on out. Show me what you've got."

Before the Sheriff could respond, Dr. Forbes tapped him on the shoulder and whispered to him.

"Now that we know his position, I'm going to cut around to the loading dock door. That way we'll have both points of entry covered."

The Sheriff signaled a thumbs up. But Forbes leaned in, one more time. "Don't let him rattle you. I know how vulnerable she is, but just—"

"I've got it," the Sheriff whispered, becoming a Marine again. He eyed Forbes' Beretta. "How many more in your mag?"

"About six, plus one in the pipe."

"Then take this," He handed him his Sig-Sauer with an extra mag.

And with that, Forbes took off—exiting out through the window. Despite the pain in his leg, he ran back around the smokestack and up onto the loading dock. The door into the slaughterhouse was unlocked, so he moved in with stealth.

Just then, from above, Axel used the remote to crank up the deafening metal track. He yelled down to the Sheriff.

"Where's the cripple? I should have finished him that night at the dumpsite." Forbes had now begun to climb up onto the scaffolding on the right side where Axel was perched.

The Sheriff could see him from the other doorway, so he decided to engage the killer to divert him.

"Forbes couldn't make it," he shouted. "It's just you and me."

"Don't forget Maddy," said the killer. "You can take her home in a body bag."

He fired two more bursts: BOOM BOOM inches away from where Maddy was sitting, causing Bergstrom to move out from his safe position in the doorway.

BAM BAM BAM—He pointed the shotgun, toward the scaffold, strafing the ceiling with buckshot.

At the distance of four stories the shotgun couldn't do much damage to the painting.

So the killer leaned forward and fired off a half dozen shots in succession, inches from Maddy's feet:

BOOM BOOM BOOM BOOM BOOM BOOM

That drew the Sheriff out even further. He stood up and fired a single shot that just missed the psychopath. It was so close that a handful of the hot pellets ricocheted off the wall behind Axel and grazed his neck, causing him to erupt.

"God*damn* you, I spent the last three years of my life on this."

And with that, Axel grabbed onto the rope he used to get down from the scaffold and swung down, firing continuously...

BOOM BOOM BOOM BOOM BOOM BOOM BOOM BOOM

Two of the shots struck the Sheriff, one in his leg and one in his chest, knocking him back just a few feet from where Maddy was anchored.

"Daddy, you're hit."

But as Axel dropped to the floor to finish him, Forbes fired down at him from the second stage of the scaffolding: BLAM! BLAM!

Now a running gun battle ensued, with Axel and Forbes trading shots across the huge space as they jumped from one scaffold to the other.

Back on the floor, Maddy was terrified that her father was rapidly losing blood.

"Daddy, talk to me," she said trying to reach toward him.

"It's just the leg," he said, in real pain. "Gotta vest on up top..."

But the bullet had grazed an artery in his calf and he was fading quickly. "Daddy, listen to me," She said. "Do you have your knife?"

"Negative." He ripped off his jacket and tied it around his leg as a tourniquet.

"Then listen to me... He found my knife from the belt. You know the one they gave me at Cascades? It's over there below the scaffold. Do you see it?

The Sheriff grimaced. He turned and saw the glint from the knife housing. "Yeah."

"Can you get to it?"

He nodded and started crawling toward it.

But up above Axel fired down at him and hit him in the other leg."

"Daddeeee" She realized that if she didn't get free to help him soon, he'd be dead.

62

Bergstrom, the Marine, was badly wounded in both legs, but he kept crawling. He was inches from the knife when Axel leaned over to fire another burst at him but Dr. Forbes fired a shot that missed Axel's head by a hair, forcing him to duck so, the Sheriff was able to get to it. With the last strength he had, he slid the blade across to Maddy.

It stopped just inches out of reach of her right arm, so she leaned over and strained to grab it… But she couldn't seem to make it. Her father was rapidly losing blood now, and tears began to well up in her eyes.

"You were *right* Dad. I never should have *done* this."

"Don't say that. You got this far. You're gonna *stop* him." He nodded up to Axel who had Forbes pinned down on the third stage of the scaffold above them.

Now, with whatever strength he had left, the Sheriff took advantage of the distraction and crawled toward the buckle knife. When he was a few feet away, he rolled over and kicked it toward Maddy. She grabbed it and quickly cut herself down. Lunging toward her father, she caught him by the back of his vest and pulled him into the hallway and out of the line of fire.

Her next move was to go back into the open "nave" to retrieve the Remington, but when she reached for it – BOOM BOOM, Axel blasted the shotgun away.

"Get back on that scaffold, bitch." BOOM!

He fired another shot and Maddy ducked into a corner.

Just then, Dr. Forbes emptied the Beretta at Axel.

BLAM, BLAM BLAM.

He drew him away from Maddy while she yelled up from below.

"You said you wanted to paint me alive."

"I lied."

And with that BOOM BOOM BOOM BOOM... He unloaded the last four rounds in his 26 shot mag as...

Maddy squeezed her father's hand.

"My gun's in the jeep Dad. I'll be back."

She started to take off, but he grabbed her arm.

"Honey listen... If something happens—If you can't—I want you to know..." His respiration was failing... "I'm so proud that you—"

"Damnit Daddy. *Please*... Just hang on..."

With tears streaming down her face, she took off out the back window as... Axel and Forbes faced each other on the faux marble floor. The killer was out of bullets, so he tossed the Tec 9 in a corner.

Forbes started to draw the Sig, but Axel, raging on meth, lunged forward and knocked it out of his hand.

The ex-FBI agent grabbed him by the shoulders and pushed him back, slamming him against the scaffolding.

It was just the two of them now, and Forbes, handicapped by his bad leg, commenced to give Axel the thrashing he'd been waiting to deliver for years...

"I saw what you did to that nun." He delivered a crushing elbow to Axel's jaw.

"Yeah?" said the killer spitting blood. "You want me to take my pants down and show you what she did to *me*?"

He kicked down at Forbes' thigh, sending him back against the floor. "How's the leg feel, gimp?"

Forbes dove for the Sig Sauer, but Axel got to it first.

BLAM BLAM—he fired two taps to the chest, blowing Forbes back against a wall. They had to be fatal shots, but when Axel rushed forward and ripped open the doctor's shirt, he found a Kevlar vest underneath.

"I would have made it a head shot, but I need you too."

He flex-tied the doctor to a pipe on the lowest stage of the scaffolding.

"My St. Bart was a washout. Some wino from North Racine. He didn't have the strength of character that I need. So you'll go up in his place."

Axel nodded up to the painting of St. Bartholomew in the mural.

"You remember old Bart, don't you? The Romans crucified him, then they took off his skin." Up on the ceiling in one of the panels, the Saint sat holding his own skin.

"Think about that, while I go kill your girlfriend."

Now, as Dr. Forbes struggled to free himself, Axel took off out the back window.

Maddy had just reached the Jeep when he burst out onto the loading dock and spotted her.

63

BACK INSIDE, with one hand flex-tied to the pipe, Dr. Forbes reached into his pocket and pulled out his cell phone. He prayed for a signal and got half a bar.

He dialed the number for Captain Jamal and said a second prayer that he'd still be in the CPD Homicide bullpen. By now it was almost 3:30 a.m.

The phone rang three times and then suddenly, Jamal's aide picked up. "CPD Homicide. Sergeant Edmonds."

"It's Forbes. Is he still there?"

"Captain," she said, racing across the bullpen into the control room. She handed Jamal the phone, mouthing the word "Forbes."

"You'd better tell me you *found* him," he said sternly, engaging the speaker function on his cell.

"Yeah," said Forbes. "There's an old Armour meat plant south of Kankakee, about a mile west of Route Seventeen."

Sgt. Edmonds, who was listening in, opened a book of maps. She flipped to the page on Kankakee and pointed to the location.

"Alright. I've got it," said Jamal.

He checked a clock on the wall and turned to her.

"Those choppers standing by?"

"In the parking lot behind the building," she said. "Four tacticals from SFG in each one."

Jamal got back on the phone. "We can be there in twenty."

"Better call Medivac," said Forbes. "Sheriff Bergstrom's been hit."

"What's her condition?"

"I'm talking about her *father*."

"What the hell is *he* doing there?"

"You think I flew the Sikorsky alone?"

The Captain nodded, accepting it. "O.K. but where's Maddy?"

"She escaped. The killer's gone after her. He's got me cuffed inside his lair."

"You want us to contact the locals in the meantime?"

"Not a chance. You send a couple of Barney Fifes up against this guy, he'll turn them into Spam."

"Alright. Just maintain. We'll be there." He was about to hang up when Dr. Forbes stopped him.

"Captain, wait. Call the State's Attorney. Have him send somebody up to Niles... The Traveler's Inn. It's on Waukegan Avenue."

"That's where they've been staying," said Sgt. Edmonds to her boss.

"Why? What's up there?"

"Killebrew's Axel files."

Two minutes later, as Killebrew sat in the Operations Center of the FBI's Field Office his cell phone rang. He looked at the screen and it said "State's Attorney." The time was 3:36 a.m. The SSA walked away from Metzger and Gonsalves to answer the call.

"Yeah. Unh huh. Right. Thanks. Keep me posted." Killebrew hung up the phone. His source at the State's Attorney's office had called to inform him that they were about to visit the motel.

Metzger came up behind him.

"Anything important sir?"

"Negative," said Killebrew. "Just keep monitoring the local channels to see if there's any chatter."

"Will do."

Killebrew checked the time on the phone. The IDD should be going off any minute now. By the time anybody from the prosecutor's office got to The Traveler's Inn, it would be much too late.

The alarm for the fire came in to the Dempster Street Headquarters of the Niles Fire Department at 3:49 a.m. A passing ambulance had seen the flames on the second story of the L-shaped motel and immediately notified the local P.D. which transmitted the call.

The small, two-station department in the village north of Chicago responded with its three pieces of fire suppression apparatus: a 105 ft ladder truck and two pumpers.

Built by Pierce Manufacturing in nearby Appleton, Wisconsin, the pumpers each had a 500 gallon onboard capacity. They were capable of sending 1,250 gallons per minute onto the blaze.

The Deputy Chief who arrived with the first response ordered the two trucks stationed on either side of the motel. One hooked up to a hydrant in the rear alley; the other one pumped from the parking lot.

Two members of the rescue team were dispatched via the ladder truck to the roof for venting. It was their job to relieve the pressure from the burning combustibles on the fire floor below.

Three other firefighters in masks with Scott's compressed air bottles on their backs, broke into the office and the two first floor rooms to evacuate the occupants. All four, including the night manager, were treated for smoke inhalation. None sustained any serious injuries.

The point of origin was a different story.

As soon as they used a Haligan forcible entry tool on the door of the second floor "war room," the firefighters smelled an accelerant.

Synthetic Class A foam concentrate is the preferred agent for suppressing a hydrocarbon fire caused by gasoline, but the small Niles FD didn't have that option—not at 3:55 a.m.

Fortunately, they had enough water pressure to drown it. The entire blaze was knocked down within ten minutes of the initial response and the fire was contained to the immediate motel structure, which was badly damaged.

A half hour after the three units had taken up and returned to their stations, the Deputy Chief called the CPD Bomb and Arson Squad.

Captain Winston Jamal was already airborne in route to the slaughterhouse, when Sgt. Edmonds notified him of the blaze.

Police departments like the LAPD used helicopters as key components in crime suppression, but the CPD had actually *disbanded* its airborne unit in 1979 to free up more funds for foot patrols.

But post 9/11 the Department acquired a refurbished Bell 206L4 from the city's Fire Department and in January of 2006 they used $2.1 million in Homeland Security funds to buy a brand new 206 Jet Ranger: tail number N135RP.

Now from the newer Bell, Jamal issued an order to Sgt. Edmonds:

Until further notice, the Task Force was to terminate any communication relating to the Axel investigation with the State's Attorney's Office and the FBI's Field Office on West Roosevelt Street.

Cutting the Feds out of the loop as they closed in on the killer was a clear breach of protocol, but Jamal had no choice.

The suspicious fire coming so close to his call to the State's Attorney, meant that he couldn't trust anybody outside of his own Squad. He tapped the pilot of his chopper on the shoulder.

"How soon?"

"With the head wind—another ten minutes."

Jamal nodded. He wondered if either the father or the daughter would be alive when they got there.

64

As he burst out onto the loading dock, Axel spotted the redhead running toward the Jeep. "Oh Maddeeeee!" She didn't even bother turning. She went right to the glove box and found the .380 Beretta. Quickly, she ejected the 13 shot mag. There were 12 inside with one more in the chamber. She was about to turn and engage him, when she noticed that the killer had stopped at the edge of the furnace. So she hesitated.

Axel had overpowered her more than once and now on the ground, in a yard that he knew only too well, she feared that he would do it again, gun or no gun. So she made a decision. Instead of leading him back inside and risking her father's life, she would draw him away from the slaughterhouse.

This had begun with him at the end of a rappelling line and that's how she'd end it. So she shoved the Beretta in the paddle holster at her back, grabbed the harness and started up the rusted circular steps around the smokestack. For a moment, Axel lost her in the dark and then, when the moon passed out from under the clouds, he saw her back-lit against the huge chimney. He smiled and decided that this was fitting. The round brick tower had coughed out the remains of his other subjects. So he would chase her up to the top and finish her there.

The smokestack had a special significance for the killer. He'd first laid eyes on it when he was just seven years old. After his foster parents had perished in that fire, Axel was being moved by the Department of Child and Family Services to St. Tim's.

There was another orphan in the DCFS van who had to be dropped off in Bournannis north of Kankakee. So the trip to Joliet from Metamora in Southwestern, Illinois had necessitated a brief detour. After the driver of the DCFS van veered off I-57 onto Route 17, Axel saw it in the distance—the huge smokestack sticking out of the flat farmland like an enormous spike. He had never forgotten that vision and years later, when he moved into the old Armour plant, he took some time to study the history of the massive flue vent chimney that had carried off the smoke from the carcass burns.

It had been built in 1932 by the Alpons Custodis Chimney Construction Company of New York. They'd used red perforated fire brick and acid proof mortar. From its concrete base, 18 feet wide, the tapered cylinder rose up 192 feet. It was 13 feet across at its summit, with walls three-feet thick around the lip. As chimneys went, it was a relative dwarf when measured against the leviathan of all brick smokestacks at the Anaconda Smelter in Montana.

But because of health and safety guidelines imposed on meat packing plants, this stack was unique. For cleaning purposes, its outer perimeter was surrounded by a cast iron stairway that spiraled up from the base to the rim. Long since rusted, it reminded Axel of a gigantic extended corkscrew.

In the days when he'd first put paint on the ceiling, months before the demolition plans had been announced, he would climb up the 19 stories at the end of each day and stand at the top.

From that height, he could catch the last rays of sun disappearing behind the horizon west toward Iowa. Staring across the American heartland, Axel felt godlike; secure in the belief that he was executing a work of historic significance. Later, when he rolled body after body into the furnace and looked up at the smoke from their remains, he was reminded of that famous chimney in Rome—the tiny stack above his beloved Sistine Chapel where the College of Cardinals met to elect each new Pope.

Black smoke meant that the conclave had failed to appoint a successor to St. Peter. White smoke meant that a Pontiff had been chosen. And yet, after living under the nuns, Axel felt that it should have been reversed. The Holy father, who presided over an institution that allowed for the mistreatment of so many children, should wear black.

Now as he completed his own interpretation of the Chapel ceiling he would wrap the rope around the redhead's neck and hang her from the outside of the chimney. There was no more fitting way to announce her place in the fresco when the media hordes arrived. And Axel was sure that they would come.

Within 48 hours this place would turn into a new Waco; another Jonestown; one of those killing fields that captured the attention of the media harpies who devote so many column inches and so much airtime to the coverage of "true crime."

Who could forget the shit storm when that D.C. intern Chandra Levy's body turned up in Rock Creek Park and cameras turned on the Congressman she worked for? How many hours were devoted to the death of angelic Jon Benet Ramsey or her older spring break equivalent, Natalie Holloway?

For how many weeks did the "Beltway Snipers" control the headlines? How many Americans stayed up nights keeping the deathwatch on Terry Schiavo? And then there was the Michael Jackson fiasco—two of them actually—his pedophile litigation in Santa Barbara and the trial of doctor Conrad Murray after his death.

Every year or so a tabloid spectacle would force the main events off the front pages, distracting the public from the issues that really affected them: like the endless war in the Middle East—the spiraling price of gasoline—or the financial meltdown triggered by the Ponzi scheme of selling toxic derivatives on housing that low-income people were suckered into thinking they could afford.

Those were issues that mattered. But the media sold junk news to the public the way restaurant chains sold junk food. From time to time there would be spotty coverage of some horrific case of child abuse, but the national pandemic was never fully addressed.

Every month or so there would be a news item about the settlement by some diocese of a priest-pedophile case. But when was the last time the national media focused on the scandalous foster care system? What about the ongoing hypocrisy of the Roman Catholic Church which kept young girls from terminating their pregnancies, then threw their babies into institutional prisons?

Axel, born Bobby Leroy Cole, was the rarest of all epic murderers—a serial killer with a social conscience and a story to tell. He would use his masterwork to send a message—speaking to the nation with a symbol in the same way those twisted Islamic fascists had done when they took down the Twin Towers. Granted, the price of his message was the death of three hundred people, but for Axel they were an important means to his end. And when it came to ends/means morality how was *his* any different than the FBI's?

Still, he needed that one last face in the ceiling and he was determined to bring her to ground. So now as Maddy ran up the steps, Axel moved to the furnace and turned up the heat, flinging the door open so that the flames lit up the night.

"It's in the book, baby... Matt twenty-three, thirty-three: 'You serpents, you generation of vipers. How will you escape the damnation of Gehenna?'"

Before he gave chase up the stairs, he ran down from the loading dock and into the garage where he kept the cars he used. In a storage compartment in the back of the LR-4 he'd used to take Christie, he had a .44 Charter Arms Bulldog. The David Berkowitz gun. It was nickel plated. Axel loved symbols. He flipped out the barrel and spun it. Six in six. He snapped it shut and took off for the smokestack.

65

Six minutes away by air, the two Bell Jet Rangers roared south above I-57. Capt. Jamal radioed the SWAT team in the parallel chopper.

"Now hear this. You've all breached a lot of perimeters. There isn't an officer on this mission who hasn't walked into some heavy shit. But this particular suspect is more dangerous than anything you've ever encountered."

In the other Bell, the tactical team listened as they studied pictures of Maddy, Forbes and Sheriff Bergstrom.

"If he takes any action that you reasonably construe as a threat to your safety or the safety of those three hostages, drop him."

Back at the slaughterhouse Maddy had circled the eighteenth story around the smokestack. She was almost to the top when she felt the stairway shake below her. Axel was closing in.

So she turned and bent over the railing, firing down. BAM. The shot zinged past Axel's ear, two stories below, and chipped the brick wall of the smokestack.

He touched the side of his cheek and tasted blood. "Why is it so goddamn hard with you?" he yelled. He leaned out over the railing and fired up at her—BANG…

The shot sheered a rusty bolt holding the old stairway.

Suddenly, it began to vibrate.

Axel struggled to hold on as…

Maddy figured out how she could beat him. If she could somehow shoot the stairs away below him, he would drop. So she leaned out over the railing again and steadied the .380 on the edge.

BAM, BAM, BAM.

She hit another of the bolts and, just then… POP, POP… The stairway below Axel started to pull away from the 19 story stack.

So Axel picked up speed, taking the stairs above him two at a time, using every bit of strength he had, pulling himself up along the railing with one hand and brandishing the .44 in the other.

By the time he started to round the 17th level, Maddy had made it to the top. There was nothing burning in the furnace, so she didn't encounter any smoke, but the heat from the fire 19 stories below was intense. She had to get off of the top of the smokestack as soon as she could, so she laid down along the three-foot wide rim and focused her aim.

BAM, BAM, BAM, BAM.

Maddy counted the rounds, She'd used seven. She had six more left and one of the .38 slugs had hit another rusty bolt, so the entire helix of a stairway started to buckle…

Axel, the killer with the 160 I.Q. stopped on the 18th level and realized that it was all going to collapse from its own weight. So he aimed the big .44 at the stairs immediately below him:

BANG, BANG, BANG BANG—firing directly at the section brace that held the 18th level to the one below it and suddenly…

The stairway below started to fall away. Like an enormous rusty Slinky, each story of the spiral dropped onto the story below it... Now there were only two levels between Axel and his prey at the top.

Maddy looked down and saw the glint from the nickel-plated Bulldog and realized that he was using a revolver. He'd fired five shots. That meant he only had one left to her six.

The killer leaned back against the brick, out of Maddy's range. He was standing on the top of the 18th level, with only a few rusty steps below him. It would seem that he'd run out of options, but Axel was supremely confident. In fact, he lectured Maddy on her choices.

"You've only got two ways down. Over the side or into the pipe."

"You know, you're right," she said, pushing herself back along the hot lip and quickly donning the rappelling harness.

"What would you do without me?" he said, chuckling.

"We're about to find out."

BAM, BAM, BAM.

She shot away at the stairs just below her.

The 18th story started to rattle, so Axel lunged up and grabbed onto the middle rung of the 19th level. He had to drop the .44 to hold on, and it tumbled down until it hit the soft dirt in the yard down below.

Now, from the top of the tower, Maddy could see just the hint of the sun peeking over the horizon to the east.

She had two bullets left in her gun and the most dangerous man she would ever know was crawling, hand over hand, pulling himself up onto the last rungs of stairs to kill her.

66

INSIDE THE LAIR, Dr. Forbes heard the shots. Ever since Axel had cuffed him to the scaffolding with the flex-tie, he'd been pulling at the staging.

The structural integrity of the huge scaffold depended on the four by eight foot sheets of three-quarter inch plywood fitting tightly into the angle brackets at each level. If he could move the pipes out of position, the brackets would bend and the entire four stories would come crashing down.

The trick was getting out of the way before he got crushed.

From the moment Axel took off after Maddy, Forbes had been pushing and pulling on the staging. He'd now managed to get it rocking, back and forth.

Finally, he tugged away at the pipe he was tied to and the staging buckled. The plywood sheets started to come down, but at the last second, the pipe holding him separated from its socket and he rolled free.

As soon as he got away, Forbes ran into the hallway by the office where Maddy had left her father. The Sheriff's eyes were open and there was a faint smile across his face. It was as if he'd finally made peace with his daughter. But as soon as Dr. Forbes saw him, he knew that he was dead.

He ran to find the shotgun, but Axel had twisted the barrel when he'd shot at it. So Forbes ran to the other side of the "nave" and out onto the loading dock.

Flames were licking out of the furnace, so he rushed over and slammed the door shut. Then he turned the big valve that controlled the gas and shut it down. Trying to adjust his eyes in the semi dark as the sun began to come up, Forbes looked left and right around the yard for the killer.

Just then, he spotted the nickel-plated .44 at the base of the smokestack, so he jumped down and picked it up. There was one shot left. He looked up and saw Axel, climbing hand over hand on the last remaining section of the rusty stairway.

At almost 200 feet, hitting Axel would be a difficult shot with a handgun, especially the Bulldog .44 designed for short range stopping power. All he could do at this point was warn her. If she had any rounds left, maybe she could drop him, so he called up to her.

"Maddy. He's four rungs below you."

"I can see him."

She fired another round BAM—and the remaining rungs below Axel fell away. He was clinging to the last piece of railing as it swung out and broke away from the brick wall.

"Come on, pull me up," said the killer.

Maddy flattened herself on the rim of the stack and looked down.

"You're out of your mind..."

"Can I quote you on that for the insanity defense?"

"As if you're getting *out* of here?"

The railing buckled again and the last bolt began to sheer.

Axel had seconds left and for the first time, he showed concern.

"Pull me up and I'll make your career."

"Not a chance."

"*Listen* to me. Do you think I could have lasted as long as I did without help? Huh? Think about it."

"What are you talking about?"

"Killebrew. You want to help clear your boyfriend down there? Pull me up and I'll give you enough evidence to knock down the Hoover Building."

"Tell me now," said Maddy as Forbes shouted up to her.

"Don't listen to him."

The bolt started to pull from the brick and Axel dropped another inch.

"Shoot the sonovabitch," yelled Forbes.

But suddenly, to Maddy, Axel was starting to make sense.

"Do you think this ends with 300 murders?" he said. "There were dozens more. I've been at this now for eight fucking years."

"And you're saying Killebrew knew?"

She had him directly in the .380's sight now.

"Knew? He made it *happen*, for Christ's sake. Each time the law closed in, he'd give me a pass. The fucker *needed* me like a gynecologist needs syphilis, and you can take him down—find out where the bodies are buried—literally. Think of all the families who can rest when you clear those killings."

Maddy hesitated as Axel dangled and the rusty railing, swayed…

"We don't need *you*," she said. We've already got the proof."

"What?" said Axel. "Killebrew's files?" Maddy nodded. "Does he know where you've got them? If he does, I can guarantee that they're gone."

"How would you know that?"

"I told you. I've worked with him. He sanitizes his crime scenes and he specializes in planting evidence. That DNA on I-80 that he put off on Forbes? That was vintage Killebrew."

The railing hung by a thread now. Maddy had to make a decision.

"Come on. Pull me up like you did on that mountain. As God is my judge, I promise to let you live and I'll give you everything: names, dates; the chance to clear more than four hundred homicides..."

Maddy's mind was racing. She still had three shots left. If she let him drop, she could end this. Nobody would blame her for putting one right between his eyes. After that, she could get down and see to her father.

But it was the very voice of the Sheriff that was guiding her now—leading her to do the right thing. Arrest the suspect, clear his cases and let a jury decide on his fate. Did that make her weak? Following her old man's code?

No Maddy decided that it made her stronger. She knew that her father was gone now. He couldn't have survived with those wounds. And so, in his memory, she dropped the rappelling line over the side...

"That's my girl," said Axel, grabbing the carabiner at the end of the line. He wrapped it around his left wrist as she stood up on the rim and started to pull him up. She held the .380 in her right hand and used the harness around her shoulders to take most of his weight.

Down below, Dr. Forbes had no other choice but to validate her decision. He didn't want to say another word that might distract her. So he quietly backed off and dialed his cell phone. There was just enough battery left for one more call.

In the lead Bell Jet Ranger, Captain Winston Jamal answered. He could barely hear Forbes over the sound of the rotor blades.

"How close are you?"

"Less then two minutes, said Jamal. "You should hear us any second."

"She's on top of the smokestack with Axel," said Forbes. "Just be careful you don't blow her off."

67

NOW ON THE THREE FOOT RIM, Maddy stood face to face with the madman. The sun was starting to come up and there was a grin on his face as he stared at her milky white skin.

"Even after everything you've been through, you're like a Botticelli."

"Release the line and get down on your knees," she ordered. "Hands behind your head."

"Now why would I want to do that?" said Axel.

He undid the rappelling line from his wrist, and grabbed the carabiner with both hands, tugging gently on it as Maddy tried to back away along the three foot wide rim.

"You swore that you'd end this."

"Yeah, to God… A deity who abandoned me decades ago."

He jerked on the line and Maddy almost lost her balance.

Now, down below, Dr. Forbes jumped into the Jeep. He steadied the Bulldog .44 along the roll bar. The gun had Trijicon sights. So he lined up the U-shaped rear-site with the illuminated sight at the end of the barrel.

At the top of the smokestack, Maddy could hear the sound of the choppers in the distance. With the sun starting to pour into the yard, she looked down and spotted Forbes in the Jeep. He seemed to be aiming something. He must have found the .44.

So she stalled for time.

"I still don't understand."

"What?" Axel was pulling the line hand over hand, moving closer.

"Why me? There must have been a thousand other women you could have chosen."

Axel smiled, "It's just your luck that you look like the bitch in the fresco."

The noise from the choppers was getting louder.

"You're a hypocrite, you know that?"

"Oh, that stings. Is that the best you can do at this point?"

"Alright then. You're a coward."

He pulled her closer.

Down below, Forbes angled for a shot. At that distance, he worried that it might go wide and hit Maddy.

"You hide behind some psychobabble about child abuse."

"No. You're wrong."

"Oh, really? Then what? You justify what you've done because you're an *artist*? You're gonna take me and those people on your wall to a *special* place?"

"That's exactly right."

"Horse shit. We're all gonna end up in your ash pit down below. You kill because you love the *control*. I saw how hard you got when you tied me up. As far as I'm concerned, you're nothing more than a jag-off predicate felon."

Now, Axel raged. "That is so fucking *untrue*. Those people on that ceiling down there were nameless, faceless ghosts 'til they met me." He started to lunge toward her, when, BANG! Dr. Forbes fired. The shot whizzed past Axel's face, and he stepped back.

Quickly, Maddy jerked the line from his hand and grabbed the carabiner on the end.

Axel started to rush toward her, but in one fluid motion, she clipped the carabiner to his belt and side stepped him, pushing him into the smokestack as she jumped out over the outside edge and rappelled, down, down, using Axel's body inside the chimney as a counterweight.

Finally, when she hit the ground, Maddy clipped the other end of the line onto the roll bar of the Jeep as Dr. Forbes threw his arms around her.

The two Bell Jet Rangers were just clearing the perimeter of the slaughterhouse. As soon as Captain Jamal jumped out of the lead chopper, Dr. Forbes and Maddy rushed up to him.

"He's inside the stack below the rim," said Forbes.

"Alive?"

"He *was*," said Maddy. You'd better deploy some men up there to grab him before he suffocates."

But Capt. Jamal took a moment to look over at the ash pit with the skeletal remains.

"Yeah," he said cynically. "We'll jump on that right away."

"No. I mean it. He told me that he killed dozens more. You'll never clear those cases if he's dead." She started to walk back into the lair, but Forbes stopped her. "Before you go in, you need to know…"

"He didn't make it, did he?"

Forbes shook his head, "No."

Maddy just stood there for a moment. "Why do we put off telling people the things we ought to, until it's too late?"

"Your father knew. The whole way down in the chopper, he couldn't stop talking about how proud he was that you'd picked up where Billy left off."

"He said that?" Forbes nodded and put his arms around her.

Maddy turned toward the lair for a moment, then dropped her head on his shoulder, and broke down.

By 7:45 a.m. a pair of Kankakee County Sheriff's units with two uniformed Deputies held the media mob at bay outside the gate of the Armour Plant.

Captain Jamal had quietly told Sgt. Edmonds to call the A.P. and let them know "off the record" that there might be a break in the Axel murder case. He was expecting a lot of heat from The Bureau, not to mention the Mayor's Office for cutting both Killebrew and the State's Attorney's office out of the investigation.

He wanted a full contingent of press on hand so that he could tell the story *his* way, giving proper credit to Maddy, Forbes and the heroic Sheriff from Washington State who had given his life so that the horror could stop.

68

As soon as he'd heard that Sheriff Bergstrom had been shot, when he was still airborne on his way to the lair, Captain Jamal had transmitted a 10-00 code for "officer down" to the Kankakee Fire Department's Rescue Unit. He'd followed it with a 10-0 "caution" code and radioed that an ambulance should be standing by for deployment to the Armour plant on his command.

He didn't want to risk any casualties until he could secure the crime scene with the tactical officers from the Special Forces Group. So after his call, a paramedic unit from the Kankakee F.D. was dispatched with orders to hold at the junction of Route 17 and the farm road leading to the old slaughterhouse, for further instructions.

Minutes after stepping off the Bell Jet Ranger, Captain Jamal had given the word for the ambulance to advance, and the two fire fighters, both male nurses, were now inside the hallway by the "nave" attending to the Sheriff's body.

Jamal then dispatched a pair of SFG officers to the top of the smokestack to retrieve the suspect. Another pair entered a door at the base of the stack with searchlights. Both teams were heavily armed.

It was unlikely that the killer had survived inside the huge brick tower. Even though Dr. Forbes had shut off the furnace, the team on the rim got carbon monoxide readings of 5,000 parts per million—a level considered life threatening.

So they'd radioed to the Captain who was now inside the lair, and he'd told them to secure the chimney at both ends until it was safe to go in and bring out the suspect—dead or alive. At that point as long as the psychopath was effectively trapped inside the 19 story smokestack, Jamal perceived the threat to be minimal.

Now, as he entered Axel's death "chapel," Jamal realized that of all the crime scenes he'd walked through, he had never seen anything more bizarre. The contrast between Axel's meticulous devotion to the work of Michelangelo and the cost in human life represented by the "subjects" on his "missings" wall wasn't just startling, it was downright creepy.

Even Maddy, who'd had much longer to process Axel's twisted vision, was awestruck as she looked up at the angelic face of 12-year- old Ginny Kendrick.

"I still don't understand. Why in God's name would he do this?"

"He didn't do it in the name of *God*," said Forbes, putting his arm on her shoulder. "It's like he said... Jeremiah, Chapter Twenty..." He nodded up to the citation in a corner of the ceiling: H 20:14-18. "Cursed be the day I was born."

"I don't follow," said Jamal.

"A serial killer has zero self worth," said Forbes, becoming the college professor again. "Every life he takes is an affirmation that he exists."

He nodded up at the faces. "What you see on that ceiling and on these walls are 299 affirmations. Maddy was going to be the three hundredth."

"Yeah," said Jamal, pointing to the Garden of Eden panel. "But he's got his own face on the body of Adam.

Are you saying that when he was finished with Maddy, he was going to kill himself?"

"I doubt it," said Forbes. "He'd want to be alive to savor all of this. The media attention. His new place in the history of serial homicide."

"That's pretty much what he told me," said Maddy. "He was sure that this place would be preserved."

"It will be," said Jamal. "At least for awhile."

Just then, Sgt. Edmonds walked out of Axel's office.

"It's all in his files, Captain," she said. "Nearly 300 hundred victims. He's described every single murder on an index card in amazing detail." She handed Jamal a plastic see-through evidence bag with one of the cards. "Each one has the victim's name, the time and date of his initial contact with them, the point abduction and the location of the homicide."

"It's like he wanted to make sure he got credit for every death," said Jamal. "What kind of killer does that?"

"Killers who see themselves as godlike," said Forbes. "Beyond the law." Jamal walked over to Maddy who was staring down at the bloodstain on the floor where her father had been shot. He put his hand on her shoulder.

"I can't even begin to express my admiration for what you've done here. Not just the risks you took, but the price you paid." She just nodded as Forbes pulled her toward him. "And you, doctor," Jamal turned to Forbes. "Your instincts were dead on."

"I'll feel better when I see his body," said Forbes. "Where are we on the search?"

"I was just about to make a call," said Jamal, keying in his radio. But just then, SSA Killebrew walked in, followed by SA's Metzger and Gonzalves.

"You might want to take this call first," said Killebrew," handing him a cell phone. "I've got The Director's office holding."

"For what reason?" asked Sgt. Edmonds.

"Are you kidding?" snapped Killebrew. "A whole lotta people at Justice, including the U.S. Attorney for the Northern District want to know why you did an end-run around the FBI."

"Tell the Director I'll call him back," said Jamal. "After we debrief you on the motel."

"What?" Killebrew reacted with surprise. He hesitated, then picked up the cell phone. "Yes, please tell the Director we'll be in touch with him shortly." He hung up and cocked his head for Jamal to walk with him into Axel's office where they could have some privacy.

"What motel are you talking about?"

"The one with the two alarm fire up in Niles."

Killebrew eyed the two Field Office agents. "Yeah. I heard there was some kind of incident. Metzger and Gonzalves will confirm that we got the report in the Op Center at about what? Ten after four? But that was by monitoring the open police and fire channels."

Just then, Maddy stormed in with Dr. Forbes. "You're saying there was a fire? Where? In our motel?"

"That's right," said Jamal, turning to face Killebrew.

"And our files?" asked Forbes.

"Destroyed," said Jamal. "*After* I put a call in to the State's Attorney's Office and asked them to lock down your motel rooms."

Killebrew smiled and tried to spin the story. "So that means you got some kinda leak in your prosecutor's office."

"Yeah, but to who?" asked Jamal. "See, after I got the call from Bomb and Arson I had Sgt. Edmonds call AT&T and pull the log on the State's Attorney's outgoing calls.

"We checked every one from midnight to four a.m.," said Edmonds.

"And damn, if there wasn't a call to a D.C. area code," said Jamal turning to his sergeant. "What was the number they called? 202 what?" Edmonds read from the log: "202-662—"

"Wait," said Jamal. He turned to Killebrew. "Give me your cell phone."

"You're out of your fuckin' mind," said the Supervisory Special Agent. He started to walk out, but two Tactical officers stopped him. One of them gestured for him to hand over the phone.

Killebrew ground his teeth, then gave it to him. It was a Blackberry 8800. The SWAT cop handed it to Captain Jamal who switched it off and on again.

As soon as the phone came back on, the number showed up across the screen: 202-662-4343. He nodded to Edmonds who showed them the AT&T log with that same number highlighted in yellow.

Jamal handed the phone to Edmonds. "Bag it as evidence," he said. He turned to Killebrew. "Are you going to surrender or do I have to get these men from SWAT to back-cuff you?"

Killebrew looked around, surveying his odds. Jamal snapped his fingers and the two heavily armed SFG cops moved toward him with guns drawn. Killebrew turned to the two FBI Field Agents for help, but they backed away, shaking their heads.

"Captain, I had no knowledge," said Metzger.

"Same here Captain," said Gonzalves.

"Cuff him," Jamal said to the two SWAT cops.

"Now wait just a fucking *minute,*" said Killebrew, about to explode.

But suddenly, outside they heard the sound of an *air horn*. Jamal's radio crackled. The voice from outside the lair said, "Captain, you'd better get out here."

Seconds later they were all outside on the loading dock, looking up at the smokestack. One of the SFG cops on the rim was trying to transmit on his radio. But the transmission was garbled down below.

"Come back to me," said Jamal. "I didn't copy."

Nineteen stories above him, the SFG cop in a Haz Mat suit peered down into the stack where Axel had dropped. Inside, his partner had descended on a rappelling harness, following the line down that had been clipped to Axel's belt with the carabiner. The carabiner and line were now clipped to a metal ladder that ran down the inside of the smokestack. "Sir, there's no body. Repeat…

Maddy rushed toward the base of the stack with Dr. Forbes. The SFG cops who had gone in from below, were shining their lights up into the big chimney.

"What are you fucking telling me?" said Jamal.

"Sir, we found the line he went over on clipped to a ladder about three-quarters down the stack.

"So you're saying *what?*"

"Sir, the subject is gone."

69

THE DISCOVERY THAT THE MADMAN had escaped from the smokestack caused Captain Jamal to order a "hands and knees" search of every square yard of the Armour plant site. But in the immediate confusion, SSA Ronald Killebrew ducked back into the lair. He crossed the "nave" as SFG tactical officers ran past him outside and he slipped out the back window of the office.

From there he ran to the black Suburban from the Field Office and found a set of keys in a magnetized box below the rear bumper—standard Bureau protocol for vehicles used by multiple agents during investigations.

He got into the SUV with its black tinted windows and drove to the fence at the edge of the compound. There he was confronted by two Kankakee County Sheriff's Deputies. As soon as Captain Jamal had received the shocking news that Axel had vanished, he'd ordered the uniforms at the gate to move the press contingent back to the other side of the country road.

So as the FBI suburban rolled up to the two local uniforms, Killebrew encountered no cameras or radio mikes. But the cops would not let him pass, until they asked him for identification. Without skipping a beat, he flashed his Bureau I.D. with its embossed FBI logo and the title SUPERVISORY SPECIAL AGENT in gold letters. As they eyed his credentials, Killebrew stared straight ahead behind black wired Ray-Bans.

But his heart rate was elevated. He wasn't sure if word had come down yet from Jamal to seal off the perimeter. Just in case, he unbuttoned his navy blue field jacket and popped the snap on the cross draw holster that held his Glock 38. If the local Smokies tried to prevent him from leaving, he'd be forced to resist. And though he didn't look forward to a shootout with half the Midwest media across the street, Killebrew's options were quickly diminishing.

Long ago he had crossed the line that separates law enforcement agents from outlaws and the events of the next 48 hours would define his career for years to come. In maintaining his off-the-books relationship with Axel in a way that gave him deniability, SSA Killebrew had lived the last six years of his life like an enemy in an occupied zone

Even the coveted files in the plastic folder that he kept with him at all times would not, on their face, show any culpability. It took his rival, the veteran ex-agent Forbes to decipher them. Now, at the gate as his mind raced, Killebrew ran the numbers. The call from the State's Attorney's Office was a piece of circumstantial evidence but it could hardly link him definitively to the motel arson.

He'd already put the original files into a cross-cut shredder. His only real worry was that Forbes might have kept a back up copy on the server at the place where the files were copied.

Fedex/Kinkos used Xerox 250's which automatically kept overnight jobs on a hard drive for up to 14 days. It would be simple enough to track down the location. Even in Chicago there weren't more than a half dozen copy centers that could have done the job between the time Forbes grabbed the plastic folder from the Drake to the time he'd returned it the next morning.

Once he'd located the copy center, Killebrew would use his position as a Supervisory Special Agent to get them to burn the file from their server. At that point the only loose end would be the killer himself.

Now, as the Suburban moved past the phalanx of T.V. crews and print reporters, he hit the gas and quickly accelerated to fifty on the country road. At a junction toward Route 17 a few miles north, he turned right out of sight of the plant and hit the roof rack lights and siren—screaming toward I-57 North.

Once he'd dealt with the file issue he would drive north to Milwaukee and pick up a commercial flight to D.C. On the chance that Jamal might issue a BOLO for him within Illinois, he decided to avoid O'Hare.

After he got back inside the relative safety of The Beltway, he would make an appointment to see the Director and begin the process of damage control. Since he'd been cut out of the Axel hunt, Killebrew would blame the escape of the fugitive killer on the CPD and its Captain, who he'd learned was not only the son of a notorious Black Panther Party member, but a one-time follower of Elijah Muhammed.

Killebrew's contacts at *The Washington Times* and *Fox News* would have a field day with that lead. The evidence from the Bomb and Arson Squad would show that the fire had been ignited with an Improvised Incendiary Device on a timer—clearly the work of the killer, who'd been a fire-starter since his youth.

The fact that Captain Jamal was now trying to escape blame for his own incompetence by attacking the Feds, was typical of local PD's who resented the depth, breadth and power of The Bureau.

Once he'd fashioned a media story with The Office of Public Information, he'd withdraw to the safety of the Behavioral Analysis Unit and await consultation.

With the maniac now linked to 300 murders still on the loose, there was a good chance that the Senate Judiciary Committee would push the Justice Department for the appointment of a Special Prosecutor and naturally Killebrew would volunteer his services as a consultant since he was the FBI's lead expert on serial homicide.

As he roared up Route 17, passing police and emergency vehicles heading south toward the Armour Plant, the veteran SSA smiled and realized that this latest twist in the Axel story would be good for The Bureau and particularly good for him.

That's when he felt it—the pressure against the back of the Chevy's front seat. Killebrew looked into the rear view mirror and turned fish belly white.

Axel, the psycho killer that he'd kept at large, was in the backseat pushing a stun gun to his neck.

70

"TIME TO PAY UP RON..."

"Christ. How the fuck did you get out?"

"You mean *before* you slipped me through the gate?"

Axel held the Taser against Killebrew's neck as he leaned forward and pulled the Glock out of the holster. Then he moved up across the center console and slipped into the seat on the shotgun side. He rested the Glock on the dashboard above the glove compartment.

"That's good. Hands at ten and two on the wheel. Keep the speed at fifty." Killebrew gripped the steering wheel tightly. If he didn't, Axel would see how much his hands were trembling. Inside he was ice cold with fear. But he tried to brass it out.

"So this is the thanks I get, Bobby?"

"I don't use that name anymore. You know that."

"O.K. Ax... Then, let me remind you that you are currently still breathing because of me." Killebrew had interrogated enough psychopaths over the years to know that he had to show strength. Otherwise they would own him.

"Actually, I'm still *breathing* because the chimney sweeps needed a ladder to get up inside that smokestack."

"I'm talking climate. You're talking weather. You're missing the big picture."

"And if I decide to let you live, you're going to do *what* for me?"

"See to it that you get away."

"Where? Some place in *this* country? Is there actually a Zip Code zone where you can guarantee my safety?"

"Piece of cake. I get people into Witness Protection every day."

"You're skipping a couple of beats Ron. First I have to be arrested and processed. Then I have to cop a plea, as if there's a prosecutor anywhere, local or federal, who would agree to that."

"You'd be surprised how far the insanity defense can take you."

"Meaning, I'm in the nuthouse for how long before you can move me to WITSEC?

"Couple of months, maybe."

"Bullshit. A couple of years as in NEVER! I go in and the key gets tossed. They throw me in the hole on a Thorazine drip with a straight jacket. Chemical lobotomy. No can do."

"You're underestimating the kind of clout I'll have after this plays out."

"O.K. so you get a book deal and a movie deal and then what? I relocate to Phoenix? Get a new I.D.? Open a Mailboxes Etc.? Start shipping packages for Big Brown with a squad of U.S. Marshal's on my ass? Do you have any idea how that could impact my night life?"

"We did it for Sammy The Bull and they cut him a pretty wide berth."

"Yeah and where is he now? The fucking Supermax. He got life for selling X."

"The man was greedy and careless. That's not you Bobby…"

Axel smiled. "You are one audacious sonovabitch Ron. But right now, you are shitting bricks."

"You're wrong."

Axel moved the Taser within an inch of Killebrew's head.

"DON'T FUCKING LIE TO ME!"

"I'm not…"

"Hey. Without even taking your pulse I can see your carotid artery going up and down like a cock on Viagra."

Killebrew swallowed hard. The killer had him dead to rights.

"Just tell me what you want," said the Fed.

"The password to my Bureau file."

"Not a chance."

"Give it to me and I'll let you live."

"And if I don't?"

"They'll find pieces of you all the way up I-57."

"When I'm dead it doesn't matter what condition my body's in."

"Yeah but think of poor Marjorie. She'll want to have an open coffin at the wake and—"

"Marjorie?"

"Duh… yeah. You're ex-wife. After the funeral I'll pay her a visit at the townhouse in McLean."

Killebrew flashed true fear now. The psycho knew where his ex lived.

"Maybe after that, I'll shoot up to Poughkeepsie to see the twins at Vassar. You want me to give you the number of their dorm room? Goddamn Ivy League girls school and all they can afford is one rent-a-cop on the desk from midnight 'til dawn."

"How do you fucking *know* that?"

"Preparation Ron. It's been the key to my success—that and a little downfield blocking from you."

Now with his left hand, Axel grabbed Killebrew's Glock from the dash and cocked it. He withdrew the stun gun and put it on the back floor behind him.

"I want access to my file, Ron."

He flicked the barrel of the Glock against Killebrew's right ear. Then he reached into the pocket of his cargo pants and pulled out a small plastic bag with a couple of shards of Ice—crystal methamphetamine. He ripped open the bag with his teeth and crunched down on the drug, shaking his head from the instant snap it delivered. The gun barrel trembled for a second, an inch from Killebrew's head.

"Alright, I'll give you the code. Just back the hammer off on that weapon."

Axel dropped the hammer on the double action semi-automatic. But he pressed the muzzle against Killebrew's temple.

"Ron, if you lie to me I swear to fucking Christ I will kill your ex-wife and children."

"O.K. But If you get the password you'll let me live, correct? Are we straight on that? You won't harm my family?"

"As God is my judge," said Axel holding up his left hand.

There was a long pause and then, finally…

"Alright. It's 456 forward slash, forward slash Ranger Tango Kite.

"Aw, RTK. Your initials. How sweet. What's the origin of the 456?"

"You were the four hundred and fifty-sixth suspect in our files."

"But who led the league in home runs, Ron?"

"You did." Killebrew practically whispered the words.

"CAN'T HEAR YOU!"

"*YOU DID*, Goddamnit. Now back off on that gun, will you please?"

"Sure Ron."

Axel pulled the Glock away and Killebrew exhaled hard.

"O.K." said Killebrew. "What about it? You said—"

"Yeah. I know. First let me have your shield and your wallet. All your cash." Killebrew smiled as he handed him his wallet. He was safe now.

"Are you relaxed? You feel good?"

Killebrew nodded.

"O.K. Now roll the window down."

The SSA was suddenly worried. "Why?"

"So I don't break the glass. Hmmm. Groin shot-neck shot. I don't know."

Killebrew freaked. "But you swore you'd wouldn't hurt me."

"No. I swore I'd let you *live*."

And with that he shot Killebrew in the groin and pushed him out the door, jumping into the driver's seat.

Killebrew spilled out onto Route 17, going into shock as…

Axel grabbed the wheel. He slammed the door shut, then put the Chevy into overdrive. He went to the radio and tuned it to 1240 AM. 50,000 watts of pure hellish metal out of Chicago. Iron Maiden blasted from the Bose speakers.

As he zoomed up the entry to I-57, Axel reached down and touched the seat which was smeared with Killebrew's blood. He ran his index finger through it and wrote on the windshield the words of the heavy metal song he was playing.

RUN TO THE HILLS… RUN FOR YOUR LIVES

Screaming out the lyrics, he pulled down the rear view mirror and winked at himself. Then, he eyed a sign that said "Chicago River Access 2 mi."

Epilogue

Axel disappeared on December 15th, the date that demolition had been scheduled to take down the old plant. Naturally as soon as the Chicago P.D. took command of the premises and declared it a crime scene, the destruction of the slaughterhouse was halted.

Now, almost a year later, a permanent exhibit opened in the spacious Kenneth E. Behring Center of the National Museum of American History at the Smithsonian Institution in Washington. Entitled: *The FBI: From Prohibition to The War on Terror*, the exhibit recounted the history of The Bureau, founded in 1908.

Just inside the entry there was a special series of photographs documenting Hollywood's laudatory treatment of The Bureau. From *The F.B.I.*, the signature series starring Efrem Zimbalist Jr., which ran on the ABC network for nine years, up through *Criminal Minds* on CBS, a series that was actually *set* in the BAU, the exhibit was proof positive that the entertainment industry's portrayal of the "house that Hoover built" was almost always positive and upbeat.

Conspicuously absent was Clint Eastwood's filmography of "The Director" which flirted with Hoover's alleged homosexuality and proclivity for secret files. The various display cases contained signage describing the FBI as "the nation's premier crime fighting and terrorism prevention agency." An entire wing of the 10,000 square foot exhibit was devoted to the Behavioral Analysis Unit, often referred to in the media as "The Silence of the Lambs" unit.

At the exhibit entrance there was a long corridor lined with display cases filled with grisly artifacts from The Bureau's most notorious suspects. Set off by overhead track lights, the mug shots of Bundy, Gacy, Dahmer, Berkowitz, DeSalvo, Gein and a half dozen other psychopaths were projected on the corridor's floor.

Beyond that were a series of glass exhibit cases celebrating the BAU's most famous serial killer investigations. It included a picture of SSA Ronald Killebrew, now in a wheelchair, getting The Bureau's Medal for Meritorious Achievement from Director Robert Mueller.

The FBI's twisted spin on the "Axel murders" had taken on Byzantine dimensions after the wounded Supervisory Special Agent, found near death on Route 17, was unable to excise the copy of his secret files from the server at the Kinko's on North Clark Street.

Once Dr. Forbes and Maddy had been debriefed by Captain Jamal and the Task Force detectives and were assured that every fragment of paper in their three-room motel suite had been incinerated, they drove directly to the copy center and printed out duplicate copies of Killebrew's files.

Realizing that the appointment of an independent Special Prosecutor might lead to the exposure of Killebrew's "special" relationship with the killer, the Attorney General opted for a limited investigation by the FBI's in-house Office of Professional Responsibility. During that probe, noting that Killebrew's actions could subject the Government to massive liability, his attorney brokered a deal in which the SSA was allowed to testify to OPR investigators under a grant of immunity.

Although he refused to take a polygraph and actually asserted his Fifth Amendment privilege more than two dozen times during his interview, Killebrew was allowed to retire with a full pension.

In order to cement The Bureau's official position on the entire incident, his lawyer also suggested that he be hailed a "hero" and decorated. Thus, The Bureau's criminal negligence in failing to stop the murder of nearly three hundred Americans could be viewed as a law enforcement triumph.

Director Mueller later faced the Senate Judiciary Committee and testified under oath, detailing the BAU's latest theory: that the Axel killer was now dead. That cover story had been enhanced when OPR investigators went into Axel's encrypted file—accessible online only via a password—and discovered that someone had inserted a medical report into the master file, twenty four hours *after* the killer's escape from the Armour plant.

The report, which appeared to be an FBI blood sample analysis from an I-80 crime scene, documented traces of the HIV virus in the killer's system. While the OPR agents could not explain why such a report would show up on an encrypted FBI server *years* after the purported analysis, the AIDS report gave The Bureau an out. With Axel dead, it could declare a media victory.

The blood report, suggesting that the killer had a terminal illness, also gave Axel the freedom to disappear. Ironically, he got the idea of hacking into The Bureau's server after studying several books on COINTELPRO and a biography of J. Edgar Hoover that described "The Director's" obsession with John Dillinger.

In 1934 Hoover had actually devoted a full third of The Bureau's budget to the manhunt for Public Enemy No. 1. After the shootout at the Biograph Theater, The Director began collecting Dillinger artifacts including the bank robber's gun, hat, eye glasses—even the pocket change recovered from his body.

But years later, celebrated Chicago crime author Jay Robert Nash challenged the conventional wisdom about Dillinger's death. In a series of books, Nash argued that, in fact, the man shot to death by SA Melvin Purvis wasn't Dillinger at all, but Jimmy Lawrence, a small time hoodlum who resembled the arch criminal.

Nash had uncovered early arrest records indicating that the real Dillinger had grey eyes. He produced Naval records which described the eyes as "blue," and noted that during his time as a sailor Dillinger's right lateral incisor had been removed during dental surgery. But the autopsy report on the Biograph corpse conducted at the Cooke County Morgue indicated that the subject showed scars consistent with plastic surgery. Curiously all of his teeth were intact and his eyes were *brown*.

Even the Justice Department's original "want" poster on Dillinger pegged him with grey eyes and mentioned two scars on his body that were missing from the autopsy report which also conflicted with the fingerprint description of the bank robber from FBI files. Nash even provided a snapshot of an old grey-eyed man who had sent a letter in 1963 to the owner of the Little Bohemia Lodge, the scene of a famous Dillinger shootout, claiming that Purvis had killed the wrong man.

Writing decades after the purported Biograph take down, the author reported that once he'd been given a pass, he'd move to California where he'd led a quiet married life ever since. The letter ended with the words, "The man shot had black hair and brown eyes... Yours sincerely, John Dillinger."

Nash produced copies of Dillinger's earlier handwriting which matched the longhand in the letter and adding to the intrigue, Nash noted that Dillinger's body had been encased in concrete at his gravesite, discouraging any later efforts to prove Hoover wrong via DNA analysis. After his spectacular escape from the slaughterhouse, and realizing that the FBI may have walked away from the Dillinger manhunt, Axel then contrived his own "out" and hacked into the files.

One of the great urban legends, investigated by generations of school boys who had visited the Smithsonian on high school trips, was that Dillinger had been gifted with an enormous penis that was preserved and on display in the National Museum. That myth was the result of a famous photo showing a series of morgue personnel and cops around the autopsy table, ogling the body of "Dillinger" which was on a slanted table under a sheet.

In the area where the corpse's private parts would have been, there was a large upward protrusion under the sheet, suggesting that the shootout victim had died with an enormous erection and that somehow, it was maintained long after the flow of blood from the victim's heart had stopped. The authorities later disputed the legend claiming that the bulge was caused by Dillinger's arm which had been hardened by rigor mortis.

In any case, the Smithsonian had never exhibited such a body part, real or imagined. But as thousands of visitors, moved through the FBI's exhibit in the National Museum, they did confront another curiosity. Just as Axel had predicted, his *entire* morbid replica of the

Sistine Chapel had been re-assembled in the four-story atrium of the Behring wing. It stood as a testimonial not only to the killer's audacity and hideous plan, but The Bureau's capacity to rewrite history.

Beyond a section of the actual chain link fence that had surrounded the perimeter of the plant, visitors walked under an archway worthy of an attraction at Disneyland, heralding, "The Slaughterhouse Murders;" The Bureau's new, more lurid case name for the Axel killings. The FBI's need to mask Killebrew's mishandling of Stranger 456 had resulted in the very enshrinement that the killer had hungered for. Rather than documenting another of the FBI's epic *failures*, The Bureau spin doctors had reconfigured it into a victory.

The fact that the killings had stopped and that the serial murder rate nationwide had plummeted since Axel's "disappearance," only solidified the public perception, fanned by the mainstream media, that retired SSA Killebrew had acted heroically.

Captain Jamal had insisted that The Bureau credit Dr. Forbes and Deputy Bergstrom for their pivotal role in the Axel case. In fact, if The Bureau hadn't reached a détente with him, he'd threatened to go to the Senate Judiciary Committee and reopen the probe into Killebrew.

As for the young Sheriff's Deputy who had lost her father to the fiend and the ex-FBI agent who had connected the dots between the I-80 case and the 300 others, they quietly returned to Washing-ton State. Like a pair of combat veterans who had survived a war time atrocity, Maddy and Dr. Thomas C. Forbes grew closer as the days passed.

He stood at her side as she buried her father. He helped her get through the trauma all survivors experience following a brush with violent death. He comforted her when she called him in the middle of the night after waking up with the fear that Axel would be on her again.

The families of all Kings County Sheriff's Deputies killed in the line of duty receive both a death benefit and the fallen officer's full pension. After putting her father's affairs in order, Maddy sold the house in Snoqualmie and moved to a small apartment in the U-District while Dr. Forbes finished out the semester.

The ex-serial hunter had long since given up on ever finding a woman who could understand him. But in the days he'd spent with Maddy on the Axel hunt, his feelings for her grew from admiration to true love.

By late March, unable to sleep alone and wracked by nightmares, she moved in with him. Over Easter weekend he took her to meet his parents in Little Compton, Rhode Island. He proposed in May and they were married at St. Mary's in Newport, the red stone gothic Roman Catholic church where JFK had wed Jackie back in 1953.

A year after the showdown at the slaughterhouse, he was sober and drug free; halfway through his new book *Axel: The Untold Story of The Slaughterhouse Murders*. Forbes had received a modest advance from the University of Washington Press, but he'd sold the film rights to Sony Pictures for enough money to live comfortably with Maddy for years without having to go back to teaching.

They learned that she was pregnant in August. The baby boy would be born around their anniversary. For his part, Forbes could not remember the last time he'd been so happy.

With each day of her pregnancy Maddy felt more beautiful. Unburdened now by the need to prove herself in a man's profession, she let her red hair grow long and began to embrace her femininity.

She still called him "Doc," but her heart beat faster when she heard his voice and he couldn't bear to be separated from her for even a few hours. The intensity of their love was heightened by the fact that each of them understood how quickly it could be cut short.

Forbes didn't believe for a moment The Bureau's claim that Axel had died from the HIV virus. From the treasure trove of jewelry and other valuables found at the Armour Plant, it was clear that the killer had amassed a small fortune. Given his various drops, including the off-site containers that stored his vehicles and a series of lockers with "getaway" money and passports that Captain Jamal 's detective had found at Union Station, Forbes believed that the killer was laying low. He was convinced that Axel would attempt to finish his masterpiece with the blood of his young wife, so they left the U.S.

Long ago, the ex-FBI agent had obtained a dual citizenship in Ireland, which meant that he and Maddy could live anywhere within the 28 countries of the European Union. They had chosen the warmest and the most southern point they could find in Italy north of Sicily and purchased a small stone house with a protected perimeter. Maddy threw herself into preparing the baby's room, studying Italian and learning to cook at a nearby osteria.

Concerned that the Axel would find them, Forbes had their names changed in a Dublin proceeding that his solicitor had put under seal. They had now been reborn as citizens of the new Europe; independent, untraceable and more relaxed and happy than any two battle-scarred veterans had a right to be.

But the killer had not been idle. No one with a 160 I.Q., an addiction to speed and a lust for homicide simply fades into the shadows. Once he'd escaped back up the Chicago River and ultimately into Canada, Axel had retrieved one of the many identities he'd set up when he was planning his exit.

From the Bank of East Asia in Windsor, he wired funds to Bangkok. Shaving his head and using brown contact lenses under wired glass frames, he took a Thai Air flight from Ontario to Singapore exiting on the passport of one Willem S. Van Fleeg, a Dutch national. After driving north in a hired car from Malacca to Kuala Lumpur, he took a deluxe sleeper berth on the Ekspres, the overnight train from the Malaysian Capital to Phuket the beach resort in Southern Thailand.

There he rented a small mountain villa within walking distance of a resort that had WIFI service. Axel spent his days getting tan and fit and his nights data mining the net for any trace of the two people he most regretted leaving alive: the gimp from the I-80 dumpsite and the red head who haunted his dreams.

Convinced that Forbes had vacated the States with the Deputy, the killer did some online research in Rhode Island probate records and learned that Forbes' maternal grandmother had emigrated from County Cork. The Irish had a program in which the grandchildren of émigrés could gain citizenship in the Republic and sure enough, Axel had found the notice in the "Birth Registry" showing that a T.C. Forbes had been issued a passport.

After he'd hacked into The Bureau server, Axel had downloaded a Trojan Horse to the FBI's site that allowed him access even after the 456//RTK password had been changed.

Exploiting the FBI's site he accessed the database at Interpol in Lyon, France. There he turned up an application for a name change made on behalf of a solicitor named Terrence O'Neill for a T.C. Forbes. He was now living as John Harrigan.

Working night after night through property transfer documents in each of the 11 EU countries accessible, Axel hit the mother lode when he discovered that a small farmhouse on the Isle of Capri had recently closed escrow. The purchase price had been $1.2 million Euros—about two hundred grand more than the bitch got from her father's pension cash out and the sale of their house in Snoqualmie.

Axel had already seen the notice in Variety online that the movie studio had optioned Forbes book for $250K against a cool million if the film every got made. Axel wondered who they would cast to play him and mused to himself that it was a shame Johnny Depp couldn't play twenty-eight.

After Jamal had brokered the deal with The Bureau, the Justice Department had restored Forbes' full pension with the "line of duty" injury premiums, so Axel figured he had a steady income of $5,000.00 U.S. a month—enough to live on modestly since they'd paid cash for the farmhouse.

Now, as he went to the Phuket branch of Malay Bank where he kept his valuables in a safe deposit box, the killer thought about which passport he'd use to book the ticket on Alitalia. He decided on Enzo Barbuti, a name he'd corrupted from a list of diplomats on the Atlas bundled with Windows.

Once in Rome he took the train to Sorrento and put down eight thousand Euros in cash for a month's lease on a Ferretti, a motor launch that could easily do 30 knots in the crossing from Positano to the island. Capri was a jewel in the Tyrannian Sea. Tiberius Caesar had the entire conquered world to choose from for his summer hideaway and he'd stolen away to a fortified villa on the cliffs overlooking the Blue Grotto.

Axel got hard thinking about how he'd kill Forbes first, then abduct the Madonna and child. He'd take her to a remote location on the mainland where he would keep her captive until he could paint her. One of the specialties at Faraglioni, a five star restaurant near the Piazetta, was cuttlefish. It was grilled and served with a black pasta made with the ink of the squid.

Axel found himself becoming erect when he thought about taking some of that ink and painting the red head with it. Full with child, her body would resemble more closely the weight of Eve's in the master's original painting.

Once completed, he would send the painting to the curator of the National Museum at the Smithsonian for their FBI exhibit with a note demanding that the image of her face be added to the ceiling of the exhibit. He might even include a vial of her blood, with a Google image of the curator's own home in Bethesda as an inducement for him to finish the job.

Axel would add a final touch: tattooing the letters M:10:31 to the back of the redhead's neck with the citation from Mark. He would harvest her skin and send it along with the package with these lines:

EVEN AS THE FIRST SHALL BE LAST
THE LAST SHALL BE FIRST

He decided that he would let her baby live and raise it as his own.

TO BE CONTINUED…

About the Author

PETER LANCE IS A FIVE-TIME Emmy-winning investigative reporter now working as a screenwriter, novelist and non-fiction author. With a Masters Degree from Columbia University Graduate School of Journalism and a J.D. from Fordham University School of Law, Lance spent the first 15 years of his career as a print reporter and network correspondent.

He began as a reporter for his hometown paper, *The Newport Daily News* in Rhode Island. There he won the coveted Sevellon Brown Award from the New England *A.P.* Managing Editors Association. Lance next moved to *WNET*, the PBS flagship in New York, where he won his first New York area Emmy and the Ohio State Award as a producer- reporter for *Channel 13*'s news magazine *THE 51ST STATE*.

Lance won his next two Emmys and The Robert F. Kennedy Award while working as a news producer at WABC-TV, the network's owned and operated station.

While getting his law degree, Lance worked as a Trial Preparation Assistant in the office of the District Attorney for New York County. Moving to ABC News as a field producer in 1978, Lance won his fourth Emmy in 1980 for his investigation of an arson-for-profit ring in the Uptown neighborhood of Chicago: "Arson and Profit."

In 1981 Lance became Investigative Correspondent for *ABC News*. For his very first piece on *20/20* Lance won his fifth Emmy for "Unnecessary Surgery," an exposé on an Arkansas hospital. He won two more Emmy nominations for *20/20* investigative pieces.

Over the years he covered hundreds of stories worldwide for *ABC NEWS 20/20, NIGHTLINE,* and *WORLD NEWS TONIGHT*. He tracked nuclear terrorists through the twisted streets of Antwerp and members of Pol Pot's children's army on the Thai border with Cambodia. Then, in the late 1980's, he took a break from non-fiction. Lance came to L.A. and began working as a writer and story editor for Michael Mann on two of his acclaimed NBC series: *CRIME STORY* and *MIAMI VICE.*

In 1989 Lance became the co-executive producer and "show runner" on the fourth season of *WISEGUY* for CBS and in 1993 he co-created *MISSING PERSONS,* for ABC. In later years, he served as a writer and consulting producer on such series as *JAG* (NBC) and *THE SENTINEL* (UPN).

In 1997 Lance's first novel *FIRST DEGREE BURN* became a national best seller, ranking No. 35 on The Ingram A-List: The Top 50 Requested Titles in Mystery- Detective Fiction. The film-noir mystery features FDNY Fire Marshal Eddie Burke. Later Lance adapted *VEIL: THE SECRET WARS OF THE CIA,* Bob Woodward's best-seller on Iran-Contra and William Casey for HBO. For *Showtime* he wrote *TERROR.NET,* the story of Bradley Smith, the courageous Diplomatic Security agent responsible for helping to apprehend the world's most notorious terrorists. In the year 2000 Lance returned to reporting with his best-selling non-fiction biography: *THE STINGRAY.*

Following the 9/11 attacks, Lance began investigating the origins of the FBI's original probe of World Trade Center bomber Ramzi Ahmed Yousef. After visiting Yousef's former bomb factory in the Philippines, he came away with 100's of pages of classified documents proving that Yousef had set the 9/11 plot into motion as early as 1994. Lance then went back and examined the FBI's original efforts to stop Yousef in 1992 as he planned the first attack on the WTC. The result was his acclaimed investigative book from Harper Collins *1000 YEARS FOR REVENGE.*

The book was later purchased by ABC which used it as one of three source books for its 2006 September 11th mini-series *THE PATH TO 9/11*. Lance followed *1000 YEARS* with *COVER UP* in 2004. In it he presented evidence that federal officials entered into an "ends/ means" decision in 1996 that buried a treasure trove of al Qaeda-related intelligence in order to preserve a series of Mafia-related cases in the Eastern District of New York (Brooklyn).

In *TRIPLE CROSS,* the third book in Lance's 9/11 investigative trilogy, he provided stunning new evidence that senior FBI and Justice Dept. officials may have obstructed justice in their failure to monitor Ali A Mohamed, Osama bin Laden's principal spy inside the United. States. In 2006 The National Geographic Channel aired a two-hour documentary entitled *TRIPLE CROSS: Bin Laden's Spy in America,* based on Lance's book.

In 2010 Lance was named a Research Scholar at the Orfalea Center for Global and International Studies at the University of California at Santa Barbara.

His fourth investigative book for HarperCollins, *Deal With The Devil: The FBI's Secret 30 Year Relationship With A Mafia Killer,* was published in hardcover in 2013 and paperback in 2014.

Lance has appeared regularly as a commentator on *CNN* and *MSNBC* and writes for *The Huffington Post, Playboy Magazine* and *The Santa Barbara News-Press.*

His website is www.peterlance.com

ALSO BY PETER LANCE

Stranger 456 is the thrilling hunt for a serial killer named Axel, who is harvesting bodies across all victim classes contrary to any profile the FBI has encountered. Working against a deadline as he uses the homicides to create some kind of master work, the brilliant but twisted killer is being pursued by Maddy Bergstrom a tenacious young Sheriff's Deputy and Dr. T.C. Forbes, a veteran of the FBI's Behavioral Analysis Unit at Quantico. Beginning on an icy mountain road in Washington State and climaxing in Axel's Midwestern lair, *Stranger 456* is unlike any take on the serial killer genre you've ever read.

It happens every day in the City. Gas is poured. A match is lit. Building, bodies and dreams go up in flames. Fire Marshal Eddie Burke walks among the wreckage. A different kind of detective for a different kind of crime. When a fire rages in SoHo a priceless mural from the 1930s is destroyed, a young woman lies dead in the ashes, and the victim's abusive ex-boyfriend is killed resisting arrest the NYPD closes the case. But Eddie Burke can't let it go. He knows the arsonist was a pro, not a jealous lover and that the torch is still out there.

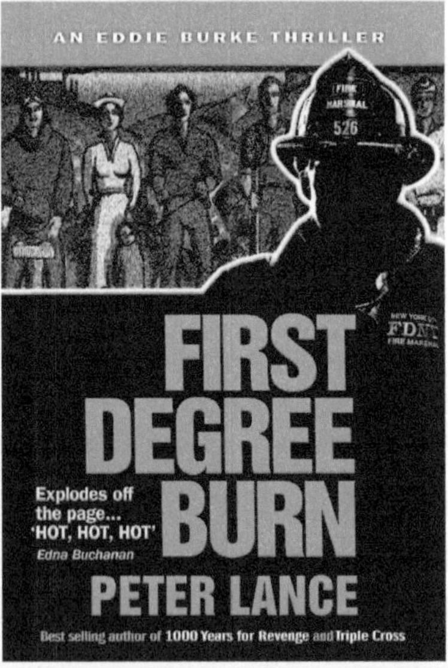

Visit www.peterlance.com

www.ingramcontent.com/pod-product-compliance
Lightning Source LLC
Chambersburg PA
CBHW020605310726
48979CB00008B/1350/J

* 9 7 8 0 9 9 6 2 8 5 5 1 3 *